for You,

HEARTS UNLOCHED

CLAIRE GEM

Claire Gem

Erato Publishing
Massachusetts, USA
www.EratoPublishing.com

CLAIRE GEM

CLAIRE GEM

Acknowledgments

My sincerest thanks go out to the following people, without whom this story would not have been possible:

Terri DelNegro, my muse and cover designer. My sister. And the best friend I could ever ask for.

Theresa Flynn, my most trusted and cherished beta reader.

Bob Marquette, who was generous and patient enough to share his knowledge and experience with scuba diving.

My dear friend and colleague, Dr. Stephano Pizzirani, who was kind enough to teach me how to swear in Italian.

And to my copy editor, Joyce Mochrie, who helped me get all the words just right.

CLAIRE GEM

Dedication

I dedicate this book, as I do all my writing accomplishments, to my husband, Clark. He tolerates my endless hours at the keyboard, listens to me spin tales over dinner and on long drives, and is, quite frankly, the reason I can write such intensely emotional romance. He taught me, over thirty-seven years ago, the meaning of

Happily Ever After

ONE

Redman's Resort - Loch Sheldrake, N.Y.
Oct. 21, 1964

A full Hunter's moon is hangin' high over the Loch, lightin' up the hotel parking lot like the one at the big Chevy dealership in Monticello. Raymond and me are gettin' ready to shut down. On a Wednesday night this late in the season, we pack it in early—usually by eleven. Gene stays on in the lobby until around midnight just in case any late night check-ins show up, or some straggler rolls in, stumblin' back from the clubhouse at the racetrack.

I'm in charge of the key cabinet. The valet lot is full of shiny steel and chrome. All the latest models from the sweet silver '62 Corvette to the brand new yellow Malibu. Ray's itchin' for the Malibu, but it's my turn to choose. I pluck the key off peg number forty-two, turn up my collar against the bitin' fall breeze, and head for the back lot.

I find Ray up against the side of the building in the shadows, his usual spot, the red tip of his cigarette bobbin' like a boat's nav marker.

"So? We doin' the Chevelle?" he asks.

I pull out my own pack of Marlboros and light up before answerin'. "Nope." I blow the word out in a puffy white stream. "Gonna roll with the 'Vette."

"Damn you, Jimmy," he mutters, then drops his smoke and crushes it out with the pointy toe of his shoe. But he doesn't say nothin' more.

I'm head valet—Ray's and Gene's boss man. And sure, we're breakin' the rules by takin' these rich folks' rides out for a spin in the wee hours. Sometimes we even take two of the hottest ones and drag the quarter mile we got marked out on the straightaway goin' toward Liberty.

But most times, we just test-drive 'em. See what they got. See what it feels like.

We all grew up in Sullivan County—farm boys. This is probably the closest we'll ever get to sittin' behind a set of wheels with its own pink slip. And without rust on the bumpers or cow shit on the floorboards.

We're just gettin' ready to make our move when a flash of headlights stops us dead.

Damn, another late night straggler. Now we'll have to wait 'til Gene pulls their luggage and grabs their keys.

But the car doesn't even pause at the lobby doors. It purrs right on by, snuggin' into the end spot beyond the area cordoned off for valet. A sweet ride, the '64 Mustang is a fastback, and the growl of its 289 vibrates in my chest before meltin' away. The taillights—three vertical rectangles of fiery color on each of her hips—glow a shade brighter right before they go black.

With the place lit up like midday under that big moon, we get a clear shot at the couple climbin' out. I remember them from earlier. They checked in around two this afternoon, all snuggles and giggles. I heard the Mister tell the bellhop, *Honeymoon Suite, 103.*

City folk. He was a big man in a black suit to match his blacker hair, puffin' on a Cuban I knew damn well was illegal. The thing's still clamped between his teeth now as he gets out and makes his way around to open her door.

She's *choice*—Elizabeth Taylor style—and built like a brick shit house. Without her coat earlier, I'd gotten a good look at her nicely rounded ass. Now she's wrapped in pale fur from her chin to her toes. The way it shimmers in the moonlight, gotta be silver fox. Like the ones me and Raymond trap up on the ridge. Their pelts bring prime cash.

Cigar no sooner slams the door when he snatches the blunt out of his teeth and drops it. Then he grabs her, clutchin' that sweet ass in both of his big hands, clear through the fur. They stand there, makin' out, 'til I'm pretty sure they're gonna go all the way right there against the car.

I look down, drummin' my fingers impatiently on the block wall behind me. Raymond pinches the bridge of his nose and mutters, "Geez-Us. They got a room, don't they?"

Then another set of headlights flashes, crawlin' down the row of cars until it shines right on the pair, like they're top bill on Broadway. Spewin' gravel, the black Caddy spins out and stops dead, right beside them.

What comes next happens so damn fast, I'm not sure I remember it right. To this day, I'm still thinkin'—and prayin'—it was all a bad dream.

~~~

Opening Day, Montlake Raceway & Casino, Liberty, N.Y.
Fifty Years Later

Kate Bardach snugged the collar of her amber, Burberry raincoat tighter around her neck and dipped into the side pocket, lifting out her compact binoculars. Excitement balled in her chest like a tightly wound bee's nest, since the next few minutes annually set the tone of her entire year. Seconds later, the buzzer sounded, and the announcer's voice echoed in the empty grandstands—*And they're off.*

Kate knew this opening day, on a weekday, a few days before Passover, she'd likely be alone in the stands. The first of April, no less. April Fools' Day. But although it may be an unlucky day for some, she felt sure she had a talisman. Her three-year-old filly was something special.

She didn't bother lifting the glasses to her eyes until the group rounded the last turn. She knew her horse—a steady, patient runner. The filly was happy to lurk in the leading third of the pack until the last stretch. Then she'd make her move.

The big gray usually stood out like a silver beacon in a sea of sorrels and bays. But today, drizzling rain had turned the track into a sea of muck. The group seemed to float over the course, hovering in a misty brown cloud like Pig Pen on Peanuts. Kate squinted through her glasses and leapt to her feet when the pink-and-white silks bearing the number three pulled ahead of the pack.

"Go, baby, go, go, go!" Kate jumped up and down. As they barreled down the final stretch, she yanked the eyepiece free and pressed her face close to the glass. "Dammit," she growled, her voice echoing in the empty grandstand as her breath puffed out in the cold air, fogging her view. She raced down to the far end of her box, center stage over the action.

Easily, the big, dapple-gray thoroughbred named *April's Here* pulled away from the pack in the last hundred yards, splashing across the finish line three lengths ahead of the second-place horse. Kate shrieked and clapped like a little girl.

This is going to be my year. *My* year. Finally.

Adrenalin sent warmth coursing through her as she flopped back into her seat and, retrieving her binoculars, dropped them into her Coach bag. Then she slipped out her phone. Thumbs flying over the keyboard, she swore again as spellcheck, along with her trembling fingers, repeatedly distorted her message to her father. *We won* morphed into *sheep,* then *erwin.* Exhilaration overcame her frustration on the second try, and she laughed out loud.

"Congratulations, pretty woman. I guess we both bet on the right horse today."

Kate shrieked and spun around toward the deep voice coming not only from behind, but above her. She'd had no idea she wasn't the only one in the stands. How could she possibly have missed *this* guy?

He appeared taller than he probably was, standing on the level above her which gave him a nine-inch advantage. Broad and imposing under a voluminous, black trench coat, he looked like an old-time mobster with his dark hair and oddly hued, light eyes. And those eyes were studying her with an expression Kate couldn't quite decipher.

Interest? Curiosity? Or downright hunger?

"Sorry. Didn't mean to scare you," he said, his voice as deep and dark as the rest of him. He leaned over the steel bars defining the boxes as *reserved* and extended a gloved hand. "I'm Marco Lareci. How much did you have on the number three horse?"

Kate swallowed her initial shock, blinked, and gathered herself back to center. This man, with his shaggy, black hair and three-day-old stubble, could be a street bum in a stolen raincoat. A twenty-first century Jack the Ripper. Or, just another racing enthusiast up from the city for opening day. But no denying one fact: he was *hot*. And his smile had chased whatever chill remained from every cell of Kate's body.

In some parts more so than others.

"Mr. Lareci. Charmed," she said, and laid her own leather-gloved hand into his. "Kate Bardach. But make no mistake, sir. I didn't merely bet on the number three. I own the mare."

His surprise rocked him back ever so slightly, his stubbled chin lifting. "Ah, and how lucky can a man get? Marco, please. May I call you Kate?"

Assessing him through narrowed eyes, Kate considered. One thing was for sure—she didn't like this vantage point, him standing so far above her. Not a position she was used to in her life. She grabbed her purse off the adjacent seat and stepped out of the box.

Hell, even wearing her four-inch, Steve Madden boots, he still towered over her by half a head. Kate cleared her throat and squared her shoulders, tossing her long hair back with one gloved hand. The damp chill crept in around her collar and sent a shudder through her.

"You can call me Kate, but only if we reconvene in the Underground. It's freaking freezing in here."

Montlake's Underground Bar, a usually dark and smoky private lounge off the west end of the casino, was as abandoned as the grandstands had been. Marco knew the main bar, Trackside, would still be closed this early in the season. But thank God the Underground was open. When he arrived a few hours earlier, he hadn't eaten anything since he left Manhattan. He'd grabbed a really fine Reuben sandwich and Devil's Path IPA there when he'd rolled into town two hours ago to meet Joshua Lieberman. The realtor who'd been handling his purchase of the defunct Redman's Resort.

He held open the heavy glass door—bulletproof Plexiglass, by the looks of it—and Kate pranced through like she owned the whole place, instead of just the mare whose win he'd won two bills on. Her hair fell in ebony waves down her back, nearly reaching her wasp-like waist.

Yeah, he thought. She was all tan and black with the coat and the hair. Add to that the confidence—an almost haughty air—and the slightly nasal ring to her velvet voice. She really did bring to mind a wasp.

Might want to watch my step around this one.

The lady wasn't the booth type. Heading straight for the bar, she hung her huge, leather bag on the hook underneath and climbed onto the barstool before he'd even had a chance to help her. Neither had said a word as they'd made their way down the escalator to the subterranean space under Montlake's recently refurbished grandstand.

"Hello, Zach. I'll have my usual. And make it a double. I'm celebrating today," she said to the barkeep, who'd paused from polishing glassware when they came in.

"All right, Ms. Bardach. Hey," he said as he pointed one thumb over his shoulder at the monitor. He gave her a high-five. "Nice going. This the three-year-old gray?"

"Yup." Kate nodded slowly, the corner of her mouth turning up. "She was well worth waiting for."

The bartender was a mature man with a salt-and-pepper crewcut and the face of a man too smooth and pretty to be anything but gay. After ignoring Marco's existence for the first sixty seconds of their arrival, he now turned to greet him with a nod as he flipped coasters down on the bar.

"And for you, Mr. Lareci? Another IPA?"

Marco caught the slight turn of his companion's head and lifted eyebrow in his peripheral view.

"No, I'll take a Dewar's on the rocks this time. Thanks."

When Zach turned to do his job, Kate shifted in her padded stool and leaned her chin on her hand. "So, this isn't your first pony ride at the Underground? No pun intended."

What was it about this woman that shot him straight in the groin? Gorgeous, no doubt. Her vivid, blue eyes rimmed with jet lashes were set at a slight angle to a Patrician nose, her pale skin the color of buttermilk. But her haughtiness, her regal air, was an attitude he usually found irritating and off-putting, no matter how hot the woman was. No, there was something about the way she used those eyes . . . studying him . . . hypnotizing him. . . .

The bartender broke the spell, delivering drinks: a martini for her and his iced glass of Dewar's. Shaking his head slightly, Marco lifted the glass and took two long swallows before answering.

"No, not my first pony ride, as you put it," he said, unable to keep the irritation out of his voice. "But you're right. I'm not a regular here. I am, however, a new property lord in the area."

Kate's eyes widened, sparked with interest. "Lord, huh? So, I'm guessing it's more than a run-down bungalow you snapped up?"

Marco slid her a sidelong glance. This bitch took snobbery to a whole new level. He should have figured. The fancy clothes, the prime spot box seat. She can't be from up here. Must be from the city. Like me.

He leaned back in his chair, resting both elbows on the padded arms. "I bought the old Redman place. I'm assuming you're familiar?"

The little huff she blew out registered shock, along with something else. Excitement?

"Redman's Resort? I know it well. It sits about a half-mile down the road from my lake house." Her smile evaporated like early morning fog, and furrows appeared between her dark, arched eyebrows. "Tell me you're not knocking it down."

Hmm. The lady likes old architecture. Must have a little bit of class going for her.

He shook his head. "No way. That place, from what I've read, is a sort of icon in this part of the county. The poshest playground in the area fifty years ago. Even for the Hollywood crowd."

Kate spun her stool toward the bar and lifted her martini to her lips, a toothpick-speared olive bumping seductively against a shapely upper lip. Marco would like to be running his tongue along that lip right now. He licked his own instead and shifted in his seat.

She sipped, set the glass back on its circular landing pad, and blotted her lips with the cocktail napkin. The white square came away with a perfect, bright-coral, imprinted kiss.

"Once upon a time," she began, speaking to the olive in her drink, "this whole area was a tourists' paradise." A touch of nostalgia laced her voice with softness.

Ah, so the lady does have a heart after all. Let's test it a bit.

"The Borscht Belt. Isn't that what they called it?"

Her eyes flashed toward him, her gaze sweeping him up and down. "Yes, they did. Of course, with a name like Lareci, I don't suppose your bubbe and poppy brought their grandkids up to this area."

Marco barked out a laugh, shaking his head. "My grandparents were lucky they could afford their old two-family in Boro Park—"

"So tell me," Kate cut in, "what are your plans for Redman's? It's in pretty bad shape. But I guess you already know that."

It was his turn to swivel away and hunker down over his glass. "This area, I believe, is getting ready for another boomtown swing," he said quietly. He'd been trying to keep this hunch pretty low-key until now. But he signed the papers with Josh this morning. He'd staked his claim.

"Get that from your crystal ball, Merlin?"

Softer side? What had he been thinking?

He fixed her with an icy glare. "I happen to be one of Fortune 500's top-rated investment specialists, Princess. My crystal ball has a pretty impressive track record of hitting the mark, dead on."

She pursed her lips. "I beg your pardon, Mr. Lareci. I had no idea whom I was dealing with."

Facetious, indignant, infuriating. He should down the rest of his drink and hit the road. The two-hour trip would easily stretch to three in this shitty weather. Who did this bitch think she was, anyway?

Stupido! Where was his brain? Why was he letting her call the shots here?

"And who am *I* dealing with? I'm guessing your lake house is only a weekend haunt," he said.

"That would be correct, Boss. I live on the Upper West Side. But I work downtown. Ever heard of Bardach & Associates?"

9

Her cynicism prickled his skin, but he still couldn't help his body's reaction to her. Not even the parts that usually reacted to a woman this sexy. Someplace higher. Like, deep in his gut.

And the way she was looking at him whispered again of a softer side, but how?

His mind clicked into research mode, virtually thumbing through the lists of companies on the Exchange. The list scrolled through his head endlessly in his sleep most every night. Filled his days with tension, on a constant hunt for the next big ticket to lay a client's chips on.

Slowly, he shook his head, causing her to cross her arms and clip that pouty lower lip between perfect, dazzling teeth. "Well, if you haven't heard of us yet, you might want to watch us. BDA on the Exchange. We're only eight years young, but we've been pretty steady for the past three."

"And what kind of commodities is BDA into?"

"Interior design. Residential, commercial, you name it. We've done some of Trump's playpens, updated the Legacy Suites at the Plaza last year. We're just finishing up a period renovation and refurnishing of the Morris-Jamel Mansion."

Marco froze, the tumbler halfway to his lips.

Lady Luck, you're definitely on my team today.

"So, interior design," he repeated, dumbly.

She laughed, a warm throaty sound that caused a tightening in his lower belly. "Yes, interior design. And you've bought a 1960s vintage hotel you're looking to renovate into a . . . what? Five-star hotel?" She lifted the martini and sipped again, this time darting her tongue out to toy with the toothpick spearing the olive.

Yes, these slacks are definitely snugging up in the crotch.

"What a serendipitous coincidence," she said. All traces of snip and snipe had disappeared, melting into warm, buttery liquid. He could almost taste the salt of the olive on her tongue.

She leaned toward him, and it was then he realized what it was about her that intrigued him so. Set his blood to simmer. Made him yearn to get closer, even through the rain of arrows her sharp arrogance spewed with every word.

It was the way she blinked. The thick, black lashes over those sleepy, slanted, blue eyes struggled to complete each and every movement. He'd never seen anything quite like it.

In a sexy, almost calculating way, the lady blinked in *slow motion*. The effect made her seem as though she were coming down off a mind-blowing orgasm. Or, perhaps, was on the prowl, actively trolling for the lucky partner for her next.

Mesmerized, Marco decided quickly he had to get to know this woman better. Study her more closely. So he asked, "I don't suppose you have a few moments to take a look at the property on your way back to your lake house?"

Forty-five minutes later, Kate followed Marco's black Infiniti along the winding drive, leading to what used to be Redman's Resort. She, of course, had insisted on taking her own car. After all, she was staying less than a mile away from the abandoned hotel. Right on the shores of Loch Sheldrake.

Although it had been standing empty for almost twenty years, it was obvious someone had been taking care of the property, a detail Kate had noticed the dozens of times she'd driven past the entryway. The new spring grass lining the road had recently been trimmed, and coach lamps glowed along its length.

But time had taken its toll on the Redman. Lingering—but badly battered from years of Catskill winters—the white paint on the craftsman-style exterior slivered free from the siding in long, curling sheets. A few of the dark-green shutters from the upper floor windows were missing. But all the glass, miraculously, remained intact.

Bright splashes of color, incongruous against the sad structure, drew Kate's gaze to two mounds of pink azaleas gracing the tops of the concrete planters flanking the front doors.

"Looks like you've started sprucing the place up already," she remarked, tipping her chin toward them as she stepped out of her pearl-white Porsche. They had parked, she behind him, underneath the portico sheltering the hotel's entrance.

Marco paused at his rear bumper, shrugging to adjust his trench coat. "Not me. There's been something or other planted in those things ever since I first looked at the place last December." He chuckled, shaking his head. "It was little pine trees then. For Christmas, I guess."

Kate arched an eyebrow. "And what makes you think they weren't Hanukkah bushes?"

A wry smile curved his lips. "Excellent point. I truly don't have any idea." He fumbled in his coat pocket and pulled out a set of keys bearing a large cardboard tag. "Just got possession of these this morning."

The frame surrounding the glass in the massive front doors, once painted a regal red, was faded and nearly bare to the oak base in spots. Still, their grand size and lavish, though tarnished, brass trim spoke of the elegance the place once held. Marco fitted the key into the lock and pulled open one side.

"After you, milady."

The building's musty sigh hit Kate's senses as she stepped over the threshold, causing a shiver to skitter across her shoulder blades. In the gloom, she was hesitant to venture any farther. The icy dampness of the day hung even heavier inside.

Marco whisked around her and made his way to the wall adjacent to the door, exposing a cleverly disguised switch panel masked within the dark paneling. Within seconds, the lobby blinked to life like a vintage scene in a period museum.

Suddenly, it was 1964. Laid bare to its bones.

Patterned carpet in an oversized diamond design, deep red and gold, contrasted sharply with the floor-to-ceiling, dark oak paneling. The lobby had been stripped bare of furniture, who knew how long ago. The only embellishment remaining in the center of the space leading up to a paneled registration desk was a gold and crystal chandelier.

But the space screamed elegance. Opulence, even. Square, stuccoed pillars dotted the open space like white-barked Sequoias, sturdy and solid and fully intending to maintain their own ground. On one side, two massive, curved staircases rose away from the ground floor to meet on the second level. They formed a heart-shaped frame around the archway leading into what must have once been a grand ballroom. Some of the gilt paint still clung to the railings, adding a golden glow to the worn but still majestic view.

"Oh, this is magnificent," Kate breathed. "Truly magnificent. Funny, I've driven by here every weekend for years and never realized how well this place has held up." She turned toward Marco, almost unable to contain her excitement. "Most of these old hotels are in shambles, as I'm sure you know. This is . . . simply amazing."

Marco's beaming smile revealed perfect, brilliant, white teeth through the dark, casual stubble on his face. An errant lock of wavy black hair had fallen onto his brow. His eyes were rimmed with the kind of thick, dark lashes women have to work so hard for. Now they glowed, not ordinary hazel, but nearly green, flecked with gold. The intensity of his gaze caused her blood pressure to spike.

Mercy, he's an attractive man. Not my usual type, but still . . . .

"So, you think it has potential? I want to make it the masterpiece it once was, but modernized. Contemporary. Sleek."

Ouch, no. She pressed her lips together and shook her head. "No. No, you can't alter this too much. You'll spoil it. Like putting a coat of hot pink paint on a classic car."

"Ah," he said, "so you know classic cars as well?"

Kate shook her head. "Not much. My mother always had a thing for the old Mustangs. But no, I've never really had any interest."

The ringing in her ears commenced at that very moment, almost the second after the words left her lips. Kate silently groaned. She drew her shoulders up toward her ears and twisted her neck.

Not again. Not now. I want this job. I can do this.

"So, what are you thinking? Surely, we can modernize this to appeal to the 21st-century tourist and still bow a nod to the original design. You can do this, no?"

But Kate could hardly hear him now, his words nearly meaningless through a buzzing static she recognized with ominous trepidation. Familiar, though dreaded. She knew well what was coming. It would be only moments before her throat closed up with spasms even her emergency asthma inhaler couldn't quell.

There was nothing here Kate hadn't been exposed to in dozens of other potential job sites. And yes, it was cold in here, even colder than outside. But it didn't explain why the hairs prickled her arms under her raincoat, and a lead blanket of sadness washed over her like a drowning wave. Oppressive. Suffocating.

There was suffering here. Perhaps an imprint of past pain, or the anguish of something more coherent. Whatever it was made Kate's chest clutch against pain so intense, she found it hard to breathe.

Old pain of massive intensity, even masked under mold, and mildew, and dust. The anguish was fresh, as raw as it had ever been. From the day of its inception.

"Hey, you all right?"

Kate blinked back into the moment as Marco approached her, concern furrowing his brow.

"Yeah, fine. Sorry. Must be the stale air in here," she stammered, struggling to draw in breaths behind ribs that felt crushed, as if bound within a straightjacket. Bruised, even broken. She struggled to put on her business face and flashed him a smile she was certain didn't reach her eyes.

"It's magnificent," she repeated, hanging on to the word like a life raft in a storm-tossed sea.

After studying her for a moment, Marco asked, "So, what do you think? Can we turn this place into a five-star hotel? Maybe add a nightclub downstairs? The basement's unfinished, but—"

"No," she snapped back. "No, I can't take on this project. I'm sorry." She turned and took three long strides to put her back over the threshold, back outside into the deepening early twilight.

Marco was right on her heels. "Why not?" Irritation poisoned the words. "It's structurally sound. I had a building inspector check out all the bearing walls, the foundation. He says the wiring needs to be upgraded, but basically, all she needs is a face-lift."

All she needs is to come up for air.

Those words shot through Kate's brain with such intensity, she winced. And then she heard the scream. A panicked, agonizing voice only she could hear.

Her heart began to race as the pain in her chest localized, escalated. As though she'd been shot or knifed. Afraid to look down for fear she'd see a dark patch spreading on the cloth of her raincoat, she started toward her car. But she was moving too fast. Stumbling on a loose stone, Kate nearly hit the ground as she toppled off one of her boots' spiked heels.

Marco caught her, his hand closing around her upper arm. He was behind her then, close—so close she could smell whatever signature scent he wore. It made her dizzy, weak. The raindrops transformed to sparkles, and for a moment, she feared she would faint.

"Hey, hey, what's wrong, Kate? Are you ill?" His words rumbled into her ear as his other arm encircled her waist from behind. The compassion she heard in his low, murmured tone broke through her already-compromised armor. She squeezed her eyes shut against the tears, but they spilled over anyway.

Before she had time to form another coherent thought, she found herself wrapped in this stranger's arms, sobbing into the lapel of his trench coat.

TWO

"What happened to you back there?"

Marco sat on the white leather loveseat in front of a massive slate fireplace covering one entire wall of Kate's lake house. The adjacent wall was glass, floor to ceiling, and framed in rustic cedar. Although it wasn't yet dark, already the lights from Loch Sheldrake's few surviving businesses on the main drag blinked in the distance, dancing in long, colorful spires on the water.

He had no idea what had just happened. One minute, he was getting ready to discuss a business deal with a pretty lady who just happened to have the exact qualifications he needed to begin renovations on his latest investment project. The next, he'd been consoling a woman who sounded as though her heart had recently suffered the loss of a parent, a child, or a spouse.

Yet, she had recovered quickly, insisting on driving her own car the half-mile up the road to her lake house. He'd followed, confused and more than a little intrigued. Once inside this lavish summer cottage—one as nice as his upscale loft in Manhattan—he'd watched as she pulled a bottle of Pinot Grigio out of a countertop wine chiller, pulled the cork, and poured two glasses.

He'd known Kate Bardach for only four hours, but he knew better than to offer to open the wine. To wait on her. To try to play chivalrous, especially once they were on her home turf.

Although she'd flashed those brilliant, blue eyes up at him once after his question, she didn't reply until she'd handed him the chilled glass and held up her own to toast.

He didn't even like Pinot Grigio. But then again, she hadn't asked.

"To memories, old and cherished. And mostly, to those better left behind," she said, fixing him with a sultry expression before performing her sexier-than-hell slow blink again.

He clicked his glass to hers and replied, "Hear, hear."

She sat beside him, though the love seat was big enough to where they were nowhere near touching. After she'd leaned back and drained half the glass in three swallows, she tipped her head back, closed her eyes, and sighed. Then she leveled her gaze at him.

"Okay, so, I have a problem with old buildings, sometimes," she began, leaning forward to set her glass on the soapstone coaster. When she did, the red sweater dress that had been hiding underneath the Burberry coat flapped open along its deep-V neckline, revealing a sumptuous view of two generously rounded mounds.

Pale, freckled skin. Oy, marrone. Funny, though, he hadn't noticed a single freckle on that porcelain face earlier . . . .

"What kind of problems?" he asked, struggling to keep his brain in control over his hormones.

She looked down into her lap, where her neatly manicured hands were folded like a schoolgirl. Her long lashes spread over her cheeks like black fans. This was a side of her he hadn't figured on.

Demure. Huh. She was all balls and brass at the racetrack.

"I know it might sound crazy to you, Mr. Lareci. But I believe buildings—homes, old houses, or places like your hotel—have their own . . . well, let's just say . . . personality." She lifted her gaze to his. "And I won't work on a project where the spirit of the place isn't welcoming."

His bark of laughter brought back the balls and brass, sparkling in her narrowed eyes.

"So, you're saying my hotel's haunted?" he scoffed, not meaning his tone to come off as deprecating as it did. But he couldn't hide his smile as he shifted in his seat and took a long draw from his own glass. "I'd imagine that could present a real problem in your line of work from time to time."

"Yes," she said, nodding slowly, her tone deadly flat. "It most certainly does."

Definitely not what Marco wanted to hear, especially from this bombshell of a woman whose very presence was about to induce him to spill his seed in his own pants. It had been a while—a very long while—since a woman had this effect on him. Even his live-in lover, Arianna, a few years back. She'd been sexy as hell and a superlative lover, murmuring to him in delicious Italian obscenities as they'd coupled.

But the spark hadn't been there...not like this. And this one, from what she was revealing to him, might well be a bit wacko. In addition, she was fiercely independent, arrogant, and too smart for her own good. Or for anyone who tangled with her.

Yet he couldn't block out the words. *This woman is something special.* They rang inside Marco's head as clearly as if he were listening through earbuds.

He knew he shouldn't. Marco knew he should finish his wine, say goodnight, and find a room nearby. And he was usually pretty good at letting his mind overrule his hormones. But tonight, something else was urging him forward. Beyond his comfort zone. Beyond his logical boundaries.

Then again, Marco Lareci never had been able to argue—and win—against his heart.

Kate didn't understand how the night had progressed as it did. One minute, this wealthy, Italian stranger was ridiculing her fear of dealing with what he called *haunted places*. The next, the conversation had drifted to more personal subjects. Where she grew up. Her education. How she'd managed to build a corporate design empire in downtown Manhattan.

Even though she personally wouldn't deal with any building with a long, lurid history. That's why she employed a team of the finest associates in the business.

What was most perplexing was how he'd managed to dodge most of her questions about his own background. But he had. As smoothly as the finest Russian vodka over ice.

"Well now you know quite a bit about me, Lareci. Now it's your turn. How long did it take you to climb from a middle-class Brooklyn boy to a big-time name on Wall Street? Pardon my observation, but you don't look old enough."

One side of his mouth quirked and he kept his eyes trained on his glass. "I got lucky. Real lucky. And yeah, I probably am one of the youngest in my field, at my level, anyway." He raised his eyes to meet hers. "I'm twenty-nine. Won't turn thirty until next month. And you?"

Ah, so he *is* younger than I am. A definite plus. He's probably not looking for anything long-term yet. If ever.

"Thirty-two," she said. "So I'm officially the older woman."

His deep, throaty laugh made her tingle in all the right places. When he moved to sit beside her on the sofa, his scent filled her head with a delicious variety of fantasies. Kate really liked the energy, the recklessness of younger men. These were the liaisons she sought out. The ones where she knew there would be incredible sex, but no chance anyone's feelings would get hurt when they parted ways a day or two later.

When he laid his hand on her bare knee, his warm, firm grip thrilled her, an electric jolt traveling straight up her leg and into her lady parts. Instantly, she felt her panties dampen.

Whoa. Good thing I don't intend to take on his project. This kind of chemistry is difficult to turn down. So there's nothing—absolutely nothing—keeping me from acting on those fantasies.

What followed in the next few hours, though, left her baffled. He wasn't like the other younger men she'd been with. Not that he was that much younger, but still. Men do mature later than women, don't they?

The man definitely took his time. He began by lifting her hand and kissing it like a medieval knight. Then he'd lifted her long, heavy mane and pressed gentle, delicate kisses, and nuzzled her neck, slow and languid, long before his mouth even found her own. Marco worshipped her body with a reverence she couldn't remember experiencing. Slow, methodical, sensual. Never before. Not quite this way.

Kate liked sex—that was true. But she accepted the act as physical, carnal. A biological need. She always laughed when her friends talked about a man *making love* to them. What love had to do with it, she had no freaking idea.

Her experience with Marco rocked her beliefs. Just a bit. Well, she'd never had an Italian partner before. Maybe there was a reason for all the fuss about Italian stallions after all.

No matter. By the time the sun came up the next morning, she'd taken care of several problems. Not only had she scratched an itch she hadn't tended to for several months. She'd also effectively warded off any further question as to whether or not she'd take on the job of renovating Redman's Resort.

"You are something very special, Ms. Kate Bardach," he said, shuffling out into her kitchen on bare feet as he tucked his rumpled shirt into the waistband of his slacks.

Kate sighed. Okay, he was a great fuck. Not a terribly creative speaker. She ran out of fingers trying to determine how many times she'd heard that one.

But she simply smiled at him through the steam rising from her mug. "You're not bad yourself, Marco Lareci." She handed him a mug of coffee. "Cream? Sugar?"

He shook his head. "No. Straight's fine with me." As he sipped, he studied her over the counter separating them, then slipped onto the wooden stool. "I guess I got lucky twice yesterday. First, by betting on your horse. Second, by meeting you. Can we round it off by making it a lucky three?"

Kate tipped her head. "I'd say, I already did. I achieved my third orgasm before you ever mounted me, stallion."

Marco blinked, then grinned. "That you did. But it's not what I'm talking about." He sipped from his mug and groaned. "Ah, caffe perfetto as well." He shook his head. "No, I'm talking about the hotel. I really want you to do it for me, Kate. I mean, hire you, as a professional. Can I make an appointment to come to your studio?"

"You can," she began slowly, "but if we take on the project, it won't be me you'll be dealing with. I already told you why."

Anguish twisted his features. "No, no, don't tell me that. I don't want one of your flunkies doing this job. I need you. *You.* I feel it," he said, pounding a fist against his chest, "I feel it here."

"Not a single member of my staff comes close to being a flunky," she snapped, irritation prickling in her chest. But she'd fully expected his reaction. Actually, she'd tricked him, and a tiny part of her felt bad about the fact. She set down her mug and drew a deep breath. Closing her eyes, she murmured, "I'm afraid it's too late for me to take on your hotel."

"What do you mean, too late? Are you that busy? How far out are your services booked?"

"No." She pinned him with a glare. "I make it my policy to never sleep with a client. Ever." Pausing, she assessed his shock and sensed a tinge of anger flaring in those pale eyes. Not green, not gray. Somewhere in between, and ever-changing. "We slept together. I can't possibly take on your renovation. But if it makes you feel better," she continued, "I sincerely look forward to sleeping with you again."

Marco screeched out of Kate's driveway with rage simmering in his chest. As soon as he pulled onto Route 17, he gunned the Q50 until the needle hit triple digits, then thought better of letting his temper earn him yet another increase in his insurance. He braked sharply and slammed the steering wheel with the flat of his hand as he swore to the empty space around him.

"Cazzo! Stubborn, calculating, Jewish American Princess," he growled.

But damn, she was like no woman he'd ever met in his life. And had an effect on him like no other woman ever had. Which, to be honest, scared the living hell out of him.

And now, he had compounded his own problems. Exponentially.

Marco went out on a limb, investing in a hotel located in what had been one of the most depressed areas of the Catskills for the last five decades. On a gut feeling. But he'd done his research. With the prosperity the new casino at the Montlake Raceway had enjoyed over the last several years, he felt certain the area was on the rebound. Ready to rise from the ashes. Real estate phoenix. An investor's dream.

So, Marco had convinced two of his best clients to take the plunge with him. The initial purchase price, they all knew, was bread crumbs compared to the mother-loaf of the cost of renovation. The marketing. The revival of a dream that had flickered and died in Sullivan County all those years ago.

Sure, there were other interior designers he could hire. Few, however, were overly anxious to relocate from Manhattan to Liberty for the months it would take for the project. Finding Kate today seemed like providence. A miracle dropped in his lap. One, serendipitously, who'd made a particular area of his body extremely happy in the hours following their meeting.

But the lady knew exactly what she was doing when she invited him to her bed. On their visit to the Redman, Marco could tell she'd been . . . what, turned off? No, there had been initial excitement in her eyes, in her voice when she first got a look at the classic architecture of the place. How it had been at least minimally maintained over the past years, and not completely abandoned to become a crumbling terrarium like the other places he'd considered. Grossman's. The Nevele. Kutsher's.

He'd simply have to persuade her a little more forcefully. Marco was not a quitter. He wouldn't have gotten to where he was—one of the most profitable investment brokers in Manhattan—without perseverance. It was what he was good at. It was precisely how he would convince Kate Bardach to head up the renovations on Redman's Resort.

No. It was no longer the Redman.

The Shelby. He would call it The Shelby Hotel.

Kate left Loch Sheldrake early that afternoon to drive back to Manhattan, stopping only briefly by her father's stables in Chester to make sure her prized filly hadn't suffered any ill effects from her maiden run yesterday. The horse was fine, the traffic was light, and although she tried not to dwell on the details, Kate was still riding the high of the incredible sex she'd shared with Marco the night before.

Memories of her visit to Redman's Resort, however, she tried to push to the back of her mind. Those experiences always shook her up, but this time, it had been painful. Actually, physically painful. That had never happened to her before.

Oh, she'd experienced a sense of uneasiness. Voices in her head, usually whispers. She'd done some research, and knew so-called hauntings came in two different varieties—residual and active. The residual kind were imprints, shadows of the past, like double exposures of two different times in the same space. These were generally harmless.

It was the active kind Kate steered clear of. These were spirits who could—under the right circumstances and with the right person—communicate with the living. Or try to. She'd like to believe the scream of agony she'd heard last night at Redman's was residual. Nothing more than a shadow of something horrible that had happened there in an earlier time.

But the pain, the searing, gut-wrenching pain, told her it might be something more. Something stronger. Much, much stronger.

Why had the place affected her so?

She handed the keys of her Porsche to her building's attendant when she pulled in about four o'clock and made her way to the elevator bank. It wasn't until she'd bolted and chained her apartment door behind her and kicked off her shoes that she realized how tired she was.

Sure, it was early. But she answered to no one but herself. Kept no one else's schedule but her own. And Kate Bardach liked it this way. She liked it this way a lot.

Once showered and wrapped in her favorite satin robe, Kate dialed security at the front desk.

"Listen, Adam. I'm ordering in some dinner from *Daniel*. Can you have the concierge bring it up when it arrives?"

"Of course, Ms. Bardach. My pleasure."

She called *Daniel* and ordered the Dorset lamb chops, then poured herself a glass of Syrah as she clicked the house phone back into its cradle. Settled down into the corner of her velour sofa, she picked up the latest issue of The New Yorker but found she couldn't concentrate. The words, meaningless to her eyes, persisted in getting up off the page and running about. Grabbing the remote, she keyed in the digits for the five o'clock news.

Huh. The cable must be out. Static filled her big screen, black and white vibrating, hissing fuzz. Eerily reminiscent of an old rerun of the Twilight Zone.

Ah, yes. She'd been forced to endure more than one of those horrifying episodes in her tender years, along with *The X-Files* and *Tales from the Crypt*. Her father was a die-hard fan of horror and sci-fi. Kate was certain responsibility for more than one of her childhood nightmares rested squarely on her father's shoulders.

But not all of them.

Just as she lifted the phone to dial the front desk to inquire about the problem with the cable, an image flickered into view. It was the face of a woman—one who looked remarkably like Kate herself. For one crazy moment, she thought perhaps her own image was being broadcast onto the screen, staring back at her like a selfie on her phone.

Until the woman began to speak.

No, not speak. Kate couldn't make out the words. Her lips were moving, but only white noise emanated from the surround sound speakers flanking the screen. It appeared she was saying the same phrase, over and over again, a sort of mantra. But the desperate look in her eyes—those brilliant, blue eyes lined with jet lashes exactly like her own—riveted Kate to the image.

A chill washed over her, and gooseflesh rose on her arms. Her cozy, secure apartment felt suddenly empty and echoey. The shadows cast by her side table lamp seemed unnaturally large on the wall beside her. Undulating. Pulsating. Moving, yet so slightly, the naked eye couldn't quite perceive it.

And the pain, like from earlier at the hotel, returned to her chest in a thudding, dull rhythm. In perfect time with her heartbeat, which accelerated crazily now. The thrumming of her own pulse in her ears threatened to drown out all other sound.

Confused, frozen with shock and more than a bit of trepidation, it took a moment or two before Kate picked up the remote, her hand trembling. She pressed the volume button up, up, up. The static was almost deafening, but through the hissing din, she made out two words.

Find me.

She stared at the image, one mirroring her own, afraid to move. But there was no doubt. The woman on the screen was saying the same phrase, over and over and over again. With a desperation Kate not only heard, but felt like a sword to her heart.

Find me. Find me. Find me.

When the buzzer of her doorbell slashed through her consciousness, Kate shrieked. The remote fell and bounced off her glass-topped coffee table to end up on the floor. Gasping for air, she slapped a hand to her chest, then pushed her hair off a now sweaty forehead, her eyes darting about.

It's the doorbell. Just the doorbell.

She scrambled to her feet, relief washing over her with the knowledge there was another person outside her door. Another living, breathing person.

The latching chain fell out of her fingertips twice, and she swore when she realized it had taken one corner of her right index fingernail with it.

Wait. Center. Common sense, girl. Security. Look through the peephole.

The distorted image of a navy blue-uniformed concierge with a severe and very blond crewcut stood outside her door, looking off down the hallway with a bored expression. She opened the door.

"Your dinner has arrived, Ms. Bardach. Shall I bring it inside?" He thrust the heavy paper bag toward her as if to say, "I'd rather you just take it right here."

"Thank you. But yes, if you don't mind. Could you bring it in? I seem to be having some difficulty with the cable signal this evening." She hated the tremor she heard in her own voice. But at this point, she was powerless to control it.

She ignored his raised eyebrow and stood back to usher him in, pointing to the side table for him to deposit her dinner.

"The cable seems to be down," she said, taking two long strides towards where the remote lay still on the carpet beside the coffee table. She lifted it and turned toward the television.

Where she froze.

Bill O'Reilly commanded the screen, dressed in his usual impeccably tailored, pin-striped suit, ranting on in his usual manner. Kate stared stupidly at the TV personality for a moment, then glanced at the concierge. The young man stood solemnly, his hands clasped behind his back, his benign smile not quite reaching his eyes.

"Ma'am?"

"Huh. Guess it was a temporary glitch," she mumbled, embarrassed. She swiped a hand down over her face. As he turned to leave she said, "Wait. Thank you. Here." She dug into her purse for a ten-dollar bill and squashed it into his palm. "Thank you. Thank you very much."

THREE

Marco was not inherently a patient man. But he could be, when necessary. He knew when it was important to be patient and when it was crucial to surge ahead. The case with Kate Bardach was one requiring patience.

Of a flavor he wasn't sure he could muster.

He waited until Monday—a full four days since he'd parted ways with her in Loch Sheldrake and returned to his Manhattan loft. Since he worked from home, the concept of a work week meant little to him. But since many of his clients did abide by the nine-to-five, Monday through Friday work week, he was fully aware of the acceptable protocol. At ten minutes past nine on Monday morning, he called in at the offices of Bardach & Associates, LLC.

In person.

"Good morning," he said, beaming into the eyes of the emaciated, anemic-looking receptionist whose pale, strawberry blonde hair fell in wispy strings around her face. "I'm here to see Ms. Bardach."

A scowl twisted the girl's face into a lemon-puckered facade as she studied the appointment screen on her computer. "I don't see as Ms. Bardach has any appointments set for this morning," she hummed. Yes, hummed. The poor girl obviously had a severe nasal condition.

Marco cleared his throat. "Well, this one might not have made it on to her calendar. We met at Montlake last week. She looked at a property I want her to take on."

Tiny furrows creased the girl's brow as she studied him with suspicious eyes. "Your name, sir?"

"Tell her I'm here representing LMP Enterprises."

Twenty minutes later, Marco found himself facing a dark, caged lioness skulking on the far side of a highly polished acre of ebony desk. Behind her, a wall of glass showcased midtown Manhattan better than any panoramic camera shot. The spire of the Empire State Building anchored the skyline, right about in the center of the frame.

"Who the hell do you think you are, prancing in here like the Prince of Wales on a Monday morning?" she hissed. She paced, hugging her arms around her excellently tailored navy suit. Her porcelain skin, flawlessly freckle-free, showcased brilliant, blue eyes rimmed in jet black with a lush fringe of matching lashes. "And who the hell is LMP Enterprises? Good one, Lareci. Good one. You got me. One for your side."

Marco smiled at her as he settled himself into the plush, leather armchair opposite her desk. "Lareci, Markovich, and Petrov. I told you I had two partners in this venture. Hey, have you ever heard this one? An Italian, a Jew, and a Russian walk into a bar—"

"Spare me!" Kate shouted, spinning to glare at him, fire sparking from her eyes. "The only reason I didn't turn you away was because I was curious. LMP, huh? I thought it stood for last menstrual period."

Marco arched an eyebrow and studied her. "Hmm. Does the regular arrival of your *monthly* concern you? Are you that worried about, perhaps getting—"

"Stop!" Kate slammed both hands down on her desk and stared at him. "Seriously, dude, you are royally pissing me off right now. What do you want? What the hell are you doing here?"

Marco crossed his arms across his chest and tipped up his chin. She was a feisty one, no doubt about that. But he'd dealt with feisty bitches before.

Scratch that. She didn't deserve such a demeaning moniker. Not yet, anyway.

Resting his elbows on his knees, Marco leaned toward her. "I didn't mean to piss you off, Kate. I only want you to renovate my hotel." He hadn't meant his tone to shift down to gentle, but somehow, it had.

Kate huffed, pinched two fingers to the base of her nose, and turned away from him, toward the wall of windows. She stood there for a long moment, saying nothing.

He could wait. It wasn't easy for him. But for her, it might be worth it.

"I told you last week," she began quietly, "I don't work on any sites I don't feel comfortable with. I simply don't feel comfortable with Redman's."

"It's not Redman's anymore," he said. "I'm renaming it. The Shelby."

When she spun toward him, for a moment, if the desk hadn't created a chasm between them, he thought she'd like to lash out and strike him. Slap his face, as if he'd called her a bad name. Uttered an unspeakable obscenity. But her eyes said it all, and more clearly than he wanted to admit.

The name meant something to her.

He'd picked it out of a hat. Totally random. But for some reason, it struck a nerve with her.

She was blinking fast, like someone either lying through their teeth or getting ready to break down and bawl their eyes out. But he didn't know which. She planted both hands on the edge of her desk and heaved in several breaths. In and out, in and out. A full fifteen seconds elapsed before she raised her eyes to meet his.

A filmy mist failed to mask the agony in those clear, blue eyes. Clear, blue steel.

"I don't know who you are or why you found me. Or, how you ended up barging into my life like a backhoe out of hell." Her chest was heaving now, and he could see the soft mounds of her breasts peeking out from under her starched, white shirt.

Complete with pale, peach freckles.

"Kate, please," he said, reaching forward to lay a hand over hers. "I mean no harm. I'm a client—a legitimate one—in need of your services. Your expertise."

She snatched her hand out from under his as though it were a hot iron. "I've already told you. I cannot take on your project. Now, if you'd like to arrange a meeting with my associates, I feel quite certain one of them may be interested."

Marco tilted his head and locked gazes with hers. The contact shot through him like a bolt of electricity, causing his breath to hitch in his chest. But he swallowed and moved forward.

"Kate, you're the one. You're the one who has to bring my hotel back to life. You know it, and I know it. It's destiny, sweetheart." He reached for her hand, snatching it before she could pull away, and lifted it to his lips, planting a soft kiss there. "Destiny."

FOUR

Kate was relieved both Yvette and Daniel agreed to go with her to assess the Redman, although her stomach was still churning a mini-tornado as they parked and gathered near her rear bumper. She could tell by the look on Yvette's face she wasn't crazy about the property already, and they hadn't even stepped inside. Daniel, her newest team member, was as enthusiastic and optimistic as any young architect she'd ever worked with.

She was also certain he was sweet on her, having invited her out for a drink on more than one occasion. Too bad he worked for her. She really did like having sex with younger men.

"Hey, this place isn't haunted, is it, Kate?" Daniel asked, laughing.

She shook her head as she lifted out her briefcase. "I wouldn't know anything about that, Dan. I'm not a believer. You know that," she said, touching his sleeve.

Liar.

Kate never divulged the details of her ability, her sixth sense, her curse. Her refusal to take on certain projects, or why. She thought it best to keep it that way. It's exactly what she did not need—for the people who worked for her thinking she was loony tunes.

Now all she could hope was she could hold it together long enough to figure out why, exactly, she had felt compelled to take on this job—one that had rocked her to her core—in the first place.

When Lareci's voice boomed from across the parking lot, irritation shot up Kate's spine like wildfire.

Pushy bastard, this guy. Figures the whole world has to operate on his schedule. Well, he'll learn fast that's not how Kate Bardach does business.

After the introductions, Marco said, "Do you want to start on the outside? Or, should we go in first?"

"I'd like to do a walk-around to check out the foundation," Daniel said. "Can't do much with what's on top if what's underneath is flawed."

Marco glared at him and replied, "I had a building inspector in before we ever signed the papers, Mister . . . what was it again?" A muscle worked in his jaw, and Kate stifled a smile.

"It's Daniel," she cut in, "and if Daniel wants to take a look himself, I see no reason why he shouldn't." She flicked her gaze from Marco, to Yvette, to Boris, and back to Marco. "But we all can go on inside and get started."

The lobby seemed a little less oppressive with the pale spring sunshine filtering in through the tall windows flanking the entrance. The light showcased the worn spots in the diamond-patterned carpet where the chandelier was casting a myriad of sparks over its surface. Although the angular shape of the reception desk might have seemed cutting-edge back in its day, Kate noticed the cuts and chips along the veneered knife-edges now.

She'd been viscerally overcome with the sadness filling the place when she'd first seen it. Now, it looked even sadder. Forlorn. Abandoned. Suspended in a time long gone.

"Whoa, got some vintage sixties going on here, huh?" Yvette said, a twinkle of amusement lighting up her usually stoic expression. "When was this place last occupied?"

Boris replied. "The last guest checked out in September of 1976. The place has been closed up ever since."

Yvette's head snapped around and she smiled, a real one. Kate could count on one hand how many times she'd seen that smile. "Ooh, nice accent. You're from...?"

"Russia," Boris said, trilling his tongue over the R in an exaggeration of his pronounced Russian accent. "St. Petersburg.

Come, Madam. Let me show you the ballroom. If you think the lobby speaks to the place's heritage, you must see the ballroom."

Kate watched, tickled to her soul, as her blander-than-milquetoast design assistant hooked her arm into that of short, dark Boris, and he whisked her away toward an archway down one end of the lobby. Kate could never remember seeing that much spring in Yvette's step since the day she'd hired her.

It wasn't until she felt Marco's glare bearing down on her that she turned toward him. "Well," she said, "looks like there won't be a personality issue between those two, at least."

The door opened then, and Daniel stood on the threshold, brushing shreds of loose grass off the cuffs of his slacks.

"Looks like somebody's been taking care of this place. The entire foundation is clear of weeds, and it looks like a fairly fresh coat of waterproofing is on there. How long since it's been closed?"

"1976." Both Kate and Marco answered in unison, then their eyes met and the tension broke. Marco smiled, she smiled back.

Warmth rose up Kate's neck, and flashes of their night in her lake house flooded her mind. On a hitching breath, she tucked her hair behind one ear and angled her body away from Marco and toward Daniel. No point dwelling on what could only remain a fond memory. It was a one-time deal and wouldn't be happening again. At least, not for a long, long time.

Daniel looked from Kate to Marco, then asked, "Have you been handling the upkeep, Mr. Lareci?"

Marco's stance softened a bit, and he shifted his body toward Daniel. "No. No, it's been maintained all through the years, at least minimally, by money placed in a trust specifically for that purpose. It was foreclosed on in 1978, but the attorneys who held the reins when we bought it have made good on keeping the place from falling down."

Daniel nodded. He turned toward Kate and said, "Let's take a look in the basement. I'll need to assess the HVAC."

He took a step towards Kate, as if to guide her by the arm. Marco didn't give him the chance.

"Let me, Kate. I know the way," Marco said, extending his elbow in the same way as Boris had for Yvette.

Again, the humor of the situation threatened to bubble out into a giggle. But Kate fought back the urge, pressed her smile into a thin line, and hooked her arm into Marco's. She followed him toward the hallway beside the reception desk.

"This way, Daniel," Marco quipped over one shoulder.

Kate didn't turn around to see the younger man's expression but was sure it was that of a wounded, and probably very pissed off, young lion.

They'd been wandering around on all three floors of the old Redman's Resort, plus the basement, for over three hours. Kate was immensely relieved the only negative vibes she'd felt from the place emanated from the silence, the dust motes, and some surface mildew on the wallpaper. No intense emotions. No shocking pain like the other day. Not a scary moment in any of it.

Of course, watching the soap opera unfolding around her had caused plenty of distraction. She was fairly certain Boris and Yvette would end up in a hotel room before the night was over. Several times, she'd had to remind her assistant to be sure and take detailed notes as to the vision Mr. Lareci and Mr. Petrov had for the newly designed Shelby Hotel.

But Kate wasn't immune to the glow she'd never seen before in Yvette's eyes. Although she herself had a strict policy against mixing business with pleasure, she'd never felt justified in imposing this rule on her staff. They were all grown-ups with their own minds. The only time she'd ever stepped in was if a personal liaison with a client had interfered with the progress of a project.

In that case, she simply switched the staff member out to a different assignment. She'd only had to do that one time.

The comedic quality of Yvette, however, towering a full six inches over Boris' height of, maybe, five foot six, did not escape her.

And Marco and Daniel's unending joust for her attention would have been downright hilarious. If not for the fact that no matter how much she'd like to jump Daniel's young, sinuous body, or replay the orgasmic events of last week with the dangerously sexy Marco, she was at liberty to do neither.

In the end, Boris kissed Yvette's fingers as she climbed into the Cadillac, and Daniel begrudgingly shook Marco's hand. It had been agreed a list of services would be generated, starting with the basics to get the property back up into redecorating condition. The details of the redecoration were still to be determined.

Kate waved goodbye as the Cadillac and Boris' Lexus disappeared around the bend in the drive. When Marco touched her elbow, she jumped.

He was tapping the watch on his wrist. "We've still got time for some lunch and a cocktail at the Underground before the third race. Isn't that when your filly runs?"

Kate closed her eyes and sighed. There was no denying it. She would be spending quite a bit of time with her new client. And the struggle to keep her mind away from the sexy, hard body she already knew—quite intimately—lurking only partially hidden underneath those tailored clothes was going to become increasingly difficult.

It was too late. She'd already tasted the poison, and it tasted just fine.

Oh, what the hell.

Her gaze locked on his as she stroked a hand down over her hair. "She does. Will you drive?"

Kate's filly won again, and Marco—again—turned a hundred bucks into two grand. This time, instead of them being strangers at opposite ends of an empty grandstand, they were a couple, tucked amicably in the front corner of Kate's box. Marco wasn't sure whether his intoxicating high was only from riding a rare streak of luck, or if something much more magical was happening.

As *April's Here* sailed across the finish line five lengths ahead of the pack, Marco grabbed Kate around the waist, lifted her high, and twirled her around in circles. They both screamed and squealed like children, and for a moment, it was exactly how Marco felt. Until, of course, her feet hit the ground and she kissed him, covering his mouth with a hunger that made him instantly hard.

There really was something special about this woman. He'd felt it from the first time their eyes met. Even though she was the complete opposite of everything he'd imagined in a future spouse, Marco Lareci found himself already thinking about using the two grand he just won on a diamond ring. For the first time in his life.

But he was no dummy, and knew—at least for the foreseeable future—he had to keep his feelings under wraps. He was quite sure any suggestion of a long-term relationship would earn him a slap on the face. And likely drive her straight away from him at warp speed.

He wasn't even sure how long it would be before she'd take him to her bed again. But he knew it would be worth the wait. In the meantime, he would enjoy this mysterious, infuriating, sexier-than-hell woman one tumultuous day at a time.

They spent the entire afternoon at the track, and Kate patiently explained the ins and outs of thoroughbred racing to Marco. He knew a little, but not nearly enough to be more than occasionally lucky with wagers. Kate grew up in the business. She told him her father had been raising racehorses since she was six years old.

They enjoyed a sumptuous dinner at the local Italian hot spot, *Frankie and Johnny's*, a mile or two up the road from Loch Sheldrake, along with a bottle of excellent Chianti. By the time they pulled back into Redman's parking lot to retrieve Kate's car, she was halfway into his lap, her firm, round breast pressed enticingly against his upper arm. When she trailed her fingers lightly along his thigh, Marco felt certain his wait might be over.

He killed the lights along with the engine.

"Why don't we leave my car here until the morning, Marco," she purred against his ear, flicking her tongue against the edge and causing an instant, rock-hard erection. He took her mouth, stroking the side of her face with his fingers as he explored and teased with his tongue. The sound of her quickened breath heightened the throbbing between his thighs.

It was impossible here, in the Infiniti. They could get creative on the hood, but the warm spring day had dropped to a chilly fifty degrees or so. Might not be the most pleasant for her, either. Cold steel on her bare bottom.

But leaving her car here made him uneasy. It was a Porsche, a very flashy, pearl-white one at that. Common sense and logic overrode the tide of lust she'd erupted in him. It simply wasn't smart to leave a car like that unattended in the parking lot of an abandoned hotel overnight.

His property. His responsibility.

"Kate, I don't think this is wise. It's not like your car doesn't fairly glow in the dark. I'm afraid if we leave it, it might not be here in the—"

Marco's words died in his throat when he noticed a light glowing from inside the lobby. Had they left one on earlier? The carriage lamps flanking the entrance were on a light sensor, but nothing inside.

"Dammit," he muttered. "Gotta go in and turn off whatever light we left on."

As he grabbed the door handle, Kate's fingers clutched his thigh. "Wait. No." Her eyes were round and wild as she stared in the direction of the window. "It's moving."

The light was indeed moving, pulsating brighter and then darker, coming from somewhere off to the left of the entryway. As though someone was coming out from the ballroom bearing a flashlight.

"Guai," Marco growled. "We haven't even begun renovations, and we've got intruders already." He snatched his cellphone out of its perch on the dash and held it low on his lap so the light wouldn't give them away.

Trouble. One quick way to extinguish an erection.

"I hope they answer 911 up here," he muttered, then hit the button to blacken his screen and lifted it to his ear.

FIVE

Kate stared at the window, terror building in her chest like hot steam. Her rational mind knew it was highly unlikely anyone would have broken into an empty, abandoned hotel. There was nothing inside to steal, except for the vintage chandelier which might bring twenty bucks at a flea market.

The whining in her ears commenced, confirming her suspicion. This was no ordinary intruder. She knew what was coming and wished now she'd at least explained to Marco what happened to her, sometimes. The panic attack and pain in her chest on her first visit to Redman's was only one way her psychic powers could affect her.

Sometimes, it was much more dramatic.

A whirling dizziness overtook her, and suddenly, she was inside the building, standing in the lobby directly beneath the chandelier. Moonlight twinkled on its crystals in the darkness—a darkness thicker and deeper than ebony velvet. And the flashes of light dancing over her face and arms and all around her feet on the diamond-patterned carpet challenged her equilibrium, and she staggered.

But there was nothing to grab on to. She was lucky she didn't topple to the floor. She recovered, though shakily, as the sparks of light began to organize and whirl around her, like a cyclone whose eye was her. The ringing in her ears grew louder, almost painful.

A sound behind her, coming from the direction of the ballroom, was like the hissing of a hoarse whisper. She turned as if in slow motion, dream-like and unafraid. Somehow she knew, felt deep in her heart, whatever was here wouldn't harm her.

But the entity definitely wanted something. Wanted to share their pain with her. That's why it had blasted her with its agony the first day she'd stepped over the threshold. How long, she wondered, had it been since this spirit could unload some of its misery on a living being? Kate often became their conduit: the only release for the suffering so many trapped souls endured, endlessly through time.

The definition of Hell.

In the blackness, she could barely distinguish the arched entryway to the ballroom. Peering across the empty space and through the far wall of glass, she could see the lake, lights glowing on the opposite shore and dancing in long streaks on the surface of the water. She didn't make out the shape, silhouetted by the oval arch, right away. Her sight had blurred, and she lifted her hands to rub at her eyes. When they blinked open again, it was there.

Her breath caught in her throat as she realized it was large, at least in breadth, its surface thick and fuzzy. Her first thought was *bear*. But then a dripping sound filled her head, and she imagined more than saw *something*—what? Water? Blood?—streaming down off the apparition's surface in dull, thudding *thwops* on the carpet. The sickening sound grew louder and louder, hurting her ears, and panic began to take hold.

Her own heart raced, and she was gasping for breath, as if she'd run a mile in heavy gear. Sparkles again filled her vision, but not from the flashes of light snapping wildly off the chandelier over her head.

Kate slapped both hands over her ears and screamed.

Yet, easily overriding her own horrified voice, two words resounded in her head. The same way as they had the night in her apartment. Echoing, pitiful. As though the voice emanated from down the other end of an underwater drainage pipe.

Find me. Find me. Find me.

Her breath hitched, and she gave in to the terror. All sounds silenced, and everything around her went black.

One minute, Marco was speaking to the 911 emergency operator, pissed off more than disturbed, by this very unwelcome interruption to his night. But as he clicked off, he nearly jumped out of his skin when Kate slapped her hands over her ears and let out a brain-jarring scream.

"What? What is it, mia cara?" He grabbed her arm and tried to turn her to face him. She fought him, screaming again and pitching her body away, whacking her head sharply on the glass of the passenger side window. It didn't slow her, and she scrambled wildly, slapping at him with both hands to free herself from his grip.

Then she finally stilled, suddenly, and opened her eyes. She looked straight at him. But Kate wasn't there. He was met with an empty, hollow stare, like a person in a coma, or one who was spaced out on drugs.

She clearly didn't see him, but was staring right through him. And whatever she was looking at with such terror in those huge, blue eyes, he was quite certain wasn't him. Seconds later, her thick eyelashes fluttered shut and she slumped, lifeless, against his shoulder.

He'd barely had time to dial 911 a second time when whirling red and white lights skittered across the wall of pines lining the driveway.

"Hello? Yes, I called a moment ago. I need an officer . . . yes. I think they're already here. But now... ," his voice grew thick with emotion. "Now I need an ambulance, too."

"What is your emergency, sir?" the robotic voice of the operator replied. "You reported a possible break-in. Are there injuries as well?" She sounded more annoyed than concerned, and her tone was the last twang on Marco's strung nerves. He snapped.

"Cazzo! No injury. . . I mean, I don't know what's happening, but my girlfriend just freaked out and fainted."

The three-second pause that followed almost had Marco slamming down the phone, but as he yanked it away from his ear, the voice said, "All right, sir. We'll send an ambulance as well."

In the instant he threw the phone to the floor, a knock on his window sent his heart into his mouth. The beam of a flashlight blinded him as he fumbled to open the door. Pressure from an officer leaning on the outside allowed it to only open a few inches.

"Stay where you are, sir. Do not exit the car. Can we see your license and registration, please?"

"Che casino! What's wrong with you people? I was the one who phoned in the call. I own this godforsaken place," he barked. Panic turned his mouth to copper. Kate lay across his arm now, limp and lifeless. "Oh, mia cara, what's wrong?" He cupped her cheek in one hand and turned her face toward him. She was deathly pale, her skin clammy and cold.

"Sir," the uniformed officer outside the door snapped, "please take your hands off the lady and step out of the car."

"Porca puttena, you just told me not to move. What do you want me to do? I can't," he caressed Kate's cheek again gently, her head still resting heavily on his shoulder, "I can't simply drop her."

When Marco Lareci's voice broke, he knew he was lost. Never, ever, in his entire life, had concern for a woman, other than his mother or his sister, brought him to tears.

Consciousness returned slowly to Kate, and she fought it with every ounce of her being. She was happy in this soft, dark place where she heard nothing, saw nothing. *Felt* nothing. Memories of her emergency appendectomy at age seven drifted back to her, and the way the nurses had repeatedly slapped her hands and patted her cheek to make her come around as the anesthesia wore off.

But she didn't want to come around this time. This euphoric, painless void was pure bliss. Coming to the surface of this deep, dark abyss promised only pain.

"Ms. Bardach. Kate. Come back to us now. Can you hear me?"

Yeah, bitch, I can hear you, Kate's mind muttered. I like it better right here where I am.

But they wouldn't leave her be. The nagging shrews.

The tapping and the slapping and shock of a cold, wet washcloth on her forehead yanked her up from the depths of her submersion so quickly, it would have killed a scuba diver.

Wagging her head from side to side, she managed enough control over the voice she'd lost touch with over the last God-knew-how-long to grumble, "What? Stop it, will you? What the hell?"

"Ms. Bardach, Kate. Can you tell us what day it is?"

"It's fucking Friday. At least, last I knew," she growled.

"Who is the president?"

She chuckled deep in her throat. "Let's not go there. Not a good idea." But in the next instant, in a lightning bolt snap, full consciousness flooded her brain, along with full memory. Sensory as well as emotional.

"Where's Marco? Is Marco here?"

By the time they brought him to her, Kate was propped up against pillows on the elevated bed, sipping from a paper cup half-filled with orange juice. Sounds from the emergency room outside her cubicle ranged from muffled, overhead pages, to murmurs between medical staff, to moans from an elderly man, she guessed, in the cubicle next to hers.

She felt relatively calm. Had collected her thoughts back to center. Had come to grips with the psychic experience she'd just endured.

Now, her biggest concern was how she was going to explain it to Marco.

Over the hum of activity beyond the curtain, Marco's voice pierced like a lighthouse beacon through heavy fog.

"What do you mean, I can't see her? Ask her, you fools. Ask the lady who she was with when this whole debacle happened."

At least he was keeping the volume of his angry voice down. He had a temper, but he also had respect for those other unfortunates in the cubicles around her.

The man, evidently, had a heart.

Best not think about that right now.

A nurse in baby-blue scrubs, who looked to be about fifteen, peeked in around the curtain and asked, "Ms. Bardach? There's a gentleman who'd like to see you. A Mr. Lareci. Is it all right if we let him come in?"

She nodded, silently, and her resolve began to falter. The bolus of anguish in her chest—the one she'd learned so stubbornly to control for the sake of appearance—broke through and filled her eyes with tears. When the curtain zinged back and she saw him, she lost it.

In the next moment, her face was buried against his neck, breathing in the good, sweaty, male scent of him and enjoying the way his stubble scraped against her temple. He held her that way for a long time, refusing to let her go even when she attempted to ease away.

When he finally did, he fixed her with his intense, hazel eyes and barked, "What happened to you, Kate? You scared me half to death."

She let out a measured breath. "I'm sorry I didn't explain this to you earlier. I'm not your ordinary date." Wryly, she chuckled, turning away as she tugged out the edge of the sheet from under her and blotted her face.

His eyes riveted hers then, and what she saw there both perplexed and terrorized her. An emotion she couldn't quite recognize. Not sure she wanted to.

"Are you ill?" he whispered hoarsely. "Something . . . serious?"

She shook her head. "No. But when I explain the facts to you, you'll probably want to drop the whole idea of doing business with me." She paused, studying him. "Professionally or personally. Get me out of here and I'll explain."

Marco sat snugged close beside Kate, together in one side of a booth in *Krum & Bell's*, a classy little bar on the lake right smack in the middle of the tiny burgh of Loch Sheldrake. It was the only place open past midnight, even on a Friday night. By the time the hospital in Harris released Kate, it was much later. They were connected, hip to hip. And he possessively kept his grasp firmly around one of her hands.

It was as though he couldn't stand not touching her, in some way, since this whole incident began. As though she'd vanish before his eyes. The very thought caused Marco's heart to clutch so painfully, he wondered if this was what his late grandfather's angina had felt like.

They'd spoken little until now, and he hadn't pushed her. She'd obviously been through a traumatic event, and the last thing Marco wanted to do was stress her further. He didn't understand what had happened, and he dreaded hearing the explanation.

Marco's grandmother had died of a brain tumor ten years earlier. Her irregular behavior had been the first symptom. Then, rapid and dramatic deterioration until, thankfully, she sank into a coma. All within the space of about six months. Memories of her illness, her odd episodes of seeming insanity, scarred him. Haunted his dreams to this day.

Once their bottle of Martinelli Pinot Noir was sitting, open, on the table before them, and the waitress had poured some into both their glasses and *gone away*—thank Christ in heaven—he turned toward Kate. He lifted his glass, nodding for her to do the same.

"Now, tell me, mia cara. What happened tonight?"

Her eyes were like deep blue pools of mystery, staring up into his own with such trepidation, it made his heart ache. Purple crescents hung beneath those beautiful eyes, and a streak of black slashed one pale cheek, which he assumed was a remnant from her now-non-existent makeup.

She was even more beautiful without it.

In a flash of ironic joy, he noticed that across her aquiline nose, there now appeared a sprinkling of freckles. Matching those on the skin of her breasts and upper arms. Huh. Why would a woman go to all that trouble to conceal a trait so genuinely, naturally, beautiful?

"First, you tell me what happened. Did the cops find an intruder inside the building?" she asked.

"No. Although either there was one earlier, or we have a strange leak in the plumbing."

She tipped her head, and he went on.

"The police didn't find a thing. But I noticed a wet spot. A puddle, almost, right under the archway leading to the ballroom."

Her gasp shocked him, and what little color had returned to her face drained away instantly.

"What? Is a plumbing leak under an archway a bad thing?" he asked, confused.

Shaking her head in snappy little jerks, she snatched up the wine and gulped half. Then set it down carefully, dragging in fluttery breaths.

"What, Kate? What?"

Dio buono, she can be such a perplexing woman.

Fiddling with the short, gold chain around her neck, she heaved out a sigh. "If I tell you, do you promise you won't think I'm a wacko?" She blinked up at him, and in a rare moment for this woman, Kate appeared uncertain. Even timid.

Laughter bubbled up from deep in his chest, and she frowned. A pouting little girl. She was absolutely adorable.

He cupped her cheek and looked into her eyes. "If I did, I would be the biggest fool to ever walk the face of the earth. You, Kate Bardach, I'm fast discovering, may be many things. But wacko is not on the list."

After holding his gaze for a beat, she blurted, "I'm a psychic. I mean, I can't read your mind, or anybody else's mind. If they're alive. But I *can* see, and communicate, sometimes, with dead people. That's what happened at Redman's. Both times."

Ah. So perhaps I drew my conclusion about her non-wacko status a little prematurely.

He cleared his throat, lowering his hand to curl around the base of his wine glass. "Okay, so, I wasn't exactly expecting that. But I'm open-minded. What makes you believe these . . . episodes you have aren't just panic attacks? The mind can do funny things to your perception when you're under stress—"

"Look. I don't expect you to believe me. But I'm telling you, I see the spirits of people who have died. I can sense their presence in a building, which is why I don't take on every job I'm offered. I already explained it to you." She spoke quickly, defensively, in a very quiet, almost threatening tone.

"You did tell me you turned down jobs that didn't feel right. But you never explained why." Marco took two deep swallows of his wine. "Were you born with this . . . ability?

She shook her head, staring into her glass. "No. I nearly drowned when I was five years old. Pulled out by the undertow at Jones Beach. They say I was clinically dead for at least ten minutes. Not breathing, no heartbeat, no pulse." She looked deep into his eyes and whispered, "But then, I came back. Ever since then, ever since I *came back*, it's as though a rent's been torn in the fabric between the living and the dead." She paused, looking away. "I guess I didn't know enough to close the door behind me."

A clutching in Marco's chest almost made him wince. The thought of a child—this beautiful little girl—nearly dying like that, then being haunted all her life by the memory of—of what? He'd heard the stories from people who'd claimed to have crossed over and then came back. Mostly, he thought they were bullshit.

But he had been raised Catholic and been taught all about the place called Purgatory. The holding tank for the souls not evil enough to banish to hell, yet not squeaky-clean enough to allow through the Pearly Gates. Yet. He always wondered what that place was like.

And just how the Pope knew about it in the first place.

But regardless of what he believed, it didn't matter. Because this woman *did* believe what she was seeing, hearing, whatever, when she had one of these seizures or panic attacks was coming from the other side.

Wherever the *other side* was.

"That must have been a terrifying experience for you, Kate. For your parents. Were these attacks diagnosed soon after?" he asked, trying to keep the suspicion out of his voice. "Ever been tested for epilepsy? Seizures?"

She whirled on him. "I'm telling you, I'm not epileptic, and this is not a physical condition you can explain away by pointing to an article in a medical journal," she snapped. "I see the spirits of those who are still trapped here on earth. In between eternal peace and eternal damnation. For whatever reason, they can't move on. *Gehenna*. I think you Christians call it Purgatory."

A chill slithered down Marco's spine. First, because it was as though she'd been reading his mind. Second, because it was one possible explanation for where Purgatory really was.

Right here on earth. The thought made him shudder.

He regarded her soberly. "What makes you think I'm Christian?"

"You're Italian, aren't you? I thought all Italians were Roman Catholics."

Well, she had a point. Most of them are. He nodded.

After a long pause, he said, "So, you're saying my hotel is haunted." A statement, not a question.

She nodded silently, her gaze dropping again to her glass.

"Does that mean you're backing out of the job?" He was almost afraid to ask the question. But there was more at stake here than just his interests. There were his partners to consider as well. Their investment.

She lifted her face slowly, her eyes glassy with unshed tears.

"I don't want to. I really don't. But I don't know if I can do this. I need a few days to think about it."

Over the next half-hour, Kate explained to Marco exactly what had happened to her the first night she'd entered Redman's. The searing pain burning straight through her chest. The overwhelming feeling of panic and claustrophobia. Then she described what she'd heard and seen on her own television screen the very next night.

She could tell he didn't believe what she was saying actually happened. But accepted *she* believed it, and so, essentially was humoring her.

Until she got to the part where she'd found out her Aunt Leah and her Italian, gangster husband had disappeared after spending their wedding night at the Redman. That, she knew, got his attention.

And that his last name was Shelby. That got his attention.

Furrows appeared between Marco's dark eyebrows, and he leaned closer to her. "I've heard the rumor. The one claiming Loch Sheldrake is chock-full of sunken corpses, victims of mob killings." He drew in a deep breath and raked a hand through his hair. He stared straight ahead at the wooden back of the empty booth opposite them. "That's all I need," he mumbled, "is for a skeleton— or two—to show up in the walls or under the floorboards during the renovation."

Ah, he's only concerned about *his* aspect of this situation. And probably *does* think I'm a complete wacko.

"I don't think you have to worry about that," she murmured. "I'm quite certain the bodies are on the bottom of the Loch."

She drew away from him then and folded her arms across her chest, looking away. The whole idea of working on the Redman terrified her. As much as she'd felt compelled to ignore her instincts and surge ahead with the project this morning, this last experience chilled her to the core.

His fingers were warm and gentle under her chin as he turned her back to face him.

"If you feel this strongly about turning down the project, Kate, I'm not going to pressure you. I'm not that kind of man. It won't change the fact I'd love to continue seeing you." He lowered his mouth to hers and kissed her softly. "You take a day or two to think about it. But I'll need an answer by Monday. My partners are getting antsy to see some progress on their investment."

Despite the gentle tone of his voice, his soft kiss, Kate couldn't help but wonder if Marco had heard a word she'd said. Why in one breath he swore he didn't want to put any pressure on her. And in the next, laid out what sounded very much like an ultimatum.

SIX

On their way back to Kate's house, she asked about her car.

"Are we still stopping by to move it?" she asked, hoping Marco would let her leave it where it was. The Porsche, though expensive, was just another pretty thing. Nothing irreplaceable. She wasn't sure she wanted to go back near Redman's again tonight.

No, actually, she was *quite* sure she *didn't* want to go back there tonight.

"We have to, Kate. We can't leave it there. It's foolish. Asking for trouble." Marco turned toward her, his chiseled jaw glowing green in the dashboard lights. "Are you up to driving?" He sounded genuinely concerned.

"Yeah, I'm fine," she said, trying to consciously prevent the rapid acceleration of her heartbeat as he turned his car onto the winding drive.

As Marco's headlights flashed across the parking lot, Kate's heart skittered at the sight of the rusted, old, Ford pickup truck parked next to her car. Marco slammed on the brakes and barked, "Cazzo!"

Frozen, Kate held her breath.

A beam of light, much more distinct this time, was crawling over the hedges surrounding the east side of the building. They both sat there in silence for a long beat before the figure of a man appeared under one of the coach lamps flanking the entrance. A very old man.

He was dressed in faded denim below, a plaid jacket above, and was wearing a baseball cap that screamed "Yankees." The beam of light emanated from his flashlight, which he respectfully lowered to the ground as Marco threw the car into neutral and secured the handbrake.

Kate lurched and shrank back as he leaned across her, flipping open the glove compartment and lifting out a surprisingly compact hand gun. She gasped as he flung open his door.

Marco stepped out of the car in one fluid motion. "Who are you? What are you doing here?" he barked. Kate could hear the rage bubbling under his shallowly controlled tone and feared what might happen next. Marco had been through a lot tonight. The last thing he needed to be doing was brandishing a gun, though she was glad to see he hadn't raised it but kept it at his side.

The old man approached them slowly, staying within the glow of the headlights. Slowly, he raised his hands in a surrendering gesture. As he did, the beam of his flashlight crawled along the underside of the portico until it was set free to shoot helplessly up into the night sky.

"Easy, mister. Easy, now. I ain't armed. I mean no harm."

Kate thought the man had to be in his seventies, at the very least. His shoulders were broad under the quilted, plaid jacket, but his faded denim pants hung loosely, like overalls with the bib straps undone. He shuffled along at a painfully slow, uneven gate, slightly dragging the toe of one amber-colored work boot along the broken blacktop. About twenty feet from them, he stopped.

"I'll ask you again. Who are you, and what are you doing here?" Marco had lowered his voice to a threatening growl, his fingers working on the weapon at his side.

"I'm James Donnelly. I been the caretaker for this here place for nearly the past thirty years. I live up on the hill across the lake. I seen all the flashin' lights here earlier and thought I better come down and make sure the place was secure. Tried to go to sleep, but I figured out there'd be none of that until I got dressed and came down and checked everything out."

Marco's shoulders drooped before he lifted his hand to his brow and muttered another quiet obscenity in Italian. Kate was quite certain she was glad she didn't speak the language.

"Geez, Mr. Donnelly, I'm so sorry. Guess we're all just a little on edge tonight." Marco huffed out a breath, then drew his shoulders up to his ears and glanced one way, then the other. "This place can be creepy in the dark."

"It can. And please, call me James." The man reached out to shake Marco's hand.

Glancing down at the gun and shaking his head, Marco muttered, "Let me put this thing away first." He leaned into the car, reaching back across Kate to store the weapon in the glove box.

Slowly, Kate opened her door and stepped out.

"Ma'am," the old man said, stepping forward, hand extended.

"Kate Bardach," she said, clasping the cold, weathered hand he offered. "I may be renovating the place for Mr. Lareci here."

James' eyebrows rose, as if questioning the appropriateness of a woman in the renovation business. But then he quickly bobbed his head, and Kate detected a hint of a smile playing across the wrinkles carved into his face, made deeper in the glare of the headlights.

"Glad to hear it," he said. "When I heard they sold it, I was afraid they'd tear the old place down. Used to park cars for 'em in their heyday."

"Really. And became a caretaker after that?" Marco asked.

"Well, yeah, this was sort of a piecemeal job after they closed up. I'm a farmer by trade. Dairy cattle. Leastways, I was, till about ten years or so ago. Old Mr. Redman's estate attorney hired me on, part-time, to keep an eye on things. Keep an eye out for vandalism and such. Sometimes the young people in these parts get bored on a Saturday night." He lifted his cap and scratched his balding head. "It's been somethin' to keep my mind occupied," he mumbled sadly.

Kate felt a pang of pity for the old man and wondered if he had any family in the area. If watching over a crumbling hotel was his "hobby," he certainly couldn't have much going in the way of a social life.

Marco studied the old man silently for a moment, then said, "You know, it's really not a bad idea. I mean, to have somebody local who's around all the time to keep an eye on the place. Especially now since we'll be renovating." He paused and glanced back over his shoulder toward Kate, who suppressed a small smile and nodded.

Marco not only has business sense, he has a heart, too.

"So, I'll make sure my two partners agree, but if you'd consider staying on as caretaker, James, I can pay you whatever the attorney was paying. Plus ten percent."

He lifted his head slowly as he replaced his cap, squinting at Marco. "I'd like that fine, Mr. Lareci. Just fine. Would be my honor." He turned to Kate. "And Miss Bardach, I promise I won't get in the way of any of your crew, either. I'll check in a little more often. Maybe two or three times a day, and after they leave to make sure the place is locked up and all secure."

"I'd like that very much, James." Kate smiled, clasping the gnarled hand once again.

As they watched the glow of one dirty taillight of the Ford pickup—just one, the other one was out—disappear down the winding drive, Kate said, "Seems like a pretty nice old guy. I'm glad you didn't shoot him."

Marco snorted and shook his head. "Me, too." He came to her and squeezed her shoulder. "You sure you're okay to drive?"

"It's a half-mile, Lareci. You can follow me to be sure I don't get lost."

Against her better judgement, she asked him to stay the night. Kate didn't want him to drive all the way to the city at two in the morning. Or to stay in a hotel somewhere out on the highway.

"But I hope you understand, Marco. I'm exhausted, and I'm shaken to my core. Do you think it would be asking too much for you to lie with me and hold me? Nothing more. Just hold me?"

Her hands were planted on his chest as he stood uncertainly, still wearing his overcoat, a few steps inside her door. Lifting her hair away from her face with gentle hands, he kissed her, long and slow. There was more tenderness than hunger in this kiss, and a small part deep inside Kate's heart melted. But when they parted, he drew back, set his lips in a line, and shook his head.

"You've been through a lot today. I don't want to add any more stress than you've already experienced. I'm not sure I could keep my hands off you. I'll drive partway back to the city, then pull over when I get tired." He kissed her again, then pressed soft kisses all along her jawline to her ear.

Then he pinched her ass.

"Ouch, you bastard," she shrieked, stumbling away from him. But then, a giggle formed like seltzer in her chest and bubbled to the surface.

He laid a hand on her cheek. She twisted her fingers into his lapels.

"Are you sure you won't stay? I'll worry about you—"

"Bah. No need. I'll turn up Andrea Bocelli and sing along. If that won't keep me awake, nothing will."

"But tomorrow's Saturday," she murmured, fighting back a yawn and failing miserably.

He gripped both her shoulders and turned her away from him, planting a gentle smack on one cheek of her ass. "Go get some sleep. You and I both know if I stay, sleep won't be part of the agenda."

But even after the emotional roller coaster of a day she'd had—plus the half bottle of very nice wine—Kate found her eyelids wouldn't stay shut. She called him, twice, and he seemed wide awake and in a relatively cheery mood, considering recent events. When they last disconnected, he was almost home.

Still, she tossed and turned until nearly five a.m. before giving in and swallowing the two sedative pills the doctor at the E.R. had sent home with her. Light had begun creeping in around the shades of her window when she dropped into a deep, dreamless sleep.

More than six hours later, bright spring sunshine gnawed at the edges of her shade when Kate's eyes fluttered open. The red digital numbers on her nightstand said it was nearly noon. She stretched and yawned, then swung her feet out of bed and padded into her kitchen wearing her favorite plush sleep pants—the ones embossed with cartoon Ghostbuster characters. And matching terry sleep socks.

She was flipping a Keurig cup into her coffee maker when the doorbell rang, making her jump.

Noon. Okay. Not an unreasonable hour on a Saturday, but still . . .

Standing on her doorstep was a uniformed officer with a round patch on his jacket declaring *New York State Police*. Kate blinked, and for a moment, stood there, totally confounded.

There had been entirely too much police activity in her life in the past 24 hours.

"Sir? Problem?" she asked, lifting one hand to shield her eyes from the brightness flooding her doorway.

"Ma'am, are you Kate Bardach?" The officer was medium height, husky under his light, microfiber windbreaker, and wore his peaked cap square and straight over what appeared to be a blond crewcut. His eyes were pale and intense on hers.

"Yes," she answered slowly. "What's this all about? Am I in trouble?"

He shifted from one foot to the other, obviously uncomfortable with the news he was about to impart. Snatching off his cap, he held it to his chest.

Yes, she'd been right. Pale blond crewcut.

Again, for the umpteenth time in the past few days, Kate's heart rate skyrocketed off the charts. But not because of the officer's charms.

"No, ma'am," he replied, then cleared his throat. "We located a vehicle registered in your name this morning. Do you own a white Porsche?"

Kate's eyes widened as she ducked forward to peek out the door into her driveway. "Well, I *did*. It was parked right there, not seven hours ago," she said, pointing. Her voice had started to take on a screechy quality that annoyed even her.

"Well, as you can see, Ma'am, it's not there anymore. It's around on the opposite shore. You know the patch of open beach where kids like to party sometimes?"

Kate shook her head slowly, reeling and confused. "No, I'm afraid I don't."

"Well," the officer continued, "an anonymous caller reported seeing a car sinking into the mud at the edge of the water. Lucky we found it when we did, or she'd be gone. You know how sharp that drop-off is. There's a wrecker up there now trying to pull her out."

Kate stood with her arms crossed, her mouth tasting like burnt rubber. She shivered from the early spring chill rustling through her sweater and Ghostbuster sleep pants. An ancient tow truck that used to be red but was now patched liberally with rust and dried mud whined and groaned as its cables endeavored to reclaim her precious Porsche from the muddy north shore of Loch Sheldrake.

How the hell had this happened?

"It's a bit of a puzzle to us as well," Officer Crewcut said, as if he'd read her mind. "The tow truck driver said the doors are all locked and there's no key in the ignition. It's as though it flew across the lake and landed here. With a splat," he added, pointing to the mud streaking the windows, rear hatch, and roof of the car.

"Who reported it?" Kate asked.

"I told you, ma'am, it was an anonymous caller. Whoever it was had been real careful to disable the caller ID."

Kate wandered away toward the less squishy surface of the grass nearer to the narrow road winding around the north side of the lake. Water had already seeped in over the soles of her sneakers—the old, battered ones she kept around to work in the yard. The cold water sent uncontrollable shudders through her.

Then again, maybe it wasn't from her wet feet at all.

She snatched her cellphone out of the pocket of her sweater and dialed Marco's number. His phone rang three times before he answered, and she knew immediately she'd woken him up.

"Marco, was my car in the driveway when you left last night?" she asked without introduction.

She heard him cough, clear his throat, and then the rustling of cloth. Yup, he was still in bed. Not surprising. The poor man probably hadn't gotten home until dawn.

"Kate? No. I mean, yes. Sorry, I'm half asleep," he chuckled. "What are you talking about, mia cara? You drove your car home last night before I left. I followed you. Don't you remember?"

"Well, somehow, it's now inches from slipping into the bottomless oblivion of Loch Sheldrake."

"What?" Marco asked. "How? Did you go out again after I left?"

"No, you ninny. I hit the sheets right after you left and just climbed out of bed an hour ago. I took one of those sedatives they gave me at the hospital, though, so I was out cold. I wouldn't have heard a thing, even if whoever did this made enough noise to wake the dead."

Kate was combing her fingers through her disheveled hair as she watched the ancient tow truck whistle and wheeze. The slack on the thick cable they'd hooked under the frame very slowly came taut, and then the winch motor started to labor in earnest.

The officer, hovering a polite distance away, caught her eye and raised his hand to gain her attention.

"Look, Marco. I gotta go. The cop wants to talk to me. Though I have no earthly idea what I can tell him that will explain this."

"Wait, Kate. Do you need me to come up? I mean, I have a meeting set with a new client at two, but I can come up afterwards if you need me to."

A nice gesture, but Marco's tone told her he wasn't crazy about the idea of making the two-hour drive again, two days in a row.

"I'll be fine, Marco. I'll get a rental while they figure out what all the water and mud did to my car."

When she clicked off, Officer Crewcut approached. "Mr. Wagner wants to know where you'd like the car towed, Miss."

Kate sighed and pinched her fingers to the base of her nose. "Do you know of a Porsche dealer anywhere between here and Manhattan?" she asked.

The officer quirked one eyebrow, then shrugged. "Sorry, Ms. Bardach. Don't have a clue."

The winch motor died suddenly, having finished its job, and sighed as the mechanic began fastening her car to the deck with heavy chains. Kate had turned again to her phone, intending to search for somewhere to get her car fixed, when she heard the guttural thrum of yet another old engine. The rustic, blue pickup she'd seen last night appeared on the narrow road winding down out of the mountain. James Donnelly pulled his truck up beside the police cruiser and cut the engine.

"Mornin', Miss Bardach. What's all this? You get lost goin' home last night?" he asked, his voice scratchy as though he'd just woken up.

Kate lifted her shoulders and shook her head. "Not really sure what happened, James. When I went to bed my car was in the driveway. This morning, it's here."

The officer interrupted. "Good morning, Jimmy. You've met Miss Bardach, I assume?"

Kate caught a flash of annoyance in the old man's eyes as he answered. "I have. She's workin' with the new owner of Redman's. Met her up there last night. Guess you heard 'bout all that commotion."

"No, I didn't. Came back on duty this morning after a week off," the officer replied. "Trouble?"

"Naw. Same old stuff. Probably some kids snoopin' around the place with flashlights, scarin' the bejesus out of each other."

The old man coughed then, a congested, gurgling sound, and Kate felt her empty stomach lurch. He snatched a handkerchief out of the back pocket of his overalls—probably the same ones he'd been wearing last night—and wiped his mouth. She obviously hadn't disguised her disgust well because he met her gaze and mumbled, "Sorry, ma'am."

Again, Kate felt a pang of pity for him and couldn't help wondering what his story was.

The mechanic, who'd finished strapping down her car, interrupted her thoughts. "I'll take your vehicle down to my garage, ma'am." He handed her a business card with a cartoon image of a red tow truck with smiling buck teeth under the words *Wagner's Wheels*. "When you decide where you'd like her towed, you be sure and give me a call."

The officer clicked shut his clipboard and said, "I'll drive you home, Ms. Bardach. But please stop by the station later today and finish up filling out the report."

James stepped forward and raised a hand. "It's okay, Rog. I'm on my way over to the Redman now anyways. I can drive Miss Bardach home. If she doesn't mind." He glanced at Kate questioningly.

She hesitated only a moment. "That's kind of you. Thank you."

The officer tugged on the bill of his cap and nodded, extending his hand. "Fine, then. If you need anything else, my name is Sorens. Officer Sorens." He cast a sharp glance at the old man. "You get your taillight fixed, Jimmy? I can only give you one more warning before I write it up."

James shook his head and looked down. "I'll get right on that, *Officer* Sorens." He put unnecessary emphasis on the word *officer*. "But if you do write it up, make sure it's to *James* Donnelly. Not Jimmy."

Kate felt bad about her muddy sneakers, but only for a moment as she approached the old farm truck, which was obviously a work vehicle. Hunks of dried dirt—she hoped it was just dirt—and wisps of hay littered the unadorned floorboards. James held the door for her, offering her a hand as she climbed up into the cab.

"Sorry ol' Betsy's such a mess," he apologized, "but she's dependable."

As they backed out onto the narrow road, Kate asked, "You live up that way? On the mountain?" She pointed to the curve where the pavement disappeared into the pines.

"I do. Got the prettiest view on the shores of the Loch. Wanna see?"

Kate nodded. "Sure, why not?"

Unsure what it was about this old farmer that touched her heartstrings, Kate figured she could spare twenty minutes to ease her curiosity about him. After all, if she did take on Marco's renovation, she'd be seeing a lot of James Donnelly.

The lane snaked back and forth through the woods at a fairly steep grade, but not for very far before the thick pines fell away and acres of rolling pasture opened up before Kate's eyes. A modest, two-story farmhouse with peeling white paint perched at the highest point on the left side of the road. Two massive old barns commanded the opposite side, both in equal states of neglect. But surrounding them, for as far as she could see, grassy slopes rolled away from the buildings, divided in places by a gorgeous, old fieldstone fence.

"My goodness, it's beautiful up here," she breathed. "Do you own all of this land, James?"

He made a growling sound deep in his throat. "Used to. Had to sell off a hundred acres ten years ago when my wife got the cancer."

"Oh. I'm sorry," Kate said. She somehow knew she didn't have to ask whether the money had afforded the poor woman a cure.

Instead of pulling left toward the house, James turned his truck onto a rutted lane, leading past the larger of the two barns. "The view from my room upstairs in the house is the same, which is how I can see the Redman so clear from here. But seein' as I don't keep my house much cleaner than my truck, I'd rather show you the view from here."

They followed two ruts in the field, sprouting with new spring grass in places, through the empty pasture and straight up to the top. At one point where rocks had worked their way through, the truck pitched and lurched, and Kate grabbed the handle above the door and laughed. James flashed her a glance, and a hint of a smile caused his eyes to crinkle in the corners.

"Country roads. Guess you're not used to 'em," he chuckled.

"No, not really. But I've been on a farm. In fact, my father owns one. A horse farm, down in Chester."

As the truck crested the top of the hill, he slowed to a stop. Kate sucked in a breath at the vista before her. The horizon yawned open for as far as she could see. Below, a panoramic view of the Loch, the village, along with the Redman property, appeared in postcard detail. She could even see her own house, her back deck peeking out from behind the pines flanking it.

"Oh, James, this is unbelievable. You're so lucky to own property like this."

He fished a toothpick out of his breast pocket and stuck it between his teeth, keeping his attention fixed on the view before them. "I am. But even a place as pretty as this can be the loneliest place in the world sometimes."

Kate blinked and hesitated before asking softly, "How long since your wife's been gone?"

"Almost seven years. She fought it, by God. Tough gal. But it got her in the end, just the same."

"I'm sorry," Kate murmured again, realizing how lame the cliché response was, but at a loss as to what else to say.

The old man shifted in his seat and straightened. He plucked the toothpick out of his teeth and said, "So your daddy raises horses, huh? What kind?"

Grateful for the change of subject, Kate smiled and said, "Thoroughbreds."

He scrutinized her with narrowed eyes. "So, you probably run 'em up here at Montlake, then." It was a statement, not a question.

She nodded. "Daddy doesn't get involved much with the training anymore. He mostly breeds and raises the foals and sells them. I have one or two yearlings in training every year. It's my excuse to come up here and get away from the bustle of the city."

Kate could feel his eyes studying her intently, a look of curiosity and concern deepening the wrinkles on his weathered face.

Uncomfortable, she added, "You should come down and see them run sometime. That's how I met Marco. My filly ran on opening day. And won."

James shook his head and reached to shift the truck into gear. "No interest. Hard to imagine a nice lady like you, though, involved in the racing business."

She shot him a sharp glance. "Why so? There are lots of female owners. Trainers, and jockeys, too."

The gears ground as he released the clutch and eased the truck into a tight circle. "Don't know much about it," he said. "Just know parts of the business can get dirty sometimes. Real dirty."

Part of her wanted to argue, to defend her involvement with racing. And after all, what business was it of this old guy anyway? But the more honest part conceded that although she owned and ran one or two horses a season, Kate's involvement with the mechanics of the industry remained superficial. She knew stuff went on, sometimes, on the backside where the trainers made deals. But she preferred to don proverbial blinkers and pretend not to notice.

Kate simply loved the game. She didn't really care about all the ins and outs of breeding, raising, or training the beasts. She yearned for the thrill of seeing her pink-and-white silks with the number three coming down the track. Preferably, ahead of the pack.

A half-hour later, James dropped her off at her lake house, and she thanked him. Kate ended up hiring a long-distance transport company to carry her car on a flatbed, dripping and splattered with muck and green, slimy stuff, all the way back to her Porsche dealer in Manhattan. She'd rented a car from Enterprise in Monticello to make the drive home. And what do you know? Their advertisements don't lie. They came and picked her up.

She settled behind the wheel of the Q50, nearly identical to Marco's except for the color, her packed bags in the back. But she had one stop to make before heading back to her apartment in Manhattan. The nearest state police barracks, F troop in Liberty.

As Kate pulled into the parking lot next to the small brick building, she couldn't help thinking it looked more like a rural residence than a police station.

Wonderful. What kind of real help can I expect from a small-town operation like this?

The police had thoroughly examined her car before the transporter pulled it up onto the flatbed. There didn't appear to be any damage to the exterior, other than the sludge caked up to the tops of the front wheel wells. She'd handed over her key, and they'd searched the interior and the luggage compartment under the hood for anything suspicious.

Like a dead body, she'd thought with a shudder.

All the men had advised her it was best not to try to start the engine until a qualified mechanic took a look. So she'd sent it directly to the dealership. With the motor in the rear of the vehicle, she could only hope the water and slime hadn't done anything more than insult the hundred-thousand-dollar car.

The more pressing question, of course, was how this had happened. And even more perplexing, why?

Kate pushed through the glass door of the police station and was surprised to see a uniformed woman sitting behind the desk.

Ah, so maybe they aren't so behind the times up here after all.

"Hi. I'm Kate Bardach," she said, fumbling in her purse for her driver's license. "Mine was the car that decided to take a swim this morning. In Loch Sheldrake."

The officer was about Kate's age and blonde, wearing no makeup and with her long hair neatly contained in a bun at her nape. Her name tag said *Anderson*. She smiled at Kate and nodded.

"We heard about that. Mighty odd way to start a Saturday morning," she said, reaching for a manila folder from the tiered baskets on the side of her desk. "Any idea how your pretty car might have found its way to the north side of the lake? You live on the south side, they tell me."

Kate nodded. "That's right. And when my . . . companion and I returned home about two o'clock this morning, he parked right behind me. And he said the car was still there when he left a few moments later."

The woman was typing notes on a keyboard now. "May I ask the name of your companion? I mean, there isn't any chance he was responsible in any way for vandalizing your car?" Her tone had become clipped and official. Kate could tell she had shifted from friendly greeter to interrogation mode.

Annoyed, Kate folded her arms across the chest-high counter separating them. "Look, I'm not sure it's anybody's business who I was with, but I have nothing to hide. His name is Marco Lareci, and he's the new owner of the old Redman's Resort. He and two other investors. I'll be working with Mr. Lareci to renovate the property."

Officer Anderson's pale, gold eyebrows rose, and a hint of a smile quirked her lips. "Oh, that's wonderful. I hate to see how many old hotels in this county just crumble and fall down. Or burn. Does he plan to restore it to an operable facility?"

Back to friendly greeter tone. Nice lady.

"Yes, he does. But it really doesn't have anything to do with what happened to my car." Kate glanced at her watch. Quarter past four. She wouldn't make it back to the city until after dark at this rate. "The officer at the scene told me I needed to come down here and sign some paperwork."

Anderson's face sobered, and she again drew her interrogator's cape around her. "Yes, in order for us to perform an official investigation. But unfortunately, Ms. Bardach, the team who recovered your vehicle didn't find anything that could be considered evidence. No fingerprints on the door handles, and nothing left inside or in the luggage compartment."

Thank God.

Kate was grateful they hadn't found anything horrible in her luggage compartment. Illegal drugs, stashed there by some criminal. A dead body. She shuddered again.

The officer slid a sheaf of papers across the counter with a pen resting on top. "I'll need you to sign three places. They're all highlighted."

Kate skimmed the official paperwork and scribbled her name in the designated areas. As she did so, she asked, "Does anyone have any idea *how* this was accomplished? I mean, it appears the car was airlifted over the lake and dropped on the opposite shore."

When she looked up, Anderson was shaking her head, her pale lips set in a grim line. "No clue. I know you've been asked this already, but are you sure you don't recall hearing anything during the night? Any suspicious noises?"

Sighing, Kate slid the papers back across the counter. "I had an—an episode yesterday and ended up in Harris Memorial's E.R. The doctor sent me home with a sedative. I doubt I'd have heard a thing, even if a helicopter came down and picked up my car."

The officer's subtle lifting of an eyebrow was her only reaction to the term *episode*. She continued her questioning, unperturbed. "No enemies you know of? Anyone who might want to deface your property?"

Kate shook her head. "I hardly know anyone up here. I live in Manhattan. I only come up a day or two a week."

"A shame," Anderson replied. "I hear it's a beautiful and very expensive car."

"Damn straight. At least, it *was*," Kate muttered. "Is there anything else you need from me? I've really got to be getting back to the city." She took her license from the other woman and slid it back into her wallet.

"No, that should do it. We'll ask around. See if anyone else in the neighborhood heard or saw anything last night." She hesitated, tipping her head. "Ms. Bardach, the investigators were quite impressed no water had leaked inside. In the front, anyway. I mean, the way they described it, the hood of the car was submerged nearly up to the windshield. And the water level was well above the lower edge of the door."

"She's a pretty tight machine," Kate snapped. "Why do you think they cost so much?"

I'm done with rehashing this nightmare.

Every time the image of her car sinking slowly into the lake flashed through Kate's mind, her stomach did a somersault. She turned to leave.

But her clipped tone didn't seem to faze Anderson, who continued, "That's why they found it so odd there was water in the rear of the car."

Kate stopped and stared at the officer, who had stood and now had her own arms crossed on the counter.

"What do you mean, water in the rear of the car?"

"There was none in the engine compartment," Anderson answered quickly. "Which I guess is good news for you—I understand the Porsche's engine isn't up front. But the officers who searched the interior said although all the seats and floorboards inside were dry as a bone, the rear shelf was wet. Right underneath the back window. But they said it appeared to have been there awhile, since a line of mold had started to form along the edges."

She paused as Kate stared at her, opened her mouth, and then closed it.

How the hell . . . ?

"You might want to have your rear window seal checked, Ms. Bardach. It appears you may have a leak."

SEVEN

Marco's meeting Saturday afternoon went extremely well. The Irish Bostonian had been referred to him by another client and was interested in what Marco could do with a chunk of change he'd secured from the sale of one of his Manhattan locations. Their luncheon meeting stretched into happy hour at *Doc Watson's* on 2nd Avenue, but the time spent was well worth it. Marco left with a signed contract and a check for fifty-thousand dollars.

Yet, as he stepped out onto 2nd Avenue to head back toward his apartment, he couldn't shake the heavy feeling in his chest. It was more than worry about the future of his investment in Loch Sheldrake. He was torn by his conflicting—and increasingly intense—feelings for Kate Bardach.

She was gorgeous, smart, and sexy as hell. But she was also fiercely independent and a wee bit quirky with this psychic business. Marco had never been one to believe in such things and didn't want to start now—especially now. As relieved as he'd been when the building inspector confirmed there was no black mold in the building, this new threat—if it existed—could be even worse.

I own a haunted hotel on a lake where the mob used to drop murder victims.

He'd ignored the tale as urban legend when he'd toured the place and talked Boris and Eliot into going in on the deal. His research on the economy of the area had been much more exciting. All signs pointed to a revival looming on the horizon for the tourist trade in Sullivan County. With the scant number of hotels in the vicinity, and none in the boutique category, how could they go wrong?

Yet, that still wasn't what was eating at Marco's gut as painfully as his feelings for this impossible woman. When their eyes first met, he'd been speared through the heart with a silent message—*she's the one.* But his heart and his mind now warred over the indisputable facts. How could he be falling in love with a woman who was obviously not interested in a long-term relationship and was possibly a little off her rocker?

And Jewish. Marrone, he could just imagine what his Old World Italian, terminally Roman Catholic parents would say if he announced he was in love with a Jew.

Thinking of his parents, Marco pulled out his phone and dialed them.

"Hey, Mama. How are you?"

His mother's squeal in his ear made him wince. "Oooh, so good to hear from you, Marco. How's my big-shot money guy doing? You coming for pasta tomorrow?"

Marco laughed, always delighted when his mother sounded cheery, free from worry. "Yes, Mama. I'll be there about one o'clock. Lasagna this time?"

"You read my mind," his mother replied, though Marco knew she was humoring him. As the only son, he figured it was his privilege to decide on the meal of choice.

"How's Papa?"

"Well, right now he's riveted to the television. With his eyes closed." She chuckled, and Marco joined her.

Rosa and Antonio Lareci lived in a beautiful brownstone in Boro Park, the one Marco had bought for them when he made his first million. In typical Italian tradition, he believed in taking care of the family. Their modest home off New Utrecht Avenue, the one he'd grown up in, had been nearly paid off. Now, the rental income from their old home allowed his parents to live in above-average comfort.

Marco's father had worked all his life repairing watches in his rented shop on 13th Avenue. The trade, in addition to buying and selling used timepieces, provided a steady—though far from extravagant—living for his wife, son, and daughter.

"And Diana? Any changes in her situation?" Marco asked, his tone dropping a bit darker.

His mother groaned low in her throat. "It's not going to change anytime soon, Marco. We all know that."

Marco's younger sister, Diana, was only one year away from her degree in nursing, at twenty-two, when she dropped out of school. She married Dr. Peter Roselli, the plastic surgeon she'd met during her internship at New York Methodist Hospital. In six short months, his sister had gone from an A cup to a D, lost the little bump on her nose, and gained one between her hips.

Roselli was forty-one at the time—almost twice Diana's age. That was over two years ago.

"Is she bringing her beautiful baby to see Uncle Marco tomorrow?"

"Of course," his mother replied, reproachful. "Don't tell me Uncle Marco has forgotten little Angelina turns one-year-old this week?"

Marco slapped his palm to his forehead, but continued evenly, "Of course not, Mama. How could I forget something as important as that?"

Marco rode the elevator to the twentieth floor, then made his way down the highly polished black and white tiles to his door. After he changed into sweats, he fired up his cappuccino maker.

His loft apartment boasted a roomy, modern floor plan with oak flooring. He'd decorated it to suit his tastes—simply, since when he'd moved in three years ago, Marco had no intention of sharing the space with anyone else. Not yet. Not until his business had risen to the goal he'd set for himself way back when he started in the trade.

Until, of course, Cleo came along. But even though his companion had come into his life totally unplanned, Marco wasn't sorry. Cleo made an outstanding roommate.

She sauntered out now as the hiss from the cappuccino maker filled the loft, apparently waking her from a restful nap. Cleo indulged in a lot of those. But she always took the noise coming out of the cappuccino maker personally. As if the machine represented competition.

Cleo, short for Cleopatra, was an Ocicat, a domestic variety of feline that looked very much like a miniature leopard. Marco's sister had fallen in love with Cleo at a breed show in Madison Square Garden she'd attended with her new beau, the plastic surgeon. Peter had, of course, immediately delighted his wife with the outrageously expensive kitten, only to claim months later he'd developed an allergy to cats.

He gave Diana a choice—either find the cat a home, or surrender her to a shelter.

Marco had never been much of a pet lover, since his work and unpredictable schedule ruled out anything requiring much more frequent care than a betta fish. But Cleo was almost that easy. And the moment she came to live with Marco, the two bonded like rejoined, wandering souls.

Now Cleo, irritated by the hissing steam, slithered into the kitchen with her tail twitching. She fixed Marco with an expression in her golden eyes that, if he didn't know her better, might pass for threatening. But Cleo and Marco had been roommates now for almost two years. He knew her better.

"Mia cara, what's your problem? You think I'm cheating on you with another of your kind?"

He paused to pour a dollop of cream into a crystal saucer, one of several he kept scrubbed and stacked on the shelf above his sink. Especially for Cleo.

"Here you go, Queen of the Nile. Did you miss me? Or, are you sbronzo I've disturbed your nineteen-hour nap?" Marco squatted and ran his hand along the cat's sleek, spotted fur as she lapped at the cream. The only response she gifted him with was another tail twitch.

Cleo never lowered herself to purring.

After his cup was filled, he made his way through the dining room, pausing only briefly at the dining table. Wistfully, as he did every time he passed through, his gaze wandered to the grouping of sepia family photos gracing the wall over the table. Sighing, he continued on to the sofa. Over the last few years, Marco had come to prefer eating in the living room.

He settled himself into a corner of his cream leather sofa and switched on the Bose stereo, lowering Andrea Bocelli to a less glass-shattering volume. With his iPad in his lap, he scrolled, trying to decide what he wanted for dinner. No sense in cooking for himself alone, that was for sure. He lived in a neighborhood where practically every local restaurant delivered. As Bocelli crooned in Italian about a time to say goodbye, Marco struggled with the decision between Thai and Italian.

Though there was no Italian restaurant, even here in the city, that struck home like *Frankie and Johnny's* in Hurleyville. Thoughts of dinner last evening—had it been only last evening?—brought to mind, of course, Kate. He set the iPad down on the heavy, wood coffee table and leaned back, crossing his legs at the ankle.

Now, nothing sounded good. Nothing as good as a candlelit dinner with Kate Bardach. He picked up his phone and dialed her.

"Hey, Marco. What's up?" She sounded casual and almost distracted when she picked up on the second ring. As though she'd been expecting his call. Or *someone's* call.

"Hi, Kate. Where are you? Still at the Loch?" he asked, trying to keep his tone light.

"Nuh-uh," she replied. "I rented a car and drove home this afternoon. Just got here, actually." He could hear clicking and zinging noises that probably meant she was unpacking and hanging up her stuff.

Or perusing a surely extensive wardrobe for an outfit to wear out on the town.

There was the itch in his blood again. As if sensing his unease, Cleo chose that moment to leap up onto the seat beside him and bump his hand with her head. He stroked her silky fur absently.

"Where's the Porsche?" he asked.

"I had it towed on a flatbed to my dealer here in Manhattan. It was really my only choice. I'm surprised they even know what a Porsche *is* in Sullivan County."

There was a snobby quality to her words again, like yesterday morning when she'd first arrived with her team at Redman's. She was in businesswoman mode. This was not being considered a personal call.

He sipped his cappuccino. "Well, hopefully there hasn't been any serious damage," he said, matching his indifferent tone to hers.

Which evidently pissed her off. "Um, Marco, what can I do for you? I mean, I just got in, and—"

"You can consent to join me for a traditional, home-cooked Italian dinner at my parents' house in Brooklyn tomorrow." He'd blurted the words out without realizing they were coming. In the brief, shocked silence that followed, he added, "It's not like I'm taking you home to meet the family, Kate. I thought maybe you could use a distraction after the past few days."

She hummed into his ear. "Hmm, I don't know, Marco. I still haven't made up my mind about your project."

"And this would have nothing to do with our potential agreement. The last thing I want to do is pressure you. It will simply be a nice, social afternoon. I'll introduce you as a new client. My parents won't think there's anything to it beyond that." Another long beat of silence, which he cut short by adding, "Besides, it's my niece's first birthday. How can you refuse to honor such a celebration?"

Marco nodded and glanced pointedly at the cat who had seated herself next to him, posed like an Egyptian statue. Her golden eyes were fixed on his as though she were reading his mind. He raised one hand in question, and Cleo narrowed her eyes momentarily. He could swear he saw her nod in agreement.

As Kate looked down on the traffic clogging 3rd Street, she couldn't believe she'd consented to joining Marco to a family dinner in Brooklyn. What had she been thinking? She hadn't been, that was the answer. She'd been tired and distracted and simply not paying attention.

Although she'd really had no plans for Sunday at all, lounging around in her pajamas all day had been sounding very tempting. Some reading, a little Internet surfing, a movie perhaps. What she definitely hadn't imagined was doing her makeup and hair, slipping on a light sweater over silk trousers, and trotting up the street to Macy's to pick up a card and trinket for a tot's first birthday.

One she didn't know anything about, other than that her first birthday was imminent. Kate could count on one hand how many times she'd been around little kids, let alone one still in diapers and drooling. It just wasn't her scene.

But she did need to keep her mind from ruminating on the strange occurrences of the past few days. The panic attacks, then the bizarre psychic episode at Redman's. The unexplained catapulting of her car clear across the lake to land on the muddy shore with a splat.

When she saw the black Q50 pull up in front of her building, she picked up her purse, slid on a comfortable pair of leather pumps, and headed out.

Kate was surprised when, after opening the passenger door for her and coming around to slide into the driver's seat, Marco clasped the back of her neck and pulled her face to his. His kiss was sweet, not sensual, but she was still caught off guard. She'd heard Italians were a very affectionate breed, but still . . . .

"How are you, mia cara?" he asked as he maneuvered his sleek car into the steady flow of traffic.

"I'm okay," she answered in a small voice. "Tired. A little out of sorts. But okay."

"So what's the deal with your car? Heard anything yet?"

She shook her head, sliding him a reproachful glance. "It's the weekend, Lareci. It's hard enough to get a straight answer from a Porsche mechanic on a weekday, let alone on a Sunday."

"Ah," he said, tipping up his chin.

He looked delectable today, dressed in black from head to toe. Turtleneck under a linen jacket, matching trousers. Hair still wet, it almost looked like he hadn't combed it after stepping out of the shower. His stubble was a full-day's growth longer than it had been the night before when she'd bid him goodnight at her door.

The lady places deep in her core began to hum of their own accord, and she did her best to mentally slap them into submission.

"How about you?" she asked, struggling to keep the conversation light. "Recover from your overnight drive home?"

He chuckled. "I'm resilient. I had an appointment with a new client yesterday afternoon, so I had to bounce back fast or risk losing business." He slid her a conspiratorial glance. "We both know how important it is to hang on to every potential client that comes along."

Kate closed her eyes and sighed, exasperated. "Marco, I thought you weren't going to put any pressure on me."

He lifted her hand from her lap and kissed her fingers. "I'm not, Kate. Really, I'm sorry. I only meant we're both very serious business people. Sometimes, business takes precedence over our personal lives."

She sighed again, with relief this time.

"But today, we're putting business aside to celebrate my baby niece's birthday. Angelina turns one-year-old next Tuesday." His smile shot her through the middle, beaming with genuine pride and joy, as if he were the child's father, not merely her uncle.

She'd heard Italian families were tight. Guess she was getting ready to experience the phenomenon firsthand.

"Your brother's child? Sister's?" she asked.

"My sister, Diana is the only one. I'm the elder," he said.

Kate nodded, wondering for a moment what it might be like to have a sibling.

"How about you?" Marco asked, reading her thoughts. "Any brothers or sisters?"

She shook her head, pressing her lips tight. "Nope. Just me. Only child. Only girl-child of a rich, Long Island, Jewish family." She shot him a cynical glance. "How do you gentiles refer to types like me? Oh, yeah. A typical Jewish American Princess."

"Well." He continued in an even tone, apparently refusing to take her bait for a sparring match. "Today, you'll be taking a walk on the wilder side. A traditional, close-knit, Italian family. And a traditional meal, complete with antipasti to start and ending with cannoli." He grinned. "Still wondering how Mama plans on getting the birthday candle into the crust of the cannoli."

His parents' lovely townhouse on Louisa Street boasted its own parking, a definite plus in this busy area of Boro Park. A generous front porch was topped by a second-story balcony, and Kate guessed the structure could easily house two families. Somehow, she knew the only ones residing under its roof were Larecis.

A young woman, presumably Marco's sister, with voluminous, dark brown hair came bursting onto the stoop as he opened Kate's door for her.

"Marco. You came," she said, almost reverently, as she approached him and framed his face in her hands. She was a tiny woman, barely over five feet tall, but filled out her pale pink sweater in a way that actually made Kate jealous. And Kate was far from being flat-chested.

Perhaps she's still nursing. How long does that sort of thing go on, anyway?

For a moment, Kate felt as though she might have become invisible, watching this pretty woman stroke Marco's cheek and gaze lovingly into his eyes. She murmured something in Italian before kissing him full on the mouth. Then, she suddenly stumbled back and threw her hands up beside her face.

"And what did you bring for my sweet Angelina?"

Marco laughed and grabbed Kate by the elbow, pulling her close to his side. "I brought her an acquaintance of mine. A dear, sweet friend. Diana, this is Kate Bardach."

So, not exactly introduced as a business associate, but Kate didn't have time to think of what a proper reaction might be before Diana grabbed her shoulders and kissed both her cheeks in turn.

"My pleasure, Kate."

Kate noticed the woman's smile didn't quite reach her eyes.

Marco leaned into the back seat and extracted a huge gift bag bearing the image of a sparkly, pink teddy bear on an aqua background. Kate's much smaller package dressed in the same colors paled in comparison as he lifted it out as well.

Oh, well. Not my niece.

Inside the door, Kate was bombarded by more introductions to people whose names and family titles left her confused. There were several old women—really old—whom Kate could only assume were great-grandmothers, perhaps a great-aunt or two. His mother was a short, stout woman with salt-and-pepper hair cropped short. Rosa Lareci scrutinized Kate with narrowed eyes when Marco introduced her. Again, as a dear friend.

"We're business associates," she said through a nervous chuckle. "Marco is hiring me on to renovate his hotel investment."

One of his mother's straggly, gray eyebrows lifted suspiciously as her eyes shifted from Kate toward Marco, and back again. Marco was oblivious, having scooped the pink-cheeked child out of his sister's arms and was busy blowing loud air kisses into the crook of her neck. The child squealed with delight.

"Welcome to our home, Ms. Bardach," Mrs. Lareci said, a thick, Italian accent failing to warm her measured tone. Not a trace of a smile lifted her age-wizened features. "Please, make yourself comfortable."

Kate watched Diana follow her mother down to the end of the narrow space and disappear around a corner into what she assumed was the kitchen. But her heart nearly stopped when she realized that following on the heels of the younger woman was the diaphanous image of another small child.

She blinked rapidly to clear her vision, but she was not mistaken. A child, barely able to walk, floated close behind Diana, clutching at the hem of her sweater. Kate couldn't be sure, but somehow felt certain, gauging from the simplicity of the child's shirt and trousers, it was a boy.

But Kate could see clearly through the child's form, easily able to decipher where Diana's long, pink sweater ended and the dark blue of her jeans began. This was a shadow figure. A residual image of a life no longer present here, in this moment, in this place.

A chill skittered down her spine. Diana reappeared from the kitchen holding two tumblers, each holding different colored drinks.

"Mimosa? Or Bloody Mary?" Diana asked.

"Oh, mimosa for sure," she replied, eagerly accepting the drink. Casually, she dropped her gaze to Diana's side. But the shadow figure of the child was no longer visible.

Marco took the other glass and called, "Mama. Come out here. It's time for a toast."

Kate found the day to progress exactly as Marco had predicted, with antipasti served shortly after their arrival. A choice of either Screwdrivers or Bloody Marys to start. Breadsticks wrapped in a salty, spicy ham Kate learned was called prosciutto. Little balls of fresh, baby mozzarella floating in basil-laced olive oil. And some more familiar fare— steamed shrimp with cocktail sauce.

Kate was full before they'd even brought out the main course.

By three o'clock, the wine bottles had claimed their place on the table, and talk was easy and disjointed. Marco's dad was a short, quiet man who took little time away from the Sports Channel to join the festivities. He, and two other men she later learned were Marco's uncles, looked like a boxer who'd missed his calling. Broad and stout with a nose reminiscent of that of an aging cockatiel, Peter Lareci proved to be the least of Kate's concern during the afternoon.

Instead, she found herself surrounded, and duly intimidated by, the strong, outspoken women of the Lareci family. Marco's mom, Rosa, his sister, Diana, and a cousin who'd only been introduced as Marisa. They said more with their eyes than with words, long silences punctuating conversations Kate felt were not their norm.

Diana scrutinized her with the most intent, sitting down the far end of the table with her sleepy baby girl dozing on her shoulder.

And, from time to time, the diaphanous image of a shy, sad-faced, redheaded little boy peeked around from behind her chair. His manifestation remained translucent, and the child seemed to acknowledge no one but Diana and the baby Angelina in her arms. Every time Kate caught sight of him, the stab in her heart made it difficult to stay engaged in the conversation around her.

When she did allow her gaze to travel from one face to another around the table, they all seemed to be staring at her. Yet, between the vision of the boy child, and the fact that she felt truly out of place in the midst of this close-knit family gathering, she found it nearly impossible to participate.

Marco sat beside her but made a point to acknowledge her regularly, often with a soft word or a touch on her hand or arm. Certainly not as one would treat a mere business associate. He was treating her more like a woman of interest. To him.

She could only imagine what his family was thinking. A complete stranger commanding their precious son/brother/grandson's affectionate attention. And the way Kate was acting, she figured they thought her either arrogant or a complete airhead.

"What was it you said you do?" Diana asked, lifting a cup of espresso to her lips after the dinner had been cleared away.

"I'm an interior designer," Kate replied. She thought to substantiate her reputation by naming some names, then hesitated.

That's not how these people judge you.

"I'm hoping," Marco began, lifting his wine glass as if to toast, "Ms. Bardach will take on the job of renovating the Redman for me."

He smiled in a way that spiked a nerve of irritation in the same moment as it stroked a note of pleasure within her. She tipped her head and stared at him, not knowing at all how to react.

Silence settling over the table was her answer. If Kate decided she would, in fact, take on this renovation, this was not going to be considered a happy day for the Lareci family.

"Well, beloved brother," Diana said quietly, "let's hope everything works out the way you have planned."

The drive back through Brooklyn to the streets of Manhattan was quiet in Marco's car. He'd had a little too much to drink to be driving, Kate thought. His family—although they'd been superficially polite—made it plain she was considered an outsider, and she could tell Marco had felt it, too. It had made him nervous, and she'd seen him drain his wine glass more quickly, and more often, than wise.

"You enjoyed yourself, I hope?" he asked as they merged onto FDR Drive.

"I did. Your family is lovely," Kate said, trying to keep the hurt out of her voice. She'd clearly felt their resentment. Not that they'd been overt. But there was no denying the sentiments underscoring the entire day.

Marco sighed. "I worry about Diana. With her beautiful baby. What will become of them?"

Kate glanced over at him in shock. "I know her husband wasn't there, but I got the impression she's happily married. He's a prominent plastic surgeon, right?"

"Yeah, he's all of that," Marco growled. "I'm not worried about their physical welfare. But Peter's an egotistical, self-centered bastard who couldn't care less about his wife and daughter. He's almost never home. And Diana isn't working. She's home all alone, taking care of Angelina all by herself. She gets very depressed."

Kate laid a hand on Marco's arm. "I'm sorry. I didn't realize."

"No," he snapped. "Most people wouldn't. She keeps the truth of her farce of a marriage conveniently camouflaged."

"So, the other child," Kate began tentatively. She had to ask about this. She had to know. "When did she lose the boy?"

The lurching of the car had Kate screeching and grabbing for the oh-shit handle. For a moment, she thought for sure they'd bounce off the retaining wall and end up in the East River. When Marco regained control of the vehicle, he glared over at her with shock and horror twisting his features.

"How did you know? Who told you?" His tone was accusatory, defensive.

Kate crossed her arms over her chest, her glare a silent challenge.

I am not a wacko. Now is my chance to prove it to you.

"Nobody told me about anything. I saw him. A little boy, older than Angelina. Two, maybe?"

"Rompicoglioni, Kate." Marco swiped a hand down his face. "You're freaking me out." Then he turned to glare at her. "Who told you? I doubt it would have been Mama."

"Why not?"

He flashed her a glance as he drove, his pale eyes haunted. Even if he had been a little tipsy on leaving his parents' home, the shock of what she'd revealed had done one thing—snapped him back to full sobriety.

"Kate, who told you about the boy? It's our own horrible, painful secret. The proverbial skeleton in the Lareci family closet." Marco's voice, tight and emotional, pierced Kate's heart.

"I'm sorry. I don't mean to pry or dig up painful memories," she began quietly.

He stared straight ahead as he took their exit off the highway and screeched into a gas station on the corner. Once the car was safely stopped, he spun to face her.

"How did you know?" he repeated. "There are no photos. At least, not in my parents' house. Mama made Diana take them all down after the funeral." His voice grew thick with emotion.

Kate hated this part of her gift. Made it feel more like a curse, since often the things she saw opened old wounds for people who'd like nothing more than to forget about their loss. But the facts remain, as do the souls of some who have left this world physically but are unable to move on.

He turned his face away from her and muttered, "Tell me what you saw." His voice broke, and Kate laid a hand on his arm.

"Marco, I'm sorry. But I had to tell you. The tot looks so very sad. And he clings to Diana's side almost every moment."

His shuddering breath made her heart ache for him. "Describe him," he barked, a desperate command.

Kate folded her hands in her lap and stared at them. "He's about two, like I said. Walking, but not well. Of course, it's difficult to tell because whenever I saw him, he was clinging so close to Diana's side, he could have been actually holding on."

"Holy Christ," Marco muttered thickly.

"He *is* holding on, Marco. The boy doesn't know he's passed and doesn't seem to understand why Diana ignores him, paying more attention to Angelina than to him. I got the feeling he was very sad, very confused."

Kate jumped and shrank away as Marco's fist came down on the steering wheel. But he didn't say anything, and for a long moment, they sat there. He kept his face turned away from her, but the quaking of his shoulders told her he was crying.

When he was finally able to control his emotions again, he repeated, "Tell me what he looked like, Kate. I'm sorry, but I don't believe you. I think you are perhaps a very perceptive person, one who surmised this loss from something Diana must have said. You can't possibly have been seeing . . . the boy. We laid him in the ground almost three years ago. He had a Christian burial."

She understood his denial, knew he wanted with all his soul to discredit what she was telling him. It was a common reaction, and Kate had learned not to take it personally. In this moment, though, it hurt a bit more, coming from Marco. But she chose not to dwell on the reason for *his* doubt to bother her any more than from a stranger.

"He had the biggest, roundest, blue eyes I'd ever seen on a child," she began gently. "He wore dark pants, bumpy around his butt as though there were a diaper underneath. His shirt had a red car on it. A cartoon caricature with eyes, too, as big and round as the boy's."

Marco shook his head and covered his face with both hands. Through them he croaked, "And his hair?"

"A tousled cap of curls." She tipped her head and studied him, perplexed. She recalled now that his entire family, other than the graying elders, had been dark-haired—brunette to black. Even little Angelina sported a slick coating of silky, jet hair clinging to her cheeks in wisps. "It puzzles me, Marco. If I hadn't seen him with my own eyes, I wouldn't question it. But the manifestation of *this* little boy had bright-red hair."

EIGHT

Normally, there was no way Kate would have consented to go back with Marco to his place. Tomorrow was Monday, and she knew she had a lot of thinking to do before she gave him a final decision as to whether or not she'd be taking on his project. But as they sat there in his car under the streetlight in a corner of the Citgo gas station, he looked so shaken, so vulnerable. She felt for him.

"Come home with me?" he asked quietly. "Please? Just for a little while. Some cappuccino . . . ."

It was as though he were in some kind of shock, and even though she didn't know the man very well—and knew damn well she shouldn't care—she couldn't help herself. She was worried about him.

"Okay," she said, "but only for a little while."

He lived in a studio loft in a lovely old, brick building with a curved corner-hugging edifice on the Upper West Side. A parking ramp led underneath the building, and he handed his keys to the attendant, then helped Kate out of the car. Neither of them said anything as they rode the elevator to the twentieth floor.

The apartment, open and spacious, was warm and inviting, yet definitely screamed male. The entire west wall featured original faded brick. Buttercream, textured wallpaper covered the opposite side, ideal to muffle sound bouncing off all the hard surfaces. Kate immediately noticed the cluster of framed photographs placed in a group over a small sideboard, flanking the wall near the dining table.

There was little wall art other than these. They must have significance.

As they entered, a spotted cat curled up in the corner of the leather sofa raised its head, huge golden eyes alarmed.

"Oh," Kate stopped in her tracks. "You live with a—a leopard?"

Marco chuckled as he stepped around her. "Va bene, Cleo. Amica."

A leopard that speaks Italian, no less. Kate had never been one much for any kind of household pets, and truth be told, was a little freaked out by cats. Apparently, Marco's roommate wasn't interested in whatever his explanation for her presence had been. Standing, the cat stretched up into a Halloween silhouette, yawned to bare impressive teeth, then landed on the hardwood with a thud. As it sauntered away, the creature cast an indignant glare over its shoulder in Kate's direction before disappearing around a corner.

"Cleo isn't much for company," Marco said as he made his way to the kitchen. "But don't take it personally. She's an independent bitch. I guess I'm lucky she lets *me* live here."

While the cappuccino maker hissed and steamed, Kate wandered over to study the photos hanging in the dining area. At first, she thought they might be pieces of random people by modern fine-art photographers. Like the ones gracing the walls of many Italian restaurants she'd visited. But as she drew closer, she began to recognize some of the faces she'd seen only a few hours ago.

Marco, a decade or so younger, laughing at the beach, his arm around a teenage Diana. His parents, sitting on a bench in front of a church, studying a book shared on their laps—most likely a bible. A group shot of the long dining table she'd eaten at earlier today, with all the now familiar faces of the people she'd met.

She was smiling at the warmth and love reflected in these photographs, tinted to sepia which made them seem timeless. Framed in slick ebony, the rectangular shapes were identical, except for size and orientation. Until her eyes finally landed on the photo in the center.

This one was different, framed in oval, ornate, carved gilt. The frame itself Kate recognized as an antique; no reproduction. The image it curved lovingly around made her blood chill to ice.

She jumped when Marco set the cups of cappuccino on the table behind her.

"My parents were not very happy when Diana came home to announce she was pregnant. She'd just started college, nineteen years old, and she didn't have a clue as to where her life was headed. Or, how difficult that journey can be." His voice, more controlled now, was dark and somber.

He pulled out a chair and motioned for her to sit, using a cloth napkin to dust off the chair first. "I don't use this area much anymore. Not since it happened." Pausing, he looked up at the photograph and sighed. "But I can't bear to take him down. It would be like burying him all over again."

Not knowing what to say, Kate laid a hand on his stubbled cheek and met his gaze. "Three years ago, you said?"

He nodded, then sat down facing her. Lifting his cup, he held it up as if to toast. "Here's to Matthew."

"What's Matthew's story, Marco?" she asked, getting the impression he was ready to talk about it. *Needed* to talk about it.

He set his cup down and crossed his arms on the table, staring into the steam rising off the foam. "Diana got tangled up with a fellow she met in a pub she and her girlfriends used to frequent Saturday nights. Guess his jaunty accent and red hair fascinated her. What she didn't realize was that he was a nothing. A nobody, working construction, freshly immigrated from Ireland."

She could see the spark of anger—rage, even—simmering still in his pale eyes. "Or, that he was old enough to be her father. And she had no clue he had a wife and three little kiddies of his own, waiting back in Ireland while Ol' Paddy spent his paycheck on beer at the local pub."

"Oh, Marco," Kate whispered, and reached for his hand. She didn't know what else to say.

"God forgive her, my sister always had a thing for older men. I guess he bought her enough beers to cloud her judgment, then took her to a sleazy hotel across the street."

"My God, she's lucky she didn't end up dead," Kate said. "Or, with some horrible STD."

"We are grateful for that." He nodded and heaved a huge sigh before continuing. "And of course, Ol' Paddy was long gone by the time the pregnancy test came back positive. Diana finished out her first semester at NYU, then moved back into my parents' house. The following spring, she gave birth to a fat baby boy with wispy, red curls."

A joyous addition to their family, Matthew had been like a pink-cheeked angel, Marco said. A happy baby, quiet and easy to please; his only fault had been he was terminally obsessed with his mother's touch. Diana had moved into her own apartment and was working, but whenever she dropped Matthew off to stay with his grandparents, the boy had melted down into a tiny tyrant.

A sudden, dark cloud engulfed the joy on Marco's face, and Kate instinctively reached over to grasp his hand as he continued to the end—the tragic end—of his story.

"Matthew was barely two. Well," his eyes drifted up to the stuccoed ceiling, "he would have been two the very next month."

A stab of pain pierced Kate's heart as though it had been *her* loss, yet she couldn't explain why. She'd never had children. Never even been around them much.

Marco drew in a shuddering breath. He rose and lifted his cup toward her. "A bit of whiskey? I think I need a bit right now."

Kate shook her head and watched as he moved toward the sideboard and opened a cabinet underneath. He poured two fingers of Jim Beam into his cup, then returned to his seat. After taking a long, slow sip, he leveled his gaze on hers.

"It was Easter Sunday. God knows, the holiday will never be the same, for any of us. Diana had just arrived with Matthew, having gone home to change him out of his scratchy, church clothes into something more comfortable. His Disney Cars shirt and corduroy pants."

"Don't." Kate reached forward with both hands and grasped Marco's. There was no reason for him to relive this agony again, not now. She pretty much could surmise what had happened. Whatever the tragedy, it had ended in the death of a toddler.

"No." Marco's eyes were squeezed shut, and he was shaking his head vehemently. "You already know the ending. It's only fair you know how it happened."

With a gut-wrenching twist, Kate watched a single tear roll down Marco's cheek. He did not open his eyes until the tale was told.

"Down on the street. Diana had walked the three blocks from where they were living, holding dear Matthew's hand diligently the whole way. When they came within sight, Mama burst through the door and called to them, her arms open wide. But Matthew . . . ." He paused and wiped the tear from his cheek with vengeance. "Matthew saw something, or someone. He broke free from Diana's grip and dashed into the street. Gone."

Gone. Like, forever. Tears rolled down Kate's cheeks as Marco continued describing the end of a tiny, precious life. Of a life wasted.

"He was a perfect stranger." Marco struggled to keep his composure, but a sob punctuated the strangled words as they freed themselves from his throat. "Later, Diana confessed, the man across the street did look like Matthew's father. It wasn't him. But somehow, for some reason only God Himself knows, the boy was drawn to him. Ruddy complexion, red hair. Matthew stepped off the curb and was struck dead by the Chrysler careening around the corner, making a beeline for that last, precious, open parking spot. Whose driver is probably undergoing therapy to this day."

Initially, she'd only meant to hold him, comfort him. His grief was so palpable, so intense since she'd ripped off the scab. They sat close on his sofa after he'd refilled his glass of whiskey, and made her a cup of chamomile tea.

Huh. Imagine that. The man just happened to have my favorite relaxation balm, chamomile, in his pantry. And he'd fixed it just like she asked, with extra sugar and a touch of cream.

"Even though," he said, shifting a glance toward the hallway, "I'll be in big trouble if Cleo finds out I've shared her cream with you."

They couldn't seem to exist in the same space, breathe the same air for very long before the natural chemistry between them took control. Her head tipped to rest on his shoulder, which led to a gentle, almost platonic kiss. At the touch of his lips, his taste and scent filled her head. When she opened her mouth to invite him in, he answered eagerly. The kiss set them both on fire. As though neither had any control over their reaction to one another.

Dawn crept stealthily around the Roman shades on Marco's bedroom windows when Kate blinked into consciousness. She hadn't intended to be swept up into this man's life, his drama. She hadn't meant to sleep with him yet another tumultuous, incredible night. But she had. And now, it was Monday morning.

What now? Did she regret it? A crucial question. Lying here in Marco's sumptuous king-sized bed, staring at the stuccoed ceiling, there was only one logical conclusion. Though Kate hated herself to admit the honest answer.

Everything happens for a reason. She was here for a reason. Marco had sought her out to renovate the Redman for a reason. There was no turning back, and somewhere deep inside, she knew that.

Damned fate. You just can't turn the bitch's tide, no matter how hard you try.

She looked over at the broad, muscled back of the man beside her, his dark hair a sea of rumpled waves against the pristine white pillowcase. His scent filled her senses, as well as the odor of sweaty sex clinging to the sheets. He was an amazing lover, no doubt. Generous, caring, patient. Yet, there was a savagery in his abandon, once he was certain he'd pleased her six ways to heaven, that made her shudder in the memory.

When they say Italian men are passionate lovers, they—whoever *they* are—know damn well what they're talking about.

She slid out of bed as quietly as she could, not wanting to wake him. Gathering her clothes was going to be more like a safari, and not one confined to the bedroom. And the last thing she wanted to do was cross paths with his resident leopard, especially naked. So she crept into the bathroom and clicked the door shut behind her, hoping to find his bathrobe on the back of the door, or an oversized bath towel, at least, to don after she bathed. The hot water cascading down from his rain shower fixture felt glorious against her back, her face, her hair.

After what must have been twenty minutes, though it seemed like as many seconds, Kate heard the bathroom door unlatch. Through the frosted glass enclosure, she could see his outline, massive and dark against the white-tiled wall. Then his voice, deep and velvety.

"May I join you?"

She slid the door open a crack and stepped back, allowing him entry. God, he was a beautiful man. His skin tone, olive to her alabaster pale, thrilled her with its richness. And he was hairy, like most men of Mediterranean origin, she guessed, though she'd known few, slept with even fewer. Yet, the coating of black curls on his chest, his legs, and of course, between his thighs, was just enough. Enough to be alluring and exciting, without any similarity to a wild beast.

Well, perhaps a little. But just enough.

Marco wasted no time, but backed her against the now warmed tile surface, combing her wet hair away from her face with gentle hands, careful not to catch in the tangles. His kiss was sweet and probing. He tasted minty and fresh—he must have brushed his teeth, and how glad she was she had done the same before stepping into the shower. They would have coupled again, there under the warm spray, had she not stopped him.

"Marco, a condom. I'm sorry. I'm on the pill, but for your protection as well as my own . . . ." The fire flashing in his eyes startled her, and he dropped his hands immediately to his sides. He didn't say a word as he angled his body away from her. Grabbing the soap, he sudsed himself quickly, then his hair, bathing as though she'd suddenly become invisible.

Kate hesitated a beat before sliding open the door from the other end of the space and stepping out.

Twenty minutes later, Kate had dressed in her rumpled, yesterday clothes and snugged her purse under one arm when Marco stepped out of the bedroom. A black, velour bathrobe covered all the amenities she'd been enjoying only minutes ago. But his chiseled, stubbled, sexy jaw was set in a hard line.

"You won't stay for coffee?" he asked, his tone neutral.

She shook her head. "I've got a meeting with my team at ten." She glanced up at the enormous, oval, wall clock hanging on the brick wall. "To discuss your project."

His shoulders rose and fell with a sigh she couldn't tell was annoyance or trepidation. "So, you're still not sure? Or, you're sure, and you don't want to break the news to me until after your meeting?" He made his way into the kitchen and began fiddling with the elaborate coffee maker, the one he'd made the cappuccino with last night. One Kate was certain she couldn't operate if her life depended on it.

"Do you still think I'm a wacko?" she blurted.

Now where had that come from? Even in her own mind, Kate wasn't sure.

He raised his hazel eyes to hers, and she saw again the pain she'd seen when she'd described his late nephew to him the night before. Oh, how she hated this part of her . . . gift? Surely, the term didn't fit the ability she had. Curse, more like.

"No. I know now, for a fact, you see what you say you see. There's simply no other explanation for what happened yesterday." His tone was dark, ominous, like thunderclouds before a hellacious midsummer storm. He held her gaze intently.

So intense she found she couldn't hold it herself and had to look away. "Then you'll understand if I find it necessary to delegate your project to another member of my team." In almost a whisper.

"No, I won't understand," he shouted, and she jumped. He had taken two steps forward to grip the counter separating them, his knuckles white with tension. Then, shaking his head, his chin dropped to his chest as he muttered, "I will respect your decision, but I will not be happy about it."

As she turned to leave, movement caught her eye, and she glanced down the short hall. There was Cleo, perched like an Egyptian statue, her tail switching from side to side in short, irritated snaps. In the dim light, her yellow eyes glowed as if electrified. A shudder danced across Kate's shoulder blades.

She reached for the door as she heard Marco growl, "Do me one favor. Please, spare me having too much interaction with your boy-toy."

Kate whirled and tipped up her chin. "And who, pray tell, would that be?"

But the man had already turned back toward his coffee maker, shaking his head in disgust. "I'll need an answer by day's end. For *my* team," he said.

She closed the door behind her with a little more force than was necessary.

How, how, how could this have happened? The mantra thrummed through Marco's head as he worked his way through his morning ritual—strong, black coffee, two cups. Separating yesterday's clothes into two piles, one for the housekeeper and one for the dry cleaner. Booting up his laptop and scanning the forty-seven emails in his inbox.

Yet, through it all, through every act of automation of his daily routine he usually found so comforting, flashes of memory slashed at his heart like static electric shocks. Impossibly round, blue eyes rimmed with jet fringe. Pale skin, every inch covered with a smattering of peach freckles once the makeup was gone. Lips so full and soft, he got hard just thinking about how they felt against his. Their taste. Her unique, seductive scent.

He had it bad for a woman who was absolutely the wrong one for him. Not only was she a hard-headed, independent businesswoman who didn't need *any* man, but she made it no secret she took her pleasures with as many of them as she desired. She was an only child—a spoiled, rich, modern-day woman who thought of marriage and family as velvet-covered anchors. And she had this . . . this weird psychic ability.

What the hell was he thinking? He needed to call her office right now and tell her to forget about renovating the Redman. Take it off her to-do list. This path he was on was a crash course, a disaster getting ready to unfold.

Marco knew that. But he also knew, deep down inside a part of his soul he'd kept sequestered for so long, it was already too late.

Marco Lareci was falling in love. Falling in love with a woman who not only didn't believe in the word, but appeared to harbor true disdain for the concept.

And one who saw dead people.

NINE

Kate hailed a taxi and rode the six blocks uptown to her own apartment, clenching her teeth the entire time. An exasperating man, this Italian stallion. He barely knew her, yet acted as though he owned her. She wasn't used to scenes like the one this morning. Wasn't accustomed to so much drama attached to the simple, enjoyable, physical act of sex.

So why did it hurt so much, the memory of the anger and pain in his eyes as she'd left his place?

Kate enjoyed her choice of a number of men, but tended toward the younger ones. The ones eager to get her into bed, but not mature enough to be interested in anything more permanent. She watched the early morning bustle of people along Broadway from her taxi window and sighed. One of the things she liked about Manhattan was the ability to remain anonymous, unattached, yet still interact with countless people every day.

Enjoy a social evening, a great night of sex, then part without so much as exchanging email addresses.

Yet, she found herself, especially over the last year or so, drawn more and more toward the lake house in Sullivan County. Toward the peace and serenity of the country. The wind in the pines, towering over her hot tub on the back deck. The gentle sloshing of water up on the shore beyond. The birds chattering to wake her in the morning, and the crickets singing her to sleep at night.

An hour later she was home, dressed and ready for work. She was getting ready to head out the door when her cell rang. Her heart leapt with the hope it was Marco.

What the hell was wrong with her? She'd never pined over a man this way. No matter how good the sex had been.

But even her internal reprimand didn't stop her heart from sinking when she saw the caller ID said *Mother*.

"Hi, Mother. What's up?"

"Lunch today, Kate? There's something I'd like to talk to you about."

Kate froze, her hand hovering over the door handle. "Is something wrong? Are you and Father okay?" But her mother's tone wasn't ominous.

"Everything is fine. You just got me thinking about . . . things the other day when you asked about your late aunt. I dug out some old photos I'd like you to see."

Photos? This was creepy, and a complete turnaround from the usual way Mother reacted to any discussion involving her late aunt. Kate could never remember seeing any photos of Leah. Didn't know any existed.

"Okay," Kate answered slowly, "but why now, Mother? Is it because of this Redman job I'm considering?"

"Partly. But there's more to it than that. Let's have lunch, okay? *Brasserie*? About one?"

Needless to say, by the time Kate walked into the offices of Bardach & Associates, she felt much less pulled together than was her usual style. She checked her hair and makeup in the brightly lit mirror of the ladies' room and yanked on the lapels of her rose linen suit. She looked okay, on the outside. Normal, sophisticated, lady-in-charge Kate.

But on the inside, her stomach was doing a tango, and her heart felt strangely sore, like a fresh bruise. Like it had been beaten with a bat. She didn't like feeling this way. She didn't like it one bit. Yet, she wasn't really sure who was to blame—her mother or Marco Lareci.

Her team was waiting for her when she whisked into the conference room at five past ten. Daniel had a third of the round table covered with various drawings and a set of what looked like old blueprints. Her administrative assistant, Luanne, sat with her laptop propped on the table in front of her. Its screen reflected distorted text off her tortoise-shell readers, which were tethered around her neck by a beaded chain.

Kate blinked in surprise when she took a closer look at Yvette. Her normally conservative, highly organized design assistant, looked almost . . . disheveled. Her short red hair, usually neatly tamed with some sort of product, sprung up in flirtatious waves all over her head. Her cheeks were pink, but it didn't appear to be from any sort of cosmetic.

Hmm. Maybe she'd been right about the sparks she saw flying between Yvette and Marco's partner, Boris. If she didn't know better, she'd say Yvette was wearing that *just fucked* look.

Kate smoothed a hand down her own hair, feeling a pang of . . . what? Regret? Envy?

"Good morning," Daniel said, a broad smile lighting up his face the minute he saw her.

"Good morning," she replied, then made her way around to her usual seat. She flipped open her iPad and propped it in front of her. "Let's get started. We have a lot to discuss today. What have you all found out about the old Redman Resort?"

Kate was impressed—they'd found out plenty. After they'd left the hotel that day, Daniel and Yvette had discovered a local museum only a few miles up the road in Hurleyville. The elderly director there had been most helpful, digging through old file cabinets and extracting a folder crammed full of newspaper clippings, photographs, and postcards—all about the Redman.

"It was the place to be back in the 50s and 60s," Daniel said. "They had some big names in entertainment up there—Sinatra, Dean Martin, Bogart, even Liz Taylor. Then, in the seventies, people started boarding airplanes for vacations instead of driving up to the mountains. By the 90s, Sullivan County, other than the racetrack, had become a ghost town."

No kidding, Kate thought, a chill skittering up her spine.

Yvette sat forward and clasped her hands atop her portfolio. "There's a rumor, or a legend, from what the old guy at the museum said, the Mafia used to dump bodies in the lake. So, it might be more of a ghost town than people realize."

Laughter rippled around the table, but Kate found it difficult to muster even a wan smile. "Okay, so enough folklore. Let's talk facts. What did you find out about the structure, Daniel? Did you get in touch with the building inspector Mr. Lareci said approved it before the sale?"

"I did. And it's held up amazingly well," Daniel said. "I guess the bank—the one who's owned it for the past twenty years—had a caretaker who kept tabs on the place. A local. He's apparently done a pretty good job."

Ah, so the old farmer—James?—wasn't making up stories.

"Anyway," Daniel continued, "I've got tons of photos of what the place looked like when it was prime, inside and out. Dated, for sure, but I think if we knock out a few walls, open up the spaces a little, it won't take much for it to shine again."

"So, it's structurally sound?" Kate pressed.

"Yes, quite. It's going to take some money to bring it up to today's codes and aesthetic standards, but it seems like the Lareci group has plenty of that."

"I'm sure they do," Kate said, tapping her stylus absently on the table. "I do have to wonder if they're going to be tossing a bunch of cash down a big, black hole."

Luanne's head popped up from her task of taking notes on her laptop. "So, you haven't heard yet?"

"Heard what?" Kate replied, glancing around the table. Yvette and Daniel both shrugged, seemingly as clueless as she.

"I think Mr. Lareci may have made a very wise investment after all. And in the nick of time, before the property values in Sullivan County shoot sky high." She tapped a few keys, then turned her laptop screen around so Kate and the others could read the headline.

Rockin' Hard Café Coming to Montlake Raceway and Casino

Marco had seen the headline only minutes after Kate slammed out his front door. He should have been overjoyed. And he was happy, or more, relieved. Even if Bardach & Associates refused to take on the renovation, Marco was certain now he'd have plenty of design firms waiting in line for the job. And he could press forward with the confidence he hadn't misled Boris and Eliot when he talked them into investing in the Redman.

But Marco couldn't ignore the incessant ache in his gut. Her words in the shower rang in his head, sending needles through his veins.

For your protection as much as for mine.

She was probably banging that boy-toy architect of hers on her lunch break most days. And God knows how many others.

He was jarred out of his bitter reverie when his cell rang. *Boris.*

"Comrade! I trust you heard the good news," he boomed into Marco's ear.

"I did. You see? I know what I'm talking about, Boris. The Borscht Belt is on the verge of a comeback. Only this time, it won't be limited to attracting only the wealthy Jewish population of our city."

In mid-sentence, his phone dinged again, and he glanced at it quickly. "I've got Malkovich trying to call in. Guess he's read the headline as well."

Boris chuckled. "I'm sure. He's scanning the stock pages long before you and I even empty our morning bladders."

Funny guy, this Russian. Weird way of putting things.

"So, do we have a design team or what?" Boris continued.

Marco braced his forehead against his hand. "I'll know by the end of the day. You, and Eliot, will be the next to know."

"Well, if her sexy, long-limbed assistant has anything to do with it, we're in." Boris chuckled. "I've already been in."

Marco sighed. Too much information, Comrade.

After two hours of formulating a basic contract, Kate waited as Luanne went out to retrieve the document from the copy room.

Daniel and Yvette both bent excitedly over the blueprints and photos, discussing floor plan options to include in the portfolio to present to Lareci, Malkovich, and Petrov. Kate hadn't yet decided whether she'd be running the show, or if she would hand it over to Daniel.

Spare me having too much interaction with your boy-toy . . . .

Marco's words echoed in her brain, sparking her irritation. She'd love nothing more than to do just that—hand over the project completely to Daniel. But the move would be spiteful and childish, and Kate was, above all, a cautious businesswoman. Her new architect was talented and enthusiastic, but the key word in the phrase was *new*. Fresh out of school. And this job, in light of the new info about The Rockin' Hard Café, could well turn out to be a game changer for Bardach & Associates.

"How about lunch when we finish up?"

Kate blinked back into the moment to realize Daniel had moved behind her, his mouth close to her ear. Too close. She discreetly rolled her chair away enough to reclaim her personal space.

"I'm sorry, Daniel. I already have plans for lunch today," she replied, trying very hard to keep her tone cool and businesslike.

He nodded and said, "Another time, perhaps."

She didn't reply.

Luanne came back through the door, carrying a stack of a dozen or more papers Kate would have to read through and sign. She checked her watch. Should have enough time to get them done and still make it to *Brasserie* on time.

"How are you planning to handle the distance factor, Kate?" Luanne asked. "I mean, you have the lake house up there, but the rest of the team—"

"I have a suggestion about that, Kate," Daniel said as he rolled the blueprints. "The ground floor has a small suite behind the lobby. Must have been an apartment of sorts for the staff at one time. Shouldn't take too much to get the space livable, at least for the weekdays."

Yvette's head snapped around to glare at him. "Are you suggesting we *live* there while the renovations go on?" She sounded as though he'd suggested they pitch a tent in a graveyard.

"Not all the time. But it would be nice to have it fixed up so we could spend the night, shower, and brew some coffee during the week. There's no way we can commute that far every day. And it sure would be a hell of a lot cheaper than a room at the racetrack's hotel in Liberty."

Folding her arms, Kate said, "A really good idea, Daniel. I'll be right up the road during the entire project, but it would be nice to know my architect is on-site, especially in the beginning stages." She smiled at him approvingly before glancing at Yvette. "You won't need to be up there more than once or twice a week until the construction crews are nearly finished anyway."

Yvette sighed, settling like a recently fluffed bird.

"So, we're on," Daniel said, beaming. "As soon as you get our clients to sign off, I'll start taking bids from local contractors."

Kate decided to walk the three blocks to the restaurant. She needed to clear her head. Get lost amid the crowds on the sidewalks, the honking horns, and the exhaust fumes. Figure out how she was going to swallow her pride and let Marco know he'd won.

Brasserie was one of her mother's favorite spots to meet for lunch, Kate knew. It always had been one of hers as well. But today, as she stepped into the long, narrow space, the brick lining one wall brought back images of Marco's place. And another pang of regret at how they had parted so coolly that morning.

Had it really been only five hours ago? It seemed like forever. A lifetime.

Damn it, she missed him.

Her mother was already seated at their favorite table near the back, in a cozy corner nearly hidden behind a spot-lit lemon tree. Joan sat with her hands folded atop a faded ivory folder tied with yellowed ribbon. The red smear on the lip of her wine glass told Kate she'd started without her.

And her mother was nervous. Joan Bardach was not one who usually drank wine with lunch.

"Hey, Mother," Kate said as she bent to brush a kiss across her mother's temple.

"Katherine," Joan replied. "Wine?"

Very nervous. And quite serious.

After the waiter had delivered her glass of chilled Pinot Grigio, Kate sipped, then met her mother's gaze.

"So what's this all about?" she asked.

Joan curled her fingers under the edges of the folder before her and stared at it. "It's about time I shared a little bit about your aunt with you. I know it's always been a taboo subject. A part of my family's history I wished would go away."

Kate laid a hand over hers. "I know it's painful for you to talk about, Mother. But I don't understand why it's so important for you to dredge all this up now. After all these years."

Joan's eyes shone with unshed tears when she looked up. "Because, Katherine. I understand you may be spending a great deal of time at Redman's. In the last place—that very same building— where Leah was seen." She lifted her wine glass, and Kate could see how violently she was trembling. Three swallows, and it was empty. "And we both know how you sometimes . . . you know, see things," she murmured, blotting her lips with her napkin.

"Mother, if my working at what used to be the Redman bothers you this much—" Then what? She wasn't going to hand this job over to her newbie architect. Kate began again. "I'm sorry this is upsetting you so, Mother. But it's business."

"You don't understand. It's not that I don't want you to take on this project." Joan managed a weak smile. "I'm actually hoping you can help me. Maybe your *ability*," her mother always said the word encased within invisible quotation marks, "maybe, for once, you'll be able to put it to good use."

Kate flopped back in her chair, her jaw slack. Her *ability* had been another taboo subject in the family for most of her life. She could hardly believe what she was hearing. "You mean, you're hoping I can find out what happened to her? Leah was last seen at the Redman, Mother. But there's no evidence she *died* there."

Her mother shrugged and tilted her head. "Is it so bad for me to want some closure? Perhaps there's . . . *something* left there. Some way you can find out . . . ."

A chill started at the base of Kate's spine and, like frost spreading on a winter windowpane, crawled up until it reached the back of her neck. She'd seen dead people, spirits, of countless other families' lost loved ones. An elderly woman shuffling along in the market with the shadow figure of an old man flanking her side. A somber girl on the subway, the translucent image of a handsome, young soldier hovering over her. And yesterday, little Matthew, clinging to Marco's sister. But they'd always been strangers.

Never anyone she'd known, or family. It had always been as though she subconsciously blocked any encounter with potential to strike too close to home.

Kate started when her mother slid the folder across the table to her.

"These are all originals, so please, take care with them. I thought it would be best for you to have them, not copies. I want you to know what you're looking for, so if you see her, you'll recognize her." The waitress delivered another glass of wine, and Joan lifted it. "To Leah. I hope you'll be able to find out what happened to her."

Marco waited until four o'clock, pacing back and forth in his apartment, raking his hand through his hair again and again. He'd clearly told Kate he needed an answer today. Her meeting was at ten this morning. How long did it take for a bunch of high-browed creatives to make a decision?

Rompicoglioni. This woman sure knows how to break my balls.

He could be a very patient man. But Marco also didn't like to be kept in suspense. If it had been anyone other than this woman, he'd have been blowing up her phone by lunchtime. He'd almost called her office at noon, then thought better of it.

This was a woman who demanded kid-glove treatment. Part of Marco seethed with anger at himself, at his own unwillingness to push her. Another part was terrified if he did, he might lose her forever.

He was so lost in his own ruminating that when his lobby buzzer went off at four twenty-five, his heart leapt into his throat.

"Yes?" he barked into the speaker next to his door.

"Marco?"

It was Kate. Relief, exhilaration, joy spread through him, warming him from the inside out like the first swallow of good whiskey.

"Come up. Please." He buzzed her in, then stared at the door, waiting.

TEN

Marco had every intention of playing it cool, staying businesslike, professional. All of those good intentions evaporated when he opened his door and saw her.

"I'm sorry," she said quickly. "I know I should have called first."

He stepped back silently, waving her in with an open arm. Then closed both arms around her the minute the door latched shut.

Burying his face in her hair, breathing in her scent, Marco felt a thick ball of emotion rise into his throat. He swallowed against it, but for a long moment, couldn't speak.

She hadn't pushed him away, yet hadn't returned his embrace, either.

Finally, he held her at arm's length and studied her expression. She was even paler than usual; dark crescents hung under both eyes, and her full lips were trembling. Her pretty pink suit was wrinkled, her jacket pulled off kilter by the leather portfolio slung over one shoulder. But she met his gaze full on, and that, if nothing else, gave him hope.

"I've been waiting," he said.

"I know. I'm sorry. Been a hell of a day," she replied, swiping under eyes that had suddenly started leaking.

"Mia cara, come in. Sit down. Let me get you something. Wine? Or, do you prefer cappuccino?"

Kate snorted into her hand, a half laugh, half sob. "Do you have any vodka? Hell, your business partner is Russian. Please tell me you have some vodka."

Marco put some soothing instrumental piano on the overheads and shook her a very dry, dirty martini. They sat close together on his couch, which felt so right. He looked down at her bare feet, toes wiggling against the hardwood floor.

Yes. This is exactly where you belong.

He waited, longer than he thought he was capable of, before asking, "So, what's got you so upset? Do you have bad news to deliver to me?"

She nearly choked on her mouthful of good Russian vodka. Calmly, he handed her a cocktail napkin, then tucked her long, black hair over her ear. The three diamond studs lining its pink, curved edge sparkled in the beam of the recessed lighting. As she set down her glass, she smiled up at him.

"I hope not. I've brought some papers for you and your partners to sign."

Marco dropped his head back and uttered a silent prayer. As long as he could stay connected to her on this project, there was still hope he might be able to win her heart. Why was he so sure of this urgent desire of his? He had no earthly idea. Probably would be one of the biggest mistakes of his life, offering his heart to this difficult, independent woman.

No matter. The situation was already well out of his control.

"Is that why you are so upset, Kate? Because you'll be working for—with—me, for at least the next several months?"

She shook her head adamantly. "No. Not at all, Marco. It's just all these strange things have been happening in my life. Ever since," she hesitated, her eyes locking on his, "ever since I met you."

He chuckled and settled back in his seat, sipping his cappuccino. "I've been known to cause some rather supernatural experiences for women, from time to time," he growled, wiggling his eyebrows at her.

But she didn't smile. "You pompous ass," she said, though her tone held no malice. "I'm not talking about your sexual prowess." She arched one dark eyebrow. "Nor am I arguing its merits."

He smiled into her eyes, searching for something underneath the facade. Something soft and malleable hiding under the emotional armor defining Kate Bardach. Something vulnerable.

Some. Way. In.

"What, then? What strange events?"

She closed her eyes and blew out a breath. "You already know how the Redman affects me. You, unfortunately, have had to endure that phenomenon firsthand. Then, my car. Now, my mother."

Marco tilted his head. "Your mother?"

Kate sipped her drink and then shook her head. "Sorry. Didn't mean to blurt that out. It's just, my mother, she gets on my nerves sometimes."

"And whose mother doesn't?" he asked.

They both laughed, and Marco could feel the ice between them breaking up. Thank God.

"What's the deal with your car? Have you heard?" he asked.

Kate's lips pressed into a thin line. "Yep. I got lucky, I guess. No major damage. A big mess, to be sure. But I should have it back before the weekend." She hesitated, furrows wrinkling her brow. "There was water on the back deck, beneath the windshield. And . . . mold? Yet, the shop couldn't find any leaks in the window seal."

"That's odd. Maybe condensation, no? They cleaned it up, right?" he asked. He didn't understand why such a minor issue seemed to bother her so. "Have the police found out who might have snatched your car?"

Kate shrugged and shook her head. "Nope. And I suspect they never will." She shifted, obviously wanting to change the subject. "I've got a preliminary contract. If you and your partners look it over and want anything changed, we can set up a meeting. Otherwise, the sooner we get started on this project, the better. Hopefully, we can have it finished by the end of summer."

Back in business mode. Her safe zone. Marco felt like a fisherman, dancing with a finicky fish on the end of a line.

Kate downed the rest of her martini—impressively fast—and rose, reaching for her briefcase. "I've got to get going." She slid out a thick, manila envelope and laid it on his coffee table. "You'll let me know?"

"Let me take you somewhere for dinner first, Kate. Or, I can order in—"

But she was shaking her head and already headed for the door. "I'm exhausted, Marco. I don't think I could even eat anything. I had a late lunch with my mother."

After she'd gone, Marco flopped down on the couch and slid the contract out onto his lap. He'd scanned the first several pages when his eyes caught on Item 36: *Right to Inhabit Property—Bardach & Associates will prioritize renovation of the studio suite behind the lobby on the first floor. Client agrees to grant permission to member(s) of the Design Team to inhabit such quarters during the renovation process, including but not limited to, architect and/or design assistants.*

Sure. Why hadn't he seen this coming? What better way for her boy-toy architect to stay close to the action—and to Kate—than to move in?

"Cazzo!"

Marco smacked the papers on the table. Of course, her *architect* knew damn well Kate's lake house was a half-mile up the road. Guess he should be grateful she hadn't simply invited Daniel to move in with *her* during the project.

He scrubbed his hands down over his face. Dio buono, he was going to have to get hold of his emotions. Suppress this ridiculous jealousy of a woman who made it quite plain she did not belong to him. No matter how much he wanted her.

When she got home, Kate showered, made herself a piece of toast and a cup of chamomile tea, and curled up in her favorite chair near the window. The lights of the city were beginning to wink on, and the flow of rush hour traffic had settled back into its normal, steady thrum. A giant moon, almost full, hung over the skyline so brilliant and perfect, it looked fake.

It was time, she knew, to look at the photos. Pictures of the aunt she'd never known, knew next to nothing about. After all, Joan had only been twelve when her older sister disappeared. Over fifteen years before Kate was even born.

The folder had been tucked inside her briefcase all day and pushed as far to the back of Kate's mind as possible. She was glad her mother hadn't insisted she look at them there, at the restaurant. With no small trepidation, Kate trusted her mother's judgment—it was probably best to see them for the first time when she was alone.

Sighing, she rose and retrieved the folder from her bag. The ivory, cardboard covering was velvety with age and smelled like the sachets her mother kept in her lingerie drawer. Ah. So that's where she'd kept them hidden all these years. Settling back into her chair, Kate laid the folder on her lap and gently untied the securing ribbons.

There were pockets on the inside, the one on the left holding several yellowed envelopes. On the right, folded tissue encased what Kate assumed were the old photographs. *Acid-free* tissue, no doubt, knowing how fastidious her mother was.

She lifted out the letters first. There were four of them, all addressed to *Miss Joan Plischner,* and the postmark dates ranged from April to October, 1964. Her mother had told her, just today, that when Leah left home right after her eighteenth birthday, she'd written letters to her little sister, rather than call on the phone.

This way, I don't have to listen to Mama or Papa's lectures, Leah had said.

Her aunt had gotten involved with an older man, Joan told her. A swarthy, cigar-smoking, fast-talker who their parents thought was probably involved in some kind of illegal activity. Probably the mob. He called himself Bart Shelby, but they knew it was an alias. The man was obviously Italian.

Kate wondered absently how her mother would react if she brought Marco home. Probably not well.

Doesn't matter. Not going to happen anyway.

She slid out the first letter, dated April 1, 1964.

Dear Joanie,

I'm going to try and write you as often as I can, but Bart got me a job working in his club waiting tables. I don't mind really, since that's where he is most of the time. It's better than sitting home in this empty apartment all day. But we go out afterward, and I come home very tired.

Sometimes I feel sad, missing you, remembering how nice it was living in our pretty house and not having to work. But Mama and Papa would never have let me go on seeing Bart if I stayed. And I love him, Joanie. I know he's a lot older than me, and life may not be quite as easy from here on. But love changes a girl. Makes you do things you thought you never would. Someday, I'm sure you'll understand.

And Bart says business is going good. He's going to take me shopping next month, he says, for a ring. Isn't that exciting? I'm getting married! Probably not until the fall—when Bart says his "ship should be coming in." I'm not sure what ship or from where, but as long as I have a ring on my finger and him on my arm, I don't care.

Please don't tell Mama and Papa about the wedding. It won't be in a synagogue or anything like that. Bart doesn't want it to be religious at all, since the only religion that matters, he says, is our love for each other. He's so romantic.

I'll write again soon, Joanie. Work hard in school and get good grades. And keep drawing—I really think you have talent. I know Papa will get you into the best art school in New York.

Love you, Sissy. Take care and miss you.

Leah

Kate carefully folded the yellowed notebook paper and slid it back in the envelope. This was a glimpse into the past she'd never expected. Seeing her aunt's handwriting, reading her words sent shivers through Kate. She could almost hear what Leah's voice must have sounded like.

Now she needed to see what she looked like. The tissue was neatly creased and folded around a dozen or so photographs. Some had wavy edges, and the paper was thick, like lightweight cardboard. Originally black and white, the image on the top photo had faded to shades of gray.

It was a shot of the two sisters, Kate guessed, Joan and Leah, when her mother was about seven or eight years old. Both dressed in plain, dark skirts and blazers; the girls were standing together, holding hands near the fountain in Bryant Park. Kate wouldn't have recognized her mother—she was such a gangly, long-limbed little girl. Her sister was a head taller than she, and heavier, already developing womanly curves. Leah wore a wide, toothy smile, and Joan was laughing.

Quick tears blurred Kate's vision, though at first she wasn't sure why. These were images from a time so far past, they should have no power to affect her emotionally. But it was the joy captured in the moment, the obvious closeness of the sisters, that got to her. With no siblings of her own, Kate could only imagine what it might feel like to have a best friend who was also your kin.

And then, to lose her.

She leafed through the rest of the photos, all similar snapshots of outings, or holidays, with the two girls posing together. Kate watched her mother and aunt grow up in a series of eight faded photographs. Almost always holding hands, or hugging. And laughing. Happy. Nearing the end of the stack, Kate began to recognize her mother's heart-shaped face and her fine, straight hair, lighter than Leah's by several shades.

And a disturbing sense of déjà vu came over her as Leah's image neared adulthood.

The last photo was encased in a cardboard folder of its own, and was larger than the rest. Before she even lifted the cover, Kate somehow knew what she was about to see.

It was a professional portrait, and this one was in color. Leah was wearing a formal, probably her senior prom gown. It was mint-green, covered with white lace, a strapless bandeau. Her shiny, black hair was teased to a high bouffant at the crown, a fringe of bangs brushing arched brows. Thick, loose waves covered one shoulder.

The other shoulder was bare, revealing pale skin liberally sprinkled with freckles.

Kate's heart was beating so fast she felt the pulse in her throat, and she swallowed hard. She lifted her hand to her mouth, a wave of dizziness making the room in her peripheral vision spin and tilt. Closing her eyes, she fought back the panic and struggled to slow her breathing.

I will not faint.

The woman in the photograph, with round, blue eyes and sensual, full lips, looked back at her from another age, another era. From fifty years in the past. But there was no denying the doppelgänger effect.

Kate was her Aunt Leah's double.

When her cellphone buzzed on the glass end table, Kate shrieked and dropped the folder. The contents scattered on the floor around her feet, and she burst into tears. For a moment, shaken and confused, she wasn't sure whether to gather the photos and letters or pick up the phone.

She grabbed for the phone. *Mother*.

"Have you seen?" Joan asked, not bothering with any greeting.

Kate choked on a sob, and for a long moment, couldn't say a word. In the silence, her mother's voice continued, "Now you see why I think you might have a chance to connect with your Aunt Leah. Sometimes, when I'm with you," Joan's voice broke, "I can almost believe God's given my sister back to me."

ELEVEN

Two weeks later, having worked out some very minor details in the contract Eliot had taken issue with—naturally, he was an attorney—Marco packed an overnight bag and headed to Sullivan County. He'd secured a hotel room at the Days Inn in Liberty—far from The Ritz, but decent and within a twenty-minute drive of the Redman.

Kate had been distant and reserved throughout the entire negotiation process, watching as Marco and her architect sparred on a number of issues. Finally, they'd agreed to disagree, adding a clause to the contract providing for "flexibility on all parties as the project progresses." The only time Kate had stepped in, she'd been openly belligerent. Naming the project, of all things, had gotten her back up. His group insisted on changing the name of the project from the Redman Resort Restoration, as BDA had designated it, to the Shelby Hotel Renovation.

Why the hell should she care *what* we call the place? She'll get paid, regardless.

Still, Marco couldn't quench his attraction to Kate. He wasn't the kind of man who gave up easily. But she'd turned down his offers to take her out for dinner twice. Even refused casual drinks at his favorite pub the third time.

He also usually wasn't the kind of man who asked three times.

Marco had come to terms with the cold, hard fact—a relationship with Kate was a bad idea. It didn't change the fact that his heart leapt whenever he met with her, at the sound of her voice on the phone. Berating himself every time his thoughts drifted to those two glorious nights they'd spent together, he accepted it had been great sex, but nothing more.

It wasn't like Marco was a lovesick teenager. He'd had plenty of women—smart, beautiful women—but not usually only for one or two night stands. Marco was a little old-fashioned that way, and believed in developing some sort of relationship with a woman before seducing her.

Not this time. He'd known her only a few hours before he fell into bed with Kate. Let his hormones override his brain. Well, he sure slipped up on the wrong woman. Let down his guard, succumbed to lust. And look where it got him.

Traffic was light on this Monday morning heading north on the Thruway, an unseasonably warm day for late April. His GPS estimated his arrival time in Loch Sheldrake at a few minutes before ten, his appointment time with Bardach & Associates. The initial walk-through. A ball of optimistic anticipation buzzed in his chest. He was anxious to get started on the renovations.

Or, was it because he knew he'd be seeing Kate?

He had to stop this. It wasn't normal for him, nor was it emotionally healthy. Maybe he'd spend some time at the casino tonight. See what kind of crowd, particularly of the female variety, the Montlake Casino attracted.

As he crept up Redman's winding drive, he could see that although he was early, he was not by far the first one there. Two pickup trucks, one attached to an open trailer, were parked alongside the dumpster that had already been delivered. The black SUV he'd seen Kate's associates driving the first day was parked in the shade of the pines on the opposite side of the parking lot. The hotel's ornately framed front doors stood wide open.

As Marco climbed out of his car, he heard the growl of an engine and looked up to see Kate's white Porsche crawling up the drive. He took a deep breath, straightened his Gucci sunglasses on his face, and waited for her to park.

She took her time getting out. Through her tinted window, he watched her, assuming she was on a phone call. Hands-free, unless she was talking to herself, she gesticulated wildly with both hands. There was no one else in the car. He stifled a grin.

Might be some Italian blood back there in the pedigree after all.

When she did swing open the Porsche's door, his breath caught in his throat. She was dressed in mint green today, a shirt-dress with white buttons all the way up the front. Well, almost all the way. The top few had been left open to reveal several inches of pale, freckled cleavage.

Damn her. She's taunting me.

"Good morning, Ms. Bardach. Happy opening day," he called, remaining where he was, leaning on the rear bumper of his Infiniti.

She paused a moment and swung her head around, tilted as if in question. "Oh," she chuckled. "Right. Opening day for the project. For me, the term brings to mind racing season."

"Ah, yes it would," Marco replied, remembering how they'd met that day in the lonely grandstands of Montlake Raceway.

Had it really only been a few weeks ago? Marco felt like their meeting—and those few days after—were a dozen years in the past.

"How's the nag been running, anyway?" he jested. "Been up to see her run again since then?"

Kate opened the luggage compartment at the front of her car and lifted out a large, flat portfolio, along with her briefcase. Not the red one today. Of course not. Red would have clashed horribly with the green dress. Today's briefcase was a mellowed, chocolate brown.

Her lips twisted, trying hard—but not quite succeeding—in hiding a smile. "I have. Came up last week to speak with a couple of the contractors bidding on the job. Daniel and I caught the last few races of the day, and wouldn't you know it? *April's Here* was on the roster and won again. By four lengths this time."

Daniel. Her boy-toy architect. So that's why she's been so distant. Marco felt the old familiar itch in his veins.

No. He wasn't going there. It was over, and he had to let it go. Let her go.

Hard to let a woman go and free your mind of her when she's standing ten paces away from you with a glorious rack on display. How silly of him. He'd been thinking it was to taunt him. More likely, it was for the benefit of Daniel the boy-toy.

The coffee Marco had sipped, and enjoyed, on his trip up until now had his mouth tasting very much like motor oil.

And it was none other than Daniel who greeted him, in Marco's face, before he'd stepped more than three paces over the threshold of the hotel.

"Good morning, Mr. Lareci." Daniel interrupted the conversation he was having with one of the jeans-clad contractors and approached with hand outstretched.

Marco was surprised at the firm confidence behind Daniel's handshake. Hell, he didn't look old enough to have a high school diploma. Let alone a degree in architecture.

"Good morning, Daniel. Is this one of our crew?" Marco asked, nodding toward the other man.

Daniel introduced the head contractor, Jeremy Pike.

"Please, call me Jeremy," the man said.

Marco knew he should say *Call me Marco*. But he couldn't bring himself to do it. He hated the admission, but he kind of liked this division of class. Maintaining his position as Mr. Lareci while he used the other men's first names. Particularly boy-toy.

Daniel didn't appear ruffled. He pulled the clipboard from under his arm and took control. "I'd like to go over the plans for the studio behind the lobby first, if you don't mind. Since that's where the men will be starting. This way, Mr. Lareci."

Oh, yeah. The place where boy-toy will be *living* in just a few short weeks.

He nodded and followed the men through a doorway to the left of the ancient reception counter. The door was stuck in its frame, no doubt from humidity and age, and Jeremy had to use a little shoulder to convince it to open. As it did, musty, stale air drifted out.

"This shouldn't take much to spruce up," Jeremy began. "The wood paneling is real, and it's in pretty decent shape. A coat of paint on the ceiling, some carpeting on the floor, and some apartment-sized appliances. Then it should be ready for occupancy."

Marco studied the space—dark and narrow with only one dirty window looking onto the front parking lot. Built-in bunk beds lined the other narrow end.

Seriously? He hadn't seen bunk beds since he was in grade school.

"Will those be staying?" he asked through a chuckle.

"No," Daniel replied, striding toward them. "This space is actually wide enough for a queen-sized bed. We'd planned to remove these. Add a futon in the living area, then erect a separating wall here," he motioned along the floor, "to provide a degree of privacy."

Privacy. Why bother? Kate has an extremely nice home right around the bend. With a king-sized bed. A very comfortable one at that.

"Mr. Lareci?"

Uh-oh. Dropped out of the conversation there for a bit.

"I'm sorry, what did you ask, Daniel?"

The child-prodigy architect leveled his gaze on Marco and paused a beat too long before answering.

"I didn't ask anything." His tone was level, punctual. "I explained that Jeremy believes this is the most economical way to redesign the space. Economical, both in dollars and days. We do, however, need your approval to proceed."

"Fine with me," Marco mumbled, and made his way out of the studio.

When he re-entered the lobby, he spotted Kate and another man wearing paint-spattered, carpenter's overalls standing under the archway leading into the ballroom. Kate was pointing to the floor, and the carpenter was peering at the molding overhead.

"I don't see any evidence of a leak, Ms. Bardach. Of course, we'll check and see what's up there in the way of plumbing. But it doesn't appear there's been any water damage here." The carpenter stooped and ran his hand over the threshold between the rooms. Two different-colored hardwood surfaces, joined with a flat board. "Nope. There's no evidence of leakage at all."

Kate was frowning down at the floor, her arms crossed. As Marco approached, she glanced up at him and said, "I thought you said there was a puddle on the floor here that night—"

"There was. I swear. I pointed it out to the cops, though I don't think they paid much attention." Marco crouched and ran his fingers along the threshold. "I'll be damned. There was water here. Not merely a few drops. Like, half a bucket's worth."

When he glanced up, Kate had gone pale, her eyes very round and wild. He stood quickly and took her by the elbow.

"Let's get a little fresh air, okay? I think all this dust and mildew is getting to you."

He didn't release her arm until they'd reached his car, where he made sure she was propped against it before he let go. She hadn't said a word, but hadn't resisted him, either. Her full-body trembling, though, had telegraphed through her elbow to his hand without mistake.

"What's wrong, amore mio?" he asked, lifting her face with two fingers under her chin.

Damn. I've got to stop treating her like she's *my love*. She's not, nor will she ever be.

Kate blinked up at him, confusion clouding her eyes. "I thought you told me—"

"I did. And I swear, there was water there—a giant pool of it— that night when I went back through with the police. We can call the station. Maybe the officer noted it on his report."

"No. It's okay. I believe you. I knew it was there. I saw what caused it." Kate stared at him with such desperate conviction, a chill washed over him. Even standing in the unseasonal warmth of the late April sun. "What freaks me out, Marco, is you saw it, too. It wasn't a manifestation only I could see." She blinked rapidly, her eyes filling. "You saw it, too. You may not have seen the . . . the figure. Whatever it was, standing under the archway, water streaming down what looked like its thick coat. It looked like fur." She laughed nervously. "I really thought it was a bear. But that's impossible. A bear would have broken a window, crashed through a door."

He stared at her, unsure what she was talking about. She hadn't even been inside the building at the time, but sitting next to him in his car. A bear?

"I was in there," she said, breathless. "I saw something in the archway. During my—my episode. I thought it was a wild animal. A bear, perhaps."

Marco skimmed back through his memory to that night. Kate had gone blank beside him, he remembered, as if she'd dropped into a trance. Temporarily catatonic. Then she'd screamed, scaring the bejesus out of him. Right before she fainted. He wasn't sure what was happening to her, what she thought she'd seen, but—

"This has never happened before. No one has ever . . . *ever*," she paused, reaching up to touch his cheek, riveting him with such intensity, his knees grew weak. "No one has ever *witnessed*. Been able to substantiate something I saw *that way*. During one of my weird episodes. A manifestation." She smiled through her tears. "I'm not crazy, Marco. This proves it. Unless you are, too."

Kate had no intention of another liaison with Marco Lareci. Especially now that she was working for him and in such close proximity to her lake house. But something clicked when she realized he not only believed in her psychic abilities, but had been a witness to evidence of the apparition. Physical evidence.

And he didn't look at her like she was a wacko when she described her vision. Not like the first night.

The team worked straight through until four o'clock, when Kate announced quitting time, and the contractors began the process of packing up. She'd followed Marco and Daniel all day through the abandoned rooms of the hotel, taking notes, making suggestions, volleying ideas for decor style with both men.

That first hour in the same space with them sparring had felt like the warm-up to a WWE wrestling match. There was so much testosterone floating around, Kate could almost smell it. When they began discussing specifics of the design plan, tensions increased. Kate became increasingly concerned with the disparity between the men's drastically different visions for the place.

Especially since, no matter what Daniel wanted to do with the hotel, Marco and his partners were the paying customers. They'd have final word on everything from paint color to lighting fixtures.

She tensed further when Daniel approached her after the contractors were gone, motioning for her to step aside for a word with him alone. She could almost hear the static crackle from Marco's glare as she turned to follow Daniel.

"Dinner tonight, Kate? We have a lot to discuss about today. Strictly business. I understand there's a very nice Italian place not far from here." Daniel was smiling into her eyes with such eager sincerity, for a moment, she actually felt pity for him.

"I'm sorry, Daniel. No. I've had about all the shop talk I can handle for one day. I think I'm going to hole up in my lake house and call it a day."

Pressing his lips into a flat line, he nodded in acceptance. He looked more like a puppy kicked away from his bone than a talented, young architect gathering up his portfolio. "In the morning, then. Same time?"

She nodded. "Ten sharp. Have a great evening."

After he'd gone, Marco sauntered in her direction, his hands stuffed into the front pockets of his jeans. He'd dressed casually today, a wise move considering all the dust and grime they'd traipsed through. But his designer jeans fit perfectly in all the right places and looked sharp under the crisp, white shirt and navy, linen blazer he wore on top.

In short, he looked good enough to eat.

Damn it. Down, girl. He's a client now, not a sex partner for an evening or two.

But the way he was looking at her, with eyes the hazy green of the lake, she could tell he was thinking about the same thing she was. How good they had been together.

"Plans for this evening, Ms. Bardach?" he asked, one side of his sculpted lips quirking up.

He'd shaven this morning, and Kate was surprised at how sexy his lips were, naked and free from their usual frame of black stubble. The sculpted fullness stirred a memory. Where had she seen lips like that before?

On Batman. What was the actor's name from The Dark Knight flick? Oh, yes, Christian Bale. The only thing Kate could remember about the old movie was that with most of Bale's face covered, her eyes had been drawn to the shape of the man's mouth. Sharply defined, perfectly formed.

Blinking, distracted, and more than a little turned on, Kate couldn't take her eyes off those enticing lips.

"Hey, where'd you go?" he prompted, gently holding her elbow with two fingers.

It was then she realized he'd asked her something.

Tonight. Plans. Yes. That was it.

She chuckled, embarrassed and a little knocked off her game. "Yes. I mean, no, not really. I thought I'd just go back to the house and chill. It's been a long day." Meeting his gaze, she asked, "Where are you staying? I mean, *are* you staying? Or driving back to the city?"

Marco shrugged and angled away from her, his hands still in his pockets. "I've got a room. In Liberty."

"Oh." It was all she could muster. She knew she should leave it alone. Let him go to his room, to his own plans for the evening. But a part of her was nudging to make another suggestion.

"I thought I might check out the casino at Montlake," Marco continued. "They've got a pretty nice bar there. See the sights. Mingle with the locals." He made an exaggerated show of pushing up the cuff of his sleeve to check his watch. "Should have time for a shower, maybe even a nap. They have food there, too, right?"

"Yes, they do. A fairly decent buffet," she said blandly. "If you're into buffets."

Kate began to fidget. Running her fingertips along the studs lining the cusp of her ear, twirling her hair around one finger. Shifting from one foot to the other. She didn't like being in this position. Wanting something, some*one*, this badly, and having to ask.

Fortunately, she didn't have to.

"What I'd really like to do," Marco said, moving closer to her and searing her with those electric eyes, "is to pick up a bottle of wine, swing by *Frankie and Johnny's* to grab some dinner, and meet you back at your place. But," he hesitated with one dark eyebrow arched, "we can't always have what we want, can we?" His tone had dropped a shade deeper—gruff and sexy—hitting Kate hard about midway between her navel and lower.

She worked her mouth, trying hard to suppress the smile weaseling its way to the surface. "I would like that, actually. Very much."

While she waited for Marco to return to her lake house, Kate pulled out the folder her mother had given to her. Again. Its pull on her had become magnetic. And besides, she hadn't read all the letters. Her overwhelming, emotional response to reading the first one had drained her, the words playing over and over again in her brain the whole night through.

She was glad she'd brought them with her. Now, after spending the entire day in what used to be the Redman Resort, an obsession to read another overtook her.

June 16, 1964
Dearest Joanie,

I'm sorry it's been so long for me, but life has been busy! Bart and I have moved into a bigger apartment, the downstairs unit in a lovely brownstone in Boro Park. Business, he says, is going very well—much better than he'd anticipated. I don't have to work in his club anymore.

119

But he's gone most nights, leaving at dusk and not returning sometimes until almost dawn. I began to worry, you know, about his being unfaithful. When he returns home, though, his clothes smell only of cigar smoke, and he looks very tired. He's taken to washing his hands the minute he walks in the door. Stripping down, scrubbing up to the elbows, almost obsessively, before he'll allow me to touch him. He says it's because he's spent a great deal of time in the basement where the liquor crates are kept, and doesn't want me exposed to anything from the rat droppings down there.

This leaves me with nothing to do during the evening hours but read and daydream of the way our life will be once we're married. Bart says once his ship comes in, he won't have to work nights anymore. In fact, he's even spoken of selling the club and moving upstate. Buying a country home in the mountains. I told him about Mama and Papa's property on Loch Sheldrake, and how much I loved it there.

I guess you're out of school for the summer by now. I hope you get to go out to Jones Beach again, like we used to. Though I remember now that the ocean scares you. Guess you sure have a good reason why. Perhaps the family vacation will be somewhere up in the Catskills instead.

Some nights, I'll admit, I get terribly homesick. If I can offer you any advice at all, little sister, it's this: don't fall in love with a man your parents reject. Of course, love doesn't pay attention to social or religious lines in the sand. Like me, you may not have a choice. Even so, it's all worth it, I assure you. The way I feel when Bart looks into my eyes and tells me he loves me extinguishes any doubts I might have when he's away.

I hope you are well and not missing me too much. Perhaps we can meet somewhere, near the Ell, some afternoon this summer and share an ice cream soda? That would be simply wonderful. You could tell Mama and Papa you're spending the day with a friend in the city. It would be lovely if we could make that happen.

Know I love you and think of you every day. I'll write again soon.
    Your big sister,
    Leah

With tears welling in her eyes, Kate folded the brittle paper back into its slitted envelope and slid it into the folder. Her Aunt Leah must have been a truly brave woman. One with a very strong conviction that her decision to give up her family for a man she loved was the right one.

How had it all gone so terribly wrong? What had happened after October 18, 1964—the date on the last envelope—to make her stop contacting her sister? Kate would like to think it was a fairy tale ending. That perhaps her knight, Bart Shelby, had whisked her away to a princess' life in Paris or London. Rome, more likely, or Venice, considering his assumed nationality.

Yes, he'd probably had family there, and once they'd welcomed Leah into their fold, she'd had no need to look back.

Yet somehow, an ominous foreboding in the pit of her stomach told Kate the ending was more like a horror flick than a fairy tale. Bart's nighttime dealings, she guessed, had been seedier than sweeping rat droppings off cases of liquor. The Mafia, she knew, hadn't died with the raid of the Mafiosi meeting in 1957.

This *love* her aunt spoke of was an emotion Kate had never been able to identify with. Oh, her friends spoke of the euphoric exhilaration of being *in love* with their newest beau. But Kate knew better.

Lust was a powerful, almost hallucinogenic drug, the ultimate aphrodisiac. Physical desire could delude your brain in powerful ways. New *love* sparked like a gasoline fire, flared bright and hot, but quickly died, leaving only cold ashes. Kate was smarter than to be taken in by lust's deceptions.

Wasn't she?

An hour later, with the late afternoon sun flooding Kate's back deck, she lay on her Shorea lounge chair, wearing her most comfy jogging suit with a floppy, straw hat covering her face. She heard Marco's Infiniti pull into the drive and the engine die.

"I'm back here, Marco," she called, tipping up the brim of her hat.

He appeared from around the side of the house, a large paper bag in one hand, a bottle of wine under his arm. In his free hand, he held a giant cluster of red roses wrapped in green tissue paper.

"Good afternoon, Ms. Bardach. You ordered dinner and wine? I'm your friendly delivery boy," he said with a grin as he mounted the three steps to her deck. "Where would you like these?"

The laugh burst from her so unexpectedly, she snorted. "You goofball," she muttered, covering her mouth with her hand. She motioned toward the French doors leading into her kitchen. "I set out two glasses. Pour us some wine?"

He returned a few minutes later with a glass in each hand, shoving the door closed with his foot. The jacket was gone, and he'd rolled up the sleeves of his shirt, revealing shapely forearms dusted with dark hair. Kate felt that buzzing sensation low in her belly again.

Patting the matching recliner beside her, she said, "Sit," and swung her feet to the patio boards.

Marco set the glasses down on the small table and was gazing out over the surface of the lake, one hand shielding his eyes from the late afternoon sun. "It sure is a pretty spot here, isn't it?"

Kate turned toward the water and realized how long it had been since she'd looked at the view. Really *seen* it. The lake house had been in her family for so long, she'd grown to take the view for granted.

"It is," she murmured. "It's a peaceful spot. The geese will be coming soon, though, and then it can get a bit more musical." She dropped her head back and looked at him quizzically. "Funny, but until now, I'd forgotten all about the geese invasion every spring."

Marco studied her, his expression serious. "Methinks, Ms. Bardach, you invest way too much of your life in your career. There's more to life than work, you know." His tone was gently scolding.

She found she couldn't maintain eye contact very long. Intense, as if he were looking for a way inside her mind, and the sensation frightened her. Blinking, she focused on the side table and lifted her glass toward him. "To discovering what's more to life than work."

It was a lame toast, she knew. But it must have pleased him, because his throaty laugh echoed out over the water, sending a warm thrill through her. He clinked his glass to hers. "To discovery."

They ate lasagna out of foil pans on their laps on the back deck as the sun dropped below the line of trees on the opposite shore, casting the lake into shadow.

"This is excellent, but you haven't had lasagna until you've had my mother's." Marco kissed his clustered fingertips and raised them toward the sky. "Now, there's a woman who can cook." As he broke off another piece of crusty bread, he asked, "Do you cook, Kate?"

"Ha!" She laughed. "It's an art I never learned. Never cared to learn. I'm good with charcoal, but not the kind you grill with."

He tipped his head in question.

"You know. Charcoal? Sketching? Interior design, remember?"

It was Marco's turn to snort, chewing. He raised a finger into the air until he'd swallowed. "Well, you're in luck then. Because I do cook. And quite enjoy it, by the way. But it's a waste to cook for one. I much prefer preparing a sumptuous meal for two." He grinned over at her. "Or more."

"Is that so? I might ask you to prove that claim to me sometime in the near future." Kate sipped her wine and studied him. "What other talents do you have I don't know about?" His lips quirked and she felt the heat rising up her neck. "The ones I don't know about," she repeated.

"Well, I threw a pretty strong forward pass in my college days. But nowadays, I like the game better from the stands than on the field." He hesitated and reached for his glass. "Oh, and I scuba dive. A buddy of mine owns a diving school out near Montauk."

Kate settled back in her chair. "Wow. Cool hobby. Have you ever gone down to any of those shipwrecks off the Island?"

"I have. Did the Cornelia a few years ago, and the Catamount last summer."

Yes, cool hobby. But Kate couldn't ignore the cold, raw fear that washed over her. Like an ocean wave.

"You should come out to Clive's with me sometime," he continued. "He'd get you going down within only a few lessons."

Shaking her head slowly from side to side, Kate lifted one eyebrow. "Me? No way in hell. Remember what happened the last time I took a dip in the ocean? I nearly died. And came back a freak."

As though someone had pinched him, Marco lurched forward in his seat and plopped his dinner tray on the table.

"You're not a freak, Kate." Brows furrowed, he reached for her hand and rubbed it between his own. "It's true, you have an unusual . . . gift. But you're no freak. You're just very, very special."

It was the warmth in his tone that got to her. Or, maybe those pale, gold-flecked eyes riveting her, studying her with such sincerity. The clutching began in her chest, rose to squeeze around her throat, then spread warmth throughout her entire body. His image swam in quick tears.

What's going on with me? This isn't simply lust. What's happening here is different. An experience new and wondrous, yet terrifying, too.

What was it her Aunt Leah had written in her first letter to her mother?

Love changes a girl. Makes you do things you never thought you would.

Well, look where that kind of reckless thinking got Leah. It got her—gone. Frightening. Terrifying.

But please, don't make it stop.

They talked until the sun had disappeared behind the mountain and full dark settled over the lake. When he could barely see her face across the distance between them, Marco rose and capped the half-empty bottle of wine. Much as he didn't want to, it was time for him to leave.

"Where do you want this? Here, let me help you clean up before I go," he said, gathering the foil containers from their dinner and stuffing them into the paper bag.

Kate scrambled to her feet. "You don't have to leave so soon. It's still early. Why don't you join me in the hot tub for a bit before you go?" She motioned toward the teak-slatted cubicle tucked on the side of the house facing the woods. Rubbing her arms, she continued, "A good night for it. Dropping down kind of chilly tonight."

Hmm, hot tub. I've been doing pretty good keeping my hormones in check tonight, but not sure I can make it through a hot tub session.

He hesitated for a beat before stepping into her kitchen to deposit the wine and the trash. "I can't," he said over his shoulder. "My trunks are in Manhattan."

"Who said anything about swimsuits?"

A quick flash of lust shot straight through him to engorge his man-parts so fast, Marco felt a bit light-headed.

Whoa. Didn't see that one coming.

He cleared his throat and turned to study her expression. She was standing in the open doorway, leaning against the frame with arms crossed.

"Sounds too good to pass up, Kate. But... ." He turned, and when he saw her face, his words of self-preservation died in his throat.

This was not the come-hither, half-smirk, half-purr she'd seduced him with the first two times. Her gaze on his was level, her expression open. Something had changed in those eyes. She seemed softer somehow.

"Please? I'd really like you to stay."

With those words, and the way she'd said them, it was Marco's *heart* that squeezed, more painful than the tension in his man-parts. This, he knew, was dangerous. And probably all a fabrication of his own mind. He knew what kind of woman Kate was—she'd never made any secret about the way she viewed relationships.

She didn't believe in them. Kate was a woman who liked men and loved sex, but not as much as she loved herself and her own independence.

He studied her face, considering. Then she hit him with another one of those slow, sleepy blinks. Damn her.

Marco shook his head and scrubbed his hands over his face. "I don't know, Kate. I know to you, this is easy. Carefree. But it's different for me. With you, my feelings are headed down a treacherous path."

She was right there, so close her scent filled his head like intoxicating incense. The effect those clear, blue eyes had on him was undeniable—had been since the first day they'd met. But tonight, it was different.

Tonight, those eyes weren't cold, impenetrable blue. Maybe this was just wishful thinking, but if there was a chance he was getting through to her . . . .

Standing on tiptoe, she planted a soft kiss on his lips, then on the corner of his mouth before pressing one warm cheek against his. His reaction, as her hair fell across his face and her breath tickled his neck, was unusual.

A knot formed in the base of this throat. Not where it usually lodged.

With her mouth on his ear, she whispered, "You're getting to me, too, Lareci. Damn you and your romantic Italian heart. You're getting to me, too."

TWELVE

Kate was smarter than to be taken in by lust's deceptions. Wasn't she?

The thought echoed back to her, hours later, after an enchanted evening with Marco on her back deck. But now, she wasn't so sure. They'd shared not only a meal, but some of the most relaxed conversations she could ever remember.

Of course, there'd been wine involved. But not that much. She'd held her hand up after the second glass, and Marco hadn't even finished his first. Kate knew well how alcohol could amplify emotions—and sensations—way out of control. She wasn't about to let the same thing happen tonight.

But she found she couldn't keep her body away from his. His scent, his strength, the way his hair fell rakishly over a forehead already developing creases—fallout, she guessed, from his intensity for life. All she wanted to do was hold him, smell him, be enveloped in his warmth. When she pressed a kiss to his perfect mouth, she'd felt him shudder, and she knew damn well it wasn't from a chill.

So, he felt it, too. That was the scariest part of all.

"Let me pour you another glass of wine—"

"No," she said, laying a finger on his lips. "I don't want anything to dull the sensations of this moment."

They dropped their clothes to the floor near the French doors leading outside to the spa. The space was cleverly screened with slatted teak boards for privacy and shielded by a thick wall of pines. Silently, he helped her lift the cover off the hot tub. He held her gaze intently as he offered his hand to support her as she mounted the steps and stepped down into the swirling hot water. Then, he followed.

The evening air had chilled considerably, sending wisps of steam to rise off the tumultuous surface. The bubbles tickled her naked breasts and between her thighs, and she found herself giggling like a silly schoolgirl. Marco slid close beside her, smiling. He dipped deeper into the water and laid one arm across the tub's edge, behind her shoulders.

As if by instinct, her head tipped to rest against his.

They sat like that for the longest time, lost in the moment. The pleasure of the swirling hot water pulsating around and relaxing every muscle in her body. The steam gathering in droplets on her face and slithering down her cheeks. The steady buzz of the crickets, determined to be heard over the humming of the spa's pumps, filled Kate's head and made her feel sleepy, dizzy.

Happy. Heady. Euphoric.

Yet lust, at least right now, had nothing to do with it. Yes, anticipation hovered, a silent promise of what was to come. But in this moment, all that mattered was their two bodies, skin to skin, enjoying each other.

She started when he spoke, his voice gravelly and gruff. "Tell me what it's like, Kate. To see what most people cannot. To see . . . dead people. Is it scary? I would think it would be terrifying."

Her fingers trailed down his arm, the surface hard and strong beneath her touch. "Nobody believes this, but until recently, it hasn't been scary at all."

He lifted his head and looked at her, his eyes sleepy and iridescent as they picked up and reflected the green glow of the illuminated water. "Until recently? Do you mean, when you saw Matthew? With my sister?"

She shook her head, sweeping away the lock of hair lying on his brow. "Seeing the boy wasn't scary. Just incredibly sad." She looked toward the lake, even though the sun had set and it was no longer visible between the teak slats. "No, it's usually not frightening. Until the first night I entered your hotel."

He paused, his lips pressing into a thin line. "So, the place really is haunted. Isn't it?"

Breathing out a long sigh, she said, "Probably not for most. But I seem to have a vested interest, you see. My aunt . . . you know. I've told you the story." Her wry bark of laughter surprised even her. "Lucky me."

Kate wasn't sure how long they'd dozed there, cuddled together in the corner of her spa. But the entire enclosure was thick with steam. Her hair, though she'd had it twisted into a clip loosely atop her head, was coming down in places, long strands tickling her cheeks as moisture followed their path to her neck. Marco's head rested on her shoulder, heavy now, his breathing slow and regular. She grinned when his next breath sounded a soft, but audible, snore.

Tracing her fingers along his shoulder, she said, "It's no good to spend an entire night in a hot tub, Marco. We'll both wake up shriveled like old prunes."

He lifted his head and blinked awake, his expression disoriented for a brief moment. Then he smiled. "Sorry. Truth is, I've never been so comfortable in my entire life." Slowly, he brought his face closer, rubbing the tip of her nose with his. "You're all pink," he said through a chuckle.

"No doubt. Isn't that what happens to lobsters?"

But he didn't laugh, just covered her mouth with his and kissed her, long and deep. He smelled clean and tasted a little salty, the sweat on her lips and his mingling. Still, he didn't touch her—other than with a mouth Kate was certain belonged on a Greek god.

When the kiss ended and their eyes met, Kate felt breathless and light-headed. He was studying her with eyes glowing the same exact hue as the bubbling water around them. A long, magical moment suspended them in time and place, an unspoken connection spiking an electric current jolting from his eyes to hers.

Then he reached up and chucked her under the chin. "Come on, lobster girl. Time to dry off."

He stepped out and reached for the two towels on the chair, wrapping one around his waist before offering his hand to help her step out. She felt his eyes on her naked body, but he said nothing as he reached around her, lifting her arms to wrap her in the plush, terry sheet. She glanced back over her shoulder and flicked off the spa.

"Help me with the cover?"

Marco helped Kate slide the leather-bound cover into place, feeling sleepy and relaxed and tingling all over. The night air had dropped down very cool, a slight breeze through the slats causing a chill on his bare shoulders. That sensation quickly vanished when Kate bent over, reaching across to adjust the flap on the opposite side of the spa. The sight of her generous hips—even hidden as they were by black terry—shocked his libido with a jolt.

Stepping forward, he pressed the now obvious bulge under his own towel against her bottom. She gasped and pushed up on her palms, pressing herself against him in answer. It was all the invitation Marco needed.

Starting with light fingers, he caressed her from the nape of her neck, down over her shoulder blades until he reached the towel's perimeter. With one hand, he lifted the fallen strands of damp hair and pressed his mouth into the curved space between her neck and shoulder. First light kisses, then circles with his tongue. When she moaned and bumped him again with her bottom, he nipped her gently.

"Take me to bed, Marco. Please," she murmured, her breath coming faster as she lifted both hands to clasp around his neck. But he caught her wrists, guiding them back down onto the surface of the spa cover.

"You keep those hands right there for a few more moments, little lady. I have some exploration to do."

He skimmed his hands up her arms and down her back, then around to the front where he worked the twisted edges of the towel free. As it fell open, he slid his hands under her breasts and she gasped as her head nestled into the crook of his neck.

"Oh, Marco," she breathed, and a jolt of desire made his erection twitch.

For a moment, he simply held those gloriously generous breasts, cupping their weight in his palms. He continued to nuzzle her neck, kissing and licking and nipping her skin, all the while murmuring sweet phrases in Italian. Words he knew she couldn't understand.

Professions of his feelings for her, those she undoubtedly would not want to hear.

She wiggled her bottom against his arousal, and he groaned. "Please, Marco. Touch me here." Her hand came up to move his fingers toward her nipples, but he caught her wrist again and pressed it back down on the pad.

"Ah, ah, what did I say? Let me explore a little first. I like to take my time."

Kate's shoulders heaved under his chin, but he continued to hold those beautiful, heavenly mounds in his hands as he worshipped her neck with his tongue and teeth. She groaned again, becoming more impatient. Her one foot began stroking along the back of his calf, and she ground her bottom against his now nearly painful erection.

He wasn't going to last much longer at this rate. Cazzo.

Without warning, he skimmed his palms over her tight, pebbled nipples, and she gasped as her knees buckled against the side of the spa. He'd momentarily disarmed her, and he smiled, purring into her ear, "Is this what you want, mia cara? Is this where you want me to touch you?"

Kate struggled to turn toward him, but he caught her wrists again and forced them, palms down, before her.

"No," he scolded. "You're not playing fair. I'm giving you what you asked for. Hold still a little longer and let me do what you want."

Her breasts, like the rest of this incredibly sensual woman, were exquisite. Her entire body was rounded curves and velvety skin, with a natural scent that drove Marco wild. The taste of her sweat on his tongue was an aphrodisiac, sending his own need into overdrive with every passing second. As he stroked and kneaded and tickled her sensitive peaks with his fingers, he felt the urgency of his own need escalate.

The next time she tried to turn around, he let her. But before she could kiss him, touch him, inadvertently send him over the edge prematurely, he swept her off her feet, into his arms, and carried her inside. The edge of her towel trailed behind, trapped between their bodies.

He shoved the French door shut behind them with his foot, using perhaps a little more force than wise. He winced when the glass panes vibrated alarmingly. She chuckled against his neck and whispered, "Don't worry. They're thermal panes."

Kate felt like she was floating in a euphoric, erotic dream as Marco carried her. She was chilled from the evening air, but her internal heat was so intense, she imagined her skin might actually be steaming. She was trembling, not from cold, but from anticipation of what she knew was to come.

Yet, he caught her by surprise when he stopped walking in the middle of the dining room and lowered her to her feet.

"What?" she searched his face, but Marco wasn't looking at her. He had snatched the towel as it fell from between them, and was busy folding it. "What are you doing?" she laughed.

His expression remained serious, furrows between his dark brows. "I'm in need of a snack first," he said.

"Oh, for God's sakes," Kate snapped and looked away, annoyed as she folded her arms across her bare chest. "You men. Struggling constantly between two basal needs—food and fu—"

"Shh." He laid a finger over her lips, then proceeded to arrange the folded towel on the edge of the heavy, wooden dining table. Without another word, he wrapped his hands around her waist and lifted her, settling her bottom on the thick, padded surface.

In shock, Kate was speechless. She'd had some creative lovers in her life, but most had been much younger, and not nearly as experienced as Marco. Coupling on the dining room table wasn't something she'd ever done. Or considered. Couldn't be very comfortable, no matter how many towels you spread on the surface. Her king-sized, memory foam mattress was only a few feet away.

"Marco, really, I don't think this is going to be very comfortable—" But she fell silent when he dropped to his knees before her and gently nudged her thighs apart. When he looked up at her, his eyes had gone dark, his pupils huge in the dim light streaming in from the porch. His hair was wild, tossed across his head in disheveled waves, and he was breathing hard. One lock nearly obscured his left eye.

"Let me explore you a bit, if you don't mind, Ms. Bardach."

Kate could count on one hand how many times a man had wanted to pleasure her with his mouth without being asked. And without reciprocation, of course. Her excitement spiked, and she dumbly whispered "Okay" before leaning back with both palms on the table.

One leg at a time, he lifted hers and set them on his broad, muscular shoulders. Then he began his journey on the inside of her knee. One beside the other, ever so slowly, he planted soft kisses, working his way along her thigh until his hot breath tickled her sex. But when she went to tangle her fingers in his hair and pull him in, she found her wrists again held captive.

"Now, what did I tell you? Just lean back, and let me pleasure you. I don't want you to do a thing." His voice had dropped an octave lower and gone rough, its tone sending a hot passion over Kate in waves.

Again, he began at her knee, the other one this time, kissing all the way up to within an inch of her sex. Maddeningly, he drew away a second time.

"Marco, you're driving me crazy," she moaned.

"Uh-huh," he said, returning to the first knee, but with his tongue this time. He drew tiny circles on her trembling skin, linking them together like a chain, inch by inch, until he nearly reached her spot.

When he moved away again, she shouted, "No, Marco. No more. Take me now." Before he could stop her, she raked her fingers into his hair and pulled him in.

She'd been nearly on the verge of shattering before he ever touched her. But the pleasure was so sweet, so exciting, she struggled to hold back the tide, fighting her release for a few seconds longer as he bathed her sensitive core with hot strokes of his tongue. Right before she was about to lose control, he stopped, blowing gently on the throbbing, wet spot.

"My snack is very, very hot," he growled.

"Oh, Marco, please, please."

When his tongue stroked her again, she came apart, tangling both hands in his hair as wave after wave of mind-blowing ecstasy shook her body and sent fireworks exploding in her brain.

THIRTEEN

As Kate's sweet core pulsed and throbbed beneath his mouth, Marco began mentally thumbing down the stock rolls of the New York Exchange. It was the only way he could stop from spilling himself onto the towel beneath his knees. He'd gotten nearly down through the *As* when she finally stopped screaming.

And yes, Kate Bardach was most definitely a screamer.

He stumbled to his feet and gathered her to his bare chest. She responded by wrapping her legs around his waist, burying her face against his neck, and bursting into tears.

"Mia cara, what's wrong? Don't do that. Makes me feel I've done something to hurt you." Her entire body was quaking, though he couldn't tell if it was from cold, or her sobs, or aftershocks.

"You *are* hurting me, Marco. You're breaking down every wall I've spent so many years building around my heart." She sobbed again, then hiccupped.

A thrill zinged through Marco's chest, and he sent up a silent prayer her words were true, and not merely lust-blind emotions that would evaporate with the morning-after mist. He tried to downplay the moment as he carried her to the bedroom.

"We have really good chemistry, you and me. It's something special. A joy we should cherish as long as it lasts."

He set her down beside her huge bed and watched as she released the clip still struggling to hold most of her hair in a messy knot. It tumbled down over her shoulders, sumptuous, black silk streaming over pale, speckled skin. When she raised her face and met his gaze, her eyes sparkled wet, her lashes dark spikes rimming impossibly blue eyes.

His heart clutched in his chest. This was more than just sex. Maybe the first time or the second they'd coupled, it had been purely physical. Those heady, passionate tumbles in the beginning when they didn't even know each other. Now, for him, what they shared went far deeper.

Was it possible she was feeling something deeper too?

Yet Marco knew he had to keep his emotions under wraps. With every fiber of his being, he struggled to show his feelings only in actions, since words, he knew, would most likely drive her away. She'd made it clear from the moment they'd met exactly how she felt about emotional entanglements.

So the only way he could express his love was to make love.

She raised to her toes and kissed him, soft and sweet, wrapping her hands around the back of his neck. Her nipples brushed his skin, hot and still hard with her desire, and he felt his knees wobble. Cupping her buttocks in his hands, he pressed her against him, letting his arousal throb painfully against her belly.

When he felt her tangle her fingers in the hair on his chest, he opened his eyes and saw her smiling.

"I liked when you were behind me out in the spa. It was very exciting. Can you do it again? Can you take me that way?"

A wave of passion nearly overtook his control. He dragged his mind back to the Exchange list. What was the first company on the Bs? BAK Capital, Badger Meter, Baker Hughes—"

She turned away from him and climbed up on the bed on her hands and knees. Backing up to the very edge, she peered at him over her shoulder. "Please?"

Marco hesitated, searching the floor frantically for his trousers. "Wait, I need to get protection."

"No. It's okay. I told you, I'm on the pill." She met his gaze with gut-wrenching intensity. "And I haven't been with anybody but you for a very long time."

He swallowed. Neither had he, but making love without a condom meant there would be no barrier to dull sensations. He raked a hand through his hair and laid a hand on one soft cheek of her bottom.

"I won't last very long," he muttered apologetically.

"It will be worth it." She smiled, her eyes mischievous. "For both of us."

He slid into her slowly, dropping his head back with pleasure as her silky heat closed around his bare skin. Marco couldn't remember the last time he'd had sex without wearing a raincoat.

Then again, he reminded himself, it had always been just sex. This, at least for him, was making love. For her, he could do this. To heighten her experience, he would force himself to hold out a little longer.

Once inside her up to the hilt, he held very still for a long moment, taking deep breaths and trying to slow the pounding of his heart. Thankfully, she seemed to understand and didn't move, merely uttered a gasp. Which was a maddening turn-on in itself. It took him a full thirty seconds before he could move without exploding.

He slid his hands up her sides and cupped her heavy mounds again, rubbing circles over her nipples as she moaned. Then slowly, he started moving in and out of her. Although he tried to keep the pace easy, he knew he wouldn't last long. No matter how hard he tried.

Especially when her peaks suddenly tightened, hard nubs between his fingers, and her groans morphed into shrieks.

Damn if the woman isn't going to climax again around me.

And she did. As her screams drove him higher, he grabbed her hips with both hands and pumped hard into her, her silky heat pulsating around him and pushing him up and over the edge.

When Kate opened her eyes, she wasn't sure how long she'd slept or what day it was. Daylight peeked in around the edge of the shade, but it was pale and dim. Could be dawn or dusk. But no, it had been well past midnight when she and Marco had finally spooned in the center of her bed, the duvet pulled up over their heads. Every time she was close to dozing off, he would mumble something into her ear in Italian and tickle her. Or, pinch her ass, damn him. Kate couldn't remember ever feeling so young, so carefree, or so damned happy.

When the boom of thunder shook the entire house, she squealed and spun to huddle against Marco's chest.

His arms came around her and he pressed a kiss to the top of her head. "What time is it? I think I died and went to heaven last night." His voice was gruff from sleep.

Kate lifted her head enough to see the bedside clock. "Nine fifteen. What day is it?"

"It's Tuesday, Bardach. What time did you tell Boy Wonder to show up?"

She smacked his arm playfully. "Stop. Why do you hate Daniel so much? He's a nice kid. Really good at what he does."

He tipped his chin down to frown into her eyes. "And what exactly would that be?"

Kate nuzzled his neck. "He's a very innovative architect. Daniel will do an absolutely outstanding job on your hotel. You, Mr. Lareci, are an innovative expert in some other, much more strategic areas."

He pinched her bottom again and she squeaked. "Stop it, Marco. I've got less than an hour to shower and put on my business face." She threw back the duvet at the very same moment as a flash of lightning flickered through the space beside the shade. The boom of thunder right on its heels had her diving back quickly into Marco's embrace.

"You're not stepping foot in the shower until this storm passes. Call Boy Wonder and tell him we'll be late."

It was nearly eleven by the time they pulled up into the Redman parking lot. When Marco drove under the portico, Kate said, "Don't leave your car here, Marco. The guys will be coming in and out with ladders and all kinds of debris. They're hoping to finish demo on the first floor this week."

She watched from the doorway as Marco parked and ran through the still steady rain, hunching his shoulders against the onslaught.

"Good morning, Kate." The voice behind her startled her, and she spun to see Daniel standing with his hands on his hips. "We've been waiting for you . . . both of you. We have a couple questions for Mr. Lareci." His tone was cocky, annoyed.

Too bad. What I do with my personal life is none of your damned business.

"Marco," she said as he stepped over the threshold, "Daniel has some questions."

Marco grabbed the collar of his raincoat and gave it a shake, then raked his hand through his wet hair. "What? We have problems?"

Over the next hour, Kate listened as Daniel and Marco played verbal volleyball over the proposed redesign of the lobby. Again, Kate thought it reminiscent of watching a heavyweight wrestling match. It started out slow, Daniel pointing to his clipboard and then up at the paneled walls.

"I know you requested some partitioning of the lobby space, but open and edgy is what this building is all about. We can leave the walls dark. Re-panel with a restoration product. I've got some images here on my iPad of some carpeting patterns I think would be dynamite in here." Daniel glanced at Kate. "As long as they meet Kate's approval."

"No carpet!" Marco shouted, throwing one fist into the air. "We are not doing historical restoration here. I'm not into flower-power, or whatever they called that psychedelic retro look. And neither are my partners."

"All I'm suggesting, Mr. Lareci, is we nod to the era in which this building flourished. Keep the colors in alignment with those of the times—pea green, peach, some saffron—"

Marco stepped forward into Daniel's face. "The look I'm after— the one my partnership is after—is Ritz-Carlton. I want guests to step through our doors and out of Sullivan County, into Manhattan.

Light neutral walls, polished oak reception counters. Gleaming marble floors. What part of this don't you understand, Boy Wonder?"

"Okay, okay, that's enough, Marco." Kate stepped between them and placed a hand on Marco's arm. He shrugged her angrily away. She turned to face Daniel, whose face had gone red, his eyes narrowed. "We can discuss colors, patterns, all of those details later. What we need settled right now is basic architecture. And no matter what the building's design wants," she paused, glaring into her architect's eyes, "it's what the client wants that matters. Map it out, the way Mr. Lareci wants it. Then get the blueprints to the builders."

Marco had stormed off toward the windows, his hands shoved in his pockets. When Kate reached his side, he slid her a glance before returning his gaze to the rain filling the puddles in the parking lot.

"I'm sorry, Kate. I was out of line. I'll apologize to him if you'd like."

His words knocked her back, and she actually did stagger in shock. No doubt, this man had a ferocious temper, iron will, and lived every element of his life with passion. But he was not, as she'd feared only minutes ago, a mindless, raging bull.

There was a softer side of Marco Lareci hiding under his macho facade.

"I don't understand why he's bringing this all up now, so early in the project. We haven't even stripped the rooms of the old, musty bedding, for God's sake. And he's already picking out carpet colors," Marco growled.

Kate stepped around in front of him, blocking his view of the parking lot. After a long moment of staring at the floor, he finally raised his eyes to meet hers.

"He's passionate about what he does, too, Marco. He's an artist and likes to envision the finished project before he authorizes a single wall to be put up, or taken down." She stroked his cheek with her fingers, her heart clutching when he riveted her with eyes the color of the lake in the morning sun. "What I said is the way we operate. The client is always right. No matter what."

Marco blew out a breath and scrubbed a hand over his face. "You know, I have to go back to the city today. I tried to move a meeting I had scheduled with a new investor. But he's flying out of the country tomorrow. I have to go back."

"It's okay." Kate smiled and reached up to kiss his cheek. "It's okay. When will you be back? I'll be waiting for you."

"It's a dinner meeting. But I'd rather not drive up so late at night—"

Kate struggled to disguise her disappointment. She forced a smile and said, "Tomorrow is soon enough, Marco. Until tomorrow, then."

Marco's drive back to the city was the most miserable he could ever remember. The rain was torrential at times, producing small lakes on the road that challenged the maneuverability of even his high-tech sports car. The Palisades Parkway, he soon realized, had been a poor choice with its winding dips and curves. Traffic screeched to a stop about five miles from his exit, and there he sat, waiting for an accident to clear up ahead.

He'd left Sullivan County at noon to make a two-hour trip, and didn't pull into the underground parking garage of his building until nearly four o'clock.

The drive had given him entirely too much time to think. Replay the ecstasy of his night with Kate, and remonstrate himself for his childish behavior this morning. What was happening to him?

He knew the answer, and it frightened him half to death. He'd fallen in love with Kate Bardach. Which was probably the biggest mistake he'd ever made in his life.

Kate sighed as she watched Marco's Infiniti disappear down the hotel drive. As if on cue, Daniel appeared at her elbow and huffed, "What is it with him? Is he a hothead or what?"

She shook her head. "No, he just knows what he wants and doesn't care what he has to do to ensure he gets it."

Painfully true. A trait that, most likely, applies to me as well.

Kate set up a temporary office in the reception area and opened up her laptop. After scrolling down through seventy-six emails, her finger twitching on the delete button, she came across one from her mother.

How are things going up there? Any clues yet?

She dropped her forehead into her hand, taking a deep breath and counting to ten before typing her reply.

We only just started demo, Mother. I'll keep you posted if anything turns up.

Moments later, something did.

One of the contractors came out of the efficiency apartment they had first on their list carrying a stack of old ledgers. There had to be a dozen or more of them, bound in pale green linen with what used to be gold-toned edges. Filthy and faded now, some of their covers were awkwardly warped. So, the stack wouldn't stand on its own at the end of the counter where the workman tried to balance it.

"What do you want done with these, Ms. Bardach? We found them in a cabinet under the bottom bunk when we went to tear it out."

Kate rose and helped the man slide the books into four separate piles so they wouldn't topple over. "Probably trash. But let me take a quick peek before we dump them." She smiled, and the workman touched the brim of his Yankees cap. "Thank you, Carl," she said.

But her breath caught in her throat when Kate opened one of the covers and realized they were registration logs. She flipped through the stacks frantically, coughing from the dust and mildew they spewed into the air around her. The one on the very top of the pile was dated April-October, 1974.

What were the chances they would go back another whole decade?

Heart beating wildly, she could barely hear for the blood whooshing in her ears as she slowly slid the books off each pile, one at a time. Most were all dated for the same months, April through October—peak season. She came across only two for the winter months.

Winter 1969-1974.

Winter Season, 1965-1968.

They only went back to 1965. Kate's heart sank. Her Aunt Leah's last letter to her mother was dated October of the year prior. She flopped down in the creaky old office chair and chewed on a thumbnail, sputtering when she tasted the tang of mildew from the registers.

Too much time had passed. There was no one left to ask, and nothing but her aunt's letters. Those she'd had the courage to read all the way through. Simply touching the paper Leah had touched—reading her young, naive words to her younger sister—stirred Kate more than she wanted to admit.

Oftentimes with psychics, she knew it was like that. Contact with a familiar item, a piece of clothing the deceased wore, even seeing a photograph could open up a channel. Kate was torn, part of her desperately wanting to solve the mystery and bring peace to the family.

Another part of her was terrified of what truths she might uncover.

"Here's one more, Miss Kate." Carl rounded the corner from the apartment and paused, clearing his throat. "Sorry, ma'am. I meant to say Ms. Bardach."

Without hesitation, he laid another register on the counter before her. Kate stood and read the dates on the cover. *April-October, 1964.*

Kate froze with her heart in her throat. She was almost afraid to touch the book. As though if she did, the memories of what happened that night all those years ago would come flooding back, into *her own* brain, as if they were *her* memories. Snatching a tissue from her pocket, she dusted the cover off gently, then closed her eyes and clutched the book to her chest.

Later, she thought. I'll go through these pages of names and dates. Later. But her thoughts wandered back to the last of Leah's letters.

October 1, 1964
Joanie,
You won't believe how exciting life has been for me the past few weeks! For one, I'm engaged. You should see the rock Bart put on my finger two weeks ago. It's a full two carats all together, with a 3/4 carat baguette in the center—that means it's rectangular— and set in white gold. Which means it looks silver, but it's really gold. All the rage now. It's so gorgeous, Joanie. I wish you could see it. Little petal-shaped leaves fan out from the center stone, and each has its own, perfect, round diamond.

I know Mother has an exquisite engagement ring from Father, but she would go so green with envy if she saw mine.

And that's not all. We've set a date. October 21st. We'll get married at the King's County Courthouse in the morning, then drive up to the mountains. Bart reserved us a honeymoon suite at the Redman—can you believe it? The Redman Resort, right on Loch Sheldrake.

He says he has two more surprises for me, but I can't see them until the day before the wedding. Oh, Joanie, dearest sister, these are all such wonderful moments in my life I wish I could be sharing with you. If only family, stubborn pride, stupid differences over nationality and religion didn't stand in the way. . . .

I promise I'll write after we get back and give you all the details. Well, maybe not all of them. But maybe when you're older. In the meantime, sister dear, know I love you forever. Wish me luck! I'll be a bride before the Harvest Moon rises.

Missing you,
Leah

FOURTEEN

Work on the first floor of the Redman didn't wind down until around four o'clock, when the contractors left. They'd accomplished a lot so far, and Kate was pleased. Daniel walked her through, and Kate counted eight of the fifteen rooms on the ground floor had been stripped of old furniture, drapes, and carpet. Even the fixtures were gone from a few of the bathrooms.

"How are they doing on the efficiency, Daniel? I hate to think of you living out of a hotel room," she said as they made their way back to the lobby.

Daniel shrugged. "It's not the Marriott, but it's not bad. The guys say they should have the apartment ready for me to at least sleep in by next week."

"Good. They're working fast," Kate said absently, her eyes landing on the register still perched on the reception counter. She rounded the desk and pointed to her laptop. "At least the first thing Lareci did was hook up the Wi-Fi."

They sat together in front of Kate's computer and held a Skype meeting with Yvette and their project coordinator, Syd. He confirmed the fixtures Lareci had picked out would be delivered by week's end, and he'd scheduled a plumber to start work first thing Monday.

"The project is moving right along," Kate said. "We might even have the place ready for a Grand Opening in time for leaf peepers, huh?"

"As long as we don't have to tango with Lareci on too many more issues," Daniel mumbled as they signed off. Then, brightening, he glanced at Kate. "Dinner? I know you don't have any other plans *tonight.*"

Kate bristled at that, catching the knowing tone in her architect's voice, his direct reference to Marco's absence. She slammed her laptop closed with a little more force than necessary.

"Nope. No plans. Other than to check out the library in Liberty." She glanced at her watch. "They're open until seven on Tuesday nights. I'll have about an hour if I leave right now."

Kate didn't go to the library, remembering as she pulled out of the drive it practically backed up to the hotel where Daniel was staying. Knowing him, he'd follow her there like a desperate puppy.

She was glad she would be alone tonight. She was feeling a little claustrophobic from all the attention she'd been getting lately and needed some time to think.

Kate seldom cooked, but had gotten a few things in at the lake house since she knew she'd be staying there—at least during the week—for the foreseeable future. A veggie omelet sounded like the perfect dinner for her this evening. Onions, mushrooms, peppers, some black olives . . . yes, she had all of those items in to go with the eggs and cheese she'd picked up at the market in town. Accompanied by a piece of that good Jewish rye she'd gotten from the Kosher bakery, the meal sounded absolutely perfect.

The rain, after tapering off to a steady drizzle through late afternoon, had stopped. Blue sky was peeking through the clouds as Kate carried her briefcase and the register into the house. After she'd showered and slipped into loungewear, she began extracting everything out of the fridge she'd need to concoct her dinner.

As she chopped vegetables at her kitchen counter, her view of the lake was unobstructed through the French doors leading onto the deck. The sky had cleared completely now, and the sun was an orange ball settling over the top of the mountains on the opposite shore. Her parents had done an outstanding job in choosing this spot and constructing the house in such a way as to maximize the gorgeous views.

She was glad they'd decided the Catskills weren't their thing for vacations anymore and deeded the lake house to her last year.

As she sat and ate, her eyes strayed to the end of the table where, only twenty-four hours ago, the surface had served as more than just a dining area. She smiled, remembering catching Marco this morning, spraying the surface with disinfectant, then polishing it to a high sheen with lemon oil. He was an impulsive man, letting nothing stand in the way of what he wanted. But he was considerate and caring as well.

A good man. The kind of man she thought her father was. The kind of man her aunt had thought Bart was. As she crunched the last crusty bit of her rye toast, she wondered *how do you know?* How do you know the difference between a good man and one whose ultimate interests are primarily his own?

After cleaning up the kitchen, Kate emerged with a cup of chamomile tea. Her gaze landed on the old hotel register, still lying next to her briefcase on the table inside her front door. Sighing, she wandered near enough to run her fingers over the faded cloth cover. The surface was pilled and pebbly from age and friction, like an old bed sheet. A tingle started in her palm and worked its way up her wrist, as though the book were somehow electrified. She shuddered.

Odd. Very odd. I must be more exhausted than I thought.

Snatching her hand away, she thought, no. She simply wasn't up to sifting through those pages of signatures tonight. Didn't want to go anywhere, and a trip through that historical record could well take her somewhere she *knew* she didn't want to go. At least, not tonight.

She flipped through the channels on the TV, wasted a few minutes on social media, even tried to read the latest James Patterson novel she'd brought with her. Nothing held her attention. Although she was tired, her body was still buzzing with some sort of restlessness. Too much on her mind. She knew she wouldn't be able to fall asleep right away. The chamomile, she hoped, would do the trick.

Kate carried her mug to the glass patio doors overlooking the lake. The moon was full and huge, hanging low over the distant mountains. Its reflection formed a v-shaped path to her shoreline that wavered gently on the water. In the darker sky to the north, tiny stars struggled to compete with its brightness. A beautiful night—so peaceful and serene—the world had settled after the thorough shower nature had used to wash it clean all day.

Until a jolt of lightning rippled across the sky, cracking it in two from right to left.

Kate gasped and staggered back, sloshing hot tea over her fingers and dripping some on her bare toes.

That's impossible. The storm is long gone. There isn't a cloud anywhere.

For a few seconds, she was afraid to move. She held her breath, squinting at the clear night sky and wondering if thunder would follow the flash. But none did.

She must have imagined it. Pinching the bridge of her nose between two fingers, Kate moved to her favorite chair and set the mug down on the side table. The stress of this whole project, and being so far out of her element—the city—for so long, these were playing on her mind like mischievous gremlins. She picked up her watch and saw it was only nine o'clock. But obviously, she was more exhausted than she'd realized.

Finish your tea and go to bed, Bardach.

But as she drained her mug, a patch of sky to the north of the moon began to glow—a pulsating, orb of light in an otherwise inky sky. Kate leaned forward and squinted. *A plane, perhaps? Maybe there's a carnival going on in Liberty, and a spotlight is shooting into the sky. But there are no clouds to catch the light. Actually, it looks more like a giant flying saucer.*

The ridiculous thought didn't have time to bring a smile to her lips before she watched in shocked horror as, from the midst of the glowing circle, another bolt of lightning split the night sky, arcing in slow motion until it struck the surface of the lake.

Silently. No thunder. Not a sound.

Except for Kate's shriek and the crash as her tea mug hit the floor and shattered. Temporarily blinded, she sat blinking, her heart a pulsating lump in her throat.

How can there be lightning? There are no clouds.

Before another thought could form, a third bolt struck, this flash the most terrifying. As it cut a jagged path from the sky to the water, the bolt split—one arm again cracking the sky almost horizontally. Kate screamed and scrambled to her feet, feeling the jab of broken ceramic plunge into the arch of her foot. But what happened next riveted her to the spot as a warm puddle of blood formed under her foot.

A flaming ball of fire broke free from the horizontal bolt and hovered over the lake's surface, not a hundred yards from shore. Kate sobbed and covered her mouth with her hand, unable to tear her eyes away from the glowing orb as it changed color, from white to orange to blue, before flaring again and taking flight due south— straight toward the Redman.

Although heavily-leafed branches later in the season obscured Kate's view of the hotel, she could still usually see it, early in spring, through the pale, new growth on the branches overhanging the shore. *During the day.*

But full dark engulfed the view. Yet, this fireball lit up the entire back end of the building, and Kate could clearly see the rear parking lot and boat ramp, as if they were under stadium lights.

The entire episode lasted less than three seconds. The bolt, a whirling fireball, screeched to a halt a few yards from the shore. Then, as if some god had grown tired of playing with it, the flaming mass dropped, disappearing into the water without a sound. Everything went black.

Kate stood frozen to the spot for several minutes, afraid to move. The sky had returned to its inky serenity. The moon had risen a little higher now, the North Star shining clearly through the night.

What had just happened?

Even being psychic, Kate didn't believe in extra-terrestrial beings, knowing in her heart there were enough unexplained mysteries here on this planet to boggle the most curious mind. What she did fear were the real threats, from people, like terrorists. But terrorists caused destruction and death. This phenomenon—whatever it was—had been, as far as Kate could tell, completely harmless.

Well, not completely. The bottom of her right foot began to throb now that the shock was wearing off, and her toes were sticky against the hardwood with her own blood.

She hobbled to the bathroom, flicked on the light, and sat on the closed commode to observe the damage. A shard of the broken ceramic cup had sliced neatly into the very tender center of her arch. Not a very big cut, but deep and jagged. Wielding cotton balls and peroxide, she dabbed at the wound, wincing at the sting of the disinfectant. Pressing down on the area didn't seem to indicate any sharp fragments left inside. She cleaned it up, squeezed some antibiotic ointment on several cotton pads, and secured them snugly around her foot with bandage tape.

It took her another twenty minutes to clean up the trail of blood splotches she'd left on her way to the bathroom, as well as to gather the broken shards of ceramic from around her chair. Before she even began, though, she closed the blinds over the patio doors.

Not a good idea to indulge in any more stargazing tonight.

Kate had almost settled back to normal as she washed her hands in her kitchen sink, though was still pondering the bizarre light show she'd witnessed. She'd heard of ball lightning, but without an inciting storm? Perhaps there had been storm clouds beyond the mountains on the north side of the lake.

Sure, that would explain it. The receding edge of the weather system they'd been enduring all day.

She dried the few dishes she'd used for dinner and put them away. From her kitchen window, she could see the glimmer of the security lights edging the Redman's parking lot flickering through the trees. Peaceful, serene, normal. Kate shook her head and chuckled to herself. Perhaps she'd imagined this whole crazy episode tonight. Dozed off in her chair and dreamed it all up, then woke with a start when she upset her mug.

Fatigue and stress can play funny tricks on the mind, and she'd been struggling with her fair share lately. Sighing, she poured herself of glass of milk and reached to flick off the light over the sink.

Maybe I'll start the Patterson book after all. Prop myself up in bed and—

Kate's heart seized as a hand smacked against the window pane, inches from her face, with a loud, wet splat. A scream tore from her throat and she staggered back, watching in horror as desperate fingers clawed, nails squealing on the glass as they struggled to gain purchase before disappearing beneath the lower edge of the frame.

The police arrived at precisely nine forty-five, only fifteen minutes after Kate put in the call. The whirling lights of two patrol cars had turned her front and side yards into a kaleidoscope light show. Still, she wouldn't unbolt the door until they flashed a badge up to the peephole. One of the cops, a female officer, took one look at her and led her by the elbow to a chair at her dining room table.

"Are you hurt, Ms. Bardach?"

Kate shook her head, but then paused and lifted her foot to rest on one knee. "Just my foot," she said weakly, confused and a little dizzy. "But it's okay. There aren't any shards left in it."

"Which window is broken?" the officer asked, shooting an urgent glance over her shoulder toward her partner.

"No windows. My tea mug. I saw . . . I saw . . . ."

The whirling lights, her rapid breath, the whooshing of blood in her ears, the pounding pain in her foot. All at once, Kate couldn't seem to take in enough air. The face of the police officer bending over her wavered and grew blurry. And then, she was gone.

Marco's dinner meeting had ended in limbo, the client wobbling on how much to put in his trust and exactly what kinds of investments he was interested in. He knew he pushed the man too hard and drank too much wine. By the time they parted ways in the lobby of the Core Club, Marco realized he'd wasted two-hundred dollars on a meal and an entire night when he could have been in Kate's arms.

On his way home in the cab from his fruitless business dinner, Marco couldn't reach Kate, either on her cell or at the lake house. He checked his watch, and it was almost ten o'clock. Where the hell was she? He knew cell service up in the mountains was patchy, but she should be home by now anyway.

Stop. You've got to stop this right now, Lareci. You don't own the woman, no matter how badly you may want her.

No matter the fact she already owns your heart and soul.

He spent an endless, sleepless night. He rose at four and made himself a pot of coffee so strong it made even him, an espresso drinker, wince as the thick, bitter brew slid down his throat. Standing in front of his apartment windows in silk boxers, he waited until the sky above the eastern skyline began to glow. Then he dressed, threw a few fresh changes of clothes in his duffel bag, and grabbed his keys. After checking to be sure Cleo's food and water towers were full, he headed down to the garage.

Once he reached the parkway, he was traveling in the opposite direction of the rush hour traffic. This morning, the Palisades was beautifully scenic in the spring morning light. Pale color had started frosting the bare branches along the roadway, like a day or two's growth of green beard. Absently, Marco rubbed his jaw.

Forgot to shave again. Oh, well. Kate seems to like it, especially when I scrape it lightly along her bare skin.

It was still early when he took the Anawana Road exit off Route 17, winding through the small burgh of Hurleyville and down the hill toward the Loch. His dashboard clock said nine thirty, and he knew Kate didn't usually meet Daniel there until ten.

Would it be presumptuous of him to bypass the hotel drive and go directly to her place? Yes, it would. Suppose when he got to her house, she wasn't alone?

Stinging little bubbles of jealousy skittered through Marco's veins. He had to get over this. Had to realize Kate Bardach belonged to no one. And certainly not to him.

He pulled into the hotel parking lot and saw the contractors were already at work, probably had been since sunup. As he stepped out of his vehicle, he watched two, dust-covered men carrying a broken section of old sheetrock out the propped-open front doors toward the dumpster. He was surprised to see the huge container was already showing signs of filling up.

Good. They were making excellent progress. Boris and Eliot would be pleased. There was a good chance they could open before the end of the season.

As expected, Kate's Porsche wasn't there. But Daniel's Escalade was parked under the trees on the far side of the lot. Great. Exactly *not* who he wanted to see first thing this morning. Boy Wonder.

He checked his watch again. Kate should be here in a few minutes. Maybe he'd scout out the building and see how far along the demo had come.

"Hey, Carl," Marco said as he spotted the carpenter in the lobby. "Looks like you guys are making great headway."

Carl slapped his hands together to knock off the dust before reaching out to shake Marco's. "We are. It's going pretty quick. Usually demo's a bitch. But this place is coming apart easier than we thought." He tipped his head toward the efficiency. "Should have your architect a place to sleep by the middle of next week."

"Hmm. That'll be great." Marco pressed his lips together. "Where is he? I see his vehicle out there."

Carl's eyebrows drew together, and he leaned around Marco to peer out the windows. "Oh, hadn't noticed. Haven't seen him yet. But he must be around somewhere."

Nodding, Marco asked, "Is it okay if I check out how the first floor rooms are coming?"

"Be my guest. We're about done ripping out everything in the front rooms, but haven't gotten to the suites down lakeside."

Marco remembered the first day the realtor had taken them through the vacant building last fall. On each of the three guest room floors, those on the end overlooking the lake were oversized and lavish. At least, they had been at one time. The realtor said they were most often reserved as honeymoon suites, with entire walls of glass overlooking the water and mountains beyond.

They would be called the Shelby's Executive Suites, Marco had decided.

He ducked his head in the first few rooms, stripped bare now of everything down to sheetrock. A workman was sweeping up in one of them and touched his cap to acknowledge Marco, but said nothing. Hands stuffed in his pockets, Marco headed down toward the lakefront room.

Patios would be nice, he'd thought. He wanted to take a peek and see if there was enough wall space beside the huge picture window to break through a doorway to an outdoor space. Maybe they could add balconies on the floors above.

He'd gotten halfway down the hallway when he thought he heard Kate's voice, but not coming from behind him. Unable to make out words, it sounded like she was murmuring, then a tinkling laugh cut through more clearly.

She must have slipped past him when he was perusing one of the rooms down front.

As he drew closer to the suite, her voice came through again, louder this time, but no words. Moaning, then more laughter. When he heard the deeper, male voice mutter something in response, Marco's blood ran cold.

She's in there with *him*. She and Boy Wonder, doing God knows what. Certainly not working.

Che casino. I know exactly what. I've heard those sounds from her before.

He reached the end suite, number 103, and wrapped his fingers around the brass handle. It turned easily—they hadn't even been smart enough to throw the lock. Sucking in a deep breath, he laid his shoulder against the door and thrust it open.

Marco stumbled into a room completely empty, except for a pair of daisy-printed drapes, horrible in their shades of faded orange and green. One length had broken free from its mount and lay crumpled in a dusty heap on the floor. Brilliant sunlight streamed through the wall of glass, which, although streaked and cloudy with years of age and weather, failed to disguise the beauty of the view beyond. No furniture, and no Kate. Or anyone else.

But he could still hear them. On the floor above, maybe? No, the voices were too near. And echoing. They must be in the bathroom. He could nearly make out the words, but not quite. Hear the heavy breathing, the groans . . . .

Panting, his hands balled into fists, Marco stormed across the empty space and kicked savagely at the pea-green painted door. It gave way easily and bounced off the tiled wall behind, sending a shower of ceramic chips raining to the floor. The echo of the impact rang in his ears. But when it faded, the voices did, too.

There was no one inside the ugly, outdated bath.

"What the hell do you think you're doing?"

Marco jolted and spun around to see Daniel standing inside the doorway, annoyance transforming his pretty-boy features into that of an angry child.

"We're doing fine with the demo, Mr. Lareci. We really don't need any help, but I would appreciate your wearing a hard hat the next time you come in to wander through while we're knocking down walls." The facetious hint of his words sent acid prickling through Marco's veins.

"Where is she?" he hissed through gritted teeth.

"I was hoping you could tell me. She hasn't shown up this morning, and I've tried her cell and house phone numerous times." Daniel pulled out his cell and scrutinized the screen with a furrowed brow. "I was actually beginning to worry. She's usually here by now."

After again dialing Kate's house phone and getting no answer, Marco jumped into his car and drove up the road to her house. Her cellphone had gone directly to voicemail. A chill settled over him when he saw her car parked in the driveway.

She had yet to give him a house key, and after several moments of ringing the bell and pounding on the door, he seriously considered breaking it down. His heart slammed against his ribcage so hard, he felt light-headed and knew he needed to calm down a minute and think. Swiping a hand over his face, he stuffed his hands in his pockets and stood on the front steps, consciously trying to slow his rapid breathing.

Although she hadn't answered either phone last night around ten, her cell had rung a half-dozen times before switching over. Now it clicked to voice mail immediately, as if it were turned off or dead. She wasn't with Daniel, one small consolation. But then perhaps something was terribly wrong. Either she had gone somewhere with someone else, in their vehicle, and never made it home, or she was inside, unconscious, maybe hurt . . . or—"

His heart leapt when he heard footsteps inside, irregular and slow, thumping across the hardwood floor. Then someone fumbled with the chain and threw back the deadbolt. The door swung open and Kate stood there, blinking in the bright morning light. For a moment, he could tell, she didn't even recognize him. Relief and dread balled together in his throat.

"Mia cara, what's happened to you?" The question sounded more like a croak.

Her hair was wild, matted on one side and sticking out as though she'd been struck by lightning. Yesterday's makeup smudged both eyes in raccoon fashion. She stared at him in silence as his eyes skimmed down her crumpled tee shirt and flannel pajama pants. When his gaze landed on the taped white bandage mummifying her right foot, a stab of horror stopped his breath.

"Cazzo, who's done this to you?" He stepped forward, forcing her to stumble out of the way to let him pass. He caught her arm to steady her and kicked the door shut behind him.

Kate fisted both hands in the front of his shirt and searched his face pathetically for a moment before collapsing against him, burying her face in his chest with a sob.

FIFTEEN

Frustrated at her own loss of control, it took Kate several minutes to compose herself enough to speak. The sedatives the E.R. doctor had prescribed, she knew, were still fogging her brain. But this wasn't like her—this bleeding-heart, damsel-in-distress feeling. It was easier, of course, to blame her weakness on Marco than on herself.

She drew back and pushed him away with both hands. He stepped back, shock and confusion contorting his features. Lifting both hands, he asked, "What? What have I done?"

"What are you doing here? I thought you were back in the city. A business dinner, right? Isn't that why you left me here alone last night?" Even she could hear the accusation, the acid lacing her words.

She was acting the spoiled bitch, and she knew it.

But no. If he hadn't left, none of what happened last night would have transpired. There would have been no inexplicable balls of lightning tearing across the night sky. She would not have broken her favorite tea mug and then gashed her foot open with the shards.

No manifestation of a desperate hand would have slapped and scratched at her kitchen window. Not if Marco had been there.

Or would it?

"Kate, I've been trying to reach you since last night. No answer, anywhere. Where were you?" Now his tone carried a tinge of suspicion, resentment, which only served to spike her rage higher.

She spun on her good heel and limped to the sofa, where she plopped down awkwardly and lifted her bandaged foot into her lap. The pain from the stitched wound had escalated exponentially the moment she'd swung her feet out of bed to answer the door.

His fault, too.

Bending over her foot, she rocked and sucked in deep breaths against the sharp jabs of pain now shooting clear up her leg.

"I was home until nine forty-five," she hissed through gritted teeth. "Until the police came and searched the house, while another nice officer called an ambulance."

Marco dropped to one knee in front of her, reaching up to lift the curtain of tangled hair away from her face. She swatted him away. "Don't touch me."

Yet, he remained amazingly calm as he asked, "The police? Searched the house . . . for what? What happened to your foot?"

The gentle, soothing tone of his voice overrode what little Kate had left in the way of stubbornness, and anger, and pride. She covered her face with both hands and sobbed, "Some creepy shit happened here last night, Marco. And I think it has something to do with that." Kate lifted a trembling finger to point at the dusty, faded register she'd brought home from the hotel the previous evening, still laying where it had on the side table near the front door. "Apparently, my late Aunt Leah is a rambunctious spirit. And she's bound and determined to get my attention."

Marco made her tea, scouting out the matching mug to her favorite she'd broken the night before, and sat next to her on the sofa. Slowly, the sedative fog on Kate's brain began to lift, even though her pain had sent Marco to her bedside to retrieve the Percocet she'd been prescribed. As she came back into herself more clearly, she realized how foolish she'd acted.

Here was her knight in shining armor—come to her rescue—and she was doing her damnedest to kick him in the groin plate. *Marco is such a patient man* was the phrase running through Kate's brain like a taunting mantra.

"So, what the hell happened here last night, Kate?" Marco asked, his voice tight and not quite succeeding in maintaining a modicum of control. He sat down next to her and laid one hand on her knee. But then he waited silently. She could almost see his face in her peripheral vision. But she kept her eyes trained straight ahead, thoughts tumbling inside her brain.

Images flashed into her memory like snippets from a movie trailer. Kate struggled to center herself, concentrating on the warmth of the tea mug between her palms. After a long moment, she sucked in a breath and began.

"Somehow I knew, when I brought home that register from the hotel, I'd brought part of her with me. Part of someone. Some*thing.*" She shook her head and lifted one hand to cover her eyes. "It was terrifying, Marco."

She felt him scoot closer to her on the sofa, and then his strong hand squeezing her leg. "Tell me, mia cara. I already know these episodes you have are horrifying. You can tell me." His fingers lifted her chin, and when her eyes fluttered open, two electrifying, pale, hazel ones stared back at her. They were filled with nothing but concern. Worry, even.

Not a trace of skepticism. Maybe he does finally believe I'm not a complete wacko.

"First, the lightning." She held his gaze intently. "I know you were in the city last night, Marco, and it had rained here all day. But before dusk, the weather front passed, and the sky was perfectly clear. A full moon rose over the mountains, and there were stars beginning to wink in the night sky."

Marco nodded. "It wasn't raining anymore in Manhattan when I left my meeting, either."

Kate went on to describe the violent lightning that seemed to bolt out of nowhere, the ball of fire sailing through the night.

"I was terrified to begin with, but when I saw it heading for the Redman, my heart stopped. I thought for sure the strike would burst the entire building into flames."

"Che casino. That would have been terrible."

She couldn't tell, as she told her story, whether Marco really believed her or not. His dark eyebrows quirked at certain parts, and she could tell he was thinking maybe she'd hallucinated the entire event. Yet, his warm fingers remained wrapped securely around her leg, just above her knee. And he never took his eyes off hers.

Until she got to the part about the hand on the window.

"Dio buono," he barked, rising suddenly to his feet and heading toward the kitchen. "Did they find anything? Evidence of an intruder?"

Kate waited, watching from the sofa, while Marco surveyed every inch of her kitchen window. He checked the latch and ran his fingers along the edge of the frame as though he might find a clue there. He had turned and was headed to the front door when she spoke again.

"They didn't find anything, Marco. Nothing. There are monstrous azalea bushes under that window. Nobody, without a ladder, could have gotten within ten feet of the window. And there was no damage to the bushes, no imprints in the soft sod beyond."

Marco halted halfway between her and the front door, staring at her.

"You think it was her. Don't you?"

She barely heard his low murmur of half-disbelief, half-horror.

Kate nodded slowly, pointing to the book on the side table near the door. "Carl found all of the old registration books underneath the bunk bed in the efficiency. I didn't think they went back far enough, but then he came out with the last one." She pointed again. "I think she wanted to make a point, Marco. She's already appeared to me, at least once, with a distinct message. *Find me.* She's there, somewhere. Or, what's left of her."

Marco jolted as though she'd slapped him, then swiped a hand down his face as he swore again in Italian. "I would think with all the demo, by now they'd have found any . . . remains."

"No, you dumbass. I don't think her body is *in* the hotel. But it is the last place she was headed. For her honeymoon. And the proof of her arrival is probably in that old guest book."

Kate slammed her cup down on the table and struggled to stand. But as her weight settled on her three fresh stitches, she winced and thought better of the move.

"Wait. Don't get up. I'll bring it to you." Marco glanced from her face to the book and back. "But do you want to look at it now, Kate? Are you up to it?"

She dropped her head back and let out loud, a wry, tortured laugh. "I'm afraid if I don't, next thing my aunt will do is drag me down into the lake by my hair."

Marco retrieved the dusty book and sat close beside her, laying it on their laps. She sucked in a deep breath, then lifted the cover and began to turn the pages.

"Her letters said my aunt—Leah—was to be married in October of 1964. Something about a harvest moon. The book starts from April on. Let's see if the entries go that far."

As she flipped through the pages, the dust and woody scent of old paper made Kate sneeze a few times. August, September, October. The number of names on the pages' lined surface dwindled from dozens per day to only a few per page by mid-September. In early October, the registrations surged for the first two weeks. Apparently, early frosts that year had bumped the leaf-peeper season up by a week or two.

Kate ran her finger down the column of names until she stopped abruptly, sucking in a short gasp.

"There it is. Leah's husband's name was Shelby. October 21, 1964." She met Marco's eyes, suddenly remembering the first day he'd brought her to the Redman. "How did you know? Is that why you're renaming it the Shelby?"

Marco's eyes widened. He started slowly shaking his head. "I didn't. The name just came to me, popped into my head." Pausing, he looked away. "The day after I met you."

A chill skittered up Kate's spine. This was too eerie to really be happening.

The signature was slanted, jerky, and rushed. This wasn't her aunt's handwriting. It was nothing like the round, loopy script in the letters. This was the hand of the man Leah married. The man she loved. The man for whom she'd given up her family.

And, quite probably, her life.

A wave of emotion crashed over her, along with a sense of disbelief and wonder. How could you care for any one person that much? *Love* someone with that intensity? So much you'd be willing to give up everything? Freedom. Control. Independence. Family.

She met Marco's gaze. "We have to find her, Marco. She won't rest . . . won't let me live in peace, until we do."

"The rumors about Loch Sheldrake," he began. "You think your aunt ended up in the lake, don't you?"

She nodded, unable to speak around the huge ball forming in her throat. "I have no idea how she expects me to find her."

Her heart clutched in her chest as he answered her silently, with only his eyes. Hazel, but a puzzling color that couldn't decide between green and brown, sparked with flecks of gold. They were filled with pain and confusion, reflecting back the emotions in her own heart. Understanding it, sharing its burden. She felt a single tear leak out and trickle down as his warm palm cupped her cheek.

"Mia cara," he murmured, swiping the tear away with his thumb.

Kate realized then, with no small measure of trepidation, she was skating very close to understanding *exactly* why her aunt had given up everything for a man. A strong-willed, stubborn, Italian man. Probably much like the one silently speaking to her now. With only his eyes. As if history were repeating itself, fifty years later.

A terrifying concept, on multiple levels.

Several hours later, after Kate had cleaned herself up and taken another pill, she let Marco help her to his car. He'd argued there was no need for her to come to the job site today, but Kate knew she should. She must. This was her livelihood, her strength, and her independence. No matter how much she felt like staying curled up against Marco's side on the sofa all day, she had to put on her big-girl panties and go back to work.

Walking, however, was a bit of a challenge. The bandage over her stitches prevented even her comfy, Cole Haan loafers from sliding on. She finally settled for her softest canvas sneakers, with the laces loosened all the way. Even though they looked ridiculous underneath her khaki dress pants.

Leaning heavily on Marco's arm, Kate made her way into the lobby of the Redman, where all activity abruptly ceased as the men turned to stare her way. Daniel's clipboard clattered to the countertop as he spun towards them.

"What the hell happened to you?" His voice was half-curious, half-indignant, a tone Kate didn't remember hearing from her architect in the past.

Or, perhaps it was just the contrast to the gentle concern in Marco's voice. One she was rapidly becoming fond of.

Kate squared her shoulders, puffing herself up as best she could while obviously dependent on Marco's grip to stay upright. "A little incident with a broken tea mug. An inconvenience. Nothing more." Her gaze swept the lobby, and she tipped her chin toward the one remaining wall, standing like a lone soldier in several inches of dust and debris. "How's the demo going? We about ready to wrap it up and get started with the rebuild?"

Hating how helpless she felt, and nauseated from the pain and the meds, Kate managed a hobble-through inspection of the entire first floor before collapsing, exhausted, into the chair Marco found for her.

"How are you feeling? You're pale, Kate," he murmured, waiting discreetly until the workmen had all dispersed toward their duties.

"I think," she stammered, swallowing hard against another wave of nausea, "I think I need to put something in my stomach. It's tossing the Percocet around like a beach ball."

"Come on. We'll get some lunch." Marco helped Kate to her feet. He tucked his arm beneath hers, acutely aware she was depending on him for support much more than when they'd arrived.

They had almost made it to the front door when the old, blue, Ford truck clamored up the driveway.

"Oh, it's James," Kate said with a weak smile.

Marco flashed her a surprised glance. "I'm surprised you remember him. You were pretty out of it the first night."

Kate chuckled. "I've been pretty out of it a lot lately." Her smile faded. "Ever since I met you."

Ouch. That wasn't exactly a declaration of love. But she's right. Seems like all I've brought into her life is calamity.

Memories of their last night together flashed through his brain. Nestled together in her hot tub, and the incredible sex afterward. His heart did a somersault as heat rushed his body.

No. Not only calamity. Definitely more than calamity.

Marco pressed his lips together and said nothing as they waited under the portico for James Donnelly to climb out of his vehicle. No dirty overalls today. A crisply pressed plaid shirt topped his jeans, and the ball cap was gone. The sparse hair rimming his balding scalp was wet, scored with fresh comb lines.

"Afternoon, Mr. Lareci." He nodded toward Kate. "Miss Bardach. I thought I'd stop by on my way to the museum."

"Hello, James. I appreciate your keeping tabs on the place. Looks like the men are making good progress." As he spoke, Marco felt Kate wobble beside him. He shifted his grip on her forearm.

The old man's brow furrowed, and his gaze dropped to the bandage peeking out from Kate's sneaker. "By God, what's happened to you, Miss Bardach? You didn't step on one of those rusty ol' nails, I hope."

"No, just a clumsy encounter with a broken tea cup," Kate replied. "What takes you to the museum?"

"I volunteer there two days a week," he said. "More for me than for them. I love goin' through all the ol' stuff there." He paused with an embarrassed smile. "Nostalgia, you know. Brings me back to my boyhood days."

Marco studied the man, wondering. "That's right, you grew up here. Didn't you say you worked at the Redman for a time?"

James nodded and looked at his feet. "I did. Not among my most glorious memories."

"What did you do here?" Kate asked.

165

Marco quickly calculated in his head. The man must be well up in his seventies, maybe older. Is it possible he was working here when—

"I parked cars. For a couple summers. Not the most glamorous job, but my buddies and me sure had some fun testin' out those rides."

Kate wobbled again and clutched harder on Marco's arm. He glanced down to see a shine of perspiration now slicked her pale face. When she closed her eyes and swallowed hard, he grimaced.

Gotta get her off her feet and something to eat, or she'll pass out on me.

"Look, James. Miss Bardach isn't feeling very well. I was just taking her for some lunch. Would you like to join us?"

The old man glanced at the ancient Timex on his wrist. "I'd love to, but I'm due up at the museum in ten minutes. Maybe 'nother time. I sure hope you get to feelin' better, Miss Kate."

And she did. After an excellent Reuben on good Jewish rye and not one, but two fountain Cokes, Kate felt like herself again. Almost. The throbbing in her foot had subsided to a bearable level. Work was progressing well on her project, and her client was pleased.

Her client, the very handsome man with the unruly dark hair and pale, hazel eyes, was sitting across from her, his cellphone pressed to his ear. He'd apologized when the business call came in as they finished eating.

"Sorry, Kate, but I really need to take this."

She watched him as he spoke with one of his own clients, his conversational style a sophisticated mix of professionalism and friendliness. But it didn't really matter what he was saying. Kate's heart rate kicked up a notch at just the sound of his voice. When he caught her watching him, he smiled and laid his hand over hers.

And when he looked into her eyes, she finally understood what she saw there. Because she felt it, too. The bubbly sensation in her chest wasn't from the fountain drinks. It was a brand-new, exhilarating, mind-blowing high, one of an intensity Kate had never imagined.

Her phone buzzed in her purse, breaking her trance.

"Yes, Miguel, what is it? Problem with April?" Kate's instincts snapped to high alert. The trainer at her dad's farm almost never called unless it was an emergency.

"No, no, no," Miguel answered in his thick Mexican accent. "Not by a long shot, Miss Kate. I've got *good* news. Wonderful news."

The foal. Kate mentally slapped herself. She'd been so distracted, so tied up with Marco, the Redman project, all the weird things that had been going on, she'd totally forgotten she had a mare ready to give birth any day.

"Oh, heavens, Miguel. Tell me. Tell me! Do we have another filly?" she asked, squeezing her eyes shut and crossing the fingers of her free hand.

"Ah, you should be happy, though not so happy as that," Miguel replied, his tone sobering. "No filly. It's a colt. But a fine, strapping colt he is."

Kate felt all the air leave her lungs in a whoosh. Damn. She so much preferred fillies. At least they stood a better chance of a career after racing than colts.

"Is everything okay, Kate?" Marco had lowered the phone from his ear and was studying her, vertical lines creased between his eyebrows. "Problem?"

She shook her head and closed her eyes, returning her attention to Miguel. "Well, that is wonderful, Miguel. Is he healthy? Up and nursing yet?"

On the way back to the job site, Marco fired one question after the other toward Kate about her new baby horse. He racked his memory, but he didn't think he'd ever seen one, other than in a distant pasture or on a Super Bowl Budweiser commercial. Oh, he'd seen plenty of horses up close, particularly the weary-looking monsters pulling buggies around Central Park at certain times of the year.

But never a baby racehorse.

"I want to see the little guy," he said excitedly. "Can we go tomorrow? After we check in with the crew? I have to go back to the city tomorrow anyway. I don't like to leave Cleo alone more than one night."

He glanced over to see her staring at him, the corner of her pouty lips quirked. "It's not a big deal, Marco. I've been watching colts and fillies grow up at Father's farm ever since I was a kid. They're . . . horses. Only, smaller."

"Well, it's a big deal for me, dammit!" he barked, and slammed his palm on the steering wheel. She jumped, and he quickly continued. "I'm sorry, Kate. I know I'm acting like a little kid. It's just...I love babies. Puppies, kittens—you know, that's how I ended up with Cleo. The spotted witch stole my heart from the first day I saw her. I was almost glad when Diana's asshole husband said she had to get rid of her."

Marco couldn't tell if Kate's sigh was from exasperation or capitulation. It didn't matter, though, when she replied softly, "Okay. But not until after we get everything checked out at the Redman."

"The Shelby," he shot back, almost reflexively. Then he remembered what they'd discovered that morning and felt an instant jab of regret. He reached for her hand. "I'm sorry, Kate. I will talk to my partners about changing the name. I understand how having the place with that name on the marquis might be upsetting to you."

"No," Kate barked. "No. It's okay. It's not necessary." She laid her other hand over his and clasped it between her own. "As long as you help me sort out this mystery, Marco. If we can find out what happened here fifty years ago, maybe somehow, my aunt's spirit will be set free. That's how it works sometimes. The living aren't the only ones who crave closure."

"What do you mean?"

She blew out a breath. "When someone dies, they get stuck here somehow. Their soul, I mean."

Marco cleared his throat. "Like my nephew." He felt the old familiar jab of pain stab him through the heart.

"Yes, like your nephew. With children, it's often because they don't understand what's happened to them. They don't know where they're supposed to go from here."

The thought of a precious child floating about, confused and helpless, made Marco's guts clench. "So how can they be saved? A priest, maybe?" He shot her a glance. "Or a rabbi. Is that what an exorcism does? Do rabbis have a similar ritual?"

"They used to. But exorcism is to release evil spirits. That's not what I'm talking about," she replied quietly.

Marco couldn't believe he was having a discussion—a serious discussion—about spirits. Ghosts. But Kate was no wacko. She had *seen Matthew*. Described him down to the clothes he was wearing when he died.

He swallowed the ball of emotion clogging his throat to speak. "So, what can be done, Kate? For Matthew, or for your aunt?"

She reached for her purse and snatched a tissue out, blotting under both eyes. "For Matthew, I'm not sure. He was so young . . . he truly doesn't understand why nobody pays attention to him anymore. He'll probably wait until someone else in the family, who knew him, passes. Then he'll follow."

Marco crossed himself and muttered an Italian curse.

She daintily blew her nose before continuing. "My Aunt Leah, though, she wants something. She wants somebody to know what happened to her. Where her body lies. I think then, her spirit will rest."

Marco's thoughts drifted back to that morning at the hotel. "I heard them, you know," he said quietly.

Her head snapped to face him. "Heard who?"

An eerie chill slid over the back of his neck as he recounted what he'd heard. About the voices, the laughter. How he'd felt sure it was *her* voice he was hearing. How there had been nobody there.

He left out the part about his suspicion and his rage. And kicking in the door.

"I guess I shouldn't be surprised. We know Leah and Bart were there. I know, from her letters, how much she loved him. And after all, it *was* their honeymoon."

She was silent for a long moment, staring straight ahead at the road before them. Then she said, "He was Italian, too, you know."

He snorted. "With a name like Shelby? Not likely."

"Mother is certain it was an alias. She told me our whole family suspected he was involved with the mob. Mother thinks Italian is another word for Mafia."

Marco rubbed his jaw. "So, she's probably not going to be thrilled to find out about you and me, then. Is she?"

He already knew it was an issue with his family. One they'd get over. Hell, they'd gotten over all the shenanigans his sister had been through with men. They certainly better not give him any flak about a Jewish girlfriend.

Or wife, possibly.

Kate folded her arms over her chest and turned toward the window. "Probably not. She'll probably freak out and swear fate is threatening to repeat itself."

Wow. Sucker punch. What the hell did she mean by that?

"I have nothing to do with the mob, Kate. I'm simply a good, Catholic, Italian boy."

But by then, they were pulling into the hotel parking lot. Boy Wonder, Daniel, was standing out front, facing off with Jeremy, the head contractor. Daniel clutched his clipboard in one hand while the other waved wildly in the air around his head.

"Oh, boy," Kate muttered. "What have we got going on here now?"

SIXTEEN

Kate climbed out of Marco's car before he could get around to help her. Leaning heavily on the open door, she shouted, "Boys! What's the problem here?"

Daniel spun toward her, his face red and twisted with rage. "Our head contractor here tells me his men left the job site early today because they were *spooked*." He put air quotes around the word. "Supposedly heard voices coming from the empty rooms. Apparently, they've taken too much stock in the local lore."

Marco had reached her side by then, and she slid him a glance. She was unsure how to react. But he stepped forward and said, "That's ridiculous, Jeremy, and you know it. Old buildings creak. Settle and sigh sometimes. Especially with all the demo going on. Surely your men—"

"I was telling Daniel here—I'll have a word with them in the morning," Jeremy said. "I'll bring in my portable radio, let them play some of that modern crap they like to listen to. It might help to keep their imaginations from running off." He shoved his hands into the pockets of his paint-splattered jeans and looked down, scuffing the dirt with the toe of his work boot. "I'll admit, the place is a little creepy. And you already know the stories about the Loch."

Kate stiffened and raised her chin. "What I do know, Jeremy, is if your men aren't back on the job on time tomorrow morning, we'll be bringing in another team. This project has a deadline, and I mean to stick to it. The Shelby *will open* before the fall colors peak, haunted or not."

As they watched Jeremy climb into his truck, Daniel grumbled, "I think they did this on purpose today. The lobby apartment is finished. First, they tell me I can move my stuff in here tonight, then they all scatter because they hear voices." He spun on his heel and headed inside, muttering, "Haunted, my ass."

Kate looked at Marco and shrugged. Although the rest of her team didn't know the whole story of her psychic powers, they had come to accept the fact there were certain buildings she couldn't work in. Daniel hadn't been around long enough to witness one of Kate's mysterious visions.

She narrowed her eyes at Marco, though, when she saw him struggling to suppress a grin.

An hour later, Daniel drove to his hotel room in Liberty, packed his things, and checked out. Damn if stupid local superstition would keep him from moving into the newly renovated studio at the Redman. Or Shelby. Or whatever the hell Mr. High-and-Mighty Lareci wanted it called. The Internet service at the hotel sucked, the bed was lumpy, and the room smelled like dirty socks, even right after the maids left. Everything in the studio was clean and brand-new. And the Wi-Fi was top-of-the-line fast.

One thing about the arrogant Italian bastard—he wasn't afraid to spend money on the best that money could buy.

Daniel picked up a six-pack of Yuengling and ordered an overstuffed sub from the sandwich shop on his way out of Liberty. He usually didn't drink beer or eat processed meats, let alone nearly a pound of them. But he was in a foul mood and felt like acting out. Being horny as hell only compounded the problem.

Daniel was certain once he and Kate started working so closely together on this project, he'd get into her pants. Although he'd been barely six months with Bardach & Associates, he watched his new boss with a critical eye. On the last Friday of every month, Kate invited the whole team to a happy hour at the pub around the corner from the office. And every month, he watched Kate leave with a new, much younger man who'd caught her eye during the evening.

She may not be old enough to have earned true cougar status, but there was no mistaking it: Kate Bardach preferred veal to sirloin, hands down.

So, why not me? I've got to be at least six or seven years her junior. And there was more than one co-ed who clamored for my attention in graduate school at the Pratt Institute.

But no, this Italian stallion moves in and takes over her every waking minute, so I don't even stand a chance with her. He looks to be in his mid-thirties, probably even older than her. Why this sudden change in her M.O.?

Daniel was so engrossed in his own mental gripe session, he'd hardly been aware of the music playing on his radio, his favorite Sirius station, AltRock. But as he pulled off the road onto the Shelby's winding drive, the disconcerting notes of something completely unfamiliar penetrated his bitch bubble.

What the hell is this?

He glanced down at his screen and read *The Sounds of Silence*, Simon and Garfunkel.

Oldies Party? Where did this station come from? I never even heard of it.

But mashing the tune keys on his steering wheel did nothing. He tried the manual station search. Nothing.

Great. Now there's a problem with my radio. Gonna be a long ride back to the city on Friday.

Grumbling to himself, Daniel parked his SUV under the portico and let himself into the lobby. Dust still hung in the air like smoky fog and sparkled in the slanted rays of sunlight streaming in from the ballroom windows. He paused, clutching the bag with his sandwich in one hand, six-pack perched on his hip, and surveyed the space around him.

The framing for the new partition sliced the lobby in two, sending a jolt of fresh irritation crackling through him. Such a nice, open space with all those windows. Why couldn't the stupid bastard see how he was defiling the original architecture of this place by trying to turn Catskill retro into Manhattan posh?

He stormed into his apartment, slamming the door behind him. He needed to get over this, and fast. This was his job, and whether he liked it or not, he was working not only for Kate on this project, but for Lareci as well. He damned well better get used to doing things their way.

The first beer tasted so good, Daniel wondered why he'd sworn off the stuff. The bottle was practically empty by the time he booted up his laptop and unwrapped his huge, animal-fat-and-preservative-laden sandwich.

Damn, that tastes pretty good, too. Why was it again I got on this health food kick?

The computer took unusually long to boot up, and he wondered if it was time to trade it in on an upgraded model. He really needed to pay attention to those updates more often. Finally, his desktop loaded, and he clicked on his browser.

You are not connected to the Internet.

Shit, now what?

But no matter how many times he ran the connectivity diagnostics, it didn't solve the problem. Daniel grabbed his iPhone and checked. Yup, just as he'd suspected. The Wi-Fi was down.

He spent the next twenty minutes trying to reset the router with no results. And for some reason, he couldn't even get the hotspot on his phone to connect.

Damn these mountains. Well, by God, the Italian stallion is going to hear about this in the morning.

The second beer went down as fast as the first—so fast, it had him checking to make sure they were actually twelve-ounce bottles and not shorties. He decided he'd finish working on the blueprints for the patio and balconies Lareci had asked for. Daniel had to admit, though only to himself, those additions were a damn good idea.

The sandwich was way more than he could eat, especially when he was used to salads and tofu. He wrapped what was left and slid it into the small refrigerator they'd installed earlier that morning, snatching out a third beer at the same time.

Measurements. He needed to take measurements of the wall space in the end unit so he could order the right-sized doors. His metal tape roll was in his back pocket, where it always lived. With his beer in one hand and a notepad in the other, Daniel headed out through the lobby and down the hall.

Dusk had darkened the interior of the building to near blackness, so he grabbed a flashlight from the front desk on his way out. None of the wiring for light fixtures anywhere other than his apartment had even been started yet. He hoped he'd be able to juggle his flashlight and the tape measure to record the dimensions right.

Who the fuck cares, he thought, as he hiccupped on his way down the hall. If the doors don't fit, Lareci will just have to pay to send them back and order new ones.

But there was still some light spilling in through the huge bay window in the end suite. The sun had set over the mountains on the other side of the lake, and its afterglow radiated off the water like orange fire. Daniel set his beer down on the floor and got to work, taking measurements.

He was jotting numbers down on his notepad when he swore he heard a woman laughing. It sounded like Kate—he'd worked with her long enough and fantasized enough times about her; he'd know her sexy, throaty laugh anywhere. The sound echoed from down the other end of the hall. Back toward the lobby.

Good. They're back. Maybe Lareci can make a call and get the Wi-Fi back up while he's here.

But when Daniel returned to the lobby, there was no one there. No cars out front. He walked up to the glass door and rattled it. Still locked and dead bolted.

Wow. Now I know why I don't drink beer.

Still, he couldn't ignore the chill that ran across his shoulder blades, making him shudder. No heat yet in the main rooms, either. Daniel mentally patted himself on the back for remembering to ask them to order in a space heater for his apartment. Gets pretty chilly after the sun goes down up here in the boonies.

A half-hour later, Daniel had altered the blueprints for the door additions and decided it was time to call it a night on work. Maybe he could catch a good movie. Shutting down his computer, he picked up the remote and switched on the modest-sized flatscreen. But white static was all he could get on any of the channels.

Damn it all to hell, don't tell me the satellite's out, too.

He slammed the remote down on the countertop with such force, the plastic casing cracked. Then he chuckled to himself. Oh, well, Lareci can pay for another one of those as well. The pompous, rich bastard has more money than God. He can afford it.

At least the bed was comfortable. Daniel opened his fourth beer and set it on the small nightstand, slipped off his boots, and stretched out. The memory-foam mattress felt heavenly on his back, and the brand-new linens smelled clean and freshly starched. The little space heater was doing a fine job of cozying up the place. In fact, he might have to lower the thermostat before he turned in.

He nearly fell off the bed when he heard the scream slice through the silence from somewhere outside his door.

Stumbling to his feet, Daniel stood barefoot on the new carpet, frozen in a listening crouch. So he *had* heard a woman earlier. Must have been coming from outside, in the back parking lot maybe. And whatever she'd thought was funny a half-hour ago was certainly not making her happy now.

He fumbled into his boots and grabbed his flashlight and phone. Should he dial 911? No, he'd better go investigate himself first. For all he knew, it could be the two lovebirds—Kate and Lareci—had decided to park near the water to watch the sun set. She probably saw a snake.

But on his way out, he unzipped the hidden compartment of his suitcase and slipped out the 9mm handgun he always carried. If it wasn't Kate and Lareci, he might need it.

The lobby was full-dark now and creepy as hell. Keeping his flashlight off, Daniel crept through the space, setting each foot down carefully to avoid stumbling on a stray fragment of sheetrock. If there was anybody skulking around outside, he sure as hell didn't want to give them the heads-up he was about to catch them.

The windows on the far side of the ballroom glowed with the light from the security lamps illuminating the back parking lot. He could just make out the rapidly fading silhouette of the distant mountains on the opposite shore, still backlit from the sunset. There were no longer any drapes masking the wall of glass, so he would have to approach slowly, carefully, to avoid being seen. Drifting toward one wall, he pressed his shoulder against it, figuring he'd be harder to spot that way.

The second scream nearly had him pissing his pants. It shot through the night so sharply, so close, it almost seemed as if it came from inside his own head. Still six feet away from the windows, he froze, his heart hammering against his ribs. He held his breath, fingering the cell phone in his hand. Maybe he should have called 911 after all.

In the far corner of the parking lot, he spotted a car. No, two cars, side by side, snugged right up beside each other. But he couldn't make out details because their outlines were fuzzy and wavering. Daniel rubbed his eyes. Damn, why had he drank so much beer? He hated this compromise on his senses.

One car was light-colored and smaller than the larger, darker one. And there were silhouettes of people—two, or three he couldn't be sure, sandwiched between. Then a pop sounded, like the launch of a bottle rocket. The heads he'd seen hovering between the vehicles diminished by one. Instinctively, Daniel lifted his cellphone and touched the screen. It flared to life, and he unlocked it, his fingers trembling as he fumbled for the keypad icon.

But when he looked up, there was only an empty parking lot with amber-hued security lights shining down on cracked pavement. He caught himself a second before hitting dial.

Had he really imagined all this? Shit, if this is what alcohol did to a person's brain, it should be deemed as illegal as meth or cocaine. He scrubbed a hand down his face and squinted out into the night. Nothing. The faint glow of the recently set sun still highlighted the crests of the Catskills in the distance.

Marco and Kate left early the next morning. *Crazy* early. Marco couldn't believe she'd talked him into setting the alarm for four thirty a.m. and being on the road before dawn.

"They'll be breezing the two-year-olds," Kate told him. "I know it's early, but it's thrilling to watch. I get a lump in my throat every time I go."

It better be *really* thrilling, Marco thought as he tentatively sipped his too-hot coffee from the to-go cup. He was driving his own car, since he was headed back to the city afterward. As he followed Kate's white Porsche out onto the highway, though, he couldn't deny the fact he was excited. This would be an entirely new experience for him.

He realized, with no small amount of trepidation, that everything—even the most mundane routines in his life—had seemed entirely new since he met Kate. He was falling fast. And although his heart told him he was headed true north, his guts kept screaming *wrong move*.

Perhaps his judgment of his sister's disastrous relationships had been premature, and too harsh. Perhaps, when it came to relationships with the opposite sex, Marco was no smarter than she.

The horizon was beginning to glow as Marco followed Kate's car onto a winding drive off a country lane, about three miles off the highway. *Bardach Farms* was scripted in gold on a shiny, black sign at the entrance. He drove along the nearly quarter-mile driveway as it wound through a thick patch of woods and over a stream before he caught sight of the farm. Then he whistled through his teeth at the panorama opening up before him.

When Kate talked about *my father's farm*, she made it sound like a backyard hobby, except the backyard was located a hundred miles northwest of their Long Island home. If this was the man's hobby, he wondered what he did for a living.

Funny, he still didn't know that. He didn't know anything about Kate's parents at all. Yet, *she* had been to *his* family's home and met immediate as well as extended members of the Lareci tribe. The thought made the coffee in Marco's stomach turn suddenly sour.

There it was, the cold hard fact. He really didn't know Kate Bardach very well at all. Yet, his heart was telling him he had fallen in love with her. He'd been so focused on gathering her into his own family fold, he hadn't taken the time to learn about hers. What kind of environment she'd been raised in. Were her parents even still married? An only child, she'd said. A spoiled-rotten only child.

And maybe one who had no sense of conventional family values. Hell, she'd told him she was a free spirit, enjoying life one moment at a time. What a blind, stupid fool he'd been.

By the time Marco climbed out of his car, his heart felt sore, as though it was infected, or bruised. And the coffee in his stomach had turned to pure acid.

He yanked on the lapels of his light jacket, wishing now he'd grabbed the wool overcoat. Even though it was nearly May, at this hour of the morning, and out in the country, the air was damp and very cool. Kate stood at the entrance to the barn beside huge sliding doors, already open. As he approached, one side of her mouth quirked up and she crossed her arms, leaning against the frame.

"The air here is different, isn't it?" she asked. "Not like the city, and oddly, even different from the Catskills."

Kate's gaze scanned appreciatively up and down his body, one side of those pouty lips quirking. Then she did that slow-motion blink thing again, and he felt the blood rush to his groin. Damn, this woman had cast an evil spell on him, and there wasn't anything he could do to convince his manhood everything wasn't okey-dokey okay.

Marco cleared his throat and changed the subject. "Hey, how's the foot?" He tipped his chin in the direction of her low-heeled boot.

Kate lifted her damaged foot forward. "Much better. Lucky I had these boots—bought them because I fell in love with them, even though they were a size too big. Today, that came in very handy. With an extra sock to pad those stitches, I'm as good as new."

"Good. I'm glad," he said around a yawn. It was just after six a.m., for God's sake. An ungodly hour.

But even though he should still have been half asleep, he'd never felt more alive. Strange new scents flooded his nostrils. Freshly cut grass, the tart tang of morning dew. A woody aroma, like pine. And there was no mistaking the distinctive fragrance of leather—the only one Marco felt familiar with.

Kate unfolded her arms and spun on one chunky boot heel on the concrete aisleway. "Come on. I'll introduce you to our staff."

Staff. A horse farm has *staff*?

Obviously, this was part of the racing industry Marco never considered. Oh, he knew the horses down on the track had to come from *somewhere*. Be housed and trained *somewhere*. He really never gave it much thought beyond that.

Now, he felt like a complete ignoramus. This place was huge. The barn—stretching out from the central entrance for hundreds of feet to his left and right—probably housed fifty horses or more. And was tidier than some people's homes. The concrete floors were swept clean. The pine smell he'd identified emanated from the wood shavings padding each horse's individual cubicle, nearly to their knees.

And Marco hadn't ventured more than twenty feet into the barn when he realized the horses were a lot bigger up close than he'd considered.

"Hey, April baby, how you doing this morning?" Kate walked up to the third cubicle on the right and didn't hesitate a moment before lifting the twisted steel latch and sliding the door open. She stepped inside, sinking into the fluffy, white shavings up to her ankles. A sudden surge of fear clutched in Marco's chest.

This gigantic beast could trample her to death without taking more than a twenty-second break from its breakfast. The horse towered over her, its head the size of two-thirds of her torso. Yet, it seemed peaceable enough, perking its ears forward and closing its eyes when she pulled off her leather glove to scratch behind them. It continued to munch methodically away at the leafy, green hay piled in a slotted bin hanging from the wall.

Huh. Like Cleo's food tower. Only a hell of a lot bigger.

"Dio buono. They look a lot smaller from the stands. Don't they?" he said.

She laughed. "Not to me. When my April prances out onto the track in my signature pink-and-white silks, she's a steel-gray goddess. Nothing gets bigger or better than that."

The clop-clop of hooves on pavement drew their attention to the far end of the aisle. A short, dark-haired man wearing a denim jacket and ball cap was leading another one of the horses out of its cubicle. This one was dark brown and was suited up with a tiny, flat saddle.

"Julio! Cómo estás?" Kate called, sliding the door shut behind her as she stepped away from her horse.

"Miz Bardach. Good morning. Here to see the rabbits run today? Been awhile," the man replied, a brilliant, white smile slashing across his ruddy face. "How is Mr. Bardach?"

"He's doing well. This the Carlington colt you're taking out?"

Marco followed Kate as she strode boldly down the aisle and right up beside the tall, lanky, young horse that looked like he hadn't yet grown into his legs. Or his ears. Like an awkward teenager. Yet still, the beast towered over Kate, so tall he doubted she could see over its back.

"Yes, ma'am. Carlos should be up from the track any minute."

Over the next two hours, Marco learned more about behind-the-scenes horse racing than he'd ever imagined. The staff arrived well before dawn to feed and water the horses and to clean their cubicles—which he learned were called *stalls*. There were six staff members: two resident trainers, three stable hands, and one groom. By the time the first fingers of light curled over the horizon, the horses in training were groomed, saddled, and taken down to the farm's private half-mile track tucked into the valley behind the barn. To be *breezed*.

"We build up their stamina this way, increasing the distance and the speed a little bit every week," Kate explained. "Their bones harden to the stress, and their lung capacity increases. And by the fall of their second year," she winked and snicked her tongue, "we know whether we've got a good one or not."

They'd followed Carlos down to the track after he'd pumped Marco's hand, tipped his hat to the lady, and swung up onto the tall animal's back with the ease of a trapeze artist. The horse—seemingly excited about its upcoming jaunt—jigged and danced in tiny, prancing steps as it made its way down to the gate. An early morning mist hung over the track, obscuring all but the near straightaway.

"Damn," Kate muttered. "We won't be able to see them go along the back side."

"Is that bad?" Marco asked, feeling completely out of his element. The sensation was uncomfortable, but he'd never backed down from a challenge yet. If Kate was this involved with the horses, he would learn.

She tipped her head, lifting her shoulders. "Not really. It's really nice to see them open up when they come out of the second turn." She flashed those impossible blue eyes at him, pursing her lips. Lifting one gloved hand to cup his cheek, she murmured, "I wanted this to be special for you."

When she locked her gaze on his, he felt the flare in his man-parts again. But something else, too. A sensation even more disconcerting. Like a jab to the heart. He took a step back and swiped a hand down his face.

Can't get myself too wrapped up in this woman. She's bound to break my heart.

They leaned on the white, wooden railing as Carlos steered the colt out onto the track. The rider—jockey? Trainer?—began bobbing up and down in the saddle to the beat of the horse's trot, taking him back and forth in a long oval on the near side.

"Carlos is the best. He likes to get them good and warmed up before he lets them go. So they don't risk an injury." Kate's eyes shone with pride and excitement as she watched the horse and rider work up and down the track.

Marco had been to about a dozen races in his life. As a spectator, in the grandstand. Never up close and personal like this. He forgot the damp chill of the morning air as he watched the huge, powerful animal prance by them, chewing on the bit so that foam dripped from the corners of its mouth. Steam began to rise from the horse's neck and hips as a sheen of sweat darkened its chocolate-brown coat. The smell of wet earth rose as its hooves stirred the dirt track.

After a few more minutes, Carlos nodded pointedly at Kate as he made the last swing by them. She slid her phone out of her pocket and opened the stopwatch app. Marco watched as he then gathered the reins in both hands until they formed a taut bridge across the horse's neck.

"Ready, set, go!" she shouted, and they took off down the track.

Kate bounced up and down like an excited child. "Here we go. This is the part that gets my blood pumping and gives me goosebumps all over." She leaned forward over the rail, watching the horse and rider gallop off and disappear into the haze shrouding the far bend in the track.

"Damn the fog," she said again, stomping one foot. Her attention shifted back and forth between her phone and the opaque mist.

Marco lost sight of the horse and rider completely. But you could hear them. No, it was more like *feel* them, the horse's hooves pounding against the track. The shock waves sent a three-beat pulse through the ground under Marco's feet, like the rumble of an oncoming train. No, more like a stuttered heartbeat. The vibration penetrated clear through into his chest. His own heart rate picked up the rhythm, and though he had no idea why, he felt the thrill of anticipation, too.

As the hoofbeats faded to a whisper, Kate's eyes swept the horizon, still heavily cloaked but patched now with the bright glow of the rising sun.

"There," she shouted, pointing to a short length of fence on the far side now visible through the haze. "Bada bump, bada bump, bada bump . . . now!"

As though she had radar trained on the racing animal, it appeared right on cue. Marco caught a fleeting glimpse of the horse, at one with its rider who was hardly visible, molded close to the horse's neck. But after barely three seconds, three strides, they disappeared again.

A tingle started at the base of Marco's spine and slithered its way up to the back of his neck. This was, truly, a beautiful sight. He'd always loved watching the horses run, but never really understood how one could invest thousands of dollars to participate in a sport where chance and luck determined the dividends. Now, he understood. This jolt, the adrenaline high, could easily justify the risk.

Kate was barely contained, bobbing on her toes in excitement. Her eyes sparkled, and she wore a smile he hadn't seen on her before now. Was it just the thrill of the chase? Or, did she really love these horses?

She must. He'd seen excitement, anticipation, ecstasy in those huge, blue eyes. This was something different. Maybe someday, he prayed, she'd wear this glow when she looked at him.

The pounding grew louder, his heart still synced in rhythm. He gripped the top rail with both hands, and Kate clamped one of hers over his. She leaned into him, her soft breasts pressed to his arm. Her breath was warm on his neck; her scent enveloped him, and his loins stirred again.

God, please, let her wear this glow for me.

She pointed to the place off to his left where the white fencing curved out of sight into the fog. "There. Here they come," she whispered.

Seconds later, horse and rider appeared like ghosts, the mist swirling away and mingling with a cloud of dust they left behind. Carlos crouched even lower now, throwing his hands forward toward the horse's ears. Within seconds, they thundered past, and an electric thrill shot through Marco.

Kate checked the stopwatch and her mouth curved downward. "Not too bad for a colt," she muttered.

Marco studied her. "You mean for a young horse? They get stronger and faster with age, right?"

As she slid her phone back into her purse, she lifted one shoulder. "They do. And this time wouldn't be bad for a two-year-old filly. But a colt's got a lot higher goal to reach."

At the risk of sounding ignorant, Marco said, "Wait. The colts run faster than the fillies?"

Kate nodded. "Some people think so. Sexism exists even in the equine world, I guess." She chuckled and linked her arm with his as they headed back up the grassy hill toward the barn. Sighing wistfully, she said, "Come on. Let's go look at my new colt. At least I have two more mares bred this year. Still two more chances for a filly."

Marco halted and stared down at her. "Wait, Kate, I'm confused. You're disappointed this baby is a colt, but they run faster. I know nothing about the ins and outs of horse racing, but—"

"I told you yesterday. Colts have a limited shelf life."

SEVENTEEN

"Shelf life?" Marco repeated, his dark brows drawing together. "What does that mean?"

Kate sighed. This was the part of racing she disliked—the realities. Explaining the details to people outside the industry made thoroughbred breeders sound callous, even cruel. But it was a business, like any other. Surely, Marco would understand.

"A breeder can own about as many broodmares as they want. They're an asset. Once their racing career is over—even if they didn't run all that well—there's always the potential breeding them to the right stallion could produce the next Triple Crown Winner. But colts turn into stallions. You can only own so many of those."

"Why?" he asked.

Kate sighed and crossed her arms over her chest as they walked. "Colts don't play nice with other horses. They can get mean, dangerous, even. A stallion has only one thing on his mind, and that's breeding. Keeping one means special quarters, solitary turnouts, and staff who know how to handle them without getting themselves killed."

They'd reached the crest of the hill, and the long barn stood to their right. Kate touched Marco's elbow and steered him left.

He resisted. "I thought I was going to get to see your baby colt?" he said, sounding indignant. "Surely, they can't be dangerous when they're babies."

"They're not, silly. But the breeding barn is over there." She pointed to a smaller, shedrow-type barn barely visible in the fog.

Kate led Marco up to peer through the vertical steel bars lining the stall's upper edge. The mare, bits of wood shavings stuck to her shiny red coat, stood with her head in the corner, dozing. Her gangly colt swayed on splayed legs beside her, still a bit unsteady. But the way he was bumping his head against her udder, it appeared his appetite was strong.

"My father gave me Priscilla when she was still wet from the womb. She was my Preakness winner two years ago. She's five now, and this is her second foal." Kate couldn't hide her pride. "She was the first one Father let me manage all on my own. The barn's first big win in three years."

Marco wrapped his fingers around the bars, and Kate noticed how the smile on his face made him look younger, his angled features softer.

"He's so damn cute. But big!" he said. "I didn't realize they were born this big. Poor Mama."

Kate chuckled. "He's actually one of the smaller colts we've had. But his legs are straight, strong. He'll grow fast." She sighed, knowing he would grow *too* fast, race a couple years, and then his career would be over.

Marco was studying her with a perplexed expression. "Why do you sound sad? This is a beautiful, brand-new life you helped create. How can that be a disappointment? So he's a colt, not a filly. So what?"

She absently picked a fleck of shaving off her trouser leg. "Because in a couple of years, unless he turns out to be the next Affirmed, I'll have to figure out how to get rid of him."

Marco dropped his hands to his sides and stepped back, staring at her. "Get rid of him. What do you mean, get rid of him? How?"

The horrified tone in his voice told Kate that, businessman or not, Marco likely would not understand how the racing industry worked. Or accept it.

"It's a business, Marco, like any other. With assets and liabilities. If a colt doesn't blow them away at the track, he's got no future as a stallion. So we geld them and send them to auction."

Marco didn't know a lot about horses, but he did know what a gelding was. There'd been a few in one of the races he'd seen, and he'd looked up the term on his phone. An equine eunuch. The very thought made his balls shrivel.

Anger flared in his chest. "You mean to tell me this precious little boy horse has nothing to look forward to but getting his balls cut off after running his heart out for you? And then being auctioned off like a . . . a slave?" His fingers curled into fists at his sides.

She was avoiding his gaze now, pulling a compact out of her purse. She peered into the mirror and tilted her head, examining her makeup in the morning light. "Afraid so." She snapped the compact shut and dropped it into her purse. "Now maybe you understand why I prefer fillies to colts."

As Marco drove back to the city, his mind chewed the morning's events over and over. He'd ridden an emotional roller coaster today. First, awe and wonder at the gorgeous and efficiently run farm Kate's family owned. Then, the exhilaration of watching those majestic creatures do what they were bred for and seemed to love—run like the wind. His heart squeezed, remembering the soft, round eyes on the baby horse, brand new and the image of pure innocence.

But his stomach churned every time he thought of the cold, callous way Kate had talked about the baby's probable fate. He was right—he didn't know this woman very well at all. This was a side of her he didn't like very much. Not very much at all.

Not that Marco was an animal activist or a vegetarian. He tried not to think about where the veal for his parmesan came from. He also savored a good steak now and again, medium rare.

But this somehow seemed wrong. Cattle were bred and raised for food. Not used for entertainment, instruments for gambling, and monetary gains. Chattel. Used, and then tossed aside like yesterday's old news. Like a casino's deck of cards destroyed when it showed only slight signs of wear.

Is that how Kate views the things she values in her life? Temporary playthings to be discarded when they're no longer useful to her? No longer capable of lending the thrill or providing her enough pleasure?

As he maneuvered along the West Side highway in heavy afternoon traffic, Marco's mood darkened from gray to black. When his cellphone rang through his Bluetooth system, he glanced at the screen and muttered a curse. The last person he wanted to talk to right now was Boy Wonder.

"Lareci here," he barked after connecting. "What's the problem, Daniel?"

"The problem," Daniel began, "has apparently resolved itself now. But you need to check on the Wi-Fi and Satellite connections here. They both went down about seven o'clock last night." Daniel's tone was sullen.

Oh, poor boy-toy. And on his first night staying at the Shelby. Marco was almost sorry he hadn't planned the outage deliberately.

Wonder what Danny boy did with his time while I was up the road making passionate love to his boss?

There it was again. That familiar jealous itch, like seltzer in his veins.

"Lareci, you there?" Irritation pitched Daniel's voice a notch higher than his normal boyish tone.

"I'll make some calls and check into it. Everything else on track?" Marco grumbled.

A pause. Then, "We may have had some locals tailgating in your parking lot last night. I heard laughter, and I thought I saw—" He broke off, and Marco heard Kate's voice in the background. "Never mind. It was no big deal. I surprised them at the ballroom window with a flashlight and scared them off. Kate's here. Gotta run."

The call disconnected, and the itch in Marco's veins turned into pinpricks of pain congealing around his heart. The truths he'd learned this morning about his lady love closed over him like a suffocating blanket.

No matter how hard his heart argued in her favor, his analytical mind continued to shove undeniable facts in his face. Love wasn't a word a woman like Kate could even begin to understand. No doubt, his body couldn't resist her. But he needed to remember—for her, it was sex, nothing more. There was no making love with Kate Bardach. Nothing more meaningful or longer lasting than sex.

Kate was pleased to detect the pungent odor of fresh paint as she stepped over the threshold of the hotel. The doors were fixed wide open, no doubt to dispel the fumes. The crew must be moving faster than she'd realized. She wondered if the bathroom fixtures had arrived.

"Hey, Jeremy," she called to the foreman, who was opening a five-gallon bucket of paint with a metal tool. "I assume your guys got over their willies about this place?"

He nodded and replied with a grunt, but didn't smile.

Daniel was on the phone but disconnected quickly after she walked in.

"Good morning, boss lady." He glanced at his watch. "Or, should I say, good afternoon?"

Kate shot him a threatening glance and felt her temper coil, but chose not to engage him. She'd worked very well with Daniel before this job. Was it her relationship with Marco? Or this place? It seemed they'd all been on edge since they started here.

"How was your first night in the apartment? Comfortable?" she asked, struggling to keep her tone light.

Daniel scoffed. "If you consider no television or Internet connection a nice way to spend the evening."

She tilted her head. "What happened?"

"No clue. I just got off the phone with Lareci. He *says* he's on it. Hope he is before the day's out, or I'll be headed back to the hotel in Liberty." Daniel shoved his phone into the back pocket of his crisply pressed jeans and faced her with his hands on his hips. "And you? Have a pleasant evening?" His tone oozed sarcasm.

Now her temper spiked. "That, dear boy, would be none of your goddamned business."

Daniel's head rocked back as if she'd slapped him, but he didn't respond. Fortunately, the crunching of wheels on the driveway

190

interrupted them. Kate turned to see James' battered Ford pull up and park.

"Mornin', Miss Bardach. Daniel." The old man touched the brim of his ball cap as he climbed out and approached the open doorway. He nodded toward Kate's foot. "Your foot feelin' some better?"

"It is, thanks." No fancy duds today, Kate noticed. He was back in his baggy, denim overalls, a faded, plaid shirt underneath. Dried brown clumps—she hoped was mud—patched his yellow work boots.

"Saw you were all here. I was stoppin' by to take a peek," he said. "Think there's a chance I could get a tour? I haven't been inside this place since I was a young fella."

Daniel glanced at Kate, whose gaze drifted down to James' boots briefly before saying, "Sure. The floors aren't in yet, and they're just starting to paint. But I'm sure Daniel wouldn't mind taking you through."

The glare Daniel fixed on her told Kate he definitely minded.

Tough shit. It's my project, and I'm the boss. You, my boy, are merely an employee.

She didn't like feeling this way, like a bitch on steroids ready to explode at any moment. Probably because she got up so early. Because of the friction with Marco.

Better take it outside and cool down some.

Kate set her briefcase on the reception counter as Daniel handed James a hard hat. "While you boys do that, I think I'm going to check out the waterfront."

The morning chill had dissipated quickly, and even up here in the mountains, the sun was warming the air to a balmy, spring day. Kate shrugged off her jacket and tossed it into her car, then made her way to the far side of the parking lot. Edged with a low stone wall, the raised pavement snugged right up to the water's edge. She peered over to see the rocky shore disappear into the greenish water at an alarmingly steep angle.

She suppressed an involuntary shudder.

At the north end of the lot, an opening in the wall revealed a concrete pad leading down into the water. A boat ramp. Kate strolled in that direction, raising her face to the sun and breathing deeply. It was peaceful up here. So very different from the life she'd become accustomed to in the city. But a serenely welcome change. One she was beginning to crave more and more often.

What was happening with her lately? Could she finally—after hitting the ripe old age of thirty two—be ready to give up her roaring twenties?

Carefully, she slipped off her low-heeled boots. She was glad she'd worn trousers today and not her customary dress or skirt. She straddled the large, flat boulder at the wall's end.

This was as close to a natural body of water as she dared get after her childhood incident. Yet, being so close, perched mere few feet above the softly lapping waves, was a punch in the solar plexus. A thrill, like taking a dare. Fear mingled with a sense of power and control. Closing her eyes, she leaned back on her hands. The smooth, stone surface felt warm and rough under her palms.

When the vision hit, it overtook her with such swift force, she had no chance to block it. Like a movie screen opening up behind her eyes, she was watching a scene. Here, but not now. Not on a balmy, spring afternoon, but at night.

And instead of relaxed pleasure, sudden terror clamped around her heart.

Pictures, still shots, flashed in stuttered frames in her brain. Dark, cold. Anticipation.

Hmm, can't wait to get back to the room.

Arousal, something tickling her nose as strong arms enveloped her body.

My fur. I love my fox coat, Bart. You're so good to me.

When those words sounded in her brain, Kate gasped and opened her eyes. With a sickening dread, she knew these thoughts were not her own. These were echoes of the past. Residual memories. *Residual hauntings.*

Of her Aunt Leah.

No, must be my imagination running away with me. I know she's been here. My mind is playing tricks.

I'm tired. Early morning. Marco . . . too many questions. Judgments.

But before she could complete another coherent thought, it hit again. This time, having her eyes open made no difference. It was as though she'd gone blind. The only sight she had was of events that had occurred in the same place, but in a different time.

In October of 1964.

She could smell him. A foreign, male scent, tinged with smoke of some kind. Pipe? Cigar? Kate had never dated a smoker—was completely turned off by it—so she couldn't tell. But now it didn't seem so bad. Almost . . . familiar.

He tastes like brandy. Yes, they'd had brandy as their nightcap before they left the racetrack bar. And oh, the thrill of his massive body against her own. She feels his arousal, hard and huge, even through the thick fur wrapped around her. He squeezes her buttocks, pulls her hard against him. But then he pinches—too hard—and she squeaks.

"Ouch, you bastard," she snips, pushing him away.

But then there are headlights, blinding them. A car pulling in, too close. What the hell is the carhop thinking? This is her brand new car. Her beautiful Mustang.

The scene in Kate's mind flickered then, like poor reception on cable when a storm comes in. A quick movement. The man she was holding turning away, pushing her behind him, shielding her. Men, two of them, dressed in black. Coming at them, fast.

Static.

Another image, a strange, popping sound, and then . . . terrible pain in her chest, making her knees go weak.

Oh, no. God, no please. Bart's been shot. They shot my Bart.

Static. White noise. Kate struggled to bring her consciousness back to the present, back to her own mind.

It was only the firm grasp on her upper arm that brought her around. Blinking, she looked up, dazed and confused. Daniel was holding on with not one, but both hands gripping her arm. Too tight.

Ouch.

"Wha-what's happening?" she managed, reading the alarm on her architect's face and not understanding its reason. How had she gotten here? Where was she?

Who was she?

"What's wrong with you, Kate? For Christ's sake, you almost fell in," Daniel barked.

As though she'd woken from a deep sleep, it took Kate a moment to realize not only Daniel, but also James was standing over her. She was still seated on the rock near the boat ramp, but she'd apparently slumped forward, and her feet had slipped off the pavement. Her socks, the bandage on her foot, and her pant cuffs were soaked with numbingly cold water.

Daniel was right. She'd passed out and nearly fallen in.

To them, of course, that's exactly what it must have looked like—like she'd fainted, or fallen asleep. She knew differently, and the thought sent icy fingers of fear to crawl across her back. But she needed to pull it together, and fast. She never shared details about her visions with her staff. Daniel was too new to the company to know she had them at all.

Scrambling to her feet, she yanked her arm free from Daniel's grasp. "I'm fine. I dozed off. We got up pretty early this morning, and I'm not accustomed to that." She rubbed her arm where his fingers, she knew, would leave a bruise on her pale skin. How would she explain it to Marco? "And ouch, Daniel. Did you feel the need to be so rough? Why didn't you just wake me?"

His blue eyes narrowed and turned to flint. "I called your name a half-dozen times as we came running over here, Kate," he hissed through clenched teeth. "We both thought something had happened to you."

Daniel turned on his heel and stormed away toward the hotel, muttering something inaudible. But James remained. He stood, looking down at her, holding his cap against his chest, wearing an oddly perplexed expression. The way he was studying her face sent the hot flush of embarrassment to her cheeks. She looked after the architect stomping away.

"I'm sorry. Daniel is young and fairly new to my team. Apparently, he can be a bit of a hothead. I'll have to speak with him about his temper."

But when she looked at the old man again, he was staring past her, down at the water's edge, where the boat ramp and the rock wall met. His eyes, wide with alarm, made Kate think he saw a snake. Another jolt of fear surged.

She stepped away and turned, following his gaze. At first, she saw nothing. Only the shallow reeds swaying with the water's movement. But she knew—from years of vacationing on the lake's shores—how the lake creatures could make themselves just about invisible.

"What is it, James? A snake?" she whispered.

Slowly, he began shaking his head, but he'd gone pale under his tanned, leathery skin. Whatever he saw obviously scared this man to death. Kate watched as he replaced the cap on his head and slowly stepped down onto the boat ramp. Water swirled nearly to his ankles, causing the soil on his boots to dissolve around them in a dusky cloud. He braced one hand on the rocks, and with the other, reached down among the weeds and greenish algae floating on the surface.

When he stood, he held a rectangular piece of what looked like plastic in his hand. It was translucent, and it was red.

"What the hell is that?" Kate asked.

And why the hell do you look like you've seen a ghost?

James was still shaking his head, almost imperceptibly. She wondered how old this man was, and if maybe he suffered from bouts of senility. Or the palsy, because his hands shook violently as he turned the thing over and over. She watched him in silence, unsure of how to react. God knows, if he were senile, she didn't want to embarrass him.

But when he raised his watery eyes to hers, they held no sign of confusion. There was pain and sharpness of understanding as he searched her face.

"What is it, James? It looks like just an old piece of plastic. Maybe part of a child's beach toy—"

"You look exactly like her, you know. Doppelgänger. Dead ringer." His voice was low and rumbling, almost ominous.

Cold washed over Kate like the icy Atlantic wave that had dragged her under all those years ago. She blinked, never taking her eyes off his, but she felt suddenly very dizzy. She swayed slightly, and he reached out to steady her, gently grasping her elbow.

"I think we should have a talk, Miss Bardach. There's somethin' I need to tell you."

Kate hesitated when James insisted she go with him in his truck for their talk.

"What I have to tell you, Miss Bardach, is some scary, serious business. I ain't talked about it to nobody since that night. And that was fifty years ago."

She went inside to tell Daniel she'd be gone a half hour or so. When she came out, James was holding the truck door open for her, his hand extended to help her in.

"Where are we going?" she asked, her nerves still jittery and stretched taut from her vision. And now, this.

Marco had mentioned something about the old guy having worked here in the sixties. Was it possible he knew something about what happened to her aunt?

"I'd like to take you back to my farm, Ma'am. Remember the high knoll in the pasture where the view is so pretty? I feel safe there. The closest I'll probably ever get to heaven. It's about the only place I've felt safe after what I saw that night."

A shudder ran through Kate like an electric shock.

"Okay," she answered slowly.

As they drove in silence around the lake and up the winding road leading to James' farm, Kate found herself wishing Marco were there. She had the feeling what she was about to hear was a key in the mystery about what happened here all those years ago.

Or maybe not. Still, she yearned for the warm comfort of Marco by her side.

James navigated the turn onto the rutted path through his pasture and shifted the truck into low as they climbed the steep hill. Spring had blossomed the farm into an Eden, with lush grasses waving in the gentle breeze. Wildflowers bobbed their purple and yellow heads along the rock wall boundary. The surrounding forest—with its stately old oaks and maples—wore their full, green summer coats already.

As they crested the hill, Kate spotted a fuzzy head popping up on the other side of the rock wall. A shaggy pony, gray and white with a bushy forelock nearly covering its eyes, stared at them as they approached.

"You've got a pony, James. I didn't see it the last time I was here," Kate said, smiling. Her memory flashed to her own first horse, a fat, palomino pony she'd named Dusty. A twinge of nostalgia ached in her chest.

His mouth quirked into a crooked smile. "Bought Gracie for my granddaughter. Her grandma and me got it for her fifth birthday." He slowed the truck to a halt and turned off the engine. "This is sort of her retirement home, I guess. My granddaughter's grown now, married, and lives in California." Sadness tainted his words.

"Cute. My father keeps some ponies out in the pasture where the yearlings run," Kate said. "Helps keep them company, calms them, after we wean them."

James bobbed his head, still staring at the pony that continued to chew on the mouthful of tall grass hanging from its mouth. "I feel kinda sorry for Gracie. Figure she probably gets lonely sometimes, too. But there's no way I could move her. Too old. It would probably kill her." He shifted in his seat to face her. "What do you do with them racehorses once they retire?"

Kate avoided his gaze. "The mares we keep. We sell the colts if they're stud material. But the geldings . . . ." She'd explained this once already today, and the realization of cold, hard facts—and Marco's reaction—hadn't exactly made her proud.

"Well, I've got a hundred acres here, with nobody eatin' on 'em but old Gracie. If you ever need a place to keep'em, retire'em, I'm sure Gracie would love the company."

She smiled. "That's really nice of you. I might take you up on your offer. In fact, I most definitely will."

The silence stretched out for a long moment, and Kate sensed the tension spiraling between them.

"Why did you really bring me here, James? Not only to offer your pastures for my geldings."

He shook his head and his face sobered. He began wringing his weathered hands together.

"Like I told you, Miss Bardach. You look just like a woman I seen there, at the Redman, fifty years ago. It's a story I feel like you need to know." He scrutinized her face, knitting his brow. "Not likely I'd remember some random patron of the hotel. But you're a dead ringer for her. And after what I saw happen, I'll never forget her face as long as I live."

EIGHTEEN

Marco spent a miserable afternoon trying to catch up on work. He'd let everything slip over the past few weeks. His clients had taken a back seat while he spent entirely too much time on his own investment interest at the Shelby. Reality crashed down over him like a lead blanket.

If he didn't keep his clients happy, he risked losing everything. It was high time he got his mind back where it belonged.

What made him even angrier was the fact he knew most of his distraction was because of Kate. His obsession with her, his ridiculous fantasy that she was *the one*. The thought spiked his temper and made him furious with himself. He was usually much more logical, more controlled than that.

He'd been using his head, all right. Just not the right one.

He sat in his home office, three monitors glaring at him like biased jurors. The center screen displayed the goings-on at the Stock Exchange, numbers and letters scrolling in an endless stream. On the left, an Excel spreadsheet listed his clients and their holdings. On the right, the Nasdaq Investment Calculator. And Marco had never found it so hard to concentrate on numbers in his entire life.

He was struggling so to stay focused that when Cleo jumped into his lap, he nearly fell off his chair. She'd appeared out of nowhere and wasn't usually a lap kitty.

"Hey, Queen of the Nile, what's your problem? Your kibble tower empty again?" he crooned, stroking the cat's sleek, spotted coat absently as he returned his attention to the screens. But Cleo was having none of it. When bumping her head under his chin didn't elicit a response, she sunk the claws of both front feet through his trousers and into his thighs.

He started and cringed, but was careful not to knock her off. "All right, all right," he growled. Wrapping his hands around her middle, he gently lowered her to the floor and rose. "Let's see what your problem is this time. Dirty litter box? Water a little funky?"

But he checked all three, and nothing seemed amiss. He'd gotten home a little after noon and taken care of all her needs then. That was only three or four hours ago. Yet, Cleo continued to weave her body in and out of his ankles and had begun an ear-splitting symphony of meows that sounded more like yowls.

"What is your problem, Cleo? Did you miss me so much?" Marco squatted and spoke to the cat, his hands lifted in question. He'd never seen her this agitated before. Was she sick? He checked the clock on the kitchen wall. After five already. If a trip to the vet was warranted, it would have to be the emergency clinic.

He stood and reached for the fridge door. "How about some cream? Nice, fresh cream always seems to soothe you." Retrieving her china bowl from the window ledge, he'd begun to pour the thick, white liquid. The cat's sudden snarl caused him to slosh cream all over the counter.

When he looked down, Cleo's back was hunched high, and her spotted hair was standing on end. She was staring at his door, her amber eyes were huge and round, and a threatening growl rumbled from her throat. Marco followed her gaze, half expecting to see a rattling door handle. But there was nothing. A glance to the keypad on his security system told him it was set and armed.

Perhaps there was someone lurking outside his door. Cats could sense things like that. But how could they have gotten past lobby security? He hadn't buzzed anyone through.

He jumped when Cleo screeched again and bolted, scrambling around the corner into his office. Seconds later, he heard a crash and his heart sank.

Cazzo. Which one of my monitors just met its demise?

Scraping his fingers through his hair, he set down the cream carton, threw some paper towels over the mess, and headed off to survey the damage. He had nearly reached his office door when a faint movement in his peripheral vision caused him to freeze in place.

His front door, painted white on the inside, appeared to be *wet.*

Marco blinked hard and squinted. Yes, there was water running in rivulets down the surface, gathering in an ever-increasing pool at its base. He watched as the beige area rug inside the threshold darkened to light brown as it absorbed the flow.

What the hell? Was there a leak upstairs?

He reached for his phone, still lying on the coffee table where he'd left it.

Got to call the super and see what the hell is going on here.

Several possible scenarios flashed though his mind. A burst pipe? A filling bathtub, forgotten?

His fingers had curled around the phone when another movement made him look up. The phone dropped to the glass tabletop with a clatter. It was Kate.

She was standing inside the doorway, wearing a voluminous, white fur coat enveloping her from chin to ankles.

Marco's heart seized in his chest, shock and disbelief striking him temporarily dumb. How had she gotten in? And why the hell was she wearing that coat?

He stared at her, realizing with growing horror that he could still see the door handle, the peephole, and his security keypad. All items *behind her.*

He was looking at them *through her.*

A wave of nausea rushed him as fear turned his blood to ice. *Was* this his Kate? Had something happened to her, and in passing, she was coming to say goodbye?

He swallowed hard against the bile rising in his throat and struggled to speak. "K-Kate?"

The wavering image didn't respond, just continued to fix him with an eerie, blue stare. It was then Marco noticed a dark patch had appeared on the front of the coat. It crept outward in an ever-widening circle. A growing, creeping splotch of red.

Blood. Within seconds, the liquid began trickling down the front of the white fur. The entire pelt itself was wet, as if she'd run through a torrential downpour. He watched in horror as water and blood dripped in sickening *thwops* onto the carpet beneath.

Marco stumbled backward, grabbing for a chair to keep from hitting the floor. He could barely hear over the whooshing of blood in his ears, and a wave of dizziness made sparkles cloud his vision. He'd never fainted in his life, but he had a feeling that was about to change.

He plopped heavily into the chair, never taking his eyes off the vision on his threshold. *Something's happened to Kate* rolled through his mind in waves, over and over in a horrifying mantra. Until the woman opened her mouth and spoke two words.

Find me.

They echoed, more inside his brain than in the room. The voice sounded muffled and far away. Desperate, yet demanding.

And exactly like Kate's.

Then, as suddenly as she had appeared, her image wavered, flickered, and faded from view. Marco sat blinking, breath heaving in his chest, and trembling all over. Terror boiled bile into his throat. Thank God for the trash can easily within reach inside his office door. He scrambled to grab it, dropped to his knees, and vomited convulsively.

Something's happened to Kate.

Wiping his mouth on his sleeve, he staggered toward the coffee table for his phone. As his hand hovered inches above the device, it suddenly buzzed and quivered against the glass. A guttural scream broke from his throat and he jumped back.

But the phone was simply ringing, silently. He'd left it on vibrate.

He snatched it up, relief swelling his heart when he saw the caller ID. It was Kate.

"Kate. Dio buono. Are you okay?" His voice was gruff, panicked, broken.

And he knew immediately, she was not okay. He heard sobs choking her before she could manage an answer.

"What's happened, Baby? Where are you?" he sputtered, emotion clogging his throat.

"Marco. She's down there. The car. James told me what he saw."

It was nearly ten p.m. before the limo finally arrived. Marco had called a half-dozen companies before he found one out of Monticello willing to send a car to pick up Kate and James from Loch Sheldrake and drive them to Manhattan—immediately. The price had shocked him, but it didn't matter. He knew there was no way he could drive. From the way she sounded, Kate wasn't in any condition, either. He doubted the old man's truck would even make it that far.

He'd paced while he waited, still pondering the mystery of what he'd seen. Upon closer examination, his front door was perfectly dry, and the puddle of water and blood he'd witnessed pooling on his floor was gone.

Was he losing his mind? He already knew his obsession with Kate wasn't healthy. The stress of the past few weeks—the emotional roller coaster ride he'd been on—was it costing him his sanity?

No. Although the puddle was gone, when he stepped on the area rug inside his door, he felt cool wetness seeping into his white socks. The entire edge remained wet, though thankfully, it appeared, only with water.

He buzzed them in, and the minute Kate came through the door, she fell into his arms. He buried his face in her hair, breathing in her scent and silently thanking God she was alive. They stood that way for a long moment, holding on. Marco wasn't sure what he was about to hear, but he knew whatever it was had shattered the ice armor Kate Bardach normally wore and sent her spiraling downward.

He was glad to be there to catch her.

When he finally looked up, he saw James standing on the threshold, wringing his ball cap in his gnarled hands. He looked embarrassed, and very nervous, his eyes darting from one side to the other. Completely out of his element.

"Come in, James, come in." Marco closed and locked the door behind him and motioned for him to take a seat in the living room. Without taking his arm from around Kate's shoulders, he led her to the sofa and sat close beside her.

"Can I get either of you anything? I know it's been a long drive," Marco began.

Kate was shaking her head. "We asked the driver to pull in at the last rest area on the Palisades Parkway. I'm fine."

James shook his head in agreement. "Nothin' for me right now."

Marco drew in a deep breath and blew it out. "Well, if neither of you mind, I think I'll pour myself a drink. Something tells me I'm going to need it."

He poured his partner's favorite Russian vodka over ice in a tumbler and rejoined them in the living room. After taking a long sip, he savored the burn as it made its way down his throat.

"Okay, so what's this all about?" he asked.

Kate cleared her throat and dug a wad of tissues out of her purse, one that looked like she'd been using them for awhile. "It seems James here worked at the Redman . . . the Shelby. Whatever. He parked cars for them back in the sixties."

Marco's gaze flashed back and forth between Kate and James, who was staring at the ball cap still clutched in both hands. When thirty seconds passed and neither said anything more, Marco's patience ebbed.

"Yeah, I think you mentioned that, James. What does this have to do with Kate? With my hotel?"

"It has to do with my Aunt Leah, Marco. James saw it happen." Kate's voice cracked at the last words, and she pressed the tissues to her mouth. Her distress doused Marco's irritation like ice-water on embers.

He took a deep breath. "Tell me. What did you see?"

The old man started at the beginning, describing what his job was, and how he'd been there when Leah and her new husband had checked in that day.

"I parked their car," James said. "And I couldn't help but notice the lady. She was the most beautiful girl I'd ever seen. Long, dark hair. Big, blue eyes. And built like—" He broke off and shifted uneasily in his seat. "She was gorgeous. Not a face you forget too easy." He hesitated and looked at Kate. "She was Miss Bardach's double. When I first saw you, Ma'am, that night at the Redman, I thought I was lookin' at a ghost."

Tell me about it, Marco thought. An eerie chill washed over him. Kate had said she looked just like her aunt. He took another sip of his vodka and swallowed. "Go on."

"Well, they was honeymoonin', you know. Checked into one of them suites, and nobody saw them for four or five hours. Then they come out and ask us to bring up the car. A beauty, it was. Brand-spankin' new Mustang. Fastback. The thing was sweet."

Impatience bubbled in Marco's veins again, and he nodded quickly. "Okay, fine. Nice car. Then what happened?"

James drew in a deep breath and raised his eyebrows. "They went out for awhile. Long time. Nearly midnight by the time they come back in. Raymond and me was gettin' ready to shut down. We was out behind the building, smokin' in our secret spot. The man—a big, swarthy guy puffin' on a cigar—parks the car himself. Then he gets out and comes around to open her door.

"They started makin' out up there on the side of the car, you know. We thought they was gonna—" He cleared his throat and slid a glance toward Kate. "Sorry, ma'am. But they was. Then all of a sudden, this other car pulls in. A big, black Cadillac. It pulls right up beside 'em, close, and screeches to a stop."

Marco drained his vodka glass, the ice tinkling as he set it down on the table. He felt Kate trembling beside him, and looked up to see tears streaming freely down her face. But her eyes were fixed on James. He laid his hand on her knee and squeezed.

"What happened then?" Marco asked in a low rumble. Although he had a feeling he already knew.

"Two guys jump out of the Caddy. One fists his hand in Cigar's coat, and there's this flash of light and a loud pop. It echoes out over the water. I figure they had one of them silencer things on a gun. Shot him point blank."

Marco slumped against the back of the couch, staring at the old man. James had witnessed a hit. Most likely a mob hit.

"What about the lady?" he asked gruffly.

The old man dropped his cap into his lap and swiped his hands down over his face, as though trying to erase the picture from his mind. "They got her, too," he said weakly. "They popped the lady, too. Threw her in the back seat like a furry sack of feed. Then dumped Cigar in the front."

Kate let out a strangled sob, and Marco wrapped his arms around her and crooned, "It's okay, Baby. We have to hear this. This is what you want to know, right? Your family needs to know. What happened to Leah's body." He kissed her hair and smoothed the back of his hand down her cheek.

After a long moment, he turned back to James. "What did they do with the car?"

"Well, me and Raymond, we're horrified when the Caddy starts pullin' away. I'm thinkin', *Great. They're gonna just leave 'em like that. Two dead bodies in a baby-blue Pony in my parkin' lot.* Well, not *my* parkin' lot, but the one I'm responsible for." He glanced at Kate again. "Sorry, ma'am. But I was only a kid."

Kate blew her nose, then said, "It's okay, James. Go on. Finish telling it."

"They didn't leave 'em. The one guy gets into the Mustang and drives it over to the boat ramp."

Marco didn't have to hear any more. He already knew how this story ended. But they'd come this far in the tale. He had to be sure. If he was going to do anything at all to try to help Kate find her aunt's remains, he had to be sure.

James had paused and leaned forward in his chair, elbows propped on his knees. His eyes were intent on Kate's face. "Are you sure you want me to tell this part again, Miss Bardach?"

Another sob wracked Kate's body, and it might as well have been a sword through Marco's heart. He wrapped his arms around her again and rocked her, eyeing the old man over her shoulder. "That's enough, James. We get it. The car's in the Loch. Along with Kate's aunt."

But Kate placed both hands on Marco's chest and pushed him away, her gaze desperate on his. "No, Marco. You have to know it all. This explains why my aunt's spirit won't be free until we find her. You have to know the whole thing."

He studied her face, anguish and horror written all over it. Leah got shot and then dumped in a bottomless lake. In her brand new car. On her honeymoon, no less. How much worse could it get?

"Please," Kate pleaded. "I've already heard it. You need to hear it, too." She rested her head on his shoulder and muttered, "Go on, James. It's okay."

James stared at some unseen spot in the distance, as though he wasn't truly seeing either of them or anything in the room where they sat. His mind had traveled back fifty years and a hundred miles north. To the fateful night in the parking lot of Redman's Resort.

"Me and Raymond, well, we ran over to the boat ramp after the Caddy screeched away. We felt so helpless, but there was no way of stoppin' it. They'd put her in drive and she was driftin' down into the water at a pretty good clip. By the time we got to the ramp, the front end of the car was already under water. They'd left the driver's door ajar, so she was fillin' up fast. That's when we realized the lady wasn't dead. Not yet, anyway. She wasn't dead."

The old man's voice broke as he covered his face with both hands. "We saw her. She popped up from the back seat, screamin'. She saw us both standin' there, but there was nothin' we could do. We ran down into the water, and Raymond and me both grabbed the bumper. But the suction of the sinking car was too strong. Within four or five seconds, she was gone."

Marco's heart stilled in his chest and felt icy, as though it had frozen solid.

Oh, my God. She didn't die from the gunshot. Leah drowned. Just like Kate almost did.

James uncovered his face, beet red now and wet with tears. He looked up and whispered, "The last thing we saw was her hands. Those bloody fingers, clawin' at the glass. It's a sight that's haunted me my whole life."

Marco felt Kate go stiff beside him, and she buried her face against his chest. His breath caught, and he quickly crossed himself. Death from a gunshot wound is bad enough, but this was beyond someone's worst nightmare.

How much worse could it get? *That* much worse.

Dio buono. No wonder Leah's spirit couldn't rest. No wonder she was insisting somebody find her, release her from the purgatory she'd been sentenced to.

Struggling to keep his own voice level, Marco asked, "And you never reported what happened? What you saw?"

But Marco already knew the answer. This was clearly a mob hit. If he'd revealed himself as an eye witness, James wouldn't be sitting here right now. He'd have been dead, disappeared himself, a long time ago.

James' shoulders lifted and dropped as he swiped his eyes with two roughened hands. "We were scared to. Never said a word to anybody. Me and Raymond made a pact. To protect ourselves and our families." He coughed and swallowed hard, his Adam's apple bobbing in his throat. "And if you folks do decide to try to locate that car, or them bodies, don't expect me to repeat this story again. I'll swear I knew nothin' about it. I never saw nothin'."

Marco nodded solemnly, completely understanding the man's fear, even after all these years. Although his family had nothing to do with the Mafia, Marco knew enough about them to know the dirty organization was still very much alive. They were still running their games in several big cities around the country.

Shoulders sagging, James seemed somehow smaller. Shrunken, as though telling the tale again, twice in one day after so many years of sworn silence, had nearly drained the life from him. Raising bloodshot eyes to Marco, he murmured, "If you wouldn't mind, Mr. Lareci, I'll take that drink now. Before I get back on the road for home."

NINETEEN

Marco blinked, shocked. "There's no way you're going home tonight. We'll arrange for a limo in the morning—"

Kate laid a hand on Marco's arm, her eyes pleading. "James made it clear before we left Loch Sheldrake, Marco. He wants to go home tonight. The limo driver is waiting."

"Please, Mr. Lareci. I don't feel comfortable in the city. God knows, I've avoided it like the plague ever since. I've been so afraid someone would remember. Would recognize me."

Marco stood and straightened his shoulders. "James, everyone who had anything to do with what you witnessed is long dead by now. But to ease your mind, I will alert the limo driver to be cautious and to notify the authorities if he suspects he's being tailed. Don't worry. You'll be fine."

Marco personally accompanied the old man to the street, watching as the limo driver opened the rear door for him. Marco extended his hand.

"I don't know what to say. Except, thank you. You may have just settled the unrest of Kate's entire family. Granted them closure. Slain the demons torturing their memory."

James looked older, drained, and even paler than he had an hour ago as he clasped both hands around Marco's. "I feel lighter, too, Mr. Lareci. It's been a burden I've been carryin' around my whole life. Maybe now I'll be able to sleep at night."

While Marco went down with James, Kate dragged herself into his bathroom and splashed cool water on her face. Her reflection in the mirror was haggard. And wincing, she remembered she'd brought no clothes, no makeup with her. She knew by morning

Marco would see her—the real Kate—bared to the bone. Nothing to soften the realities of who she really was.

And who was that, really? Kate wasn't sure anymore. She'd experienced emotions over these past weeks since she met Marco she didn't realize existed. Maybe it was reading her aunt's letters. Although Leah had lived a short life, it had evidently been filled with not only passion, but love. A concept Kate wasn't quite sure she understood.

Ever since she could remember, her parents had been little more than amicable roommates. They lived together and raised their daughter in a secure, nurturing environment. Kate had never lacked for affection, but most of it came from her mother. But as she'd matured into adulthood, even her mother had backed off from sharing with Kate the complexities of an intimate relationship.

Hell, she'd even pawned off the "sex talk" to Kate's long-time nanny, Selma Ridley. Kate was thirteen before Selma sat her down to have "the talk."

"You know, I told your mama this would be a whole lot less uncomfortable coming from her than from me," Selma began, sweat beading across her forehead on that hot August afternoon.

They'd been up at the lake house, ironically. The same place where she and Marco had spent an unprecedented, passionate night a few weeks ago. Kate's thirteenth birthday had come and gone. Although her mother had provided sketchy details about why her body had begun to change—and why she'd started bleeding for five days every month—she'd divulged very little more information.

Selma was from the South, herself and her people having been born and raised in Atlanta. The only reason Selma lived in New York was because three of her sons—three of the five—had taken jobs in the big city and relocated with their families to Long Island. Her daughters both married West Coast businessmen and moved out that way.

Selma had served as Kate's nanny, and confidant, since she was five years old. And she had been the best. Even when the job duties got difficult, like explaining the birds and bees to the young Kate Bardach.

"But I don't understand, Selma," Kate had protested. "You're explaining basic biology to me here. I *know* what mating is," she'd insisted, rolling her facetious, teenage eyes. "The male sticks his thing in the female, and babies are born. So, what's the big deal? If I don't want babies, I won't let a male stick his thing in me."

The look of horror on her nanny's face, including a healthy, white rim around her irises, told Kate she'd rocked Selma's world. She giggled. Kate had been there when Father had brought the stallions and mares together during breeding season. She'd seen them *do it*—yuck and disgusting though the act was. Violent, nasty, messy.

And the message Father had related was clear: unless you want a baby, don't do this with your boyfriends.

"Child, child," Selma began, lifting Kate's fingers to her lips as she rocked on the bed beside her. "You have no idea how much more complicated it can be. This isn't only about mating, Kate. There's a whole lot more that goes with it. When it's folks you're talking about, and not horses or dogs."

Kate wasn't sure, even now, staring at her own gaunt reflection in Marco's mirror, she understood the "more that goes with it" any better than she had as a teenager. What she did know was this: the physical act was not, as she'd thought back then, nasty or icky. It was fabulous. Enticing. Addictive. But what was happening to her guts when she was around Marco went far beyond a simple coupling. More than sex.

And that knowledge frightened Kate half to death.

When Marco returned to the apartment, Kate was stretched along the couch. She'd showered, and since she had nothing else, pilfered one of his terry robes to wrap herself in. When he came through the door, she sat up, adjusting the ample folds to be sure she'd adequately covered herself.

After locking the door and setting the alarm, he came to her. She couldn't resist melting into his embrace, reveling in his musky scent, the strong, hard feel of his muscles holding her tight against his body. When she sighed and relaxed against him, he mumbled something in Italian. She didn't understand the words, but they were soothing. A reassurance.

Or a prayer.

"It's after midnight, Kate. We've both been up since four thirty this morning. It's time to sleep. God knows, we both need to get some sleep."

He lifted her as though she weighed a feather and carried her into his bedroom, laying her gently on his bed.

"I'll be back. Shower," he said, his voice guttural. A sensuous zing rang through her belly as she curled into a ball on his sumptuous bed.

She could still hear the spray of the shower in the bathroom when she felt the jolt on the mattress. Turning, she spied Cleo, who had easily sprung from the floor to the mattress at her feet. Kate froze.

For a moment, they eyed each other, like uncertain adversaries. Cleo's golden eyes were huge, but her coat remained sleek, her back level. Slowly, without breaking eye contact, the cat began its saunter from the foot of the bed. Toward Marco's pillow, Kate assumed.

Ten minutes later, Marco stood in the doorway of his bathroom, nude. As he scrubbed at his wet hair with the towel, he studied the scene before him with a mixture of relief, humor, and joy.

Kate lay curled in a semi-circle, still wearing his robe. One arm was crooked under her head, with the other cradling something close to her side. She was sound asleep.

As was Cleo, who lay snuggled close to Kate's body as she purred. A sound Marco seldom heard her make.

Morning came too soon, creeping around the edges of the Roman shades in Marco's bedroom. He opened his eyes but didn't move, lying very still. He didn't want this night to end, to spoil this moment. Because this, Marco realized, was how he wanted to wake up from now on. For every single day of his life.

Spooned behind Kate's nude body, one arm wrapped around her waist, his face buried in the hair at the nape of her neck. Last night, he'd crept under the duvet carefully, not wanting to disturb either her or Cleo. But sometime during the night, Cleo had decided sharing the bed with not one, but two humans, was demeaning and had slunk off to one of her secret sleeping places. Kate had slid out of Marco's robe and into his arms.

They hadn't made love. Instead, Kate had buried her face against Marco's bare chest and cried, softly and for a long time. Until his chest hair was soaked with her tears, her pain. With his chin resting on her head, he'd rubbed her back and murmured comforting words until finally, she'd drifted back off to sleep.

Marco knew now what he had to do. Perhaps, he now knew why they'd been brought together in the first place. Whether or not their serendipitous meeting would guarantee any sort of long-term relationship, he couldn't be sure. But he was certain, beyond any shadow of a doubt, what his role was in this drama.

Especially after last night. Dear God, had he really experienced a ghostly vision? There was no denying it. The weirdness of the event had been predicted—and confirmed—by the reaction of his cat.

How ironic his hobby was diving. He needed to call his friend Clive, the man who'd trained him. The man who was also a licensed seek and recovery diver. He wasn't sure if the Mustang was even still within reach, since rumors claimed the bottom of Loch Sheldrake had never been found. But for Kate, he had to try.

Hell, for his own sake. It seemed clear, from last night's macabre vision, Leah wasn't about to let this go without him at least trying to find her. Marco wasn't psychic. He wasn't used to seeing ghosts, and wasn't sure his sanity could take another vision.

It was bad enough he owned a haunted hotel.

Kate stirred in his arms then, squeaking as she stretched and yawned. Turning toward him, he felt her naked breasts brush his chest, her nipples peaked and taught. Instantly, he was hard. There was no denying his physical attraction for this woman. No matter how his logical mind argued, Marco knew that in the end, his body would take control every time they were together. He simply couldn't deny her. Sadly, his feral instincts would, undoubtedly, drag his heart along, too.

Neither said a word. Her blue eyes, spidered with a web of tiny red lines from her tormented night, locked with his and bored right through to his soul. How had he fallen in love with a woman like this? Marco knew damned well this affair would not end with wedding rings and baby booties. Kate Bardach simply wasn't made that way.

But if this was all he could have with her—mornings like this when he could delude himself into believing there was a chance for a real future with Kate—he would take them. Every minute he could spend gazing into those huge, blue eyes, worshipping her glorious body, and giving her comfort and pleasure, would be well worth the pain and heartache afterward.

He hoped.

Kate's heart felt bruised. It was the only word that came to mind to describe the sensation after hearing the lurid tale James had told. He'd not only shed light, undeniable light, on what had happened to her Aunt Leah. But, in some subtle way, he'd also charged her with the task of recovering Leah's remains. She felt it now her duty to find them, have her family's rabbi bless them, and lay them to rest in a respectful, traditional way.

Bringing closure to her mother, who had carried the tortured secret in her heart all her life. The taillight lens of the Mustang surfacing where it did, *when* it did, was undeniable evidence. Now, it was her job to find her aunt.

What might be left of her. If the car was even still reachable. Hadn't plummeted to the unknown depths of a lake that nobody had completely explored.

The man holding her right now might be able to help her. Kate buried her face against him, reveling in his musky, male scent. The rough brush of his chest hair. The feel of his strong arms around her. The security she felt with his muscular legs entwined with her own.

And the long, thick hardness of his arousal.

She had a job to do. A mystery to solve. A sunken car to locate. But for right now, all Kate could think about was how much this man seeped into her body and soul. Taking control.

And how, even though she'd never before been the kind of woman who relinquished control to *any* man, now she embraced the sensation. Falling into his arms. Relishing the security and comfort he offered. Letting down her defenses until she felt, truly, at his mercy.

Falling. Falling. Fast.

She reached for him, closing her fingers around his stiff shaft as she covered his lips with hers, hungrily. He moaned into her mouth, answering her furtive tongue with his own, but only briefly before pulling away.

Gazing down at her, he asked, "Are you sure you're up to this? Now?" His hazel eyes glowed with passion, but the furrows between his brows told of his concern for her feelings, too.

Such a patient, generous man.

Kate said nothing before resuming the kiss, deeper and more insistent this time. His scent, his taste caused her body to react in ways she'd never imagined possible before. And truth be told, Kate was no stranger to sexual coupling.

That's not what's going on here. The thought jolted through her mind like the mysterious lightning she'd seen at the lake a few weeks ago. Wild, powerful, almost sacred in its intensity.

And completely beyond her control.

Breaking away, she threw back the duvet and rose to her knees, admiring the god-like male form lying on his side before her. She was amused by the perplexed and slightly disappointed expression on Marco's face. Then she cast him an evil smile. Slowly, her hands and mouth began a purposeful, sensuous journey down the front of his chest.

His Mediterranean background had furred his body in all the right places, and just enough. Curly, dark chest hair continued down his torso, narrowing around his navel. She pressed kisses all along the way, running her tongue in small circles every inch or so, until she heard him growl. When she got to his navel and dipped her tongue inside, he groaned as he fell over onto his back.

"Oh, Kate. Mia cara. My waking fantasy," he murmured.

She felt her own arousal soaking her inner thighs with desire. But this morning was for him. He'd always been such a generous lover, insisting she reached her pleasure—at least once, usually twice—before he thought about his own. It was her turn now to give back.

His shaft was hot and hard, her hand barely able to encircle it. The skin was soft and velvety, thrilling to touch as it pulsed beneath her fingers. A small bead of moisture had already formed on his swollen head.

When she closed her lips around him, he bucked and let out a guttural cry. She tried to take him all in, but found it difficult. Hell, she'd never been with a man this big. And she wasn't into the gag reflex thing. She'd have to improvise.

With one hand wrapped around the base, she used her tongue and teeth to tease him into a frenzied state of ecstasy. Licking, sucking, stroking. A pity he didn't let her continue too long. She was quite enjoying herself when Marco raked his hands into her hair and stilled her.

"No more, mia cara. I can't hold on much longer."

But she shook her head wildly and used her free hand to bat his away. She wanted to give this to him, a pleasure she knew men coveted. One many women shrunk away from. The completion.

It didn't take much longer. His hips bucked convulsively as he neared his climax, and his fingernails dug almost painfully into her shoulders. When he came, the shudders racking Marco's body told her it was a pleasure he'd seldom experienced.

And one she hoped to give him, time and time again.

As she lay beside him, his sweat-soaked chest heaving under her ear, she marveled at the knowledge this was the first time in her life she'd ever completed this part of the sex act with a man. In this way. Before, it simply hadn't held any appeal. And up until now, pleasure had been all about her. Kate blinked.

Is that the person I'd become? Selfish? One wrapped up in my own wants and needs, oblivious to the feelings of others?

Cold reality splashed over her like a wave. Just now, she'd derived as much, if not more, ecstasy from pleasing Marco than if it had been her on the receiving end.

She dozed for a short time, curled up close against him, knowing it was still early. Thankfully, Kate knew she wasn't needed anywhere today. At least, not urgently. Any questions Daniel had could be answered via telephone. She wondered absently if he'd had Wi-Fi and satellite service last night. Surely, if he hadn't, they'd have heard from him by now.

The red, digital numbers on the clock beside Marco's bed read a few minutes past eight when she opened her eyes again. He was stirring beside her, his fingers reaching up to tangle in her hair, slide up and down her back. When Kate lifted her head, he met her gaze, one side of his mouth quirked up.

"Thank you for giving me a breather, Ms. Bardach. But I haven't held up my end of the bargain," he grumbled, his voice rough with sleep.

But Kate was not about to let go of this control high she was feeling yet. Rising to her elbow, she leaned her head on one hand and laid a finger on his lips with the other.

"Shh," she whispered. "I'm not finished yet."

In one swift movement, she swept one leg over him, straddling his body at the narrowest point—his hips. With agonizingly slow deliberation, she settled over his half-aroused sex and began a delicious kind of massage, her hot, slick heat pressed down against him. Marco growled and closed his eyes, stretching his arms over his head to curl his fingers around the metal spires of his headboard.

"Okay, milady. You're in control. I'm yours."

Within seconds, he was rock hard, his erection hot and throbbing against her lower belly. Kate smiled down at him when he freed his hands to reach for her. "Nuh-uh. You keep those hands right where they are. Unless you want me to tie them there."

Passion flared in his eyes, along with an emotion Kate wasn't sure she recognized—challenge? Pride? Or just pure sensual delight?

Yet, he didn't fight her demand, dutifully clutching the headboard frame again and his eyes locked on hers with such heat, she almost had to look away. It was hard to maintain eye contact with him when he got this way, when a door opened up in those gold-flecked, hazel eyes, straight into his soul. The sensation caused a clutching in her own chest she found perplexing, as well as disconcerting.

Love changes a girl. Makes you do things you never thought you would.

When the words from Leah's letter popped into her head, she sucked in a quick breath and stopped. Lots of things had changed about how she thought, and felt, since she'd met Marco. But she wasn't ready to even consider what that meant. Not yet. Not now.

The sex. Concentrate on the physical. It's what you know how to do, how to enjoy.

His shaft was huge and throbbing now, standing at full attention in front of and resting against her belly as she rhythmically rubbed her wet folds against him. Lifting herself up high enough to hover above the swollen head, she settled down over him, and he groaned.

"Please, let me touch you. Please you," he begged, snatching his hands free and reaching for her breasts.

But she grabbed both wrists and froze in place. "No. We're going to do this my way."

219

Creases formed between his eyebrows as a pained expression contorted his handsome features.

"I feel so helpless. Like I'm using you," he pleaded.

"Not so, Mr. Lareci. Today, I'm the one using you."

Immediately after the words left her lips, inwardly, she cringed. Did she really mean those words the way they sounded? There was a day, not so long ago, when the statement would have been absolute truth. Undeniable fact.

As she balanced on her knees over the god-like body of the man beneath her, she knew this was different. How could a woman be so shallow, so selfish and deceitful, to even consider using a man like Marco?

Not only his body, but his heart?

Concentrate on the physical, Kate Bardach. That's what you know how to do best.

With gently probing fingers, she took him into her grasp and maneuvered his throbbing shaft into position, separating her swollen folds with his head. The contact made her gasp. How easy would it be now to simply settle down on him, take him inside her body completely, and rock herself, and him, into rapid release.

But she struggled to maintain control over her body's screaming desire to be sated. She wanted more time, exactly like this. More anticipation. More buildup to the inevitable.

But for whom? For herself? Or for him?

Pushing the question to the back of her mind, Kate concentrated on the here and now. As she stroked the throbbing head on her engorged sex, she kept her eyes open, her gaze locked on his. The array of expressions crossing his face thrilled her: frustration, an agonizing struggle to maintain his own control, and a kind of sweet surrender. There was something else, too. Another emotion, speaking to her from within in the depths of those pale, hazel eyes.

Saints be damned for that something else. The way she felt when he looked at her that way, persistently worming his way into her mind, her soul.

I *cannot* love you, Marco Lareci. It's simply not possible. Not practical. Not part of my life plan.

Unable to keep the shield around her emotions any longer—nor hold her passion at bay—she freed her hand and sank down over him. She reveled at the feel of him inside her, her tender folds embracing him as she slid down his impressively large length. When her swollen and uber-sensitive clit found the roughness of his curls at the base, she gasped.

Then, time stood still. Neither of them moved for a long moment, gazing into each other's eyes. Speaking without saying a word.

Slowly, she began to rock her hips, rolling her sex over his pubic bone, pressing to increase the already-delicious friction. Still, he had not moved, not released his grip from the headboard. She was close, and she knew by the corded, trembling muscles of his forearms—holding his own release was costing Marco every ounce of strength he had.

What kind of man was this, who was willing to do anything to please a woman? She'd never, in her life, encountered one strong enough to deny himself for her.

"Now? May I touch you now, mia cara?" His words were gruff, strangled, a rumbling growl from a throat tight with emotion.

And his sweet sincerity sliced straight through to Kate's soul.

Nodding, she closed her eyes. She felt the warmth of his palms covering her breasts. They felt swollen and heavy, the nipples so hard and peaked that the stroking of his thumbs over them was almost painful. Almost, but not quite.

And the delicious sensation took her straight up and over the edge, her release crashing around her in a shower, sparks of white heat exploding in her brain. Over and over she pulsed around him until her screams of pleasure became sobs. Only when she had crested the wave did he slide his hands down her body to grip her hips. With three hard, pounding strokes, he joined her in ecstasy.

Marco had barely finished pumping into her when she collapsed onto him. Sobs wracked her body, her tears again soaking his chest. Fear and confusion flooded his brain, a brain still buzzing and befuddled by the power of their lovemaking.

"What is it, mia cara? Did I hurt you?" He smoothed her sweat-soaked hair away from her face.

Silently, she searched his face with those impossible blue eyes, tears flowing freely down her cheeks. Then slowly, she shook her head.

"Not physically. But I'm afraid—absolutely terrified—that someday, and soon, you will."

TWENTY

At first, Marco had no idea what Kate meant. Hurt her? He'd never intentionally hurt a woman in his life, either physically or emotionally. He had always been completely honest with his lovers, even the ones who became his "regular girl" for a time. And those few had ended up hurting *him* when they broke it off, eventually tiring of his jealous and possessive nature.

Women these days weren't the tender, wilting flowers of days gone by. Not that he wanted a weak woman anyway. A weak woman could never stand up to his aggressive personality.

With his thumb, he wiped the tears away from her soft, pale cheek and stared at her, uncertain what to say. Kate Bardach, he knew very well, was one of the most strong willed women he'd ever met. And she'd made it crystal clear, by her words and actions, she would not be owned, or controlled, by anyone. Especially not by a man.

But gazing down at him with haunted, pain-stricken, blue eyes—her unadorned face sprinkled with freckles she usually hid under makeup—she looked . . . different. Younger, more innocent. Vulnerable.

"What are you saying, Kate? What are you afraid of?"

Was it possible he'd finally broken through the icy shield she kept around her emotions? Marco's heart leapt at the unlikely possibility.

She stared at him for what seemed an eternity, and he waited, holding his breath. He longed to tell her he loved her, open his heart to her, and confess she'd owned him from the first day they'd met. But he could see the fear plainly in her eyes. He knew those three words would, like a sudden movement toward a frightened animal, scare her straight away from him.

The window into those blue depths remained open only a few seconds more. Closing them, she wiped her face with the backs of both hands and began shaking her head. Her next words cut him nearly in two.

"I'm afraid I may never again experience pleasure like this in my life. And that, Mr. Lareci," her tone was flippant as she opened her eyes and lightly pinched his chin, "would be a crying shame."

Ah, what a ridiculous, fantasizing man I can be. For her, it's all about the sex. Only the physical. If only that were true for me.

An hour later, showered and dressed for his client luncheon meeting, Marco fussed over the cappuccino maker in his kitchen. As usual, the hissing steam brought Cleo out of hiding. Hair standing slightly on end, golden eyes wide, and tail snapping back and forth in annoyance.

Damn, but why does this cat take an appliance's noises so personally?

But Cleo started, jumping in place when Kate emerged from the hallway. Apparently, the cat had forgotten she was there. Recovering quickly, she sauntered in Kate's direction and promptly began her attempt to trip her, winding in and out of her bare ankles like a silky snake.

"I can't believe how she's taken to you," Marco said as he poured steaming milk into the second cup. "I'm not sure whether to be pleased or creeped out."

Kate stooped to stroke the cat's back. "Why would that creep you out?" she asked through a chuckle.

Marco had yet to tell Kate about the vision he'd seen last night before her panicked phone call. He wasn't sure he believed it even happened. And he sure as hell didn't want to think about what it meant. The fact remained, Cleo had been completely weirded out by the vision of a woman who could be Kate's twin, yet had curled up with the real Kate only hours later.

He lifted his shoulders and let them drop. "Just not Cleo's usual MO. Highly unusual behavior for the prissy beast."

Setting two steaming cups on the counter, he motioned for Kate to take one of the two bar stools.

"I'm sorry to leave so soon, but I'm meeting a client for lunch." Hitching one leg up on the second stool, he lifted his cup and sipped. "Gotta keep the cash flowing in so I can pay my interior design firm, you know."

Her smile, he noted, didn't quite reach her eyes. "You make it sound so—so impersonal. I thought we'd become closer... ."

"Have we? I didn't think it's how you operated, Ms. Bardach." Marco couldn't keep the coolness out of his tone.

Not that he'd tried. He needed to keep reminding himself—to her, this was all about the sex.

She laughed wryly. "It wasn't. Remember I told you at the beginning? My policy: I don't sleep with clients." Her expression sobered. "You changed that. You've changed a lot about me in these past weeks."

"Have I? Think about it, Kate. Really think about it." He placed a finger under her chin and searched her eyes. The doors were closed again. Big, beautiful, blue doors, shut and bolted tight. "Think about it long and hard. And then you let me know."

Marco drained his cup and rose, reaching for the sport coat he had tossed over the end of the counter. "Will you be here when I get back? Should be around four."

Kate had gone very quiet and was staring blankly into her coffee cup, her hands lying limply on her lap. She nodded, but didn't reply.

He planted a kiss on top of her head as he turned to leave. He'd gotten halfway to the door when she called after him.

"Marco? I need to tell my parents what we found out last night. I'm meeting them for dinner at Del Frisco's, seven o'clock. Will you come with me?"

Marco looked at the floor and sighed. Dinner with her parents. Probably not a good idea. But it was true, they needed to let somebody know they'd found out where Leah's remains—and likely that of her husband—might be found.

And after his encounter with her spirit—was he really believing this?—Marco had the distinct impression he'd been enlisted to assist in the search. A demand, not an invitation. Whether he liked it or not.

He nodded silently, then turned and left.

That night, Marco held the cab door open and reached for Kate's hand as they stepped out onto the sidewalk in front of Del Frisco's. She looked stunning in an outfit he couldn't remember seeing her in before. The shimmer of the fabric told him it was silk, and the color matched her eyes perfectly. She'd belted it with a wide strap of finely braided gold, which showed off her sumptuous curves exquisitely.

Almost too well. He flashed the doorman a threatening glare when Marco caught him following Kate's movement through the door, his attention unabashedly plastered on her ass. Acid prickled Marco's veins.

Got to get over this. She's not yours, never will be. A great screw. Nothing more.

As they waited for the maître d' to look up their reservation, Marco leaned over to murmur in Kate's ear.

"New dress?"

She looked up at him and grinned. "I didn't bring anything with me last night, remember? I had to run back to my place to grab clothes and makeup anyway. Just so happens Saks was right on the way." Sticking her chin in the air, she tossed one side of her heavy, dark mane over her shoulder.

As she turned to follow the waiter to their table, Marco couldn't resist. He reached down and patted her bottom, then squeezed appreciatively.

"Marco," she growled, swatting his hand away and straightening her shoulders.

He winked at the maître d', who'd watched wide-eyed before amusement crinkled the outer corners of his eyes.

Her parents had already arrived and were seated at a table tucked into a back corner of the dimly lit dining room. Marco was surprised at how young they appeared. Kate was thirty two, she'd told him, but her parents were very young fifty-somethings. Her mother was a slight, petite woman with angular features and neatly cropped, light-brown hair. Not an unattractive woman, but still— one glance told Marco Kate's looks had definitely not come from her mother.

But then, he already knew that. Kate's beauty came from her Aunt Leah.

Her father was a man of stocky build whose tailored suit fit him impeccably. His hair and beard, both jet black, were cropped close and neatly trimmed. His eyes were dark as well, smallish and close-set in a round face, cool and distant behind dark-rimmed glasses. He stood as they approached the table, pulling out a chair for Kate before embracing her.

Stiffly. His somber expression never changed as he studied Marco over her shoulder.

"I'm Marco Lareci." Marco extended his hand, surprised at how pale and smooth the other man's was, with long, tapered fingers.

"Kaleb Bardach. My wife, Joan." Kaleb nodded toward Joan without looking at her.

Warm welcome, Marco thought wryly. Then again, what had he expected? He was only their daughter's client.

"I understand you've made a wise investment up there in the Borsht Belt." Kaleb didn't waste any time setting the tone for the evening's conversation. Formal. Businesslike.

Marco cleared his throat and lifted the water glass to sip. "Yes, it appears we did. My partners and I were extremely pleased to discover the Rockin' Hard's interest in Montlake."

The waiter interrupted them, and Marco deliberately waited to see if Kate's parents ordered alcoholic beverages. Then he noticed the already half-empty glass of red wine in front of Joan and breathed a sigh of relief.

He was definitely going to need a drink, maybe two, to get through this dinner.

Kate ordered a martini, so Marco didn't hesitate to order Стахоапт, pronouncing the name of the imported vodka in perfect Russian.

Kaleb's eyebrows rose, and as the waiter left, he asked, "You speak Russian as well? As well as Italian, I mean," Kaleb qualified. "Kate tells me you have quite a repertoire of Italian . . . expressions." One side of the man's too-pink lips quirked.

Marco suppressed a smirk and dropped his gaze to the table. "I speak fluent Italian. But not Russian. My partner is from St. Petersburg. I've picked up a few words."

Up until now, Joan hadn't said a word, keeping her attention trained on her hands in her lap. She seemed subdued and a little nervous, her occasional glances toward her husband revealing carefully controlled flashes of impatience.

Finally, she said, "Kaleb, we need to order dinner. You're on call. I'd hate to have you miss out on your meal."

They ordered as soon as the waiter returned with their drinks, and Kaleb quietly informed him they were pressed for time.

For Marco, this meal couldn't be over with fast enough. He felt like an extra in a play where nobody had shared the script with him. Kate referred to her parents as either Mother or Father, or by their given names directly. Conversation was halting and stilted, with long periods of silence in between. Fortunately, the waiter interrupted often, with salads appearing almost instantly.

Marco was still picking at his salad when his prime rib eye appeared sizzling before him. But his appetite had long since disappeared. Even his second vodka hadn't eased the atmosphere at the table, as if a cold, damp fog enveloped the entire party.

He jumped when Kate, apparently having slipped off her stiletto, ran her warm toes under the cuff of his trousers. When he slid his glance toward her, she smiled sympathetically.

Apparently, he wasn't hiding his discomfort very convincingly.

Kaleb did not miss his meal. He ordered sesame seared tuna that, to Marco, looked like it should still be wriggling, then consumed it in a seeming attempt to pre-empt its escape. Right on cue, a dull, buzzing sound emanated from his breast pocket the minute he laid down his fork.

"Oh, I knew it," Joan moaned. She laid a hand over Kaleb's and said, in a reassuring tone, "At least you got to finish your dinner. And to meet Marco here."

The cool fog dissipated quickly as soon as Kaleb Bardach exited the room. Marco learned Kate's father was the Site Chair of Cardiology at Mount Sinai Hospital and was often called away at inconvenient times. It seemed as though neither wife nor daughter was much surprised, or bothered, by the interruption.

In fact, they both appeared almost as relieved as Marco.

Moments after he'd gone, Joan rested both elbows on the table, visibly more relaxed. She leaned across the table toward Marco. "Kaleb was planning to leave before we opened the discussion about Leah anyway," she said quietly. "When it comes to that subject—or anything having to do with my family—he'd rather not be involved."

No wonder Kate is so clueless when it comes to close family ties. Her father not only eats cold fish, he *is* one.

Kate interrupted Marco's thoughts when she laid her fork down on the edge of her plate with a loud snap. She pressed her hand over Joan's and said, "We have news, Mother. News about what happened to Aunt Leah."

Over the next half-hour, Kate retold the tale they'd heard from James. Marco watched in silence as a gamut of emotions played over Joan's face: from relief, to devastation, to outright horror. He knew now why Joan had chosen the seat facing toward the rear corner of the restaurant. She'd suspected the news wouldn't be good and didn't want to make a spectacle of herself in public.

Marco was impressed at how well Kate maintained her composure. For her mother's sake, he was certain. Or, maybe

229

because she'd spent all the emotions she was going to, last night, during James' telling. After all, it had been the second time she'd heard the horrific story in one day.

Or, perhaps because the well of Kate Bardach's emotions just didn't run all that deep. Some innate instinct in Marco's gut wagged its finger in his face, swearing this was, in fact, the truth.

When Kate finished speaking, Joan had her napkin pressed to her mouth as tears streaked down her cheeks. Her shoulders shuddered, but she didn't make a sound. Kate glanced at Marco and murmured, "I'm going to take Mother to the ladies' room. We'll be back shortly."

While he sat waiting, Marco wasted no time in hailing the waiter to hand him his American Express card. And to order a third vodka. He was going to need all the courage he could muster—artificial or otherwise—in order to make the offer he'd already decided to make.

Joan was much more composed when they returned, even having repaired her drizzled makeup to a semblance of normalcy. She looked directly at him and said, "I'm sorry you had to witness that, Mr. Lareci. I've been a very long time in limbo. And yet now, there's still no closure. Now, instead of not knowing, still holding out some lame hope she's alive somewhere, I know exactly where Leah is. Her remains. It pains me to think I'll never be able to give her a proper burial."

"Please, Joan, call me Marco." He reached out and took both her hands in his, gazing directly into her light-brown eyes. "I might be able to help. I don't know if Kate's told you, but I'm a certified diver. The friend who trained me is licensed for search and recovery. I hope I haven't overstepped my bounds, but I've taken the liberty to call him already." Marco slid a quick glance at Kate, who looked surprised, but not displeased. "With your permission, Joan, he will alert the authorities first with our suspicions. Then, we'll arrange a dive."

TWENTY-ONE

Kate waited until Marco stepped inside his apartment, then watched him lock and latch the door. The minute his fingers left the keypads of the alarm system, she stepped up close against his body and buried her face in the hollow of his neck.

"I don't know how I can ever thank you," she whispered. "How *we* can thank you."

His arms came around her, but lightly. There was no passion and very little emotion in his embrace.

Very much like the way Father embraces me, she thought. Which, with Marco, stung a little.

"I don't know if we'll even find the car, Kate. The research Boris did at the museum way back at the beginning claims nobody's ever found the bottom of that godforsaken lake. To my knowledge, nobody's ever tried."

Or, how many bodies are down there, if the bottom *could* be found. Kate had heard all the rumors. She suspected there wasn't only a 1964 Mustang lying on the bottom of Loch Sheldrake. God knows how many other skeletons littered its depths, still chained to juke boxes and buckets of concrete. The thought made her shudder, and a wave of nausea washed over her.

"Are you okay?" Marco immediately asked, holding her away and searching her face. "You look very pale tonight."

Kate closed her eyes and shook her head. "I'm exhausted. It's been a hellish few days." She cupped his jaw with one hand. "Will you take me to bed and hold me? Just hold me?"

Marco studied her face, emotions warring inside him. He loved her. He knew that. But he also now realized, without a doubt, Kate

Bardach had absolutely no idea what love was. Nor did she show any signs of wanting to learn. She'd been raised in a cold, loveless home and grown into a woman who thought sex was the highest high you could aim for.

She had no idea how much higher love could enrich the physical pleasure.

Sleeping next to her again, holding her, and waking with her curled against his side would stir all sorts of wild fantasies in his head again. Of a forever with her. Of her bearing his children, growing old with him. He didn't know if he could steel himself against those futile hopes and dreams one more time.

But he'd brought her home with him. They were, after all, in his apartment, and he'd made it clear by the way he'd locked up they were in for the night. Before his brain could find a way out of what he knew was a certain spiral into heart-splitting agony, he heard himself saying, "Of course, mia cara."

As Marco drifted off to sleep with Kate wrapped in his arms, he said a silent prayer.

Please, God. Steel my heart to this woman. Give me the strength to separate my brain from my balls, pull my emotions together, and walk away.

Kate's phone buzzing from inside her purse woke them. She'd been dead asleep, so secure and comfortable spooned up against Marco's hard, muscled back, her arm snugging his waist. They hadn't had sex. But the few times she'd woken during the night, it was because they'd drifted apart, no part of their bodies touching. Only when they were again connected, warm bare skin to skin, did she relax enough to drift back off to sleep.

She ignored the first call, but when it began buzzing a second time, only a few minutes later, she groaned and disentangled her legs from Marco's, then from the sheets. The chill of the still air on her naked body caused her skin to pucker with gooseflesh. Snatching up the phone, she glared at the screen.

Yvette?

"Hey, Yvette. Good morning. Problem?" Kate glanced at the time in the corner of the screen and realized it was only a little past nine. Her offices didn't even open until ten. Besides, Yvette was calling from her personal cellphone. What was up?

"Sorry to bother you so early, Kate. I'm up here at the Shelby. The seamstress should be here with sketches and fabric samples in less than an hour. Did you forget?"

Kate slapped a hand to her forehead and groaned. "Shit, Yvette. I did. I'm in Manhattan."

"Oh," was the timid reply.

Her brain clicked immediately back into work mode. Kate said, "It's okay; I'll be there in two hours. And a half. By eleven thirty, the latest. Listen, when she gets there, give her a nice, leisurely walk-through, and then take her and Daniel out for breakfast somewhere. Say I got tied up in the city. Cover for me, will you, Sweetie?"

As she clicked off, she looked over to see Marco watching her, his muscular arms folded behind his head. The covers had slipped down, revealing almost all of him. Her gaze drifted from his sleepy, sexy eyes, over his beard-darkened jaw, and down his furred chest, following the trail of dark hair to where it disappeared under the duvet.

She groaned again, this time at the throbbing longing between her thighs.

"I'm sorry," she stammered. "I totally forgot about the meeting with the woman who's making your custom window treatments and duvets. I'm already hours late."

His expression didn't change, which she found disconcerting. She'd expected to see the same disappointment on his face she felt. But instead, he only shrugged.

"Can I call a car for you while you get dressed?" he asked coolly.

Another stab in her chest. What the hell? Why was he acting so distant?

"You can't drive me?" she asked, hating the whimper in her voice.

He shook his head without a moment's hesitation. "If I'm going to arrange this dive for you next week, I need to catch up on all the work I've been ignoring for the past month. It's time for Marco Lareci to come back to the real world." He tossed back the covers and stood.

No sign of arousal between his thighs, at all.

Kate swallowed hard and crossed her arms over her chest, feeling suddenly, oddly, very naked.

"I'll shower and be out of your way in fifteen minutes," she murmured. As she headed for the bathroom, she called over her shoulder, "And if you could call me a car, that would be awesome."

Kate's limo pulled up to the Shelby at precisely eleven twenty-three. The driver had taken her offer of an extra hundred to break the sound barrier—seriously. Maybe a little *too* seriously. After they'd broken free of the city traffic and hit the open highway, Kate found herself getting dizzy from the scenery zipping by at such an alarming rate. She slipped on her shades, closed her eyes, and spent the remainder of the trip leaning back on the headrest.

But her mind couldn't rest. There was an elastic band twisted around her insides, and she knew exactly why. What she couldn't decide was whether she was more upset with Marco for causing these feelings, or with herself for allowing them to develop in the first place.

Being around her parents last night had brought it all home to her. For one thing, she tried to remember the last time she'd spent any time with them—together—and couldn't. Joan and Kaleb were married and lived together, and they bore one child. But that was about as far as their relationship extended.

She knew her mother had moved into a separate bedroom years ago, using the excuse of Kaleb's erratic and unpredictable schedule being too disruptive. Joan liked to maintain order, routine in her life. Pretty difficult to do when you never knew what time of day or night your husband would get paged and disappear.

Kate hardly knew Kaleb, she realized. He'd never been a nurturing father. Other than the time they'd spent together at the horse farm, they rarely visited. The only time Kate spoke to him was the occasional phone call—always in reference to a horse. And of late, Kate felt more comfortable simply texting him whatever news she had.

Perhaps this was why Marco's attentions had gotten past her defenses. He was affectionate, doting even. His jealousy didn't annoy her so much as flatter her. And, unlike the numerous other lovers Kate had entertained, Marco was more mature. If not in years, then certainly in demeanor. It was why, she realized, she'd always been drawn to younger, less experienced men. That way she could remain in control, not only of the situation, but of her feelings.

Younger men were after Kate for her body. For the sex, a night or two of passion before they fled out of fear they'd be expected to make some kind of commitment. So Kate never had to worry about developing feelings for any of them.

Marco was completely different. She'd known it from the start, but couldn't deny the electrifying attraction she felt for him. Once her body got a taste of his brand of lovemaking, she found she couldn't get enough.

Lovemaking. There was the problem, right there, plain and obvious. Kate had never before thought of the act as anything but sex. Screwing. Fucking even, when it got rough and sweaty and dirty.

But Marco did none of those things with her. What she and Marco shared was lovemaking. With sensations reaching far beyond the physical—emotions she'd never before experienced worming their way into her heart. Making her yearn for him. Worry about him. Miss the living hell out of him when he wasn't near her.

And this morning, he'd looked at her like a stranger. Like she'd been looked at so many times before. By men who'd gotten everything they'd wanted from her and were ready to move on.

A sudden panic filled Kate's chest, and she fumbled in her purse for her phone as the limo driver pulled up in front of the Shelby and parked. He got out and came around to open her door, but she held up a hand, waiting for the call to connect.

One ring, two, three.

Hello. This is Marco Lareci. I can't take your call right now, but leave me a message, and I'll get back to you as soon as I can. Ciao.

Just the sound of his recorded voice in her ear raised a lump in Kate's throat. She clicked off without leaving a message, then handed the bills to the driver. She mumbled a thank you as she picked up her bag and turned toward the door. A tear slid down her cheek, and she angrily wiped it away.

Damn it all to hell. She'd fallen in love with the man and now wasn't sure whether it was too late to tell him or not.

The minute she walked through the door, she saw Daniel at the reception counter, his laptop open before him. She cringed. His greeting smile quickly faded once he got a good look at her face. Her sunglasses hid her eyes, but not her trembling lips.

"What's wrong, Kate? Did something happen?" He was by her side in an instant, taking her bag from her and laying an arm across her shoulders. "Come into my apartment and tell me what's going on. What's got you so upset?"

Kate sniffed and mumbled, "Could I please use your bathroom? It's the only one up and running in this place, right?"

His eyebrows drawn together, Daniel nodded and led her by the elbow through his small quarters. He pointed to the door leading to the compact, but shiny, new bathroom. When she was locked inside, Kate slid off her sunglasses and leaned against the sink, her head hanging over it. She knew Daniel was right outside, probably listening with his ear up against the door. So she struggled to swallow the sobs as she watched her tears drip in a continuous stream onto the porcelain.

I've fallen in love—something I've always been terrified of doing. And now, in all likelihood, I've smothered the seeds of something beautiful before they even had a chance to grow.

Ten minutes later, makeup repaired and having resumed a reasonable rein on her emotions, Kate came out of the bathroom and nearly plowed over Daniel. She'd been right. He'd been outside the door, listening, the whole time.

For a moment, she wished she'd made retching noises, or groaned and flushed the commode a half-dozen times.

"Where are they? Yvette and . . . what's her name? Celia something, right?" she asked, careful to maintain the cool, boss-lady tone she usually used around her team.

Daniel scrutinized her face before answering. "They just got back. I was coming in to check on you."

Right. Sure. *That's* what you were doing. And almost fell into me when I opened the door.

The afternoon dragged on forever. Celia Worthington had not one, but three gigantic fabric swatch books, which her assistant dragged in and plopped unceremoniously on the reception counter.

"My word," Kate began, her eyes widening as her stomach sank. "I thought this sort of thing was done with online photographs nowadays."

"Oh, no, not for a project of this size and complexity, Ms. Bardach. We need to be sure not only the colors and patterns are right, but that the textures will complement as well."

Kate was tired and more than a little irritable. She did her best to pay attention as she followed Yvette and Celia through the hotel. In some sections, the renovations were still far from complete. So it took some imagination to envision window dressings, upholstered furniture, and duvet covers amid the unfinished sheetrock, ladders, and tool boxes scattered about.

Kate's imagination wasn't cooperating today, no matter how hard she tried to concentrate. Yvette was tentative about every suggestion she made, always looking to Kate for approval first. But today, although usually Kate liked to call the shots, she was happy to let her assistant take control.

About halfway through the afternoon, Celia excused herself to use the restroom in Daniel's apartment. Once she had Yvette alone, Kate searched her face.

"What's your problem? You don't seem nearly as chipper as you did a few weeks ago. After you first met Marco's partner. The Russian guy. Boris?"

Yvette's lips pressed into a flat line, and she avoided Kate's gaze. "It's over. All done. A bonfire burned out all too quickly." She looked up, and Kate didn't see any sorrow in her assistant's expression. Only resolution.

Yvette shrugged. "You know how it goes for us, Kate. We ride the roller coaster. The highs are great. The lows, not so much. There'll be a new boyfriend in a week or three to warm the spot gone cold in my bed." Her shrewd smile sent shivers up Kate's spine.

My God, is that how I sound?

Kate slipped outside at least a half-dozen times throughout the afternoon, seeking a semi-private spot from which she could call Marco. Every time, his phone went to voicemail. And every time she returned, Daniel followed her every step across the lobby.

The man was really starting to grate on her nerves. Concern, okay. But she knew damn well much of Daniel's supposed *concern* translated plainly into jealous lust.

Still, she should be grateful somebody was concerned for her feelings. Even here, out of her usual city element, Kate had never minded being alone. But at this moment, there was an aching hole in her chest she knew only Marco could fill. And she'd never felt more alone in her entire life.

Finally, around four thirty, Celia's assistant began dragging the heavy swatch books back out to her van. Yvette was looking over the final paperwork while Kate wandered over to the ballroom windows. She stood staring out at the lake. In a few minutes, she'd be able to get out of here. Go back to her place, pour herself a glass of good wine, and climb into her hot tub and relax. Sit in the warm, swirling water until she shriveled up like a prune, if she wanted to.

She'd come to the realization Marco was not going to answer her calls. There was no way he'd be out of the loop for this long on a work day. Unless . . . .

Unless something had happened to him. A sharp pang of fear zinged her chest.

Turning, she interrupted something Celia was explaining to Yvette, and both looked up, surprised.

"I'm sorry. Yvette, before you sign off on all of this, has anyone discussed any of these choices with Mr. Lareci?" she asked, trying very hard—probably too hard—to sound nonchalant.

Daniel, who was sitting beside where the girls had the paperwork spread out, looked up from his laptop screen and narrowed his eyes. "I've been shooting Lareci images of the designs all afternoon, Kate," he answered levelly. "He's approved every one with no hesitation."

So there it was. He *was* ignoring her calls. The realization tore her heart in two. A gunshot wound to the chest could not have been more painful.

She sucked in a deep breath and said, "Listen, guys, I'm exhausted. Put a lot of miles between here and the city over the last couple days. I'm going home. I'll have my cell if you need anything else." She glanced at her watch. "But it's time for all of you to pack it in for the day anyway."

"Do you need a ride home, Kate? I see you don't have your car here," Daniel offered, standing and closing his laptop.

"No, thank you, Daniel. It's a lovely afternoon, and the house is barely a half-mile up the road. A walk will do me good."

Kate arrived on her doorstep twenty minutes later, shoes in hand, the heels having proved downright dangerous to walk in on a country road. She'd only stumbled a time or two when a badly positioned pebble pressed into the still-sensitive place where her stitches had been. The pavement was hot from the afternoon sun, so she kept to the side where the shade of the lush tree cover kept it cool.

Once inside, she leaned back against the door and closed her eyes. Thoughts of Marco swirled around her, infusing the air with his scent, his taste. The feel of his touch. The way those pale, gold-flecked eyes spoke to her without words. An overwhelming sense of sadness settled over her like a dark, heavy blanket.

She'd lost him, she was certain of it. If not completely, she knew his feelings for her—if he still had any—had cooled considerably. And it would take more groveling than Kate knew how to do to win his heart back.

But there was nothing she could do about that now—not tonight, from over a hundred miles away. Not when he wouldn't even answer her goddamned calls. Growling, she flung her cellphone in the direction of the sofa and stomped into her bedroom.

It wasn't until her shower and a half-glass of wine relaxed her to the point of giddiness that she realized she'd not eaten anything all day. All she'd had to drink was one icy bottle of water Jeremy had fished out of the contractor's huge cooler for her about two hours ago. She could call for a pizza delivery. It was still early, and she wasn't too hesitant to unlock and open her door before dark.

But three bites into her first slice of pizza, Kate realized she was beyond hungry. No, not beyond hungry; just had no appetite for food. The hunger gnawing inside her gut tonight was for a man she didn't have. And now, maybe, never could.

After dumping the entire pizza box into the trash, Kate poured herself a second glass of wine and headed out to the hot tub. She dropped her robe to the floor and stepped into the bubbles, settling down until the water lapped beneath her chin. At first, the heat and steam did their job and soothed her.

But as she began to relax, memories floated back into her brain. Memories of her and Marco's passionate night right here, beside this hot tub. How he'd worshipped her body, making gentle, slow, passionate love to her. Telling her plainly, without words, how he felt about her.

And the damned fool that she was, she hadn't understood a single word.

But Kate Bardach wasn't used to self-deprecation, at least not for very long. Her eyes snapped open and she thought, *he could have told me.* He could have said he was falling in love with me, instead of playing a silly, elusive game. Like Scrabble with half the pieces missing. Like watching an emotional Jeopardy game. Okay, he knew she had psychic abilities, but really? Had he expected her to read his mind?

It was plain and simple. Marco Lareci hadn't played fair.

Anger bubbled up in her throat, turning the few bites of pizza and wine into an acid bath. Cursing under her breath, Kate clambered out of the tub and wrapped her thick, terry robe around her, cinching the belt with a savage jerk. This was not her fault, damn it. And she was not about to accept the blame.

And this whole dive offer—what, did he think he would win her heart, and her mother's good graces, by playing Lancelot in a wetsuit? By God, her family could afford to hire any dive team they chose to go down after Leah's remains. Searching for where she'd left her cellphone, she made the mental decision: Marco's dive was off. She and her mother would find another means to locate Leah's sunken car, and whatever else was left. The first step was to call Mother and inform her of the decision.

But where the hell was her phone?

Dog tired and more than a little tipsy, Kate wandered around her house, from the kitchen to the dining room to the living room, searching every horizontal surface for her cellphone. She grabbed her purse and upended it, dumping the entire contents on the table. Makeup tubes, loose change, and an assortment of pens and pencils rolled off the surface and clattered to the floor. But there was no phone.

In her bare feet, she padded toward the table inside her front door, where the registration book from the old Redman still sat. Sliding it aside, she searched for her phone. Nothing.

But the book beckoned to her. Her fingers tingled every time she touched it. Standing there on the throw rug inside her threshold, she stared down at the register. Faded, dusty, the linen cover

241

tattered along its edges. She already knew what was inside. Yet still, like a magnet to her hands, the book commanded she touch it.

As she did, another odd sensation began under her bare feet. A chill ran up her entire body, prickling her scalp. Cold. Wet. Icy water squished up between her toes.

As she looked down to investigate the cause, her gaze strayed across her fingers now lying atop the old book. She blinked, her vision momentarily blurring before clearing again. And Kate froze, shock and confusion turning her to stone.

Kate was a French manicure kind of gal with pale, translucent pink covering all but the opaque, pure white, squared tips of her nails. The fingers she was looking at now sported nails clipped much shorter, filed into rounded ovals, and painted with bright-red polish. And there was a ring on the left hand.

A vintage diamond baguette nestled among white-gold petals and more diamonds. Exactly like the one Leah described in her letter to Joan.

Kate staggered backward, staring in disbelief at her hands. Not her own, but *these* hands. Her Aunt Leah's hands. When she turned them over to study the palms, she gasped when she realized they were streaked with blood. She shrieked, a sudden wave of bile rising into her throat.

Shudders of revulsion racked her body as she desperately swiped them against the front of her terry robe. But the robe felt suddenly petal-soft, silky, and smooth. Kate looked down to see she was no longer wearing terry cloth, but fluffy, white fur.

Her scream reverberated through the empty cottage. Somewhere deep in her brain, she knew what was happening. This was another vision, another direct contact from her aunt's spirit. She struggled to slow her racing thoughts and regain control over her own body. Sucking in a deep breath, she raised her face toward the mirror over the hall table.

Her reflection wasn't there. Like the blank television screen in her apartment the night after she entered the Redman, the mirror showed nothing but black and white static. Kate heard the hissing of white noise. Until the voice, sounding like *her* voice, broke through the static once again.

Find me.

And suddenly, there it was. Her image? Or her Aunt Leah's? The woman in the mirror was translucent, wavering like a candle flame, or as if she were under water.

As if she were under water. She *is* under water. Lying lost, forgotten, and abandoned on the bottom of Loch Sheldrake for over fifty years.

Find me.

A strangled sob broke from Kate's throat as she staggered away from the mirror. When would this nightmare end? She squeezed her eyes shut and fisted both hands until the nails bit painfully into her palms.

When the doorbell rang, she shrieked again and wrapped her arms around herself. What now? What horrible image would she find if she opened the door, or even dared to peer through the peephole?

But seconds later, the bell rang again, followed by pounding and a man's frantic voice.

"Kate! Kate, open up. What's happening in there?"

TWENTY-TWO

Too tired to eat, Daniel suffered through a wilted salad with watery dressing at a Mom-and-Pop diner in the tiny burgh of Loch Sheldrake. He was exhausted after the day's proceedings. Dealing with Yvette and that Celia woman, with all their talk of bouffant valances and matching, upholstered wing chairs. Helping them decide between two of the ugliest paisley patterns he'd ever seen. Playing email volleyball with King Lareci, who was apparently going to get his way with every little detail of the decor for the place.

The concept turned Daniel's stomach. What this 60s vintage building craved was *period*—retro colors with stark, clean lines. No. Instead, the place would end up looking like the Ritz Carlton, duplicated a hundred miles north. Just what boss man wanted.

He'd been pissed at Lareci for his decisions about the renovation from the start. Then, at the way he waltzed in and swept Kate off her feet. To, undoubtedly, fuck her brains out. What did this guy have so special to keep her going home with him now for over two months? This wasn't the Kate he knew. The free-spirited, one-night-stand, independent woman who changed sexual partners as often as her underwear.

And then today, she shows up looking like there'd been a death in the family. Daniel figured it was Lareci she'd been trying to call all day. Like, every twenty minutes, with no success. Kate's deflated reaction when he told her he'd been emailing back and forth with the bastard all day said it all.

They'd had a lover's spat, must be. So maybe, he thought as he toyed with a soggy, pale, pink slice of tomato on his plate, this was a golden opportunity. Kate went home alone tonight. Lareci was nowhere in sight. Maybe now was his chance to get a piece of what he'd been having wet dreams about for the past six months.

Daniel picked up a bottle of wine on his way to Kate's place. A last-minute decision, he grabbed a bouquet of flowers wrapped in green paper he found displayed in a tub of water near the register. He pulled into her driveway about eight o'clock.

The sun had almost disappeared behind the mountains in the distance, and the colors were beautiful. Orange, red, blue, and violet streaked the sky in a pattern so perfect, it looked like a watercolor painting hanging over the shimmering water. Sunsets probably looked real pretty from her back deck.

I'll be happy to be her sounding board. Hold her hand while she cries, ease her grief about whatever the Lareci creep had done, with a couple glasses of wine. Then, I can make my move.

Yes, this was his chance, Daniel thought, as he swung his legs out of the SUV and made his way to the front door, wine and flowers in hand. But as he reached the top step, he paused, listening. He could hear her through the door. Sobbing.

The heartless bastard. What the hell could he have done to upset her so? Squaring his shoulders, Daniel pressed the doorbell.

The blood-curdling scream coming from the other side sent the wine bottle crashing to the concrete step.

Was Lareci in there? Hurting her? Had he arrived while Daniel was away at the diner?

Daniel pounded on the door with one fist, shouting, "Kate! Kate, open up!" The flowers scattered as he hammered with both hands. He tried the knob, but of course, it was locked. He was about to pull out his phone and dial 911 when he heard her fumbling with the chain and deadbolt.

When the door swung open, Kate stood before him, wearing nothing but a white, terry robe. Her hair was disheveled, she was barefoot, and she wore no makeup.

Hmm. Looks way different from the Kate I'm accustomed to seeing. Hell, how does she cover up all those freckles?

Her eyes were red, and her lips were pressed into a grim line. As though she was disappointed to see him. *Him*, and not the Lareci bastard.

Great. Just fucking great.

"What's going on, Kate? I heard you crying. Screaming. What the hell?" he asked, annoyance clearly leaking out onto the words.

She hesitated, staring at him dumbly, before finally taking a step back and saying, "Come on in, Daniel. It must have been the television you heard. I was watching a movie."

Sure. He wasn't buying that story for one minute.

"Are you alone?" he asked, scanning the room for signs of another person. Of *him*.

She nodded. "Yes, and I guess," she chuckled nervously, dropping her gaze to the floor, "I guess watching a horror flick isn't the smartest move when I'm up here in the boondocks by myself." She ran her hands down over her robe and tossed one side of her dark hair over a shoulder. "I must look a fright myself," she said weakly.

Daniel heaved a huge sigh. "Well, I *had* brought wine. And flowers, too. I could see you were feeling a little down when you left today. But now they're a big mess all over your front stoop. I'm telling you, Kate; I thought you were being raped in here."

Her embarrassed grin didn't reach her eyes as she shook her head jerkily. "Nope. No, just a silly old movie."

Daniel reached out and pinched her chin between two fingers. "Are you sure you're okay?" he asked in his best I'm-really-worried-about-you tone.

Hell, it works for Lareci. Why not for me?

She nodded, sliding a glance toward the door. "And don't worry about the wine. I have some. If I get you a broom, can you sweep the glass off the porch? It's getting dark, and I'd rather not go outside right now. I'm a little spooked. From a stupid movie," she added.

Well, there goes admiring the sunset from the back deck.

A half-hour later, Daniel sat in the easy chair across from Kate on the couch, elbows on his knees. He'd poured her another glass of wine and studied her face as she sipped it. She had quieted considerably, after draining the first glass he'd poured in three or four swallows.

Time to make my move.

Daniel rose and moved to sit beside her, laying a hand on her bare knee as it peeked out from the folds of her robe. "Do you want to talk about it? About what happened to upset you so much today?"

She shifted uneasily on the cushions and kept her eyes trained on her wine glass. "I'm fine, Daniel. Really. A little over-tired, perhaps. These long-distance projects . . . the travel wears on me."

He reached up to tuck a strand of hair behind her ear, catching sight of the three diamond studs lining the edge of the pink, shell-like shape. She shuddered, but didn't pull away. *Good sign.*

Hmm, I've often imagined running my tongue over those sexy speed bumps. Maybe after another glass of wine—

"I'm not interested in what you have in mind, Daniel." She was looking straight at him now, her tone dead serious. Even a tad stern.

Uh-oh. I guess I haven't gotten her tipsy enough yet.

But Daniel wasn't going to let this opportunity pass so easily. Hell, he was *in*. She was at least two drinks on the way to mellow, and she was already half-naked. This was the closest he'd ever gotten. The first time he'd managed to break through her icy, boss-lady armor.

He let his fingers stray down to her shoulder, where he drew circles with one finger on the lapel of her robe. "I know how you operate, Kate Bardach. I know how you choose to relieve the stress in your life. I can help you with that. Tonight. No strings. Nobody else has to know."

Kate blinked at him and drew back, her eyes wide. "You're offering to have sex with me? For *my* sake? Therapeutic sex?"

Daniel lowered his voice to a growling purr, trailing his finger down the front of her robe toward where the deep V revealed a tiny slice of delectable, freckled mound. "Trust me. I know you'll feel better. Take your mind off everything. If only for a little while."

He leaned in to kiss her, then tumbled back when she lurched forward and bumped his nose with her cheekbone. Setting the wine glass down on the table, she stood and glared down at him, hands on her hips.

"Look. Up until now, I know I've come off as a wild child when it came to my social life. But let's get one thing clear. I'm past that now. My sex-for-the-hell-of-it days are over." She turned her back to him and wrapped her arms around her waist. "I'm in love. I've fallen in love with Marco Lareci."

Kate's heart had finally stopped slamming so hard against her ribs they ached. She'd been disappointed to see it was Daniel on her doorstep and not Marco. But she was so shaken by this last vision, she was grateful there was somebody there with her. Anybody.

She should have been shocked by Daniel's advances, but she wasn't. He'd been trying to get her in bed ever since she hired him. At first, she used the *I don't mess with the employees* routine.

Kate could tell after several months of his repeated attempts to ask her out that Daniel cared less about keeping his job with Bardach & Associates and more about getting her naked. After all, he was a talented, young designer in the big city. He'd be snapped up by another design firm in a heartbeat if she fired him. Or, if he left.

What horrified Kate more than anything else was how he viewed her. Mostly because it was true. She'd always considered her lifestyle modern and carefree. Apparently, to the people who knew her and worked with her, she appeared shallow. Loose. An easy lay. One who thought sex could cure everything.

Well, for a while in her life, it had. Or seemed to. Not anymore.

"Listen, Daniel. It's obvious why you came here tonight, and I hope I've made it clear I'm not going to bed with you. I'm sorry, but things have changed." She turned to face him, meeting his surprised and slightly irritated expression. "*I've* changed. But I wasn't lying when I told you I got spooked tonight, and frankly, I'm afraid to stay here alone." She glanced up at the clock. "It's too late for me to go back to the city now. Would you humor me and stay here tonight? I have a guest bedroom."

By all rights, she knew Daniel should have refused her. After all, he'd arrived with half a hard-on in anticipation of a rousing night in the sack. Now, she not only had rejected him sexually, but told him she's in love with Marco—a man he obviously despised. She expected him to storm out the door, trailed by a stream of curses. Quit, maybe.

But Daniel surprised her. Maybe he had a heart, and a brain, under that exuberant, puppy-like persona after all.

He swiped his hands down over his face and sighed before meeting her gaze again. The irritation was gone from his expression, replaced by . . . what? Sympathy? Pity?

"Okay, I'll admit it. My ego is bruised. But I'm not too proud to also admit I love working with you, Kate. And, pardon my skepticism, but I don't think this thing you have with Lareci will last very long. It might take a little longer than usual, but you'll tire of him. Appears to me as if he's already tiring of you."

Ouch. Now those were words she'd rather not heard spoken out loud. The very fear she'd been harboring all day.

"I'll stay," he continued, shrugging. "Sleep in your guest room, not try anything. You can trust me. But promise me this. When you and Lareci officially call it quits, will you give me a chance? You and I, we are alike, Kate. We value the same things in life. Good times, money, sex. They're all commodities. Disposable. You know, like your racehorses."

Double ouch. Is that how heartless I appear? How shallow I *am*?

"Once you get over your Italian stallion, let's give it a go," Daniel continued. "I think we'd make quite a team. At least," he winked, "for a little while."

Later that night, Kate lay staring at her bedroom ceiling. Sleep was off the table. Her eyes had been opened in a cruel, stark way today, and there was no way she'd be closing them for quite some time.

Daniel's words had cut to the core of the matter. To the core of her life, baring to her eyes the person she'd become. How could she have been so blind and so selfish?

First, his comment about Marco *already growing tired of her.* The image flashed in her mind of those gorgeous, hazel eyes, only that morning, studying her from his bed. The grim, emotionless, blank expression. A cool, green stare, as though he were looking at a complete stranger, or somebody he really didn't even care to meet.

How his virile male body hadn't reacted normally to her nude form.

This had been one of Kate's deepest fears ever since her first encounter with a man—they would no longer find her desirable. Rejection. It had been easier to enjoy the physical pleasures with men she hardly knew, with whom she parted ways before that could happen. Before they could cause her any emotional pain.

Then, Daniel's reference to disposable pleasures, *like her racehorses.* She'd never thought of them that way. She loved her horses. At least, she thought she did. But he was right—they were temporary playthings she tossed aside once they were no longer useful to her.

Kate would never forget Marco's expression of horror at the farm when she told him the geldings went to auction at the end of their career. Sending them off was an unpleasant part of the racing industry she'd chosen to ignore. If she didn't think about it, she could pretend it wasn't happening.

Like slaves, he'd said. Marco had seen the situation for its true worth. And her attitude toward it spoke to him in agonizing detail about her true nature.

But it's not the woman she wanted to be. Not anymore. For the first time in her life, Kate knew what it meant to love someone—

really love them—more than herself, more than her pride. Aunt Leah's words in her letters echoed in her brain.

Love changes a girl. Makes you do things you thought you never would. Someday, I'm sure you'll understand.

Finally, Kate understood. And somehow, she had to figure out a way to prove it to the man who held her heart hostage.

TWENTY-THREE

After Kate left that morning, Marco immersed his mind completely in his work for the entire day. He hadn't gotten as far behind as he'd feared, and by four o'clock had cleaned up most of his old business. He spent the next three hours cultivating relationships with new contacts.

He'd been interrupted, at least a dozen times, by emails from Daniel. Apparently, Marco was expected to bless every detail on the decor down to the color of the stitching on the upholstery.

Oy, marrone. What part of *Ritz Carlton* didn't Boy Wonder understand?

All day, he'd try to ignore the niggling feeling of loss in his gut. Marco couldn't help thinking his perfect woman had materialized before his eyes, then slowly transformed into someone he not only didn't know, but had no desire to know. Like Delilah the temptress, the story from his Bible study days. A woman of evil intent, destined to draw him in to his ruin.

Yet, there was still a nugget of doubt. He didn't want to believe Kate was intentionally cold and calculating. Maybe she simply didn't know any better. He'd dined with her parents. Seen them interact. Experienced their non-family unit. Met her heartless father.

Ha, what a laugh. Kate's father was the big cheese of cardiology at Mount Sinai. *Cardiology.* Yet, he guessed that inside Kaleb's chest, instead of a beating heart, there was only cold, hard lead. How ironic was that?

In defense of his own bruised heart, Marco had chosen to block Kate's calls. He knew well, with her intense control over his emotions, he was a lost soul. The only way to escape a sure path to Heart Hell was to cut her off, completely.

At seven thirty-five, he checked his phone. There were twenty-seven missed calls from Kate Bardach. *Persistent bitch. Doesn't like to take no for an answer. But . . . .*

Was she okay? What if something were wrong? If she needed him?

No. He knew better. His last email interchange with Daniel was time-stamped at four thirty-seven p.m. Daniel had been prudent in informing him of Kate's arrival earlier in the day, and would have mentioned a problem if there had been one.

He was still clutching his phone when it rang, and he jumped, nearly dropping the damn thing. Hands trembling, he read the caller ID. *Clive.*

"Hey, my friend, how goes it?" Clive asked. "Are we set for day after tomorrow? Loch Sheldrake, right? How the hell did you even find this place?"

Marco sighed. "Long story. But it seems, from all the evidence, there may be a 1964-and-a-half fastback Mustang down there. Most likely with the remains of two bodies inside."

Clive hummed a wordless reply. Then he said, "Yeah, I got your message. I've called it in, and it seems since there was never even a missing person's report filed, we're on our own with this one. I'm bringing my usual gear, but in a situation like this, the cops aren't interested until we have evidence of bodies. It's just hearsay."

Marco leaned his forehead on his hand. "I don't know if we'll find anything, Clive. But there's a real nice lady who's hoping we do. She needs closure. Her sister disappeared without a trace."

Clive's soft whistle streamed into his ear. "So, is this a lady of interest? Or, are we doing this out of the goodness of our hearts?"

Sitting up straighter and realigning his armor, Marco replied, "No, this is an older woman. A relative of an—an acquaintance. She's been looking for her sister for over fifty years. And I'm a paying customer on this one, Clive."

His friend's laughter was wry, yet knowing at the same time. "Okay, *Compagno.* We'll go with that as an explanation. You can fill me in on the details about your *acquaintance* later. Over a beer."

Marco ended the call and sighed, shut down his office computer, and headed for the shower.

After a largely sleepless night, Marco rose at four a.m. Damn, if he could only turn and walk away. But he knew he couldn't. For one, his investment sat right where these murders supposedly happened. If there was evidence to find, it had been dumped into the place's picturesque water view. Now didn't *that* curse his group's fancy new hotel venture?

Second, he'd already gotten Clive involved before he realized he and Kate weren't a match made in heaven. If he backed out now, there would be more questions to answer than he was willing to deal with. He'd been lucky enough to escape Kate's spell with even a trace of his masculine pride left intact. What did remain, he didn't intend to risk, especially with Clive, an old friend who read Marco like *he* was psychic.

And then there was Joan. As disgusted as he'd been that night at dinner—realizing what kind of family Kate came from—his sympathies had gone out to Joan. As far as he could tell, she was the only one with a heart in the Bardach clan. And he felt sorry for her. Her husband was a pompous, cold-hearted man focused on only his own interests. His work and his fun little hobby, the racehorses.

Never mind there were hearts, as well as lives, involved in both ventures.

For a frivolous, frantic moment, Marco wondered if Kate really did have more of her mother's sentimentality than her father's self-love. He supposed it was possible, though from everything he'd witnessed about her so far, the woman definitely took more after dear old dad.

Had he imagined the way she looked into his eyes when they were together and her defenses were down? The thought of those deep, blue depths locked on him made his heart squeeze in his chest. All those twenty-seven times she'd tried to call him yesterday. Had she realized she really did have deeper feelings for him and was desperate to let him know? Or, was she simply a stubborn, relentless woman who didn't tolerate being ignored?

Could he afford to take the chance she'd do more damage to his emotions than she already had?

Well, unfortunately, he couldn't just walk away from this whole situation and not take the chance. Undoubtedly, Kate would accompany her mother to witness the dive. It sure as hell wouldn't be her father.

Kaleb would probably be too busy bossing around the surgical residents at Manhattan's largest hospital, or arranging the next truckload of used-up racehorses to be hauled off to the auction block.

With the dive date and time only a little more than twenty-four hours away, he had to do something. His choices were limited since Marco didn't have Joan's number and couldn't call her directly. He'd either have to call Kate or drive up to tell her in person.

His logical brain told him the former was the smarter choice. His heart had him throwing a few things in an overnight bag and calling for the parking attendant to bring up his car.

It was still very early when Marco drove past the Shelby, a little past seven. The construction crews had arrived but were still huddled around the tailgate of Jeremy's truck. He always had a Box of Joe and a few dozen donuts for his men to start out the day. Sort of a construction crew's huddle, Marco thought with a grin.

Kate probably wouldn't even be awake yet. She usually got to the job site by around ten. At least, that's the time she always designated for Boy Wonder.

Marco's blood began its incessant itch again, and he swore under his breath. It irked him Daniel slept not a half-mile away from where Kate did, while he was four counties away. Had they spent time together last night? Had dinner? Her calls had stopped coming in right around four thirty yesterday afternoon. Maybe she'd given up and decided she didn't want to waste any more time on a stubborn Italian who'd ignored her calls all day.

No. He wouldn't allow himself to believe that. Kate may not be head-over-heels in love with him, but Marco couldn't accept she felt nothing for him at all. Besides, the last thing he wanted to do was show up on her doorstep at the crack of dawn and wake her sporting a bad attitude.

But his good intentions flew out the window a few seconds later. His attitude spiked to a few notches above *bad* when he pulled into her driveway—*behind* Daniel's black SUV. The itch in his veins turned to pure acid when he got to the top step and saw the purple stain on the concrete. What the hell? He stooped to retrieve the circlet of green glass, complete with cork, just visible under the edge of the shrub flanking the steps.

Had they both gotten so drunk they couldn't even make it inside the door without breaking a bottle of wine?

Rage blinded him as he mashed down the doorbell button and didn't let go. He could hear the incessant buzzing from inside, but after thirty seconds, even that annoying horn-blaring wasn't enough to satisfy his fury. He began pounding on the door with both fists.

Less than a minute elapsed before he heard the deadbolt release, and the door swung open. She'd obviously looked out and realized it was him, then prepared her façade. Because there wasn't a shred of surprise or embarrassment on her pale, freckled skin. Through a huge smile she murmured, "Oh, Marco," and stepped forward with her arms outstretched.

Seriously? Who was she trying to fool?

He took a step back, nearly tumbling off the stoop in the process. His clumsy display made him all the more furious, and he barked, "Cazzo, Kate. Did you even wash my semen off the sheets before you invited Boy Wonder to your bed?"

Kate blinked, confused at first by Marco's crude words and enraged expression. She knew the man had a hot temper, but she didn't think she'd ever seen him *this* mad. Half-asleep still, she'd forgotten all about Daniel, sleeping in the guest bedroom. After lying awake until nearly four a.m., she'd finally given in and taken a sedative.

But oh, it all came crystal clear to her now. Behind him, she saw Marco's car was pulled up so close behind Daniel's SUV, she wondered if he'd actually rammed into it. Then Marco uncurled one fist and stuck his hand under her nose.

He'd gripped the broken bottle neck so tightly, there was blood oozing out of a small cut the glass had sliced into his palm.

"Have a good time last night, Kate? Too bad the last bottle never even made it inside the door," he hissed.

All the air left Kate's lungs in a single, debilitating whoosh. This looked bad, she knew. There was no way Marco would ever believe her version of last night's events. Even though they were true. She fisted both hands in her hair.

"Marco, no. Please, calm down and hear me out. Last night . . . I had another vision. She appeared again, but this time—"

"Oh, I'm sure you had quite a few visions last night, Kate. Is this the same ploy you use with all of your lovers? To intrigue them? Make them feel sorry for you? Oh, poor, frightened, psycho Kate."

His words sliced through her heart with such sudden sharpness, she actually felt like she might be having a heart attack. She grabbed at her chest, realizing then her robe wasn't even properly closed. She'd thrown it on so quickly, the V of the neckline gaped open nearly to her waist.

This looks bad. Really, really bad.

"Marco, you have to believe me." Her voice rose, panic spilling out and choking the words around a sob. "This isn't what you think."

It was at that moment—of course—Daniel stumbled out from the hallway. "What's going on, Kate? Everything all right?" His voice was gravelly from sleep, and he was naked from the waist up, wearing only a pair of rumpled jeans. His usually neatly styled blond waves stood up from his scalp like a poorly mowed wheat field.

Bad. This is very, very bad.

She watched as Marco's eyes slid over him, narrowing, his face growing even redder than it already was.

Kate reached out and touched Marco's arm. "Please, just listen. I was afraid to be alone last night. I asked Daniel to stay—"

Marco jerked his arm free as though she was poison. "Oh, I don't doubt you did," he spat. "I'm sure boy-toy doesn't have the balls to come after you on his own. Good for him he didn't have to."

"Marco, we didn't sleep together." Kate hated the desperation in her voice, but she knew, no matter how hard she tried to explain, her words wouldn't penetrate his fury.

The way his pale, hazel eyes skimmed over her then made her skin prickle. He was looking at her like she was something his cat had puked up on the carpet. A long, tense moment froze them, all three, as if time itself hit a momentary snag.

Then Marco's low, guttural words sliced her heart yet again. "Didn't sleep together, huh? That may well be true. I'd imagine, knowing you like I do, neither of you got very much sleep at all."

She stepped out onto the stoop, but Marco whirled and trotted down the steps.

"Marco, please. Don't leave like this," she pleaded.

He stopped, but didn't turn to face her. "I came here this morning to let you know the dive will take place tomorrow at ten a.m. I'm sure your mother will want to be there." His monotone was so flat, he sounded like a robot.

Tears blurred her vision as she watched him stalk around the back of his car—if he *hadn't* rammed Daniel's SUV, his car was evidently too close for him to walk between the bumpers. He climbed in, revved the engine, and screeched out onto the street. His tires left behind a twenty-foot skid trail on the pavement.

Marco didn't care he'd just made the hundred-mile trip up from the city. Or, that he'd be making it again tomorrow morning to meet Clive for this godforsaken dive. He couldn't think past the anger pushing his blood pressure beyond the point of sanity. And he knew, if he stopped at the job site now, he would likely turn his anger on one of the innocent workers. Possibly with his fists.

He turned his car onto Route 17 headed south and wound the powerful engine up to nearing red line.

Let a cop pull me over now. Or rather, let one try.

Was he angrier with Kate or with himself? He knew it should be the latter. After all, she'd made it clear from the beginning exactly what kind of woman she was. It was wishful thinking, on his part, spinning the fantasies in his head. Since the first day he'd gazed into those impossibly blue eyes, he'd wanted, more than anything in the world, for Kate Bardach to be *the one*.

But wishing can't make it so. He'd put his heart on the line and completely deserved the humiliation he was feeling right now. Kate had never committed to him. Never told him she loved him. The woman had every right to sleep with whomever she chose.

Marco slammed the steering wheel with his palm, breaking open the small cut the neck of the wine bottle had sliced into it. He swore as he swiped his leather-wrapped wheel with a handkerchief before fisting the cloth. Logic wasn't reining in his temper very well. Not very well at all.

He wanted to break something, hurt someone. Project his pain outward so he didn't have to endure it all by himself. Twenty miles later, he knew exactly how he would do that.

Using his hands-free phone system, he dialed an old friend. One he hadn't spoken to in two or three years. Not since she moved out of his apartment. After sharing his bed for almost eight months.

"Arianna. How are you, my love? It's me. Marco." He spoke in fluent Italian.

TWENTY-FOUR

When the Bardach's house phone rang at seven thirty-five a.m., Joan wasn't really alarmed. Kaleb got calls at all hours of the day and night, seven days a week. She only thought it odd since her husband was already at the hospital. He'd left at six that morning.

Joan picked up her cup of coffee and carried it to the telephone table. Her heart *did* leap when she saw the caller ID flashing on the screen. *Katherine*. Her daughter never called this early.

"Hello? Katherine, what's wrong?"

Joan's stomach did a slow turn when her daughter's sob rumbled into her ear. "Mother. Mother, I need to talk to you. I think I've made the biggest mistake of my life."

Three hours later, Joan stood in her kitchen and fixed a cup of chamomile tea, extra sugar and a touch of cream. The concoction had been her daughter's comfort drink ever since she was a child. She carried it to the small, round, café table in the breakfast room alcove of the Bardach family home on Long Island, where Katherine had sipped the balm dozens of times.

Her daughter sat staring out at the profusion of flowers in the carefully landscaped cutting garden. The spring blooms had begun to fade, but due to Joan's careful planning, the early summer blossoms were already competing for center stage. Ever since Katherine left home almost fifteen years ago, Joan's garden had become her baby. The place where she poured out the love and attention she had nowhere else to express.

As she approached, Joan felt quite sure Katherine didn't see a single flower. Tears streamed down her face in an endless trail. She'd given up trying to catch them with tissues from the box on the table, and they dripped from her cheeks and chin onto her tightly folded hands.

Joan couldn't remember ever seeing Katherine this upset. It alarmed her. Her daughter—she'd always thought—was exactly like her father. Cool. Aloof. Strong.

Or was she?

Joan settled herself in her chair and covered Katherine's hand with her own. "Tell me, Dear. What's happened? You're acting as if someone is dying."

"I am."

The words shot through Joan like an arrow. "Oh, my God, Katherine, what's wrong? Do you have . . . cancer? Dear God, no." She collapsed back in the chair and slapped a hand to her chest.

Kate smacked her hand to her forehead. Here she was, doing it again. So busy worrying about her own problems, her own agenda, she hadn't taken a moment to consider how her theatrics would upset her mother.

"No, Mother. No, please forgive me. I'm not ill. I just feel my heart is breaking, and I don't know how to handle it."

Until recently, I didn't even know I *had* a heart.

Joan huffed out a long breath and closed her eyes. "Well, thank God you're not really dying. Don't ever scare me like that again. You selfish, impudent girl."

Yup, she's got that right.

Joan lifted her cup with shaking hands as she leaned her elbows on the table. "Now tell me what this is all about. Kaleb told me you have a new colt. Nothing's happened to him, I hope?"

Kate shook her head.

"Or to April?"

So there it is. That's the extent to which my own mother sees my emotional attachments. My horses. And even them, I toss aside when they're no longer able to race or have babies.

Perhaps this had been a mistake, to come here. Kate hoped her mother might understand the torment she was going through at having lost Marco. But honestly, why did she believe that? Joan was as much a closed book as Kaleb. In fact, the first time Kate could remember seeing her mother emotional at all was when she opened up to her about Aunt Leah.

Aunt Leah. Right. The dive. No matter what, she had to tell her mother about the dive.

Kate swallowed the knot in her throat and followed it with a sip of her tea. Then she met her mother's gaze. In typical Mrs. Kaleb Bardach fashion, Joan was waiting quietly for Kate to explain. Silent patience. Never pry. Only speak when spoken to.

A flash of hatred for her father seared Kate's already bloodied heart. She pushed it aside. Where it—where he and his attitude toward life, she'd recently decided—belonged.

"Mother, Marco has arranged the dive. Tomorrow, ten a.m. He thought you'd like to be there." Kate struggled to regain her composure, keep her voice steady.

Joan's eyes widened, and a smile lit up her face. "Well, that's wonderful news, Katherine. Perhaps we'll be able to solve this mystery after all these years. Perhaps finally . . ." her expression sobered as she stared out the window, "finally, I'll attain a sense of peace."

Her eyes slid quickly back to Kate's face, while creases formed between her pale eyebrows. "But it's good news, not bad. Why are you so upset?" Her tone darkened. "Have you had another episode?"

Kate nodded, another wave of sobs threatening to melt her into a puddle on the chair. Swallowing hard, she squeaked, "I did. The start of this whole, terrible mess."

Over the next hour, Kate told the story of what had happened last night and how frightened she had been.

"I know Leah . . . her spirit . . . I know she doesn't mean me any harm. But every time I even *consider* distancing myself from Marco, she does something to scare me to death. Right before this happened, I decided to call you and suggest we find another dive team to go down after the car. Being around Marco . . . ." She was at a loss to explain emotions she didn't understand. Unsure her mother would understand them either.

But Joan didn't skip a beat. "I believe you're in love with this man, Katherine. I knew from the first time you spoke of him." She reached forward and stroked Kate's cheek. "There's been a light in those beautiful eyes of yours these past months. One I've never seen there before."

Kate blinked rapidly, fighting back another wave of tears, her throat so tight with pain she couldn't speak. Her mother *did* understand. Joan probably knew the truth even before she did.

"I'll admit, at first, I had this terrible feeling. I mean, it's like history is repeating itself," Joan continued. "You are the image of Leah. She fell terminally in love with an Italian. Unfortunately, in Leah's case, *terminally* has become quite a literal description."

Kate lurched forward and laid her hand on her mother's arm. "But Marco isn't a criminal, Mother. He's a good man from a wonderful, close family. That's part of what has terrified me about our relationship. I don't know how to be a part of a family like his."

Joan nodded, never taking her pale, brown gaze from Kate's. "Growing up in this household," she motioned to the room around them, "I guess I shouldn't be surprised. Your father is a good provider. I don't regret my life with him. But he's never been the affectionate type."

Kate nodded, thinking. Her father had always been an enigma. Kind to her and her mother, but never very giving of himself. Monetarily, yes. But never in a more personal way.

"Marco is so different from Father. From any of the men in my life. Worlds away from the type of men I usually spend time with."

Joan nodded, a hint of a smile brightening her features. "You are right. Marco is a good, kind man. How caring the man must be to arrange a dive into that godforsaken lake with the only intention to ease our pain? And from the way he looks at you, I know he's crazy about you."

Her mother's attention again strayed out the window, yet Kate could tell by her blank expression Joan's thoughts had retreated back inside her own mind. "I had a man look at me that way once. A long, long time ago. Like with Leah, my parents weren't very happy about my choice, either. But I didn't let it stop me." She sighed and squeezed Kate's hand. "Too bad Vietnam stepped in and took him away from me."

A pang of pity shot through Kate, and she took her mother's hand in both of her own. "Oh, Mother, I'm so sorry. I never knew."

Joan patted her hand. "It was a long time ago. But when you find a love like that, you sometimes have to fight for it. This man, this Marco, I think he might be worth fighting for."

Kate's heart did a slow, painful twist. Why, oh why, hadn't she come to her senses sooner?

She had felt Marco drawing away from her—from the woman she used to be—even before this morning's debacle. Now, she'd probably destroyed any chance to reclaim what they'd had together. To mend his faith in her. To convince him she'd realized the error of her childish, selfish ways and grown into the woman he'd believed her to be.

Kate crossed her arms on the table and buried her face, sobbing. "What am I going to do, Mother? Do you think it's too late?"

She felt Joan's hand stroking her hair. "I agree, what happened today will be difficult to bounce back from. One thing I do know about men—a blow like that to their ego can be deadly to a relationship."

Kate wailed.

Thanks, Mother. Precisely what I needed to hear.

"But he hasn't canceled the dive, Kate," Joan went on. "And I don't believe he's doing this only for me. He hardly knows me."

Kate looked up, and her mother lifted her chin with two fingers.

"My relationship with Paul—my soul mate, my forever true love—it wasn't meant to be. Apparently, Leah's and Bart's love wasn't in the cards, either. But maybe, just maybe, three's the charm. Perhaps you and Marco can mend the trail of broken hearts cursing our family's women."

At nine thirty the next morning, Kate and Joan were waiting in the parking lot of the Shelby. Kate had tossed two collapsible beach chairs into the back of her mother's Lincoln, and they'd set them up close to where the boat ramp met the pavement. She had no idea how long a dive like this would take. She knew she'd be pacing the entire time, but she wanted to be sure her mother was comfortable.

The early June morning was sunny and cool, with a slight breeze coming off the water. Kate was grateful bad weather hadn't postponed the dive. She wanted this nightmare over. And she couldn't wait to see Marco again.

Somehow, some way, she was going to show him how much she loved him. Prove to him she could change. She could be the woman he'd thought she was. The woman she wanted to be.

Ten minutes later, a van crunched up the driveway. A colorful, underwater scene splashed the sides of the bright-blue van, overlaid by the words *Abyss Explorations*. Marco was in the passenger seat, and Kate started in his direction before he even opened the door.

She stopped when a sporty, red Cadillac STS pulled up close behind, and a tall woman wearing white-framed sunglasses stepped out. Her long, blonde hair fell in perfect spirals down her back. When she came around the front of the car, Kate admired the form-fitting silk dress she was wearing. Pristine white. The grommet detail was a dead giveaway—a Derek Lam, Kate was certain.

Hmm. This diving guy's girlfriend has pretty good taste.

She turned her attention back to Marco, who climbed out of the van and headed straight past her, lifting her mother's hand to kiss it. Her heart sank only slightly. How nice he was paying deference to Joan first.

But, in the next moment, the richly clad blonde was beside him, clutching his elbow.

"Joan, this is a very close friend of mine, Arianna Valducci," Marco said. "She's a field scout for the Travel Channel. I asked her to come along today in case we find anything of interest."

Marco slipped his arm around the woman's waist, and Kate's heart seized.

"Marco—" she began.

But she was cut off as the blonde stepped between them and stuck out her exquisitely manicured hand.

"You must be Kate. Marco's filled me in on this entire," she paused, slipping off her sunglasses and sliding a knowing glance at Marco, "this entire *situation*." She turned her attention back to Joan. "I'm truly sorry for your loss, Mrs. Bardach. I do hope the boys can find what you're looking for today."

Panic clouded Kate's brain, and for the moment, she was speechless. The Travel Channel? Was Marco trying to make a public spectacle of this? One look told Kate her mother was wondering the same thing.

And if not, why was this life-sized Barbie doll even *here*?

Marco had avoided looking in Kate's direction since they'd arrived. But now, he stepped forward and gazed down into her eyes with a serious, almost threatening expression. "Kate, Arianna is a close friend. Very close. And I thought it only right to give her first shot at the footage of the recovery. If we find anything."

The words were like a hot blade to Kate's heart. Joan bolted to her feet, her eyes wild.

"Footage? You mean filming? There'll be no filming of this recovery. This is my sister's remains we're talking about here. I'm certain we have rights—"

"We don't know what they'll find down there, Mrs. Bardach." Arianna laid a hand on Joan's arm. "And even if Clive and Marco do locate . . . something, there will be no proof it belongs to your kin until the forensics report comes back. By then, it will be too late to film anything. The opportunity will be lost."

Fury boiled up in Kate's chest and she hissed, "I can't believe you'd do this, Marco Lareci. I was under the impression family meant more to you than that."

His eyes on hers was as cool and green as the water lapping on the rocks behind him. "It does. But, quite honestly, Kate, I'm the one who's surprised. I really didn't think this would bother you, of all people. Not at all."

The blade made another agonizing twist in her heart, and for a moment, Kate actually thought she might be sick. She turned away and stalked to the water's edge, her arms folded tightly around her middle.

From behind her, she heard her mother mutter, "You're going to turn this into a circus. It's sacrilege. Disgraceful."

Then, Arianna's melodic voice. "We don't mean to cause you any more pain than you're already experiencing. There will be no circus. No camera crews. Marco is a certified diver, and he's also very good with an underwater camera. He'll be doing the filming himself."

This was worse, so much worse than she'd expected. Marco was not only *over* her, but he was deliberately betraying her. An obvious attempt to hurt her. And what was the story with this blonde Barbie doll? The *real* story?

TWENTY-FIVE

Kate returned to the group as the rear doors of the van swung open, and a tall, wiry man stepped down. He was already wearing a wetsuit.

"Clive, this is Kate Bardach," Marco said as he approached.

A Jacques Cousteau clone, Kate thought as she shook his hand, with his thinning white hair and deep lines etched into his face.

"My pleasure, Ms. Bardach." His expression remained serious as he studied her face. "Marco tells me you have reason to believe this might turn into a search and recovery mission."

Kate felt her cheeks burn, unsure of how much Marco had told the man about her. Her abilities. Had he explained the details? Or, just told him she was a wacko with a hunch? *Psycho Kate?*

"Yes," she began, struggling to keep her tone level and confident. "This was the last place my aunt and her new husband were seen in October of 1964. They checked in, then vanished. Along with their brand new car."

Clive nodded sagely, his gaze wandering past her to the lake. "I've done a little reading up on this particular puddle. Seems if we find any bodies down there, they might not be the only ones."

Kate blinked fast and looked down at her hands, clasped so tightly before her the knuckles had blanched. "There are rumors, yes. But I'm hoping . . . ." She paused and swallowed hard. Part of her knew her aunt's spirit would never let her rest if they didn't find her. Another part chilled with the horror of the very notion. "A tail lens washed up on the boat ramp last week. It matches the kind of vehicle they were driving," she said in a small voice.

Marco had gone to the back of the van and paused. "Do you think it's possible the car survived all this time, Clive? It's fresh water, but still, it's been fifty years."

"It's entirely possible. This water is cold. Surely, at least the engine and parts of the sheet metal would remain."

Kate shuddered and closed her eyes against the imagined image. If they did find anything, she knew this image—and countless, macabre others—wouldn't exist merely in her imagination for long.

Especially once they were recorded in digital detail.

Marco climbed into the van and appeared less than a minute later, zipping up the front of an extremely form-fitting wetsuit.

"Ah, you did bring the camera," Marco muttered, reaching inside the van and lifting out a black case.

Kate's stomach did a slow, nauseating twist as Joan buried her face in a handkerchief. She slid a searing glance toward Arianna, who was oblivious, her glittering eyes dancing as she admired Marco's muscular form in the wetsuit.

"No camera today, Marco," Clive said. "Today, we just go down and scout the territory."

Twenty minutes later, Marco followed Clive as he splashed down the cracked concrete of the ancient boat ramp, fins tucked under his arm.

Clive looked up at the clear blue sky overhead. "Lady Luck smiles on us so far. This bright sunshine should carry down as far as you're certified to dive, Marco. But," he motioned to the floodlight clipped to his mask, "I'm prepared if we need to shed a little extra light on our find."

"Be careful, Marco, please. How long do you think you'll be down?" Arianna asked.

Clive answered. "Depends on how deep we go. The deeper the dive, the less time our air holds out."

Marco flashed his sexiest grin at Arianna. "Don't worry, Ari. Clive's one of the best. We shouldn't be down more than a half-hour."

Kate fought the impulse to grab Barbie's corkscrew mane and yank a hank out by the roots.

"You do realize," Clive called as he waded deeper into the water, "if we do find human remains, we'll have to quit until the authorities are notified."

Joan sobbed, and Kate wrapped an arm protectively around her shoulders. "We understand," she replied.

"Come on, Lareci. Let's get this show on the road," Clive said over his shoulder as he slipped on his fins. Then took in his mouthpiece and adjusted his mask.

Marco was always amazed at the heady exhilaration of being able to breathe under water. Like some kind of childhood dream, like being able to fly. But today, Clive wasn't allowing him any time to loll around enjoying the sensations. Within moments of them sinking below the surface, Clive waved a hand, signaling for Marco to follow him into the dusky depths below.

They headed north. The water was greenish, cloudy with floating algae that mottled the brilliant sunshine slicing through in shimmering beams. Marco was amazed at what Loch Sheldrake looked like under the surface. *Volcanic crater* was the term that came to mind as he paddled after Clive's oscillating fins.

A shelf of jagged rock rimmed the shoreline, describing the Loch's boundary for the first twenty feet or so down before their safety check. The shelf narrowed at an alarmingly rapid rate, to the point where Marco found himself following Clive laterally in places to avoid colliding with the encroaching rocky outcroppings.

But as they went deeper, he could see the ledge ended below them. Dropped off, sheer and flat, straight down into black oblivion below.

There's no way in hell we're finding any sunken car or human remains in this lake. At least, not without a submarine. Or a diving bell.

They had to be at least 50 feet down when they reached the end of the ledge. Clive turned north and began to hug the jagged boundary. All Marco saw were rocks, some fallen and rotting tree trunks, a lost boat anchor snagged in one place, and little else. After a short time his instructor ceased swimming and faced him, shaking his head and pointing in the opposite direction. They turned and reversed, retracing their path to the south.

A few moments later, Clive paused and pointed upward toward the shore, then continued on his southern path. It took a moment for Marco to decipher his instructor's meaning, but then he realized—duh, that's where the boat ramp is.

Good thing Clive's with me, or I'd never figure out where I came into this godforsaken lake. Or how to get out.

They hadn't swum far beyond drop-in when he spotted the wreck.

At first, Marco wasn't even sure what it was. The lichen-covered shape lay about twenty feet ahead, perched on the very edge of the rocky precipice defining Loch Sheldrake's undetermined cauldron of the unknown. It wasn't until they'd nearly reached the wreck that Marco spotted the flashes of red near one end of the irregular shape.

A shaft of sunlight caught on the remaining left taillight of the Mustang, which had nearly broken free from its badly rusted frame. It was swaying gently with the movement of the water, as if waving to get their attention.

If Marco didn't already know what they were looking for, he would not have recognized the wreck as a car at all. The front end was gone, rusted away near the middle of the body. Sheet metal, Marco knew, was all that held the vehicle together. Half a car remained—the rear half. Short sections of rust-patched, mint-green metal wobbled unsteadily along the sides, hiding from view whatever might still lie inside.

The rear axle, caught on a jutting boulder, is all that had kept the entire vehicle from plunging to Loch Sheldrake's full, unfathomable depths. For almost fifty years.

A chill starting from deep in his gut spread through his veins like ice water. It *was* here. His heart rate spiked, rendering him momentarily light-headed. Would they find Leah down here, too?

Or, had her remains been sucked out when the front half broke free and sank?

Marco's breathing rate kicked up as he checked his wrist mount. Even if he weren't hyperventilating, his air wouldn't last another ten minutes. He waved to get Clive's attention—who was already swimming close to the wreck—flashing the beam of his spotlight inside. Marco was still a dozen or more feet away. When he caught Clive's eye, he gave the thumbs up sign and gradually began his ascent.

Clive caught up with him at the safety stop, and Marco's breathing had still not slowed. This was too real, too freaky, to have actually located what could be Kate's aunt's car. He couldn't tell by Clive's expression if what he'd seen inside was significant. Not surprising, since his instructor was incredibly stoic. But Marco had already decided, until he was up on top, he didn't want to know anyway.

They broke the surface at the same time, and Marco yanked his mouthpiece free, gasping for air, though his tank still had several minutes left. Kate and Joan both jumped up from their seats, their hands intertwined.

Arianna rushed to the water's edge. "Marco, are you okay?" She kicked off her shoes and splashed into the water to meet him with outstretched arms.

Marco staggered up the broken concrete surface, coughing and nodding his head. But he couldn't get the words out before his instructor. Clive had already pulled his head gear free and strode boldly past him, straight up to face Kate.

"Ms. Bardach, I believe we've located what you're looking for. At least, what's left of it. An automobile, some sort of compact coupe. Looks like it might have been light blue at one time. Green, maybe? Anyway, it's crumbling, split in half from years of deterioration. The front end is completely gone."

Kate's eyes widened, and she staggered back a step, her gaze darting to Marco. "Did you see it, too? Is it—"

Marco nodded solemnly. "It's a Mustang. I'm sure of it. The left taillight is still hanging on to the wreck. Half a car."

"But half a car is not all that's left, Marco." Clive's words took on an ominous tone. "There's something inside. On the floorboards, wedged in front of the back seat. At first I thought it to be a large animal. A huge, light-colored pelt—a polar bear came to mind, though we all know that's not possible. But then I spotted the skull." He turned back to face Kate. "It's time to call in the authorities on this one, I'm afraid. The skull inside the wreck is human."

Marco was glad—so glad—the first dive took place on a Saturday. At least he wouldn't risk running into Boy Wonder. He didn't think he could have handled that, at least not without taking a swing at him. And if the bastard had snuggled up to Kate . . . .

No. Really good thing it was a Saturday.

Yet, as hurt and angry as he'd been by Kate's betrayal, he couldn't help but feel a pang of guilt when he saw the way she looked at Arianna. He couldn't deny it. He'd done this—came up with the idea of filming the dive and called not just anyone, but Arianna—on purpose. Now he wasn't the least bit proud of it.

Kate's big, blue eyes had been unable to disguise her pain. Of course, he could have been imagining it. There he went again, fantasizing about the impossible.

Marco hadn't originally planned on Arianna actually coming with them that day, but she'd insisted. She wanted to scout out the area, take pictures of the lake and the town, talk to the folks at the museum, yada yada. But when the day came, she did none of that. She spent her time instead hanging on to him every chance she got, referring often to the good times when they'd been together.

Yeah, it had been good with Arianna. But he knew within the first few weeks—she wasn't the one. Frankly, the only reason he'd allowed her to move in and stay with him for eight months was because they shared so much in common. Italian families. Born and raised in Brooklyn. Arianna struggled her way to the top of the cable network industry in much the same way as Marco had fought his way to his own fortune on Wall Street. He thought perhaps, in time, he would grow to love her.

And, okay, she'd been good in bed. But sex only scratches part of the itch. They'd parted friends, both knowing no matter how much they had in common, they weren't in love. And never would be.

But it seemed on dive day, Arianna might be willing to give it another go. By the end of the day, Marco had to break it to her, point blank, there wasn't a chance of that happening. Not an angel's chance in hell.

Since Marco had no idea how long it would take for the authorities to set a date for Clive to do the recovery, he rode back with Clive to the city that night. Then, he holed himself up in his apartment the rest of the weekend, brooding.

He was on his second beer and watching a Yankees game on Sunday afternoon when his doorbell buzzed. For one crazy minute, his heart leaped, and he prayed it was Kate. But no. His sister's voice came across when he activated the speaker.

"Hey, bro. You busy? Got company?" Diana asked.

"Nope. Just watching the game. Come on up."

Diana was alone, and Marco couldn't hide his disappointment she didn't have little Angelina with her. His sister hugged him like she always did, kissed him full on the mouth, then scowled at his expression.

"You don't look very happy to see me," she snarled, and stuck out her lower lip.

Marco smiled and sighed. "I am, Di. I'd hoped you had tadpole with you. I could use some cheering up."

Diana wandered over to the easy chair where Cleo was perched, waiting for her pats. As she scrubbed her hand up and down the cat's back, Diana said, "For once, her daddy is spending some quality time with our daughter. I think Peter might actually be coming around. He's been getting home earlier, spending a lot more time with us. He's crazy in love with his little girl."

"Well, I can't blame him there," Marco said, heading for the kitchen. "Want a beer?"

"I'd love one. And what's wrong with you, anyway? Why so glum?"

Marco snapped the cap off the bottle of Heineken and handed it to her, shrugging. "A blue weekend, I guess."

Diana screwed up her face and glared at him, balancing the beer on her hip. "Don't try to fool me, bro. Girl troubles? I thought you and that Jewish babe you brought home to meet the family were getting it on pretty well." She lifted the bottle and slugged a third without taking a breath.

Marco chuckled and shook his head. His sister was no prim prissy. She was just another one of the guys.

Then he sobered. "What did Mama and Papa have to say about her, anyway? Did they buy she was only a client?"

Diana snorted. "No way. Not that you tried to fool anybody. Hell, the way you looked at her? Marco, I don't think I've ever seen you look at a woman like that. Not even that Ariella chick."

"Arianna. And no, Arianna, though a very nice woman, is not wife material. Not for me."

Diana blinked, her head whipping around to stare at him. "And this Jewish chick is?"

Marco groaned and headed for the couch, where he flopped down so hard his beer sloshed out of the bottle and onto his shirt. "Cazzo," he snarled.

Diana grabbed some paper towels off the counter and threw them down on his chest before she perched in the chair. "Well? Spill, dude. And not just your beer. Am I going to have a Jewish sister-in-law or what? A sister's got a right to know."

Marco stared at the television through unseeing eyes. The image of Kate's beautiful face flickered in his memory, and he felt his guts twist. He shook his head.

"Nope. It's all done. Over. She's already hooked up with her boy-toy architect." He took a long draw on his beer. "It would never have worked. I can only imagine how Mama and Papa would react to a double ceremony—with a priest *and* a rabbi."

Diana scooted forward in her chair and slapped Marco on the knee. "Hey. You've got to get over this *what will the family say* line of thinking. It's never stopped me."

He lifted an eyebrow and tipped his head. "Yeah, and how's that worked out for you so far?"

Diana lowered her head. "I know, I made some mistakes. But when it comes right down to it, Marco, Mama and Papa don't really care who we choose to spend our lives with, as long as we're happy. I mean, you know they hate Peter, but it doesn't keep them from loving the hell out of their granddaughter, does it?" She looked up and glared at him.

Marco studied her face, her dark eyes serious on his. "I'll keep that in mind," he said quietly. "For the future. But I'm afraid with the *nice Jewish lady*, it's not going to happen."

Two hours later, Diana snuggled Cleo one more time, hugged Marco, and pinched his cheek as she prepared to leave.

"Don't look so down, big brother. You're a drop-dead gorgeous guy with plenty of money and a great future. Another girl will come along and snatch you up in no time."

Marco was mortified as a lump clogged his throat, and his sister's image swam in sudden, unshed tears.

"Oh, Marco." Diana hugged him close, and they stood there, rocking back and forth, for a long moment. "If she means that much to you, bro, don't give up on her. Fight for her." Her voice was soft, kind.

"I won't fight for a woman I can't trust," he choked, burying his face in his sister's hair until he regained his control.

After she'd left, Marco turned out all the lights, except for the one in the hall, then went to the windows to admire the nighttime cityscape. His eyes shifted focus from the panoramic view outside to that of his own reflection in the glass. Haven't even showered today, he thought with disgust. He was wearing a full-day's growth of beard and might have passed for a street bum if not for the designer jeans and Ralph Lauren polo shirt—now sporting a beer stain.

I won't fight for a woman I can't trust. The words echoed back to him and reverberated inside his head. He remembered the morning Kate had left in such a hurry and how cold their parting had been. He'd been so disillusioned with her by then, he'd actually gotten out of bed, nude, on purpose to prove her naked body had no effect on him.

Could he really blame her for seeking comfort from a guy who was obviously in serious lust with her?

He was jolted from his thoughts by the screech and snarl coming from behind him. Spinning around, he looked down to find Cleo hunched up, teeth bared, her spotted coat standing out from her body as though she'd been struck by lightning. She was staring at the window.

I live on the twentieth floor. And it's dark already. What can she see?

Turning back toward the window, he saw a reflection, like his own image he'd been studying minutes earlier. But the image no longer was him. It wasn't anything he recognized as being in his apartment.

It was a mirror with a wide, gilt frame. And it was filled with black and white shimmering static.

TWENTY-SIX

Marco froze, watching in horror as an image appeared on the mirror. *Through* the mirror. It was as though he were on the other side, behind it, looking out.

It was Kate, standing wide-eyed and staring down at her hands. Her mouth gaped open, and sheer terror contorted her features. He saw her hands then, too. Not Kate's long, graceful fingers with subtle, pale polish. He knew those hands like his own, so he quickly realized they didn't belong to her.

And Kate didn't wear rings. Yet, the ring finger wore an ornate, vintage-looking diamond engagement ring.

Marco watched as she turned her hands over and screamed. Blood smeared her palms, and when she tried to wipe them on her robe, her panicked sob ripped through to his soul.

This wasn't Kate. This was Leah, wearing a blood-soaked, white fur coat.

From behind him, he heard Cleo screech like a banshee and scramble off down the hall, her nails snicking a frantic tattoo on the hardwood. But he couldn't take his eyes off the scene unfolding before him. His blood was pumping so hard, there was ringing in his ears. He staggered and grabbed the edge of the counter to keep from going down.

The scene in the mirror faded, and when he could barely see it, another came into view. Kate, on her couch. Daniel sitting close beside her, urging her to drink her wine. Leaning in to kiss her.

Nearly crashing a fist into the glass, Marco restrained his rage to punching the counter instead. Was this what happened that night? And why was this sadistic spirit showing it to him, like a newsreel, through the mirror on Kate's wall?

He turned away, fury boiling the contents of his stomach up into his throat.

I don't need to see this. Don't want to see it. I already know how the story ends.

That's when a flash of something—lightning?—lit up his entire apartment as though it were broad daylight. The crack left his ears ringing and the hair on his arms standing on end. When he tried to take a step away from the window, he found he was frozen from the waist down. Riveted to the spot.

He twisted slowly back toward the window. He shifted his feet. Funny, they worked fine in this direction.

Okay, Leah. You've made your point. You're going to make me watch this disgusting display whether I like it or not.

But he heard Kate's voice then, as sharp and clear as if she were in the room with him.

I'm not interested in what you have in mind, Daniel.

Marco watched the shock on Daniel's face as she stood abruptly, whacking him pretty hard in the nose with her high, pronounced cheekbone. His heart leapt when he heard her say: *Let's get one thing clear. I'm past that now. My sex-for-the-hell-of-it days are over. I'm in love. I've fallen in love with Marco Lareci.*

The image in the mirror began to fade, and as it did, Kate's last words echoed eerily, growing louder and louder.

I'm in love. I've fallen in love with Marco Lareci.

The mantra grew so loud that Marco clapped both hands over his ears, but he couldn't keep the words out. Over and over, as though they were coming from inside his own head.

I'm in love. I'm in love. I'm in love.

I've fallen in love with Marco Lareci. Marco Lareci. Marco Lareci.

When Marco came to, he was lying on the hardwood floor in front of his picture window with a lump on the side of his head as big as a walnut.

Geez, I only had three beers.

Marco couldn't remember the last time he'd gotten drunk enough to pass out. College, maybe? No, probably his senior year in high school.

He clambered to his feet painfully, holding the side of his head. His hand came away clean, thankfully. No blood.

Must have smacked it on the edge of the counter when I went down.

Slowly, the memory of the vision seeped back into his brain, and he wasn't sure if he should be terrified or relieved.

This could not have really happened. No, this was simply the alcohol and an overactive imagination. That woman's wormed her way so deeply into my brain, she's causing me all kinds of nightmares.

He flicked on the kitchen lights, squinting in the brightness as he grabbed a bag of frozen peas out of the freezer. As he pressed it to the lump on his head, he swore when the pain spiked even higher. Tentatively, he made his way to the window. What could he have been seeing that triggered such a weird nightmare?

Marco didn't have a mirror in his living room or dining room. And even the mirrors in his bedroom and bath weren't framed in gold, but dark wood. And where had the bolt of lightning come from? The night sky was perfectly clear, the moon a nearly-half slice hanging over the glittering skyline.

His appetite gone, Marco decided to turn in early. Tomorrow he would hear back from Clive. Tomorrow he would know the next encounter he'd have to endure with Kate, the woman who, it seemed, had stolen not only his heart, but his sanity.

Dropping his clothes on the floor, he climbed into bed and turned to adjust the overhead stereo system to some soothing, new age piano to help settle his brain. He'd barely slid between the sheets when not music, but a voice came over the speakers.

Kate's voice.

I'm in love. I've fallen in love with Marco Lareci.

The phrase repeated three times, echoing eerily, before fading to be replaced by "Canon in D" by Sad Violin.

Marco lay there for a long time, staring into the darkness. He must have hit his head harder than he thought.

Maybe I should check into Urgent Care. What if I have a concussion and don't wake up?

But then, what would it matter now, anyway?

Had the night at Kate's house with Daniel really happened that way? Or, was this another, rationalizing fantasy spun by his overwhelming desire for it to be true?

One thing was for certain. Marco vowed before closing his eyes that when he woke—*if* he woke in the morning, he couldn't—*wouldn't*—give up on Kate Bardach until he knew for sure.

Kate hated breaking the news to her mother. It turned out, to both her and Joan's dismay, none of the authorities were interested in recovery of *possibly* human remains from a *possible* Mafia hit from fifty years ago. Since James refused to give his testimony, they had no real evidence to substantiate the claim other than Kate's visions. Psychic visions, she knew, weren't a form of evidence usually allowable in court.

In fact, her claims would have hurt their plea instead of help it. They would look at her as though she were a complete wacko.

The detectives in Suffolk County, where Clive's shop was, had no interest in making the trek to witness the recovery of what Clive could only assume were human remains. Nassau County, where Joan lived, had pretty much the same opinion. And the Sullivan County police said if the front end of the car was gone, then the VIN number was, too. There would be no way to even begin trying to identify the wreck. The chief sounded bored and dismissive as he said, "There are a lot of old rumors about the Loch. But nobody's ever come forward with any hard evidence."

Because if they had, Kate knew, they'd be dead.

So, the morning of the recovery dive was set for the following Friday at ten a.m. The weather reports were again favorable. This time, Clive told Joan, he'd bring his entire crew and equipment, including the mesh bag used to retrieve small items from shipwrecks.

Or bones.

Again, Kate arrived early with her mother and was waiting anxiously for Clive's van to pull up the drive of the Shelby. Being a workday, the construction crews were in full swing, and Kate cringed knowing Daniel would be out here at some point snooping around. An encounter with Marco would not be good.

A call to Kate's attorney confirmed what Arianna had told them that morning was true: until forensics could link the bones down in the wreck to the Bardach family, there was nothing they could do to prevent filming of the recovery.

The haughty, Barbie-clone bitch. I wonder if her legs only swing front and back, like a real Barbie doll. Might be kind of difficult to have much fun with that in bed, she thought bitterly.

But Kate couldn't deny her excited anticipation of seeing Marco again. They hadn't spoken since the last dive. All correspondence had been between Clive and Joan.

And damn his stubborn Italian ego to hell, Kate was still in love with him. Desperately, achingly, still in love with the man. Even going to bed every night knowing, since last Saturday, he could be in his apartment screwing Barbie doll's brains out.

Marco and Clive were late. Fashionably so, Kate thought, glancing at her watch at ten twenty-two when the lavishly illustrated van drove up to the end of the boat ramp. But instead of a red Cadillac STS following this time, it was Marco's own black Infiniti. And with a sigh of relief, she saw he was alone.

Kate stood, rubbing her bare arms against a chill emanating more from the inside than out as she watched him step out of his car. He glanced her way, but she saw no reaction. No emotion on his handsome face. His lips were pressed in a grim line, aligning with a stiffly set jaw.

At least he left Barbie home this time. One less level of stress to add to the mix. But a black case, probably holding the underwater camera, was slung by a strap over one of his shoulders.

To her relief, he strode directly toward her and her mother with purpose. Nodding to Joan first, he greeted her simply with a cool, simple "Kate."

"Good morning," she said, hating the breathless quality to her voice. How did he do this to her? He could turn her into a mound of blubbering gelatin by simply saying her name.

"Clive brought all the necessary equipment to recover whatever we find in the wreck," Marco said, addressing Joan. "We'll bring up whatever we can. Then you can arrange for the forensic investigation—"

"Got it, Marco," Kate cut in. "So, let's be clear. You're still filming this whole thing?" She tried to keep her voice level, hating that it cracked mid-sentence.

He hesitated before nodding once. "I'm sorry, Kate. But if it turns out this isn't who we think it is, the footage is worth its weight in gold." Marco locked gazes with hers. "A valuable commodity. It's a fact I'm sure you can appreciate, Ms. Bardach. I'm quite sure."

Kate closed her eyes and clenched her teeth against the new onslaught against her personality. Her old personality. The one she never realized she owned. The Kate Bardach she didn't want to be, not for one more minute in this life.

"Besides," he continued, "even if it does turn out to be your aunt, there's always the chance your lawyers won't win that fight."

Another jab. How could I possibly love this man? He's as cold, as calculating, as—"

Kate's thoughts were cut off when Marco's head snapped sharply to the right. She turned to see Daniel striding toward them.

Oh, shit.

"Everything all right here, Kate?" Daniel made a show of eyeing the camera over Marco's shoulder, tipping his chin in that direction. "Is this bastard really going to film them disinterring your aunt's remains?" Daniel's tone was lethally threatening when he halted not three paces from Marco, taking a wide stance and perching both fists on his hips.

Holy shit. Ballsy little twit. But not very bright.

What happened next did so in such slow motion, Kate wasn't sure if she'd slipped into a semi-conscious state or not. She watched as slowly, carefully, Marco slid the strap of the camera bag off his shoulder and set the package down gently on the ground. Way off to the side. When he came up from his stooped posture, he moved so fast, she barely saw his fist before it made contact with Daniel's jaw.

The younger, slighter man actually caught air as he careened away and landed flat on his back, six feet away. While Marco rubbed his fist wearing a smug, satisfied expression, Kate bit her knuckle, wondering if Daniel's jaw might be broken.

"That," Marco said, with a self-satisfied smile, "is for making a pass at my girl." He stepped in then, close, and wrapped his arms around Kate's shoulders, pulling her to him roughly.

His kiss was savage, wild, uncontrolled. He forced her lips open with his tongue and ravaged her mouth. Unable to control her body, her soul's response to him, Kate met him, tangling her tongue eagerly with his.

Time stood still, or seemed to, as did Kate's heart. For one long moment, it was just the two of them in the whole world, and nobody else mattered.

When it did end, he nipped teasingly at her lower lip on the way out. His strong arms crushed her body so hard against him, she almost couldn't breathe. He looked down at her and spoke to her silently with gold-flecked, green eyes, glowing with passion.

With triumph. With possession.

"You *are* my girl, aren't you, Kate? If not, tell me now, and I'll walk away." His throaty grumble was so low; she knew it was only she who heard his words.

"I'm yours," she sputtered, her throat thick with emotion. "Only yours. Since the beginning."

He growled, "You know the film won't go anywhere, unless—"

"You two lovebirds can do the nasty at a later date," Clive called from the back of the van. "Lareci, get your suit on. We've got a job to do."

When Marco disappeared into the van to suit up, Kate felt a hand on her elbow. Joan stood close beside her, holding out a fresh tissue. Kate took it, laughing.

"I hadn't realized I'd even been crying." She turned, looking for Daniel. "Hey, is he okay? Marco hit him a pretty good shot."

Joan nodded. "Tough kid. He was on his feet and off to the hotel before the two of you started kissing. He looked more embarrassed than hurting."

"Well, he deserved that. Maybe now he understands, once and for all, and he'll quit trying." Kate blotted her drizzling makeup and blew her nose.

"Kate, is he still going to . . . to film this dive? Please tell me he won't," Joan asked, her features contorted with worry.

Kate sighed and squeezed her mother's hand. "Mother, I assure you, the film will go nowhere unless it turns out it's not Aunt Leah."

Nodding her head and gazing at the van, Kate murmured, "Trust me, I know the man. Family means the world to him. There's no way he'd exploit ours that way."

Moments later, the entire dive team—Clive, Marco, and another man Kate hadn't been introduced to—spoke with the ground crew in a huddle near the water's edge. They set up a folding table, on which they placed a radio receiver. Marco had Jeremy run an extension cord out from the hotel to power their communications equipment.

Clive carried a different type of face mask than what he and Marco wore for the first dive. This was a full-face helmet, which Kate realized was equipped with a speaker and mic. Clive would be able to communicate with the men on the shore while the dive progressed. The other man, whom Kate heard Clive call Roger, wore the same simple gear as Marco. Roger emerged from the back of the van carrying a three foot long, duffel-shaped, mesh bag.

For the bones, Kate realized with a shudder.

Hopefully, all that would be left were bones, and nothing more hideous. She put an arm around her mother and squeezed when she heard Joan mutter, "Oh, my."

TWENTY-SEVEN

Kate listened with her heart hammering to the intense discussion between the divers and their land crew, two men Clive had introduced as Derek and Jonathan. Standing a respectable distance away as Clive briefed his team, she couldn't make out the entire conversation. But certain words did filter through, like *jagged metal, unstable wreck,* and *potentially dangerous,* serving only to spike her terror higher.

Finally, the huddle broke up as Clive high-fived Marco and Roger, shouting, "Let's do this!"

As the three divers turned and headed for the boat ramp, Kate ran to Marco and touched his arm.

"You don't have to do this. Why don't you stay up top while Clive's team—"

"I'm perfectly capable of assisting with underwater recovery, Kate. I'm certified, same as the others." His tone had suddenly gone cold and harsh as he riveted her with his cool, green gaze. She shrank back and wrapped her arms around her waist.

So, this was a macho pride thing. Marco had initiated this entire exploration. There was no way, she could tell, this man was going to stand back and watch as Clive and his team handled the difficult, dangerous execution of the recovery.

Then her eyes strayed to the camera strapped to his belt. And oh, yes, the filming. She pressed her lips into a thin line and looked toward the ground. "Please, be careful," she muttered. But he had already started moving away.

Marco's feet made splashing sounds as he followed Clive and Roger down the boat ramp. Kate squinted against the sparks of light the sun sent shooting off the tiny waves their entry caused. Slowly, they waded in until the water lapped chest-high around them. Then, all three donned their fins and masks and disappeared beneath the greenish water.

"Clive, you copy?" Derek said into the transceiver's microphone. A few seconds passed before Kate heard his reply.

"A-okay, Derek. We'll let you know when we reach the target." Clive's speech sounded echoey and slightly garbled.

The water seemed a little clearer to Marco than it had been the day of the first dive. Or, perhaps the sun was higher, more intense. It cut through the greenish gloom in slanted rays fanning out from the surface to the rocky ledge beside them, all the way down to where it ended. That depth, Clive had told him, was about seventy-five feet. The light played in dappled patterns over the jumble of boulders, highlighting the gentle sway of underwater plants dotting the rough landscape.

Within minutes after their descent began, they reached the place where the boulders ended in a sheer, vertical rock face. Below them, Marco saw nothingness. A black abyss. Clive waved for him and Roger to follow, and they took off on a straight course, due south, hugging the shoreline. Marco remembered the wreck being not terribly far down the coast from the boat ramp.

The damned camera was slowing him down. Marco, being a much more muscular man than his lean, lithe instructor, never had been able to swim as fast as Clive could. But it wasn't only the few pounds of extra weight the Underwater UltraMax Camera added. The bulk of the football-sized housing hanging off his side felt awkward and cumbersome.

But Clive had insisted he strap the damn thing to his waist. He wanted Marco's hands free until Clive was satisfied he was in a suitable place to shoot the video. Safe and out of the team's way.

When it came to safety, Clive didn't take any chances. He knew Marco was emotionally invested, involved with at least one member of the family. And he hadn't hesitated to express his concerns about Marco's reaction on seeing whatever they might find inside the wreck. It had pissed him off, initially, but Clive was right. A recovery mission like this could quickly become highly dangerous, even deadly. Emotions couldn't be allowed to cloud the team's thoughts or actions.

The wreck came into view within minutes, and Marco's stomach twisted at the sight. Still hanging off the ledge at a precarious angle, the remaining rear half of the car was nearly covered with lichen and silt. Small fish darted in and out of the rear wheel well. They scattered as Clive approached and swam around the back of the car.

Clive had been on the other side—the passenger's side—last time. He'd been flashing his powerful light beam around inside the car when Marco had realized he was running out of air. Clive now hovered over the roofless structure, pointing down. Then he motioned for Marco to position himself behind and above the wreck on the passenger side.

He followed Clive's direction, locating a flattened place on the shelf where he could settle as he unsnapped the buckle holding the camera from his belt. He switched it on and slipped his hands into the straps on its sides before turning around. Hitting the record button, he telescoped the lens and focused on the scene beneath him.

From his perch, his view was clear and unobstructed. The entire back seat and floorboards were visible, laden with silt and mud. Clive swam over and into the space, reaching in and grabbing what appeared to be a hunk of fur. He shook it gently and pulled it off to one side, raising a cloud of silt that momentarily hid what lay beneath. But as it gradually cleared, the bottom dropped out of Marco's stomach.

No, Clive was mistaken. This is an animal. A beast of some kind. Either a lost hunter's quarry, or perhaps an unfortunate horse or cow that fell into the lake and landed on top of the already sunken car. But no, his logical mind told him. The bones lying inside the furry cocoon were slender and too small. A fawn, perhaps? Or, a tall, lanky dog, like a Great Dane?

And the fur wasn't right. Dirty and stained green in patches with algae, it was unmistakably light in color. Pale yellow or tan. Long and fluffy. As Clive had said, like a polar bear.

Marco telescoped his lens to enlarge his view, and a chilling realization hit him. Animals—wild or domestic—don't have satin linings.

The coat's lining was still fairly well-preserved. Animal fur, Marco guessed, was one of nature's best defenses against the elements. This looked like it was once a magnificent, full-length fur coat. Chinchilla, or maybe fox. After fifty years under the water, however, it was matted and stained. And all that remained wrapped within its embrace were bones.

Fighting a sickening twist of his gut, Marco continued to record the scene until his hands began shaking too badly to keep the camera steady. He dropped it to his chest and switched it off.

One by one, Roger and Clive lifted each bone, most still intact and clearly recognizable. A thigh bone. Several smaller bones from the arms and hands. They carefully laid each artifact into the mesh recovery bag. When Clive lifted a section of spine with part of the rib cage intact, Marco felt the blood drain out of his face.

This had been a life, he thought. A human life. One extinguished young and lost to her family, lying here under the water for over half a century. No wonder her spirit couldn't rest.

Closure, Marco thought, wasn't only sought by the living.

At last, Clive reached deep into the wreck and came out with a skull. He laid it carefully on the top of the contents of the mesh bag. Then he motioned for Roger to take it up before turning to glance at Marco.

The blood had, indeed, drained from Marco's head. Out of his brain. He sat there staring at Clive, confused and light-headed for a moment. Finally, Clive's frantic motion toward his watch, then his regulator gauge, shocked him back into the present. He fumbled clumsily with the camera, re-buckling it to his waist. Then he pushed off the flat rock where he'd been sitting and began following Clive around the rear of the wreck.

He was nearly directly over the car when a flash of light caught his eye. A hazy cloud of silt still hovered over the back seat and the ruined fur coat. But a finger of sunlight pierced the gloom and glinted on something. Once, twice, three times.

Flashing. Like the beacon of a lighthouse.

Marco didn't think, he just reacted. Turning course, he dove straight down toward the wreck, frantically grabbing for the tiny, glittering object. In the current produced by Clive's retreating fins, it had tumbled off the coat's lining, bounced off what was left of the door frame, and begun its descent to the abyss below.

They'd been down less than twenty minutes, yet to Kate, it seemed like hours. She'd paced endlessly back and forth across the edge of the parking lot, peering over the rock wall at every pass. Occasionally, she caught a glimpse of the rising stream of bubbles from one of the divers, glittering like a strand of crystals as it rose to the surface.

This waiting, and not knowing what was happening down there, was killing her.

Communication between Clive and Derek had been intermittent and completely uninformative. When she asked Jonathan why, he explained that the more Clive spoke, the faster he used up his air supply. They were only scheduled to be down about thirty minutes and had to make use of every single one to retrieve whatever they found and get back on the surface. The communication, he said, was more of a safety measure. In case something went wrong.

In case something went wrong. A shiver skittered up Kate's spine. She nodded and returned silently to her pacing.

Joan had gotten very quiet after the divers went down, staring off over the water with a glazed, stoic expression. Preparing herself, Kate thought. If what the divers brought up today was what they both expected, it would be the end of a fifty-year-old mystery. A relief, but a bittersweet one.

At least they'd be able to lay Leah's remains to rest. And they'd know, finally, where to find her. Even if it were only to leave flowers on her grave.

When a sudden flurry of communication crackled through the transceiver, Kate froze, straining to make out the words.

"Marco. Marco! What the fuck—"

Clive's voice sounded angry, then frantic. Kate rushed to Derek's side.

"What's happening?" she demanded.

Derek held up a finger as he depressed the transmit button. "Clive, everything all right down there?"

Silence, except for the occasional blip of static. Then Clive's voice again. "Lareci, goddamn you, what the hell are you doing?"

TWENTY-EIGHT

It's the ring. My ring.

The words rang through Marco's brain as though someone—it sounded like Kate—was speaking from inside his head. He watched in panic as slowly, gracefully, the silvery circlet of stones tumbled and glided across the satiny lining of the coat. The wake of Clive's powerful fin strokes hit it then, sending it off the edge of the cloth. By the time Marco swam close enough to reach it, it had already bounced off the metal door frame and was floating free.

Tumbling, on a beeline course. Down. Into oblivion.

Frantically, and forgetting all of his diving training, Marco kicked his legs, breast-stroking with both arms in its wake. If he could only swim faster . . . was just six inches closer . . . .

Without thinking, he reached out with his left hand and grabbed the rusted door frame, ignoring how the jagged metal bit into his skin. With all his might, he pushed off, using the frame as a springboard, giving him the extra impulse he needed.

It worked. Holding his right hand open beneath the falling ring, he watched it drift onto his palm before locking it within his grasp.

But when he turned back to resume his original course of exit, he found he couldn't. Something was holding him back, snagging him. He looked down and saw the strap of the camera hooked around a ragged edge of the door frame.

And yet, when he tried to work it loose with his free hand—the one not holding the ring—he couldn't see what he was doing. A cloud of darkness blurred his view, and it was spreading and muddying the water. From his hand. His own blood.

Good thing there aren't sharks in this water was the last thought that flashed through Marco's mind before all hell broke loose.

"Clive, come in. Do you need assistance?" Even formerly calm and cool Derek was sounding panicked now, since it had been a full two minutes since Clive's last words came through the transceiver. And in those two minutes, Jonathan had disappeared into the van and emerged, fully suited up and headed toward the boat ramp.

"He's caught. Snagged on the wreck." Clive's gravelly words were more like a snarl. "Trouble, yes. Send Jonathan. My air won't hold."

"If Clive's air won't last, then won't Marco's run out, too?" Kate sobbed, grabbing Derek's shoulder and shaking him to get his attention.

He pushed her away, though not roughly. "Jonathan's on his way, Clive. With two ponies," he said into the mic.

Kate had no idea what ponies had to do with this crisis, but was beyond reasoning with. She grabbed Derek's arm and shook it with all her might. "Tell me what's happening down there, damn you," she sobbed.

Calmly, Derek set down the microphone and faced her. "I don't know much more than you do, Ms. Bardach. But apparently, Marco's gear has gotten caught on something. I'm sure, once Jonathan reaches them, everything will be all right."

His surroundings had begun to take on a surreal appearance, and Marco was unusually calm. The brownish cloud around his left hand had transformed, organizing into a stream, rising like wisps of smoke from a winter chimney. The sun's rays, scattering from what seemed a central point on the surface, sprayed out in a perfect triangle before him, around him. For a moment, he had that dreamy feeling again, like when he'd first learned to dive.

Isn't it a miracle I can actually breathe under water?

He was jolted out of his reverie when something clamped over his shoulder, painfully. The force hoisted him away from the wreck until the belt around his waist bit into him, even through the wetsuit. He looked around and saw Clive's panicked eyes behind his mask and the gleam of the diving knife in his hand.

With two swift flicks of the knife, the belt fell away from Marco's waist, the camera along with it. He watched it drift down, past his knees, his ankles, his fins. He had no desire to go after it.

But Clive yanked on his arm, motioning frantically with the "surface, now" signal. When he struggled to comply, Marco realized he still wasn't free. Something else was holding him fast to the sunken car.

He followed Clive's gaze to his other, more worrisome tether: Marco's air line, which was hooked around one of what was left of the car's rear louvers.

Clive's look of panic and his clear hand signal for STOP in front of Marco's face finally jolted him back into full reality. The dreamy haze evaporated as his senses came suddenly alive. Facts flooded his usually logic-obsessed brain. He was seventy-five feet below the surface, his air supply was most likely running very low, and he was snagged. By his air line.

His heartbeat skyrocketed when he saw Clive's next three signals. First, he crossed two fingers, one over the other and pointed down, making a circling motion.

No shit, Marco thought. I know I'm tangled.

He then made a scissoring motion, then tapped his mouthpiece.

Okay, so he's going to cut my line and share his air with me.

Marco struggled to maintain a sense of calm as he watched Clive reach over his shoulder with the knife. He prepared himself for the explosion of bubbles he knew would burst from the line the minute the blade released the pressure.

What he didn't expect was how powerful the release would be. And how the shock waves would affect the stability of the wreck.

The whoosh of pressure releasing sounded like a small explosion beneath and behind Marco's ear. The bubbles—in those first seconds—pummeled his neck and head, completely obliterating his view of anything else. The impact had blown Clive back several feet. Realizing they were no longer connected, hand to wrist, Marco panicked.

Then another, deeper rumble reached him, one he felt more in his chest than heard, followed by a scraping and a terrible screeching of metal against rock. With horror, Marco watched the cloud of silt rising from under the wreck. The vibration of the bursting cylinder had knocked the wreckage free.

But even as he kicked frantically upward, reaching for Clive's outstretched hands, he found himself being dragged backward. Downward. His air line, though cut, hadn't broken free from where it was looped around one of the sinking car's louvers. And like he was strapped to a rocket, Marco realized he was jetting away, and down.

On the shore, they heard a small explosion—the sudden expulsion of compressed air from Marco's tank—all the way up to the surface. Kate screamed, running to the rock wall and leaning over at a dangerous angle. Desperately, she searched the water's murky depths for something, any sign of the divers. All she saw was the heaven-bound air as it broke free, boiling the surface with volcanic intensity.

"Oh, my God, oh, my God," she wailed, covering her face with both hands. "That's Marco. My Marco."

Her mother ran to Kate and wrapped her arms around her. She forced Kate's face to her shoulder, where she sobbed convulsively. A horrible premonition obliterated her every thought. Although neither of them had any idea what was really happening down there, Kate knew.

Somehow, she knew Marco—the only one, true love she'd ever known—was about to die.

Marco's initial terror faded quickly, almost instantly, as he watched Clive's shocked, horrified face grow smaller, blurrier, and farther away. Oddly, his own sense of panic was gone. He didn't even feel the urge to breathe. No choking, drowning sensation. In fact, as a result of the initial impact of the explosion, he'd lost his mouthpiece entirely, yet seemed to have weathered the shock without inhaling as much as a single mouthful of water.

As if he no longer needed air. As though he could breathe under water.

He floated, slowly sinking beyond where the sun's rays penetrated the murky depths. Only vaguely aware of the huge, metal anchor pulling him from behind, he felt no pain, no constriction. Like a stranded astronaut in some ancient, outer space flick, he was suspended in time and space. The world above him took the form of an inverted bowl of dim, greenish light, speared with golden shafts from the distant sun.

Its beauty thrilled him. The peace enveloped him, like warm, welcoming arms. Weightless, stress-free, painless. The only slightly worrisome part of the dream was the dark, brownish-red stream trailing from his left palm.

His brain knew he'd cut himself, probably pretty badly. But he felt nothing. No pain at all. And, in truth, he didn't care.

When Kate's image floated into view, at first, he was confused. Kate, he knew, was terrified of the water. And where was her gear? No. He must be hallucinating. Probably due to lack of oxygen, as his brain cells began to die.

As a child, Kate had almost drowned. It's what had caused her unusual sensibility. Her gift of seeing those who had passed. Is that what was happening to him now? Was he passing into the realm beyond life? Was he dying?

The woman came nearer, her long, dark hair floating around her head like an oscillating halo. Up close, Marco could see it wasn't Kate. No, this was Leah. Kate was a fashion queen, but somehow he knew she wouldn't be caught dead wearing a full-length, fur coat. Especially one made from the real pelts of butchered animals.

It was not until that moment Marco realized he still held the ring, clenched in a death-grip in his right palm. He opened his hand and studied it in wonder. Is this what he'd given up his life for?

He looked up and met the woman's intense gaze directly. No, it wasn't Kate. But goddamned if it couldn't be her twin. She blinked those huge, baby blues in the same slow, sexy way. No wonder Joan had hidden those photos for so long. Kate was her Aunt Leah's doppelgänger.

When she reached out her hands to him, he re-sealed his fingers around the ring and held out his arms. Her lips formed a knowing, slightly gleeful smile. He clearly felt her cool fingers encircle his wrists. Her grasp was firm and comforting. And though what was left of his consciousness told him there should be panic, and dread, and pain, there was none.

Marco woke to plenty of pain. He was lying flat on his back on ice-cold, wet concrete. His left hand throbbed like a son-of-a-bitch. His lungs felt as though he'd inhaled liquid acid as he struggled to suck in air that seared with every breath. And the first sounds he heard as consciousness returned were Clive's livid rants.

"You stubborn, stupid, pig-headed, Italian bastard. You almost killed us both."

TWENTY-NINE

The next sound Marco became aware of was Kate's sobs, and he struggled to sit, pushing himself up onto his elbows. A firm and not especially patient push shoved him back down.

"Stay put, you stupid bastard. The medics are almost here," Clive snarled.

His head bumped back down onto the pavement, and Marco drifted again, half in and out of consciousness.

It was kind of a nice place to be, he thought. Stuff doesn't hurt nearly as bad here.

He floated there, peaceful, until he felt someone prying at the fingers of his right hand. His eyes flew open and he snarled, pulling it free. "No," was all he could manage.

But when he opened his eyes again, Kate had reached his side, her face hovering like an angel's between Clive and the emergency rescue team. She leaned close over him, so close he could smell her. Her liquid blue eyes probed deep into his.

"It's okay, Marco," she sobbed. "You're going to be okay." Her fingers caressed his cheek and trailed along his jaw. She laid two fingers against his lips. A sudden and very complete peace settled over his soul.

He lifted his right hand then, riveting her gaze. Unfurling his fingers, he held out the precious contents to her and saw the look of shock and disbelief on her face.

Darkness dropped down over him then like a heavy blanket, and he neither heard nor saw anything more.

Kate stood with Clive near the nurse's station in the Emergency Room, waiting to speak with the doctor. Marco had regained consciousness in the ambulance and was madder than a wet cat they were on their way to the hospital. If Kate hadn't ridden with them, she was sure Marco would have made the ambulance driver pull over and let him walk back to his car.

Dr. Robertson—a tall, attractive redhead in her mid-thirties—came out of Marco's cubicle and approached them. She didn't look happy.

"Mr. Lareci has six stitches in his left hand, and we've given him a tetanus shot. We've run all the tests . . . at least, all the tests Mr. Lareci will *allow* us to. He seems fine, if not overly agitated. How long did you say he was without oxygen?"

Clive didn't hesitate in answering. "Less than two minutes, to be sure. Jonathan got there with two pony tanks within seconds after the wreck broke loose." He paused and drew in a shaky breath, rubbing the back of his neck with one hand. "He's one damn lucky bastard. But his hose must have broken free from the wreck within seconds after I lost hold of him." He glanced at the doctor, then at Kate. "I'll tell you, it was a miracle. I had no way of knowing the neck of his cylinder had been compromised. We check them before every dive."

"It certainly sounds like a lucky break." The doctor nodded, then continued, "Well, I'd like to keep him overnight for observation, but—"

Kate heard Marco's voice echoing from down the hallway. He was giving one of the nurses hell again. But he'd been doing that with everyone since he woke up in the ambulance.

Dr. Robertson sighed. "I don't think Mr. Lareci will consent to staying." She looked at Kate, her brow crinkling. "Is he always like this?"

Kate grinned and nodded. "Pretty much."

"You poor thing."

"Where's Kate? Kate!"

Marco appeared out of the cubicle barefoot, wearing a johnny gown a size too small and several inches too short. She covered her mouth and snorted, heading in his direction.

"Kate, will you please get me my pants? I'm ready to get the hell out of here. Where are my pants?" he barked.

She met him halfway down the hall. Without a word, she went up on her toes and wrapped her arms around his neck, silencing him with a long, provocative kiss. It took only a second before his arms encircled her waist and he pulled her to him, answering each of her tongue strokes with one of his own.

When she felt his erection hard against her belly, he broke the kiss and growled into her mouth, "I need my pants, Kate."

She tipped her head back and smiled into those gold-flecked, green eyes. "I like you better without them."

Two weeks later, Marco stood beside Kate, his arm linked through hers, at Leah's graveside. Her place, even after fifty years, was still waiting empty in the family plot at the Wellwood Cemetery on Long Island. As Kate and her parents listened to their rabbi recite the Mourner's Kaddish in Hebrew, Marco joined along in his own silent recitation of prayers he knew—the Lord's Prayer, the Hail Mary, the Apostle's Creed.

He didn't think God, whatever His religion, would mind.

After opening her parents' car door for Kate, he kissed her on the cheek and said, "I'll see you next week."

Shiva, Kate had explained to him, was the mourning period that would go on for seven days following the burial. She had wanted to stay with her mother during Shiva. Marco didn't know how he'd live without her beside him for seven long days. But out of respect for Joan, and for her family's custom, he urged Kate to do exactly that.

It had taken three days after recovering Leah's remains for the dental records to confirm they were, in fact, Leah's. But no one had any doubt they were. When Kate presented the ring to her mother, it was all the proof they needed. Marco waited until Shiva was over, then waited two weeks more out of respect. Then, he called Joan, without Kate's knowledge, and made arrangements to visit her parents at their home.

Marco half-expected Kate's father wouldn't be there, but to his surprise, Kaleb was. They invited him into their formal parlor where a maid served them coffee. A platter of rugelach and biscotti was laid out on white paper lace—side by side. A good sign, Marco thought.

Perhaps they suspect the reason for my visit after all.

An hour later, Marco drove back to Manhattan whistling a tune. He'd not only secured Kate's parents' permission to ask for her hand, but had also purchased a ring to put on it.

THIRTY

Four Months Later
Grand Opening Celebration, The Shelby Resort

Marco could never remember feeling more excited, or happy, in his entire life. While he and his partners expected to book about a third of the Shelby's rooms with their own and Kate's family, guests ended up packing the house. The caterers had done a fabulous job of dressing the ballroom with the finest linens, flatware, and china. Steamer trays of a mind-boggling array of foods, ranging from lasagna to knishes, lined the long, side wall.

And everything smelled fantastic. Marco checked his watch, grateful they'd begin serving soon. But where was Kate?

He'd left her in the third floor suite an hour ago. She'd pushed him out the door, insisting she didn't want him to see her outfit until she came down to the lobby. He glanced at his watch again, then up at the heart-shaped bridge of stairs framing the ballroom entry. Marco swallowed hard, and his stomach did a nervous flip-flop at the thought of what he was about to do.

He knew Kate Bardach was a stubborn, independent woman who liked things according to schedule—*her* schedule. No surprises. What he planned to do tonight would smack her straight out of left field. No way she would expect he'd pop the question here, tonight, in front of over a hundred friends and family. Including her own.

Kate's entire design team was there, the only exception being her architect. Marco didn't need to question why Daniel decided to bow out from the festivities tonight. Not only did Daniel hate the way Marco had ordered the redesign of the hotel, but there were other, more personal factors at play.

Oh, well. Too bad, so sad.

Marco jumped when a hand clamped down over his shoulder. He turned to see the smiling face of his partner behind him. Boris had a glass in each hand—one a champagne flute, the other a tumbler of clear liquid. Boris shoved the flute into Marco's hand.

"You look like you could use this, comrade," Boris boomed in a voice that seemed too deep for his modest, five-foot-six stature. He'd obviously been dipping into the vodka till for some time. His cheeks were a bit pinker than normal, and he was wearing a goofy grin.

Marco took the flute and drained it, relishing the burn of bubbles as they slid down his throat. "I will admit," he said, "I'm a bit quaky on this one. Not sure how the girl will react."

Boris snorted. "Well, I don't think there's another person in this hotel who doubts she'll be overjoyed. And besides, Lareci. She probably knows already anyway. She's psychic, remember?"

Marco lifted one eyebrow. It was a notion he hadn't considered. Could she read his mind? No, she'd clearly told, right from the start, that she could not. Sighing, he thought, *even if she can, if we're going to be man and wife. I wouldn't want it any other way.*

The lobby was packed, a cacophony of voices and laughter echoing off the marble floors. The new, gold and crystal chandelier glittered overhead, sending sparks of light bouncing off the crowd. He had hoped for a good turnout, but this was more than he ever expected. The marketing director Eliot hired had done an excellent job, managing to coordinate the Grand Opening on the same weekend as that of the Rockin' Hard Café a few miles up the road. Marco had to actively search the mass of paying guests to locate his own family and friends.

His parents and sister had settled themselves comfortably in the small sitting area off toward one side of the space. His toddler niece was busy showing off how she could climb up and down off the upholstered loveseat all by herself. Eliot and his wife, Phyllis, stood near the bar, speaking with some people Marco didn't know. Even James had shown up, nodding timidly at Marco as he slipped through the front doors wearing a suit Marco was sure had been in mothballs for forty years.

And Kate's parents were there, too. Joan stood next to the stony-faced Kaleb Bardach, who alternated between glancing at his watch and sipping red wine.

The clamor in the room suddenly hushed, and somebody wolf-whistled. Marco turned toward the stairs.

She'd paused on the top step like a high-fashion model at the end of a runway. And he knew, in that instant, deep in his gut, there would never be another woman, mortal or goddess, who could set him on fire the way she did. The way she was doing right now. Embarrassed, Marco felt his throat constrict and his eyes go bleary.

Kate wore red, her best color with her pale coloring and dark hair. The dress was floor-length and sparkly, shimmering as she moved toward the top step. The fabric was also obviously stretchy, because it hugged every one of her delicious curves from where it dipped low between her breasts down to her hips, cupping her perfect ass before flowing to the floor. Her ebony hair was coiled and pinned on top of her head, a bright-red rosebud tucked into one side. Tendrils swirled free from her temples and nape, accenting the creamy tone of her skin.

She descended the stairs slowly, holding on to the railing. She, no doubt, was wearing a pair of her skyscraper-height stilettos, Marco thought. The red ones. He licked his lips. He'd have to make sure she kept those on later, after the dress no longer hid them.

He met her at the bottom of the stairs, holding out his hand. She clasped it and looked into his eyes, hers sparkling with amusement. After hitting him with another one of those slow, sexy blinks of hers, her gaze trailed down his body to where he knew damned well he was tenting his trousers. When she looked up at him, he quirked the corner of his mouth and gave a one-shoulder shrug as he used his free hand to button his dinner jacket over his embarrassing condition.

When he leaned in and covered her mouth with his, a cheer went up in the room, followed by laughter and clapping. A waiter appeared with two champagne flutes on a tray, along with an empty tumbler and a small, silver knife. Marco used the knife to strike the tumbler several times until the crowd quieted. Then he handed one flute to Kate and raised the other high over his head.

"I'd like to call a toast to the incredible efforts, talent, and determination of the Bardach & Associates design team. As you can all see," he motioned toward the room around them with his glass, "they've done one hell of a job transforming The Shelby Hotel into the finest boutique accommodation in Sullivan County."

Shouts of *hear, hear* filled the room, followed by the synchronized clinking of a hundred glasses.

Marco obliged the crowd, kissing her once again, soft and sweet. When their lips parted, he drained his champagne glass in three swallows. Then, to Kate's bewildered expression, he lifted her barely-touched flute out of her hand. He set both on an empty tray nearby. Turning and raising his hands, he clapped them over his head to get the crowd's attention once more.

When the rumbling silenced, he said, "I'm not finished."

Kate expected Marco to make a big deal about the job her firm had done on his hotel. She'd fully expected—in fact, planned—the look of fire she'd see in those gold-flecked, hazel eyes when he saw her dress. What she didn't see coming was what he did next.

In front of all these people, including both of their families, friends, and at least fifty guests of the hotel, Marco went down on one knee. A hush fell over the room like a heavy blanket.

"Katherine Bardach," he began in low, rumbling voice, "you saw the potential in this crumbling building, and shared my and my partners' vision. With your perseverance, excellent resources, and magical imagination, you've transformed the defunct Redman Resort into The Shelby Hotel, a boutique masterpiece."

A smattering of applause broke out, but Marco, his back toward the crowd, raised one hand to silence them. He continued. "Somewhere along the way, Kate, I'm hoping you also recognized the potential in this jealous, overbearing, stubborn, Italian boy from

Brooklyn. Because that boy is now a man who's bat-shit crazy about you and wants to share the rest of his life with you. Only you."

Kate's hand went to her throat. Her initial reaction was shock.

Marco *never* swears in English.

But embarrassment quickly followed, laced with a tad of annoyance. What possessed him to pull a stunt like this, here and now?

The pompous, proud Kate Bardach, the woman she used to be, would have been mortified and thrown a fit to prove it.

They hadn't discussed forever. Hadn't even said the "L" word out loud to each other. Not yet.

But as Marco's handsome face blurred behind quick, unbidden tears, she realized she was no longer the same woman. A long way from the Kate who had peered up at Marco on the step above her in the grandstand of the racetrack that day. Then, his elevated perch had assaulted her sense of control, her precious pride. Now, everything was different. Her heart suddenly filled to bursting with a rush of love and joy she'd never known she was capable of.

His voice low and gruff, Marco murmured, "Kate Bardach, will you marry me?" as she watched him slip a hand inside his coat. Withdrawing it, he presented a ring, sparkling on his palm.

The ring. Leah's ring.

She felt a tear spill over and slide down her cheek.

A woman's voice from somewhere in the crowd pierced the hush. "Aw."

But Kate stiffened. Something here wasn't right. She couldn't stand it. Marco—her big, strong, stubborn Italian stallion—on the floor groveling in front of all these people. And her, towering like some sort of royal princess over him, a good four inches taller than even her normal height. For a moment, Kate wasn't sure if she wanted to grab Marco's hand and yank him to his feet, or reach down to smack him on the side of the head.

She did neither. Slowly, Kate lowered herself to her knees until they were face to face, so close she could clearly see the already-darkening stubble on his jaw. Smell his intoxicating scent, enhanced by the tang of champagne on his breath. His eyes, usually light and almost golden at times, had darkened, and she saw creases form between his eyebrows.

Meeting his tremulous gaze, she peered deep into his eyes and said, "Damn straight I will."

For the remainder of that magical evening, Kate knew how Cinderella must have felt at the ball. She was swept into a dreamlike state, with the camaraderie of her friends and family close around her, the sumptuous feast, and freely flowing wine. And the man she now knew was her soul mate never straying more than an arm's length away.

When the tables had been cleared and pushed to the perimeter of the room, a string quartet began playing lyrical melodies. Several couples immediately rose to dance. Kate watched Marco's sister, Diana, kiss her toddler, Angelina, on the cheek as she handed the child over to Grandma and Grandpa. The elder couple headed upstairs to put the sprite to bed.

Marco leaned close beside her against the wall, one arm draped over her shoulders. She could feel him studying her. He lowered his mouth to her ear. "What's wrong, Kate? You should be jubilant tonight. But instead, you look sad."

Her shoulders lifted with a deep sigh. She didn't want to spoil this magical night. But as Diana returned to the group of people she'd been conversing with, Kate could still see the shadow of the toddler. The translucent image of Matthew, clinging desperately to his mother's skirt.

"Nothing," she breathed. "I know it's cold, but will you join me on the patio for a few minutes? I need to clear my head."

They slipped out through the side door, flanking the ballroom's wall of glass onto the flagstone patio Kate had herself designed. Night had fallen, and the moon hung low over the Loch, its reflection quivering on the surface. Kate rubbed her arms and snuggled closer to Marco. Leaning on the white iron railing, she rose to her toes and kissed him, long and sweet.

When their lips parted and she opened her eyes, she froze when she saw the woman standing about ten feet behind Marco. A woman with impossible blue eyes, raven hair, and wearing a full-length, white fur coat.

Kate sucked in a breath, and Marco turned to see what she was staring at. She heard his gasp.

"I see her," he said quietly, and closed his hands over Kate's.

Her image was vivid, though translucent. But glowing in a way Kate hadn't seen before. Wrapped in pale fur from her chin to her toes, her dark, thick hair fell loosely over her shoulders. This time, though, there was no blood, no look of horror, no pain in Leah's eyes. In fact, she was smiling.

Kate knew her aunt was stopping by, one last time, to say goodbye.

"You're free, Aunt Leah. Finally free," Kate whispered.

Leah's countenance emanated peace and joy. With a slow, sexy blink, she nodded once. But as her image began to fade, Kate stepped out of Marco's arms and called, "Wait."

Time stood still. Kate pointed through the wall of glass toward where Diana stood, laughing in a group. She watched as Leah's gaze followed.

The small, red-haired boy was still clutching desperately to Diana's skirt, swaying slightly with sleepy, listless eyes. As though he'd heard her call him, he blinked and his eyes flashed toward the window. First, curiosity, then relief, even joy brightened his tiny face. When Leah crouched and held out her arms, Matthew hesitated only a moment.

Taking one last look up at his mother, he released his grip on her dress and planted his thumb firmly in his mouth. Then he turned and toddled straight through the glass and into Leah's arms.

"Dio buono," Marco muttered, his voice thick and garbled. "I see him. I see him, too." They watched as Leah lifted the boy onto her hip. Turning, she looked back over one shoulder and threw them a slow wink as she gradually faded from view.

"They're free," Kate choked on a sob. "They're both finally free."

Kate wrapped her arms around Marco's head and drew his face down into the crook of her neck until their weeping subsided. After a few moments, he drew away, frantically swiping his eyes.

A strong man with an incredibly tender heart, Kate thought. How could I have been so lucky?

She reached two fingers down into her cleavage and pulled out a tissue, holding it out to him. He choked on a laugh as he took it, sniffed, and smiled before blowing his nose.

Then he lifted Kate's hand, running his thumb around the stones of the ring. He met her gaze.

"Kate Bardach, I love you. I love you with all my heart and soul. And I will until the day I draw my last breath."

Kate swallowed against the lump in her throat and replied, "And I love you, Marco Lareci. You stubborn, jealous, Italian boy from Brooklyn. And I will for the rest of time."

Marco lifted his face toward the heavens. Then he closed his eyes and whooshed out a breath. "Thank God. There was a time I thought I'd never hear you say those words," he whispered.

Kate lost herself in the depths of those pale hazel eyes. Then, arching an eyebrow, she shrugged and quipped, "To be honest, Lareci? Me, either."

They both dissolved into laughter. Marco wrapped his arms around her waist, lifting her high and twirling her around him. The blast of chilly, damp air under her skirt sent a wave of shivers up her spine.

He set her down and ran his fingers along her cheek. "You're freezing, mia cara. Let's go back inside."

Kate pressed a soft kiss on his mouth, then tucked her head under Marco's chin as they made their way through the door. When his hand slid south from her waist, she shouldn't have been surprised. But she jumped and squeaked anyway when the now familiar, sharp twinge of pain shot through the skin of her ass.

Again!

She swatted his hand away and shrieked, "Ouch, you bastard!"

THE END

A Note from the Author

Thank you for joining Kate and Marco on their journey. I hope you enjoyed reading their story as much as I enjoyed writing it. If you want to *hear* their adventure as told by my favorite narrator, J.S., HEARTS UNLOCHED will be available on Audible.

Please, take a few moments to leave a review on Amazon and Goodreads. Reviews are incredibly important to authors, and how our stories reach more readers like you.

Also, check out my debut New Gothic Romance, PHANTOM TRACES, available in eBook, paperback, and audiobook from Amazon.

~~~

A history professor in a tweed jacket, a cheeky Goth chick, and a pipe-smoking, book-hurling ghost. Put them all together in an antiquated library and, well...

*Professor **Jack Wood**'s silver-streaked hair definitely ages him, and he can thank Killer Dawn for that. He won't be falling into the love trap again anytime real soon. But this new librarian has him curious, with her head-to-toe black Goth garb, piercings, and a defiant attitude to match. Definitely not his type of girl, but still...*

***Abigail Stryker**'s got her work cut out for her. The last two librarians didn't last a month before airborne books chased them off. But Abby's determined to make her new life a go—and to stay as far away from older men as possible. Once was enough. Might be tough to do when the library's best patron is none other than dreamy-eyed Jack Wood. And it seems the eccentric ghost may have taken a shine to her as well.*

~~~

I'm presently working on my next book, SPIRITS OF THE HEART, another intensely emotional love story set against the backdrop of an abandoned mental asylum. My newsletter subscribers receive updates first, so please consider signing up at my Website or Blog. You can also find me on Goodreads, Facebook, Twitter, and Pinterest.

Remember, when you're in the mood for an intensely emotional contemporary romance with a paranormal twist, think—

CLAIRE GEM

32572828R00201

Made in the USA
Middletown, DE
09 June 2016